MIND GAMES

ALSO BY THE AUTHOR

THE STRANGER BESIDE ME

ANN RULE

MIND GAMES

A NOVEL

SEVERN HOUSE PUBLISHERS

This title first published in Great Britain 1984 by
SEVERN HOUSE PUBLISHERS LTD of
4 Brook Street, London W1Y 1AA
by arrangement with Sphere Books Ltd

British Library Cataloguing in Publication Data
Rule, Ann
 Mind games.
 I. Title
 813'.54(F)   PS3568.U42

ISBN 0 7278 1089 8

Printed and bound in Great Britain by
Anchor Brendon Ltd, Tiptree, Essex

FOR LAURA, LESLIE, ANDY, MIKE,
BRUCE, REBECCA, AND MATTHEW.

MAY THEY ALWAYS KNOW THAT LOVE
IS THE ONLY POSSESSION THAT MATTERS.

ACKNOWLEDGMENTS

For their inspiration, patience, support, intelligence,
and friendly criticism, I owe many thanks to the following:

Fred J. Horner, former Sheriff, Okanogan County, Washington; Paul
Bernstein, former Chief Prosecutor, City of Seattle; Larry Nash, Chief,
Puyallup, Washington, Police Department; Darrel Wilsey, Head
Ranger, National Forest Service, Stehekin, Washington; Bill Wilsey,
Betty Wilsey, Margie Wilsey, Stehekin Landing Lodge; Ernie Gibson,
Chelan Airways; Miriam Giles, Barbara Easton, Gerry Brittingham,
Lola Pammenter, Charles S. Miles, Maureen and Bill Woodcock, So-
phie M. Stackhouse, and the Northwest Authors' B. and M. Society;
John Saul, Michael Sack, Donald E. McQuinn, Ann Combs, Donna
Crefeld, Margaret Chittendon, Archie Satterfield, and Jeannie
Okimoto, a stalwart, if occasionally disorganized, group.

To my agents: Joan and Joe Foley, good friends.

And to Starling Lawrence, my editor,
whose pencil is as deft as it is ruthless.

MIND GAMES

PROLOGUE

MOTHER

MAY 23, 1957

Lureen Demich might have been surprised to know that her labor pains began less than a mile from where she had conceived the child. She had been with so many men for so many reasons in the year past that she could not be absolutely sure who the father was. Sometimes she let them do it because she was lonely, sometimes for money, and occasionally she had only been bored. But never once for love.

She moved on when the carnival's tents were struck and the caravans lumbered off to the next town, and the men blurred in her mind along with the cities along the circuit: Cincinnati, Moline, Ann Arbor. But she did remember one gangling, carrot-haired boy who'd been pushed into her trailer by some drunken fraternity boys, the kid who'd stuttered as he'd shoved a ten-dollar bill at her. He must have been a smart kid to be in college even though he couldn't have been over sixteen. She saw that he was a joke to the others, that they resented him for his brains, and she heard them laugh when his book smarts and fancy words failed him where it counted.

She'd taken his money and told him to hurry as his friends chanted cadence outside. And hurry he had. Never even really got into her before he spilled it all over her thighs. Then she'd laughed too and turned away to clean up the mess.

The carnival was a thousand miles away when she began to vomit.

Lureen had drifted aimlessly for all of her short life, planning nothing, and dreaming only impossible dreams. She always expected magic and begged the card readers to promise her a better life. But she had little aptitude for anything beyond attracting men, and when each one left her, she always felt that things were a little worse than they had been before.

She was not yet eighteen when she crouched, terrified, against the cool metal wall of the Nashua trailer and felt her belly contract. She thought she might burst. She had been there all day and most of the night, attended by the blank-faced old gypsy woman who watched her with slight interest. There was no compassion, and no one to share the weight of Lureen's fear. The others had told her that the gypsy would know what to do, then left the two of them alone as if pestilence drenched the trailer house.

Lureen knew she was going to die; there was no way that she could push a baby out of her without dying. She turned her face away and gagged as the gypsy held a jelly jar full of whiskey to her lips, and then heard herself grunt deep in her throat. She bore down against the mattress beneath her hips. Her own sounds startled her; she sounded like an animal. The gypsy woman grunted with her, urging her down to darker tunnels of pain she had no wish to explore. She prayed that the baby was dead. She had never wanted it.

The gypsy woman moved toward her, blocking the window with her bulk, and Lureen closed her eyes and pushed with a shudder that shook her body. She felt herself split and something slippery and wet burst from between her legs.

For a moment, it was very quiet. She watched the gypsy rub the red and white thing with a rough towel, watched with a sense of complete removal. It *was* dead. Good. And then its mouth opened suddenly and she heard its cry bounce off the tinny trailer sides.

The old woman muttered with satisfaction and pushed the squalling bundle near her face. It lived, an ugly thing with a head drawn to a point, slick with her blood and covered with stuff that looked like cottage cheese.

She turned away, pressed her face into the mattress, and slept.

In Coatesville, Pennsylvania—when her name was still Louise—her own mother had gone away, leaving behind one snapshot for her daughter to study. The little girl had been able to discern that Dorothy Demich had been pretty (as she was), full-breasted to the point of incredulity (as she would be), and young, very, very, young. Louise understood that Dorothy could not have survived long in the half-house she shared with Pete Demich and her grandmother, Lena. She understood it more through the years when she waited her own time to flee. The house smelled of painted-over dirt and old women. There was no dining room; her father slept in the single bedroom, and Louise shared a Murphy bed in the living room with the old lady.

Once she had longed for rugs, or even just one rug, to cover the linoleum that was so scuffed you couldn't tell what pattern it was supposed to have. She even tried to wash the gray lace curtains and found the old Easy Spin-Dri in the basement full of nothing but shreds after the water drained away. She finally accepted that there was no way to change the half rowhouse from what it was. The neighbors who shared the common center wall painted their side every five years; Pete never bothered.

Louise had tried to take friends home a couple of times, but when Pete worked all night at the Lukens steel mill, he woke in the late afternoon and walked through the house in his undershirt and shorts, scratching his testicles as if the girls weren't there, embarrassing her and frightening her schoolmates. When he worked days, Lena sat in the corner of the living room in the sagging, wine-plush chair and stared at them, her clubbed fingers spewing out lengths of tatting. What use there was for the strange knots that emerged Louise never learned. Lena refused to speak English in front of her granddaughter's friends, barking out comments in Polish to Louise. The other girls gathered up their paperdolls and went home to houses with mothers who baked cookies and hugged them.

Lena Demich had never hugged her, or kissed her, or even run a rough hand over her braids in a gesture of affection. At night, the old woman snored and farted, and her great girth pulled Louise over to her side of the Murphy bed. Louise learned to sleep with one arm hooked around the bed frame.

Her grandmother was a presence. Nothing more. She seemed to have some attachment to the other old women who lived in the houses that clung to the hillside leading up from the valley floor and Main Street. Louise listened to their talk, trying to find some way to get through to her grandmother, but she never found the key. Lena and Pete communicated with single words over the supper table in the kitchen. They seemed to understand each other; Louise understood nothing.

She was not a bright child. Most of her teachers barely saw her small pale face in a sea of pupils. She neither caused trouble or excelled enough to be noticed. Over the years, an occasional teacher tried to draw her out, but there was never enough time, and Louise shrank from attention that singled her out. She was afraid they would find out that she could not read. Arithmetic was the same. What was it that other students knew that she could not learn? Why couldn't she learn?

Louise was passed from grade to grade along with the rest. As she fell further and further behind, her imaginary world insulated her from the frustrations that threatened to bury her. She fantasized that her mother would come back for her, that Dorothy would realize how much her child resembled her, that she had left part of herself behind. Louise was quite sure that her mother was an actress, really successful, who lived in a grand house somewhere. It was only a matter of time until they would be together. She lied about Dorothy at school, but no one believed her, and the popular girls in soft cashmere sweaters and coordinated skirts laughed at her. She could blink her eyes and make them go away.

Pete and Lena knew that Dorothy was never coming back to claim the strange, skinny child she'd foisted off on them. They knew Dorothy had been dead for three years, her body thrown away in an alley in Chicago by the man whose hands had closed around her neck until they left ten pale blue fingermarks in the soft flesh there. They had accepted the news of Dorothy's murder with stoicism; as far as they were concerned, Dorothy had died the day she walked out on the family, and her actual death neither surprised nor angered them. They hadn't sought vengeance, and no one was ever arrested for the crime. Pete and Lena had been relieved to have her gone, and they'd resented only that she hadn't taken her child with her. Her death verified for them their conviction that the wicked would be smitten down by the unyielding god they answered to.

They had seen no need to tell Louise that her mother was dead. Children always carried tales. When Dorothy's belongings arrived in a brown paper package, Lena picked through the clothing, papers, and bits of costume jewelry with distaste. She had always thought that Dorothy was a tramp, unworthy of a hard-working man like Pete, and the tight sweaters and flimsy undergarments confirmed her feelings. She lumbered down to the coal furnace in the basement and burned everything but the jewelry. Maybe she hadn't noticed the letter addressed to Louise; maybe she had. It didn't matter. Those who died out of grace had no right to send messages to the living.

Lena suspected that Louise carried the bad seed within her, and she watched her granddaughter closely for the signs.

Louise became Lureen in her own mind when she was fourteen, but she didn't tell anyone. There was no one to tell. She chose it for her own name, her *real* name, when she heard it in one of the Saturday after-noon movies she saw—something with Joan Crawford or Shelley Winters. Louise never identified with the main star of the movie; she liked to pick someone in the background, a young girl who was pretty and nice and always turned out to be happy at the end of the film. It might happen to her, when Dorothy returned, or it might happen when she grew up and was old enough to leave home. It couldn't happen where she was because no one could be happy there.

Louise–Lureen's body remained as slat-thin as a child's until she was almost fifteen, and Lena thanked God daily for that. But in the almost tropical heat of the August before her sophomore year in high school, the fact of her budding could no longer be denied. She lasted only a week in high school before she was called into the assistant principal's office.

"You'll have to wear a brassiere," the woman explained. "Or you can't come to school."

Louise was embarrassed to tears, and felt her skin suffuse with a wave of heat as it was pointed out that she "flopped" when she played volleyball in the gym.

"You must remember there are boys' classes on the other side of the gymnasium. There have been complaints."

Louise stared at the woman, confused. Who had complained? The boys? The other girls? The teacher? She had never really felt her own body; it had suddenly become as heavy as stone.

"You must be modest, Louise. You must show respect for yourself and for others."

The woman before her had no discernible breasts. How could she understand? Louise wished that she could have had a principal like Greer Garson or Maureen O'Hara, someone who might know that she had meant no harm.

"I'm sorry. I didn't realize. I guess I just suddenly . . . kind of . . . grew."

"A woman must be aware of her body."

"Forgive me."

"It's not up to me to forgive you, Louise. Try to be more careful."

She wore her coat for the rest of the day, feeling her face flame whenever anyone glanced at her, wondering which of them had been talking about her, wishing that she had had one friend who might have told her.

Avoiding her grandmother's half-lidded stare at the coat on a warm September day, she hurried to the bathroom and closed the door. The only mirror in the house was over the chipped basin, and she had to climb on the edge of the tub to view herself from the shoulders down. Balancing with one hand on the window ledge, she pulled up her blouse with the other.

It was true. Her breasts had bloomed, plump pillows of white flesh, centered with salmon-colored nipples that seemed much larger than she remembered. They looked peculiar to her; she was so thin and they were so big. They seemed not to be a part of her body at all. She turned from one side to the other, getting used to them. In a way, she thought, they looked nice. Movie stars had big breasts, and nobody complained. Still teetering on the tub's rim, she pulled her blouse off and draped it around her, forming a vee of material in the center of her chest.

They did look nice. They looked like her mother's breasts in the snapshot she carried. She pulled the material tighter and two round half circles popped up over the top. She was amazed that they had grown so quickly, that she had barely noticed. She smiled at herself in the mirror. No wonder the boys watched her from their side of the gym. No wonder. She felt just the slightest sensation of power, something she had never felt before.

The bathroom door opened so quietly that she heard no sound at all. She didn't hear the old woman until she was beside her, spitting out a word of Polish that Louise didn't understand. Still, she felt the force of it, and the vehemence behind it. Her feet lost their tentative perch on the tub, and she fell, crashing against the toilet stool. The floor there smelled sharply of urine and she turned her head away, tasting blood in her mouth.

"Get up, and cover yourself. What you doing in here?"

Louise stood up slowly, lifting a hand to her mouth to wipe away the blood there.

"They said at school that I need a brassiere."

"Who said? Who thinks he has to mind our business?"

"A lady in the principal's office. She says I flop."

Lena jabbed a bony finger at her and poked her breasts.

"Ahh, she's right. You're as big as a cow. Come."

Louise followed her grandmother into the living room where the old lady pulled a flesh colored harness-like garment from the cedar chest there. She wrapped it around Louise's chest, tugging, pulling and lacing until Louise could barely breathe. She looked down at her breasts and saw that they were flattened now, the bulk of them pushed against her ribcage and back under her arms. She tried to take in a lungful of air and couldn't.

"I can't wear this," she protested. "I look like a freak and I can't breathe."

"You wear it. I will go to Sears and buy you some brassieres. Now, you pull this very tight and your boobies won't stick out like you was a whore. You are like her, your mother who ran away. Big breasts. She didn't even feed you with them, too afraid they wouldn't be so big after."

Louise closed her eyes and turned away; she hated to hear Lena talk about Dorothy, hated the flat, closed look that passed over her grandmother's face when her mother's name was mentioned. She'd seen Lena naked once and had been horrified at the slack, empty breasts that hung down over her corrugated belly. She could not imagine that Lena had ever been a young girl. Lena avoided mention of anything having to do with the body, and she wondered if it was because Lena's own body was so ugly.

Still, having breasts seemed not to be as repulsive to her grandmother as having periods. Nobody had prepared Louise for the sudden rush of hot blood that had coursed down her legs six months before. That had been the worst day of her life. The terror. She had walked into the kitchen with her shoes literally full of blood and looked at Lena with a plea for help.

Lena had responded with rage, pulling Louise into the bathroom where she filled the tub with water. "Wash yourself. That is not clean blood. It is blood from the curse, and you have to wash it away."

What had she done to deserve such a curse? Lena had talked of evil spirits often, of things that happened in the old country, but Louise could not imagine what sin she herself had committed. Lena had not explained. Instead, she'd reached into the towel closet and brought out a length of flannel sheeting which she tore into squares and then folded into oblongs. Louise thought that the old lady had finally gone completely off her rocker.

"Now stand up," she'd barked. "See? See—this is how you do." Lena had lifted up her own black skirts and gestured between her legs. "It is to soak up the bad blood. You mustn't let anyone know. When the rag is full, then you wash it and hang it in the basement behind the furnace. You don't let your father see it, and don't let the boys smell the fish smell. They will know you are a bad girl. They will try to get you—to do the bad thing to you. The bad thing hurts. It is full of hurt; you must not let them close to you."

Louise had had no idea what the bad thing was, and boys never got close to her—no one did—but she obediently held the flannel rag between her legs. She'd been afraid to ask Lena for more explanation. She'd spent the next four days taking baths and washing the blood-soaked rags until the skin on her hands peeled off.

The bleeding stopped then, and one of the girls at school told her about Kotex. She threw the soiled rags into the furnace. The next month the bleeding came again, and she realized that it would come and go and that it happened to all women, not just her. But the boys did come around her, like dogs who had caught a scent. Their sudden interest disturbed and fascinated her at the same time.

Louise felt some stirring that she had not felt before; she had always longed to have someone hug her, but what she felt was different. It felt good and bad at the same time, and she wondered what she could do to make it stop. It was like listening to a song she liked and then having the music end before it was time. She felt empty, with a compelling need to be filled. She knew it had something to do with the place between her legs. When she leaned against the washing machine, she could feel it in her belly too, and sometimes the machine's vibrations made her think that the elusive ending of the song was almost within her grasp.

Louise had not the faintest notion of the sexual act. If she had been able to read, she might have found out. The movies told her nothing; the characters kissed and held each other, and then the scene always dissolved, leaving her puzzled and frustrated.

Louise came home from school on a frozen January day when she was sixteen and found Lena sitting still as a rock in the easy chair, her hands clasped around the spew of tatting. She was dead. She had been dead so long that she was stiff, and Louise could not release the chain of knots from her hands. She screamed for the old woman next door, and someone called Pete home from the steel mill.

Her father had fallen to his knees in front of his mother and begun to sob. Louise had never been more astonished, filled with wonderment at the sight of Pete rocking back and forth as tears made rivulets in the mill grime on his face. Her father had never demonstrated any emotion, nothing more intense than annoyance, and here he knelt in front of Lena and wept like a baby. Lena's laced black shoes were planted in a puddle of her own urine.

Louise began to laugh. She had never seen a man cry. In this house empty of feelings for all the years of her life she could not deal with this rush of emotion, and she could not stop laughing. She saw her father turn slowly and warn her with his eyes, and she laughed. Still kneeling, Pete raised his hand and caught her in the face. Then he fell sideways on the cracked linoleum, scrabbling at it with his hands and sobbed louder.

She ran. Past the arms raised to hold her back, beyond her father's shocked command, skittering down the ice-crusted porch steps, hardly touching them. It was only when she reached the sidewalk and drew a breath of crystalline air that she realized how nauseating it had smelled inside.

Old fool. The old fool was dead.

Louise felt no grief because she hadn't really lost anything. She wasn't sure what she felt, perhaps a renewed hope that her mother would come for her at last, now that there was no woman to care for her. Maybe it had been Lena who kept Dorothy away for all the years.

She could hear them inside, their voices rising and falling in choruses of mourning and indignation, punctuated by groans from her father, the keening of an animal left alone in the woods. She ran down the hill toward the Lincoln Highway, anywhere to get away from that sound and the smell. She would have to go back in there sometime, but not soon.

She ran past the corner where the drugstore was, only vaguely aware of the whistles and catcalls from the high school boys who lounged against a window displaying trusses and surgical collars, pock-faced guys with duck's-ass haircuts and cigarettes hanging from their lips. The cold air froze her throat and hurt her lungs. A cramp seized her beneath her ribs, drawing her gut inward until she had to slow to a walk.

Her own bladder had been full to bursting when she had arrived home to find Lena dead. Now it demanded attention. The Day-Old-Bread-Store loomed ahead, windows steamed over. She ran inside, knocking over a stack of stale sandwich loaves, bouncing oblongs of red, yellow, and blue wax-paper into the narrow aisle.

"Hey!" the Italian shouted. "You! Girl!"

"Bathroom," she cried. "You got a bathroom?"

He was so close to her that she could see the pores of his nose, the stubble of coarse black hairs on his chin. He nodded and gestured toward the back of the store, as she dashed past him and slammed the door. The toilet was dirty, but she was past the point of caring.

The Italian looked at her curiously when she finally came out. He had pulled down the shades in the front windows, casting a greenish pall over the bread inside. The past-date bakery goods looked like bodies huddled on the white metal tables.

"You O.K., girl?"

Louise bent to pick up the bread loaves scattered around her feet. Wonder Bread. Wonder. Wonder. Her fingers felt numb, and she couldn't seem to grasp the slippery loaves. She looked up at the Italian and saw that he looked funny. But everything seemed different; the whole world had changed.

"Let 'em be. They're too old anyway. I'll give them to the pig man when he comes by."

"You're closing so early? It's only four thirty."

"It's a slow day."

She liked his voice; it was soft, and she was amazed that she had someone's full attention. She walked over to the counter and leaned against it. "You always close up at five. Every day but Sunday, you're open nine to five. See, I remember?"

"It don't matter. They don't come in by now, they won't be in. What's the difference in a couple loaves of bread?"

Vito Ferrano was thirty-eight, a bachelor not by choice but by circumstance, the grudging support of a senile father and a sister whose

mustache discouraged serious suitors. Now the girls looked past him at
the guys in their twenties, guys who still had hair and hadn't the girth
that Vito had. He rubbed his hands over the white apron covering his
belly and felt the growth between his legs; this girl always did that to
him. How old was she? Eighteen? Maybe nineteen. Not a real pretty
girl, but not bad either. She didn't carry herself like the ones who
came into the store and teased him just so he'd throw in a free bag of
doughnuts. She hunched her shoulders to cover up those breasts, or
maybe it was just too much weight for her to carry up front.

He leaned forward over the counter, balancing his body on his
splayed hands, hoping the apron hid the erection that he couldn't stop.
There was something peculiar about the girl, but he couldn't figure out
what.

"You got problems? Somebody chasing you?"

". . . I don't know. Maybe. She died . . ."

"*Who* died?"

"My grandmother. You know her. She comes in on Fridays and
Tuesdays."

"Oh, yeah." He didn't know. One old lady looked just like the next
to him. "That's too bad. You feeling real sad about it, huh?"

She bit her lip and looked down, poking her finger into the yielding
white plastic package of rolls on the counter. She didn't feel sad, but
she supposed she should. It was very quiet inside the dim store, and she
could hear the man breathing.

"I just came from school and I found her. Just sitting there. Just
dead. I didn't think people died sitting up."

He watched her, seeing the rise and fall of the white blouse over her
breasts, the bones in her wrist so close to the skin that they shone
through. He reached a plump hand across the counter and patted her
hand. Her skin was as cool as water, and his own so hot he thought he
would burn her with his touch.

"It's good when they go like that. They get old, and they just kind
of stop. They don't feel nothin'; it's like you just turn out a light, you
know? Just *click*, and then no more."

She nodded faintly. He took it for grief that she could not put into
words. He moved around the counter and she leaned toward him,
putting her head on his shoulder. He held his body back. He didn't want

her to feel the bulge of his erection. What kind of a man gets a hard-on when he's supposed to be comforting a poor girl like this?

She smelled him, a yeasty odor, and his aftershave lotion. It smelled good. It got the smell of the house out of her nose. She leaned closer to him and he put his hands tentatively on the hip bones that pushed through her blue wool skirt, trying to hold her away from his lower body, but she pushed forward. She felt like a little rabbit to him, all bones, helpless, but her breasts burrowed into his chest, sending such shocks through him that he trembled.

"Don't cry," he whispered, although she wasn't crying at all. "What's your name, girl?"

"Lou— . . . Lureen."

"That's pretty. You're pretty. A pretty, pretty girl." He stroked her hair. "This makes you feel better?"

She nodded her head and moved closer to him. She felt the hardness against her belly, and wondered what it was, and yet, not knowing, liked the feel of it. She worked herself closer to him, feeling the odd stirring that she'd never been able to explain. Her legs felt weak, and she clung to him for support. He lifted her onto the counter and stood between her knees.

"You call me Vito," he whispered. "You like being here with Vito, don't you? You forget about what's outside there. You forget you're sad."

He stroked her hair, her face, and let the fingers covered with silky black hairs trail down her neck. And then he touched her breasts, petting them as if they were separate beings. Stroking, kneading, rubbing them in a circular motion. She closed her eyes. This was the best she'd ever felt in her whole life. She could never remember being touched at all, and now she was being touched in a way she had never imagined. It was so much better than leaning against the washing machine.

"Little rabbit," he murmured. "Poor little rabbit." He opened the buttons on her blouse, and she made no move to stop him. Her breasts felt as if they had grown, as if they had to burst out of her blouse. She kept her eyes closed and gasped when she felt his lips on her nipples, He touched the erect pink flesh gently and then sucked, and she felt a warmth spread between her legs and into her hips and belly.

Suddenly, he moved away and she opened her eyes in protest. She watched, fascinated, as he untied the long white apron, and stood before her in a white tee-shirt and dark trousers. He stared at her breasts and his face was so different, flushed with color, his lips parted. She could see the bulge in his pants and she watched as he unzipped himself and let a great blue-veined cylinder of flesh spring out. It seemed to have a life of its own, standing out from his open fly, the slit at the end of it touched with a drop of moisture.

He pulled at her shoulders, drawing her forward on the counter, and she spread her own legs farther apart, aware of dampness in the crotch of her panties. He was not gentle now, but fumbling and hurried as he tugged at her panties.

She knew that this must be the bad thing that Lena had warned her about, but she didn't care if it hurt. Grunting and panting, the man moved toward her, and she lowered herself onto the purplish probe, sliding down over it, wrapping her legs around his waist.

It did hurt, but only for an instant, and then Lureen felt, for the first time in her life, that the empty place inside her was filled up. She clung to him, and he lifted her clear of the counter, circling the room in a clumsy dance until at last he gave a cry and his arms lost their strength. He set her back on the counter and slumped beside her, his head on his arms, breathing so harshly that she thought he was sick.

"Vito?" She watched him with alarm. "Did I hurt you?"

"Huh?" He looked up at her and began to laugh. "Naw, you sure as hell didn't hurt me, little rabbit. You only just wore me out."

Relieved, she slid off the counter and began to look for her panties. She found them under a table and put them on. She watched him and saw him changed. He had been with her, touching her, surrounding her, enveloping her, and now he seemed so distant; he turned away and zipped up his pants, reached for his apron and tied it around him again.

"Vito?" she said quietly. "Do you still like me?"

He looked up, and his face was back to the way it always was. He didn't seem to know her. He grabbed a rag and started to wipe the counter.

"Sure, sure I like you. I like you fine."

"But you're different—than you were before."

"Well, it's always different after. You know . . . "

"No."

"Didn't you ever do it before?"

"No."

"Oh shit!"

"Well, I never did. But I liked it."

"Lureen . . . how old are you?"

"Sixteen."

He slammed one hand down on the counter and looked at her as if he hated her, and then he slumped and said quietly, "Lureen, I'm sorry. I thought you was older. I wouldna never done it if I knew."

"But I liked it."

"You gonna tell anyone?"

She considered that for a moment. "No. I haven't got anyone to tell. Can I come back again?"

"Sure. You come in anytime. I'll save you one of them pecan pies they send down from Philly."

He was walking her toward the door, his hand flat and insistent on her back, urging her out.

"No. I mean can I come back—like it was today?"

He pulled up the green shade on the door and surveyed the sidewalk outside, satisfied himself that it was empty of traffic, and unlocked the door. "Sure. Well, we'll see. You're O.K., kid. You're just a little young."

She turned against his pressing arm, trying to hold onto the good feelings, and yet seeing them vanish. "Didn't I do it right?"

"Kid. You did fine. I'll see you around. Right?"

Lureen was out the door and on the sidewalk. The ice beneath her feet looked clear on top, but she could see dirt and debris frozen into it where it coated the cement. She turned and headed slowly up the street toward the drugstore corner. It was so cold. Even the drugstore guys had gone inside. She didn't want to go home, but there wasn't anyplace else to go.

"Hey! Kid!"

Lureen looked back at him, standing outside the bread store. And she felt the loss that she would feel for the rest of her life. How could she have been so close to him just a few minutes before and be so separate from him now? How could people pull apart so completely?

She had liked the "bad thing," despite Lena's warning, but she had basked in being held. Once it was over, there was no more holding. She made a half-step toward him again, but his voice held her away.

"I'm real sorry about the old lady. You take care now. Right?"

He didn't want her back. She walked away, wondering. There was something that made men want you close, and there was the thing they could do that took away the empty place, but you couldn't count on them to want you afterward. It didn't make sense to her.

She'd expected that Pete would shout at her when she got home, but he just looked up dully when she walked in. She went to bed all by herself—for the first time—luxuriating in being able to sleep in the middle of the bed, and in the silence.

Lena's departure made so little difference to her that it was as if her grandmother had never existed. Pete went his own way, and Lureen rarely saw him. Sometimes she'd catch a glimpse of him downtown with a woman; it might have been just one woman or a series of women who looked so much alike that she couldn't tell one from the other. He gave her money once in a while and sometimes he brought groceries home. She existed on cokes and egg-salad sandwiches and Franco–American spaghetti, and used whatever money was left over for mov--ies. Pete won a twelve-inch television set on a punchboard. She found it in the living room one afternoon. It must have been for her, she figured, because he was never home to watch it.

It changed her life.

Because she couldn't read, Lureen had drawn all her information from movies and pictures in books. She could not afford to go to the movies very often, but now she could spend hours and hours in front of the television set. The square plastic Philco centered with gray images was an education for her. The soap operas went beyond anything she had ever gleaned from movies; she could be part of them, live through each day's drama on "As the World Turns," and see what a family was supposed to be. It explained things she had never been able to grasp. She realized that Dorothy had not returned because Dorothy was suffering from amnesia. On television these people who had forgotten always came home eventually, and so would her mother.

Television became far more important than going to school, and she went less and less often. When she signed Pete's name to excuse notes, no one questioned her; the only class where she understood what was going on anyway was Home Ec. The things she really needed to know about were home on TV. She could spend a whole day and half the night curled up in Lena's old chair, the shades drawn against the sun. Sometimes she yearned to crawl into the set and be part of the life inside. Time telescoped and she was always amazed when the "Star Spangled Banner" and the nightly prayer came on.

"I Love Lucy" and "Queen for a Day" and the rest erased any memories of Vito Ferrano. She forgot what he looked like; the only thing that remained of that afternoon that Lena died was a rippling sensation, an awareness of her belly. It wasn't insistent enough to make her want the funny fat man to touch her again. If he could make her feel that way, then she suspected any man could.

There *was* a man she dreamed about, a man who walked with her day and night. *Elvis.* When she saw him for the first time on Ed Sullivan, she was stunned by his beauty. He was clean and pure, and yet he moved in a way she'd never seen a man move before. The audience roared and screamed when he moved his hips that way, and the cameras suddenly focused on his face alone. But Lureen felt so much more for Elvis than the audience did; he had such sadness about him. She could see it in his eyes and hear it whispering beneath the beat of his songs. She wanted to put her arms around him and tell him she understood.

Lureen knew that she would meet Elvis sometime, although she wasn't sure how or when it would happen. There were some things a person just knew. She knew that Elvis was good, and she heard on talk shows that he was a Christian and loved his mother, and that he'd been very poor. So he wouldn't make fun of her because of the way she'd been unpopular and lonesome and because she couldn't read. Most of all, she knew he would understand that she had to find her own mother.

Lureen didn't go to school the last Friday in April; she never went on Fridays because that was the day when something important happened on all the soap operas, something that you waited for all week long. She stayed in front of the set until 4:30 in the stuffy living room, the blinds blocking the breeze and daylight.

There was no food in the house, and Pete never came home until late on Friday because it was payday and he went to the tavern. There wasn't any money in the house, but she remembered that Lena had kept a jar of pennies and dimes on the shelf in the hall closet.

It was dark in the closet and the shelf was thick with dust. The coin jar was gone; she'd figured it would be. Her hand brushed against the candy tin where Lena had kept buttons and thread. Curious, Lureen lifted it down, the old eight-sided box, its daisies and roses barely visible anymore under the scratched grime on the lid. She carried it into the kitchen and turned on the hanging light bulb there. Lena could have left a few coins hidden under the buttons; she was surprised one of the old women hadn't taken the candy box away along with all of Lena's other things.

The tin was full of costume jewelry, and she recognized the pieces as if they were from another lifetime. It was Dorothy's jewelry; she had played with it years and years before. A double loop of dusky pink beads shaped like roses, claylike and still giving off the faint fragrance of the petals they'd been pressed from. A charm bracelet with an American flag, a "V for Victory," and an "E" from the steel mill—the kind they gave out during the war, the war when her father went away for a long time—a little cracked bell, and a funny little man with a big nose peeking over a wall. She picked out a flower made of colored stones caught in a tarnished metal ribbon. There were earrings. Dorothy had always worn earrings: tiny bananas and apples, red and white squares, purplish dulled sequins, silver half-moons with smiling, top-hatted ladies on them.

She picked up a watch, shook it, and heard a distant faltering tick. She wound it, but it stopped then, one hand falling inside the scratched face.

Her mother's wedding ring was there too, a thin band of gold where there once had been three small diamonds, now only three spaces with prongs sticking up hollow. She looked inside the band and could make out some writing there. Painfully, she spelled it out: "P.D. to D.D., 11–12–39, L.o.v.e."

"Love?" Boy, that sure didn't sound like her father. Maybe that's what they always wrote on wedding rings.

She'd seen every piece of the jewelry; Dorothy had let her play with it to keep her quiet. But Dorothy had loved jewelry. Why hadn't she taken it with her? Especially her watch and her wedding ring?

Lureen yelped as her finger hit the pin to Dorothy's favorite brooch, a large enameled Dogwood blossom with a pink stone center. Sucking the drop of blood away, she carried the brooch to the bathroom mirror and adjusted it at the neck of her blouse. She could almost see her mother's face stare back at her from the mirror, remember how Dorothy had worn the pin just as she did now.

Puzzled, Lureen put the candy tin back on the shelf. She'd never seen her mother's jewelry around during all the time since she'd gone away, even though Lena had had her sewing things out in the living room often. So the pins and necklaces must not have been there before. If Dorothy had come home to visit, she would surely have waited to see Lureen. She wouldn't have gone away again without seeing her own daughter. It didn't make sense. Maybe Dorothy *had* left without her jewelry and Lena had hidden it from Lureen all these years, and then the old ladies had put Dorothy's things in the sewing tin after Lena died.

Trying to figure it out made her jumpy; she could reason it only to a certain spot and then her thoughts dissolved and she had to start all over again. She couldn't concentrate on the television. She poked around in the refrigerator looking for something to eat even though she didn't feel hungry anymore, but all she could find was an end of cheese with a fuzzy green patch growing on it, and a bowl of something she didn't recognize. She craved something sweet, like a "short-chocolate" at the drugstore. It wasn't a short-chocolate-something; it was just ice and milk and chocolate syrup. The girl at the counter had laughed when, wanting a double-size, she had first asked for a "large-chocolate," instead of a large "short-chocolate."

She dug down in the couch cushions and found a quarter and three pennies, and that was enough. There were probably more coins down there, but she needed to be outside quickly; sometimes, walking seemed to help her think better. But Lureen walked slowly along the Old Lincoln Highway—Main Street—and passed up the drugstore without seeing it.

She didn't realize that the blocks were melting away behind her. She had walked more than two miles in the failing light when she heard the sounds of the carnival. She looked up to see that the field next to the used car lot on the west end of Main Street was filled with tents and rides; a ferris wheel circled above the street, festooned with lights. Caught in the crowd, Lureen walked past the booths and the freak shows. It was so bright that her eyes hurt, and the music made her ears hum. Her vista on the world had been a twelve-inch screen for so long; now it made her dizzy to be shoved along the sawdust path of the midway.

Every stall seemed to have its own music, and a few steps past took her into another channel of sound. The night air smelled of fried onions, hamburgers, chicken corn soup (from the American Legion booth), submarine sandwiches, smoke, beer, and sometimes an acrid wafting of whiskey on the breath of men who nudged her shoulder as they passed. She saw people she recognized, faces from school, and some nodded. But no one stopped to talk to her. She was no one's best friend—not even anyone's second, third, or fourth best friend. It didn't matter; it hadn't mattered for a long time.

Male voices called to her as she was swept past the gambling booths, seducing her with their voices to come and win with the toss of one dime. She smiled at them, shook her head, and was carried on to the next coaxing pitch.

She stayed a long time in front of the freak show, wondering what it must be like for the creatures who stood on the rickety stage to be stared at. A bearded lady with hair on her chest, but with what seemed to be real breasts. A dwarf with a head bigger than any she'd ever seen, shuffling strangely on two tiny legs. A fat lady, sitting on a chair that looked like a throne. The fat lady had short curly hair and her eyes were almost hidden in a face whose red cheeks melted into her neck and her neck into her breasts, cascading flesh falling away from the polka dot, ruffled baby dress she wore. Her huge legs were planted like barrels beneath the baby dress, fat ankles pouring over little baby shoes with red bows.

It made Lureen feel suffocated to see the rolls and rolls of flesh, and she touched her own waist lightly to be sure she could still feel her ribs there. The fat lady lifted a hand slowly and seemed to be beckoning to her with the perfect, star-shaped appendage, the red nails flashing. Lureen turned away and fled into the crowd.

She heard Elvis singing, and she followed the faint thread of his voice, coming finally to a platform at the far end of the carnival grounds. "Heartbreak Hotel" played continuously as four women gyrated slowly before a gathering cluster of men. Lureen stopped, entranced, as they danced in a blue spot-light. They looked beautiful, although when she pushed in a little closer, she could see that they had on an awful lot of make-up.

"What you see here, gentlemen, is only a small sample of what those little ladies will show you inside. Every one of these dancers has been selected for her . . . er . . . particular dancing ability. This is not a family show; so we don't urge you to bring the little woman in. I'm not exaggerating when I promise you that you will never regret the price of one ticket. We're going to be full up inside; so I suggest you get in line now and get your ticket for the kind of show that you've never seen before."

Lureen studied the barker. He was slim, and he had brown hair with sideburns like Elvis. She thought he was kind of handsome, and he moved like he was full of energy or electricity. His white shirt was open at the neck and wet with sweat in his armpits. She liked his voice, and she liked the way he winked at the crowd. She thought it must be exciting to work in a carnival.

The dancing girls all wore satin brassieres and little skirts with gold fringe around the bottom. Their legs were encased in black net stockings with sequins that flashed when the light hit them.

"Now, Lila is going to give you just a short demonstration of what I'm telling you about, gentlemen. Show 'em what I mean, Lila." The barker smiled at the woman at the end of the line. She was older than the rest, and Lureen saw she had a soft layer of fat that was marked with a red line where the fringed skirt circled her waist. She stepped to the front of the stage and began to move her midsection so that you could see the muscles beneath her skin bunch and ripple up and down. It didn't seem quite right to Lureen to have Elvis singing for a dance like this one, but she did think the woman was pretty talented, even though she never smiled and chewed gum all the while she performed.

The men crowding against the platform didn't seem to mind; they weren't watching the dancer's face.

There was a scratching sound that made Lureen wince as Elvis's voice stopped, and "The Steel Guitar Rag" blared out. Now Lila put her hands behind her head and with elbows akimbo began to thrust her pelvis forward violently to the twanging music. The flesh at her waist quivered with each *Boom . . . Boom,* and the watching males sent out a kind of tension that made Lureen step back and cross her arms over her breasts. She'd seen a pack of dogs once circling a cat up a tree and the men reminded her of the straining, growling animals.

The music stopped in mid chorus, and Lila dropped her arms to her sides and stepped back into the line of dancers. All the life disappeared from her body; she didn't look at the crowd, but turned and walked back through the flap in the tent behind the stage.

"She wiggles, she jiggles, and she bounces, men. And she does more, but that's all for now. Line up over here and get your tickets. Fifty cents. One half dollar for a full show inside. Don't tell your wife, and don't tell your girlfriends. The show starts in two minutes; so have your money ready."

A couple of the men grinned with embarrassment and moved away into the constantly surging midway, but most of them dug into their pockets for coins and passed through the ticket stand. Lureen watched the last of the dancers disappear behind the stage and saw that there were spots in the sparkling net stockings that had been darned with heavy black thread.

She stood, hesitantly wondering where to go next. Part of her wished she had the fifty cents to go inside; she was curious about what more Lila could show the crowd that she hadn't done outside. She wondered what it must be like to have so many eyes watching you when you danced, admiring you. And she wondered how you could make your stomach do all those rolling movements that made it look like that.

"Hey! You! Hey, girlie!"

Lureen jumped. The man in the white shirt who'd sold the tickets was leaning over his stand and calling to her. He smiled and she could see white lines in his tanned face as the skin pulled tautly across his cheekbones. She walked a little closer, and his eyes were so blue they were almost white. He was older than she'd thought—maybe about thirty, but she found him the best-looking man she'd ever seen in her whole life.

"You mean me? she asked.

"Yeah, sweetheart. You." He jumped off the platform by placing one arm on the stage and vaulting over the footlights. His biceps stood out on the supporting arm, and his body moved as effortlessly as a leaf in the wind. He was short and that surprised her—hardly taller than she was. He stood so close to her that she wanted to step back. She couldn't.

"You with it?"

"What?

"You with it?"

"I don't understand," she murmured, trapped by the clarity of his eyes.

"You with the show, I mean. You work here?"

"Oh. No—no. I was just watching them dance. I guess they have to study a long time to do that."

He laughed, a sharp rasping bark of a laugh. "Yeah. Oh my yes, a long time. You dance?"

"Not like that. A little—at school, and . . ."

"How old are you?"

"Sixteen."

"Naw," he drawled in disbelief. "You're kidding me. You're eighteen at least. You don't look like no sixteen-year-old girl."

"Really. I'm sixteen."

"I'd say you're eighteen."

She couldn't look away from his eyes, and she shivered.

"I say you're eighteen, and you can dance like a dream."

She didn't answer.

"We've got a place for another girl. With your looks, and your figure, you'd be our star attraction. On-the-job training, free eats, free costumes, thirty-five bucks a week, and you get to travel all over the country. Get you out of this town. I mean some of our girls are on television now, in the big time."

"I can't dance like that," she murmured.

"Sure you can."

"Do you really travel all over the country?"

"You bet. Tomorrow Harrisburg. Pittsburgh. Detroit. Cleveland."

"Memphis? Do you go to Memphis?"

"Why not?"

She stepped backward, tripping over a snaking coil of extension cord and he darted out a tattooed arm to steady her.

"I have to go home now," she stammered.

His eyes still held hers, and he was still smiling. He pointed to a silver trailer parked in the shadows behind the tent. "You change your mind, you come back, hear? You just knock on that door over there. You come back before 3:00 A.M. and I'll be waiting. Just bring your little suitcase, and you knock."

She didn't know what to say. He watched her as she edged away, trying to find a space in the flow of people behind her. Then she found one and slipped in.

"Hey girlie!"

She turned and saw he was back on the little stage. He cupped a hand around his mouth and shouted over the din, "Memphis! New York! Miami!"

Lureen ran almost all the way home, and she kept seeing the man's eyes. She figured he'd been teasing her. She wondered if she'd look pretty in one of the costumes with the fringe and the net stockings, and then she was sure he'd been teasing her. Nobody was going to give a wonderful job like that to her, except. . . . She stopped, winded, walked slowly past Piscoglio's Drugstore, the windows darkened now. It was a lot later than she'd realized. Except maybe it was the same thing as Vito Ferrano. Maybe it was because of the little bit of power she had with men. She wasn't sure she wanted a job because of that. And she probably wouldn't get to see "As The World Turns" anymore since most likely you couldn't have televisions in trailers.

The front porch light was out, but she could see the lamp on in the living room. She went up the steps quietly and tried to make the staircase inside without Pete's seeing her. He didn't care how late she stayed out, but she didn't like to talk to him when he was drunk, and he'd be sure to be drunk by this late.

"Where the hell you been?" His voice stopped her, and she blinked as she walked into the living room. The room looked different somehow, but she couldn't tell what was changed.

And then she looked toward the television set. It wasn't there. She darted glances around the room and she couldn't see it anywhere. She looked at Pete in bewilderment.

"So? What's the matter with you?" he said. He was really drunk, so drunk his whole face seemed squashed and the few strands of hair he usually combed over the top of his head were down in his eyes.

"Where's my television?"

"It ain't *your* television."

"Where'd you put it?" She felt panicky. "Did you put it in the kitchen?"

"It ain't here."

"Don't tease me. I want to know where it is. I've got shows I've got to watch."

"I gave it to Myrna. Hers is on the fritz and I said she could have it. Hell, I never watch the damned thing."

"I watch it!" she screamed. "I've got my shows. I watch it all the time."

"Well, you ain't gonna watch it no more because I gave it to Myrna."

Lureen sank down on the straight chair next to the hallway. He meant it. He wasn't going to bring it back. She started to cry, wiping her nose with the back of her hand.

Suddenly Pete was standing in front of her, weaving but standing. He grabbed at the dogwood pin on her blouse and pulled it off, ripping the thin material as the pin came away.

"What the fuck are you doing with this?"

"My mother left it. It was in Grandma's stuff. It's mine now."

"Your mother didn't leave one shitty thing here, dummy. She took it all with her when she waltzed out of here."

"It's hers! She must have left it. I remember when she used to wear it."

He held the brooch high over her head, making her jump for it as he staggered away.

"She took it when she run out," he shouted. "She took every damn thing but the silverware."

"Grandma had it," Lureen said softly. "She had all of Mama's stuff, and I found it in the closet. Give it to me!"

"They sent it back." Pete stopped, turned back to his chair and lifted his can of beer and drained it.

"What?" Lureen was in a frenzy. It was her fault. If she hadn't gone out, he couldn't have stolen her television set. If she hadn't

looked in the closet, she wouldn't have found the jewelry. "Who sent it back?"

"No one." Pete studied the floor between his bare feet.

"Who sent it back? I'm going to find her. I'm going to ask her."

"You ain't gonna find her! Because she'd dead. Dead. Dead. Dead."

"No!" Lureen screamed to drown out his words. "She's got amnesia. She can't remember how to get home."

"She can't remember because she's dead, you airhead. They sent all that junk back from some morgue in Chicago a coupla years ago. She left me, and she left you, and she wasn't nuthin but a whore. Shit! Shit, why'd you make me tell you? Ain't I taken care of you all this time? You just better believe she's dead and forget about her."

She looked at him without expression. She was more shocked than Pete was when she leapt on him, raking his face with her fingernails, driving her knee into his hairy body. He covered his head with his arms as she beat on him, screaming, "Liar! Liar!"

He brought his arm back and knocked her halfway across the living room. She lay there stunned as he stood over her, blood oozing from the scratches on his face. He lifted his arm again, and then stopped. He could kill her. She would kill him if she had the strength. Her head ached where she'd hit the doorjamb.

She watched his chest heave, and then saw him lift his hand to his face and stare at it as it came away stained with his own blood. He turned and walked unsteadily toward the bathroom.

She was gone before he came out, everything she owned jammed into a shopping bag. She would never remember running back to the carnival grounds. There was no place to go back to, and no place else to run to.

She pounded on the door of the little silver trailer, saw a light come on inside, and then the man was there in the doorway. He was bare-chested and she could see he had a purple snake tattooed across his belly and over one shoulder. He smiled when he recognized her and stood back to let her in.

He looked at the shopping bag in her hand, and asked, "Now, how old did you say you were?"

She stared back with flat eyes. "Eighteen. I'm eighteen like you said."

After a few days, she saw that the baby wasn't as ugly. Its head had settled into a nice round shape, and they all came to see it and told her he was a pretty baby. Dolly Dimples, the fat lady, took care of her, bringing her food as the caravan hurtled through the nights and days, heading south. Her breasts filled with milk, and it was a relief when she nursed him. He was cute—like a doll—and he didn't cry very much. When he did cry, she discovered that she could quiet him with a teaspoon of whiskey. She didn't really want him, but she didn't hate him anymore either.

She decided to give him a really nice name, something different. Duane—because that sounded good with Demich. And Elvis for a middle name, because she still thought about Elvis sometimes, even though they never got closer to Memphis or Nashville than Wilmington, Delaware.

When she had to perform, she either got Dolly to watch him, or she gave him a little extra whiskey and he slept in a cardboard box behind the stage.

He turned out to be a really smart little kid, and the roustabouts taught him to swear when he was two and everybody thought that was funny. She didn't know what the hell she was going to do with him when he got old enough to go to school, but the kid was a fact of life, and that's the way it was.

Sometimes she thought maybe she should adopt him out, but she never got around to it, and after a while he just seemed to take care of himself. She liked him when he was good, and when he wasn't, there was usually somebody who'd take him off her hands. She guessed she wasn't cut out to be a mother.

Lureen cried a lot. Just some little thing would make her eyes puddle up, and she couldn't help weeping. She tried never to think about Dorothy, not after that last night in Coatesville, but once in a while she just couldn't help it. She still dreamed about her mother and woke to find tears streaming down her face. Little things made her cry too; she couldn't bear to see the carcasses of cats and dogs that had been killed along the highways and left there as if nobody cared about them. Sometimes she cried because of things that men said to her and did to her, but that didn't last long because there was always another man in another town.

The baby hated it when she cried. He patted her face and cooed, "Poor Reenie," and she would hold him and rock him until her tears went away. It was a funny thing about that little kid; when he looked at her with those big eyes, it seemed like he understood everything, like he was the grown-up and she was the baby. The gypsies said that meant he was "born old," and it seemed like maybe he had been. Lureen was dumbfounded when she learned that Duane had taught himself to read when he was only just past four. All that trouble she'd always had trying to figure out letters and numbers and her own kid could read better than she could. The gypsies said he was born under a Scorpio moon and that was why, but she didn't believe that; she'd seen them finagle too many suckers out of the gold in their teeth with all their spooky double-talk. Besides, Duane wasn't *that* smart. He got lost just like any kid and would stand in the midway bellering for her at the top of his lungs, crying til the snot ran down his face.

He always had a dirty face and wet pants, and he was afraid of the dark too. It was hard to figure him out. Sometimes he seemed grown up, and sometimes he was only a baby, clinging to her skirt and pulling on her until she felt like screaming.

Still, when she got to crying so bad and he looked at her and said, "Don't worry, Reenie, I'll take care of you," she just had to believe him. And she'd look right at him and say, "You do that Duane. You always take care of your mama and we'll both make out O.K."

PART ONE
DUANE
SEPTEMBER 1, 1981

CHAPTER ONE

He was as invisible as any living creature could be when venturing out
of its natural habitat. Protective coloration. A tall man, all long bones,
and yet crouched in what should be an excruciating position for even
an average-sized man. He had trained himself to remain motionless for
hours, a lesson learned from the yogi in the freak show who made the
rubes gasp when he lay down on his bed of nails. He was shrouded
behind a wall of trees and vegetation where humans could not see him,
and the woods creatures skittered by him without fear or even awareness of his presence among them.

The huge rock he'd selected for his vantage point had been deposited by some glacier eons before. Its worn surface was baked hot where
his toes gripped it, and the September sun above him seared the late
afternoon and made the air smell of baked pine needles. But the man
was oblivious to the sweat that oozed from his pores and snaked over
his body and to the dusty membranes in his throat. There was a canteen he'd stashed beneath the lowest outcropping of his perch, but his
mind was not on slaking his thirst. He felt no thirst. He felt no pain
from the cramped muscles in his calves and thighs as he hunkered
there, his long spine bent improbably forward, his elbows resting easily
on his bony knees.

He used only one of his senses: sight. The binoculars pressed to his
eyes lent him the semblance of a great brown frog alert for prey. He
could see more keenly than any hundred men without glasses, but he
had to be sure that this time she would be perfect. He had thought he
had found flawless specimens before, only to find that they were
shabby, deceptive imitations.

They had wasted his time and his energy and they had made him
angry. He'd revealed himself to them, deluded by their lies and pretending, and so he had had to deal with them. God, how he hated the
ugliness of it, but they each deserved it, and he had done what had to
be done. Each time, for days afterward, he had trouble thinking clearly.

He couldn't have that now. His mind was one of his weapons. He'd
known he was smarter than hell ever since he'd known anything, and
he never made the same mistake twice; it was just that the sluts could
put on so many different faces.

His mind had kept him alive. He had endured because of it, with no
help from a goddamned soul. Ever.

His physical development had kept pace with his mind. Six feet, five inches tall, 195 pounds, with long, long femur and humerus bones supported by taut, functional muscles that gave him the strength some men coaxed and honed in gymnasiums and on playing fields. Sports were anathema to him, an odds-on threat to the only entities he was sure of—his body and his brain. He'd seen too many old boxers with stove-in faces and scrambled minds, reliving glory days that never happened; even Broadway Joe was walking around on legs with knees three times as old as he was. Stupid.

He had only the slightest of defects, and that had occurred before he was old enough to prevent it: a slight bowing out of his shinbones, the aftermath of rickets from a diet of french fries, Coca Cola, snow cones, and never enough milk. Once he was big enough to steal or beg his own food, he'd eaten well, and become stronger than most men by the time he was twelve. He had just a vestige of hearing loss in his left ear; one of Lureen's boyfriends had knocked him across the trailer after he bit him on the leg, but that had almost been worth it—to see that fat turkey howling and jumping up and down on one leg.

He rarely thought of the raised scar that ran across his back from shoulder to shoulder like a bolt of lightning—bluish, smooth skin there, the keloid left when the burns healed. No feeling there, as if the streak of scar were full of Novocain. He couldn't remember pulling the coffee pot down off the two-burner gas stove, but he recalled the brilliant pain of the hot liquid cascading over his back and his screaming for Lureen who didn't come. He didn't blame his mother. He'd never held her responsible for any of the bad things; she'd done the best she could. Women liked to trace the slick-skinned path across his back, and he always told them he had been struck by lightning. Bitches who mothered him turned him off.

He'd had a mother. The only mother.

Lureen.

Her name whispered through the synapses of his brain cells and made his gut roll over. He missed her with a consuming ache, just as he'd always missed her. She was woman to him, and would be forever. Vague, tentative, frightened—too frightened to be with him all the times he needed her.

Sometimes when he visualized her face, he saw vertical bars superimposed on the image, and that had bewildered him for a long time, until he weighed the variables and realized he was seeing her through the slats of his crib. He could smell stale urine, feel the sodden lumps of his own feces in his full diaper. Nobody was supposed to be able to remember that far back, but "nobody" wasn't him.

He could not picture the men. He had seen them, but they were nothing to him beyond huge figures looming over his crib, or, worse, part of two locked bodies a few feet away, moving together in what had seemed to him a cruel struggle that surely hurt Lureen.

He'd sensed that some of those strangers had liked him O.K., and that others were pissed that they had to do what they did to his mother while he watched them silently, his little, useless hands clenching the crib's bars. He did remember his rage. He'd wanted to kill them before he had even known the word for it.

One of them took her away and never brought her back. He'd heard *dead* then, and whispered phrases that made him feel dead too.

He shut his eyes and blocked the memory.

The twitching in his arms accelerated, and he lowered the glasses from his brow and stretched, sending a family of quail fleeing in panic. He remembered the canteen, reached for it, and drained it of the hot, tinny-tasting water. He'd have to remember to get some salt tablets; the weather was much hotter than he'd expected. He'd always heard that Washington was cool and rainy, but that turned out to be the part around Seattle. All the sweating was making him lose potassium. Salt tablets would fix that.

He lay back on the rock, and the flat surface felt good under his extended spine. Tiny bits of sand and mica adhered to his damp skin, and he felt the difference in tactile sensation between the unscarred skin and the fibrous keloid. He would have to remember to wear a shirt to cover the scar; it made him highly describable to the law.

Research. Anything could be researched—legal or illegal—and understanding witness identification was one of his more meaningful projects. The dead didn't describe, but there were always others. He had a long headstart on any adversary because of his intelligence, and he'd bettered his odds with information. He'd tried it on brains alone in the beginning, but the sheer number of cops, even bumbling along, outweighed his advantage. Most cops were stupid assholes who went by the book, never seeing subtle movement outside the pattern, but there had been a few of them who took the time to think and they'd blocked his path.

He'd done time for the little stuff—not a lot of it, but enough to let him know he couldn't stand to be locked up. Juvey hall, which was basically a joke. A month or two in one of their "training schools," but they'd never put him in the joint, and they never would. He was almost grateful to the smarter dicks because they'd taught him more unaware than they'd taken from him; he'd vacuumed what he needed out of their heads.

He knew how to change the way he was remembered. If he slumped, he could diminish his tallness by inches. The old fart in Denver who'd handed over her savings to the "bank examiner" had been adamant that he was under six feet and over thirty; she hadn't recognized him in the line-up, picked the off-duty cop standing next to him. The bunco dick had been pissed when he couldn't get the prosecutor to file. And Duane was out of Denver on the next plane. It was a disappointment anyway. Smog. He'd expected Denver to be clear and on a mountain and it was flat and smoky, full of pretend-cowboys and dull brick houses.

Washington looked like the calendars said it did. Seattle was surrounded by mountains, and it got even better when he'd crossed over them to the east. He liked the orchards and the brown hills that looked like giants fallen asleep in the baking afternoon, Gullivers who might wake at any moment to roll over and create an entirely new skyline.

Most of all, he liked the forest. He looked straight up at the trees above him. The firs and pines seemed to grow higher as he stared, their top-most branches turning to black filigree against the sun. There was a continuity here. They must have always been here, and they would always be here, reaching stoically toward the sky. It gave him a transcendant peace that only reinforced his choice of this place.

He closed his eyes against the sun, pale green eyes flecked with hazel. From the side the pupils were not the smooth concave half-sphere others had, but notched.

Lureen's image emerged now on the nether surface of his eyelids. He could see her little face with the regular features, her huge frightened pansy eyes, the faint dusting of freckles that touched her nose and cheeks in summer, and the mouth so soft. She had such a mass of dark flyaway hair, hair so fine that it curled in tendrils around her jaw and then became as evanescent as smoke haloed around her fragile skull. She'd hated her hair and tried to tame it with endless brushing that had only set it alive with electricity. Everything about her had been ephemeral, that tiny girl-woman as transient as a dragonfly.

He sighed. At twenty-four, he was already two years older than she would ever be. Still, she was always with him, waiting just beyond the limits of his peripheral vision. He sometimes felt that, if he could only turn his head quickly enough, he would catch her and draw her back to him.

He knew *that* Lureen was gone forever. But he also knew that she did not rest, that she still wandered lost and terrified in the world just beyond the tree tops and on the other side of the mountains.

His name was about all she had been able to give him, beyond life itself. Duane Elvis Demich. One of his cell mates in the reform school had pointed out to him what his initials spelled.

"You're dead, man," the stupid ass had chortled. "Get it? D.E.D. Dead. That ain't what you'd call lucky initials. D-e-e-wane Elvis. What the hell kind of pussy name is that?"

He had slammed the other boy back against the metal bunk and held him, dangling, above the floor until he just about peed his pants. Nobody ever mentioned his name again.

She had chosen that name, given him a name unlike any other. The only material things he ever bothered to keep were the warped 45 records she'd treasured so—Elvis's records. God, when the man himself dropped dead, it had been like she'd died again. He liked to think that Elvis was with her someplace, making it easier for her until he could set her free.

Sometimes he wondered why he couldn't have looked like her, and shuddered when he imagined her giving birth to him. How could such a tiny girl have delivered the great mass of him? Had she forgiven him the pain of that May night in Michigan? He'd found his creased, stained birth certificate and seen his birth weight: ten pounds, eleven ounces; it had made him wince to think of it.

"Mother: Lureen Dorothy Demich. Born: March 7, 1940. Birthplace: Coatesville, Pennsylvania. Father: Unknown."

His hair was light auburn, thick, and wavy. His eyes were green, or gray, or hazel, depending on his thoughts. His features were powerful, chiseled, defined, where hers had been so delicate. Viewed from the side, he had the etched-coin image of a young Greek god, just as her Elvis had had when he was younger. Seen full face, he had a slightly jarring appearance; the two sides of his face had come together and joined a few millimeters from true alignment. The off-center result was not enough to make him less handsome, and most people didn't notice it, but he wondered about it sometimes. His right eye slid off just a little, drooping when he was tired, as did his cheek on that side. Sometimes, he covered up one side of his face or the other and studied the portion left to view in the mirror. The left side looked angelic and calm, but the right was evil.

What the hell. He'd only done what he had to do. Survival is the law of the jungle, and the fittest don't regret what they do to stay alive. He had surmised that morals consisted of only what one perceived as right or wrong, and that what people said and what they actually practiced rarely coincided anyway. Most of the carnies he'd known in his first world took care of each other and ripped off anyone in the civilian world with impunity. Even cons had certain standards of ethical behavior. But the straight world—outside the tents and outside the walls, anything went. That's where the real animals were.

The tree darkness overhead devoured the sun and the wind lost its warmth, reminding him he was about out of time for the day. The massive rock had turned dank beneath him. He sat up and made a sweep of the two-lane road fronting the river's edge, looking for any sign of activity. It was presently empty of cars or joggers.

He had a gut feeling that this was going to be the place. He had always sensed vibrations of what was going to be propitious for him, and he'd been almost shaken with the strength of the signals he'd picked up as he had crossed the Cascades and seen the vista of eastern Washington spread out before him. What he sought waited here for him to discover.

He was a watcher, unseen, and he had an indefinable control over those he observed; they never knew he was near. Sometimes he prowled through lovers' lanes, padding silently up behind parked cars to see what was beyond the steamed windows, a woman struggling and sighing in the arms of some horny bastard behind the steering wheel, glimpses of bare flesh and tangles of arms and legs. He could get so close he could hear them rutting there, heedless of any danger.

Although he wasn't a voyeur, he couldn't stanch the unbidden rush of blood to his groin, the erection that pushed at the fly of his jeans when he watched the fools playing at love. They had no comprehension of what real passion or commitment was, but they could mimic the act of love and trick his body to react instinctively. It annoyed him because that meant he'd have to find a place to relieve himself of the urgency in his genitals. He never thought of breaking into the cars and having the women he watched, nor did he consider having sex with the loud and pushy tramps who flocked into the Trail's End Bar back in Natchitat, sending out less than subtle signals to him with their self-conscious laughter, their compliant posture as they leaned against the juke box pretending to make selections. Women always came on that way with him. They liked his bigness, his lidded stare as he watched them over a schooner of beer, but their made-up faces fell and their giggling faltered when he turned his back on them and walked across the gravel lot to his motel room.

He had no time now for any of that, and he was irritated at the betrayal of his own body, of that male response to anything female and young and soft, or anyone who looked that way in barlight.

The Big Apple Motel lacked a lot, but it gave him a base of operations. And it was cheap, a few steps up from the shacks furnished for migrant workers who flooded Natchitat when the crop neared fruition. The manager had assumed that he was part of them, a little better dressed, a little more savvy, but basically a transient willing to pay twelve bucks a night for a single iron bed, a toilet, sink, and a hot plate.

He'd stayed at the Hyatt Regency in San Francisco, the Brown Palace in Denver, and the Fairmont in Dallas, and had been charged more for one breakfast from room service than two days rent at the Big Apple. The Big Apple stank of sweat, spilled beer, semen, and Pine-sol, a permeating miasma that seemed to be ingrained in the asphalt tile floors and plywood walls. He could rid himself of the odor only by smoking and staying out of the dump from dawn until midnight. But it suited for now. Suited his medium-thick bankroll and suited his need for anonymity in Natchitat.

He had a couple of hundred bucks, and that was as low as he planned to get, and so he worked one of the minor scams available, nothing that would take much energy or much thought. It had taken him only a day to isolate the product most needed in Natchitat. The migrant shacks were a few miles outside of town, and few of the alkies had transportation into town. He saw they would cheerfully kill each other over a half-full bottle of Tokay but would not walk into Natchitat to buy the stuff for $1.19 a fifth at the Safeway. He could buy the cheapest vinegar-wine for $3.29 a gallon, and he bought ten gallons a day. Bottling was cheap; he paid one of the winos a buck to gather all the empties he could find, and he filled the dirty bottles with his Safeway supply. He made the rounds of the camps each evening with his Harley's sidecar filled with fifths of retread Tokay, and sold out quickly at two and a quarter apiece. His daily profit was $75.60—less the buck for the bottle man.

"A goddamned savior," one of his customers had called him, as he cradled a full bottle of Tokay. Two thousand bucks a month and he was a goddamned savior to boot. He'd made ten—twenty—times more than that as a bunco man, but that had taken full days of his time, and he needed time for more than money now.

The road was offering possibles infrequently; he was spotting mostly carloads of fishermen headed home. He stood finally and whirled his long arms to ease the strain of watching all day. He pulled the sweat shirt with *Ohio State* printed on it over his head, replaced the binoculars with mirrored sunglasses, and leapt off the rock.

He disliked this part of his day the most. He would have to eat, deliver to his customers, sleep, and rise tomorrow to begin again. He resented his need to eat and sleep as much as he detested the sexual embers that flashed into fire so often. Bodily functions delayed his quest, but he was ravenous now and could think only of a raw steak and cold beer.

The bike was safe, hidden by the fallen fir and the huckleberry bushes. Even a plane overhead would not be able to make it out. If the time came when he had to ditch it, he planned simply to send it roaring into the river. He ran his hand over the bulges in the saddle bag instinctively and relaxed as he felt the outlines of the guns inside; they were both there—the pistol and the dismantled rifle.

He was pushing the bike through the last copse of trees onto the roadway when he saw her. He blinked his eyes to clear the orange outline of the setting sun, but she was still there when he looked again, his breathing suspended by her perfection.

She ran alone, her breath sounds carrying back to him as he watched from the trees. Her jogging shoes slapped the asphalt steadily, but she ran like all women, arms flung out too far from her sides, breasts bouncing. The woman's hair was tied back with a red band around her forehead, wispy, fine, black, and faintly curly.

He must have made a sound, although he was not aware of it. For an instant, she turned her head toward the woods, and he saw her full face. Her large eyes looked . . . not frightened, but wary . . . and she ran past him, stepping up her pace.

He stopped himself from calling out to her; she would not recognize him yet. He had to expect that it would take a long time, but he felt the first ballooning of joy in his gut, the first wonder that it had come about. His knees trembled as he watched her run away from him, knowing it was only for the moment, knowing that she would never really run away from him again.

There was lettering on the back of her T-shirt. He raised his binoculars to make out what it said:

Natchitat County Sheriff's Office
Wives' Bowling League

And beneath those smaller letters, a name in flowing script:

Joanne

CHAPTER TWO

Danny Lindstrom watched the red and yellow lights dotting the dispatcher's panel and saw them blur, merge into each other, and then separate. He shook his head, as if he could jar the fatigue loose with an abrupt movement.

It was 4:12 A.M., and he was officially off duty, but it was always difficult to come down off shift—especially third watch. He chose to work the 8:00 P.M. to 4:00 A.M. shift, because it gave him his days with Joanne. But he knew also that the hours of darkness were when everything happened, and the sights and sounds and smells set his mind at a pitch where adrenalin flowed as a natural component of blood.

When it was hot and the moon was full, like tonight, almost every radio squawk brought situations laced with danger and excitement. He wanted it as much as he feared it. Hell, he sought it out; he was bored with routine police work and even after eight years he still got a kick out of flipping on the blue lights and jamming his thumb on the siren button. But it left him drained physically and emotionally and always with that fine edge of anxiety when it was time to pack it in and go home.

It was hard to let go.

He remembered now the hassle with Joanne. He hated arguing with her just as he was leaving for work, but she was determined to go out jogging by herself, no matter how many times he'd warned her that being a policeman's wife was no automatic guarantee against rape. And that had made her madder. Everything set her off lately. He knew what it really was; it was the same old argument about the baby, or, rather, the fact that there was no baby. Every time she started her period, she cried.

"You don't just pull babies out of a hat," he'd told her.

"No, you don't, Danny. At least, we sure don't. If you could just see past your precious ego and go have those tests, maybe we'd find out what's wrong with our hat."

"*My* hat, you mean," he'd said, and slammed out of the house, and immediately felt rotten. What she was asking of him wasn't that much, but he couldn't bring himself to jerk off into a bottle.

He rubbed his eyes, trying to close out the picture of Joanne, her jaw set, her eyes furious. He hadn't even thought about her all night. Since he and Sam had reported in at a quarter to eight, neither of them had had time to think about anything, take a leak, or have a cup of coffee or a meal break. That was one way to avoid thinking about marital problems.

It had begun with a squaw fight at the Bald Eagle—two of them clawing and scratching over the sorriest buck of a man he'd come across in a long time. When it was over, there'd been blood all over the Bald Eagle, and enough spilled beer to float the whole place right down Main Street into the Columbia River. One of the old gals had her breast laid open from her collarbone right through her right nipple, and the other had fought and kicked and bitten them as they wrestled her into their patrol car. Sam was nursing a dead-center hit in his family jewels and their unit was missing a back window. The object of the ladies' jealousy had sat at the bar boozing quietly throughout the fray, never looking up. Hell, he'd been smart; *his* balls weren't hurting.

Danny glanced over at Sam who sat gingerly on the edge of the report desk, scribbling out the Field Investigation Report on the pickup they'd stopped right after midnight, an old beater full of bearded punks who'd given them a Seattle address and a lot of flak about being pulled over. Something was wrong about that truck, but they hadn't scored a hit on Wants and Warrants, and they'd had to let them go. They'd both figured the rig was a mobile cocaine stash, but they couldn't search it: no probable cause. The inviolate rights of the American citizen. Sure as hell, they'd get a call from the coast on that one in a week or so, but the old truck would be long gone by then.

Danny sighed. He wondered sometimes why they bothered. Every time they made a stop like that one, they were flirting with having a .45 shoved up their noses.

The state cop—Richards, yeah, Richards—had bought the farm on the same stretch of highway last winter, just walking over to some vehicle he'd stopped. He and Sam had found the poor bastard sprawled face down in the snow with his ticket book still in his hand, his gun still holstered. Richards's body lying there wasn't as bad somehow as the imprint left behind in the frozen bank after the hearse left. Angel in the snow. The perfect outline of arms and legs and head there, and the great splotch of red where Richards's blood had melted the snow beneath his heart.

They'd thrown a great funeral, though. Cops from Spokane. Cops from Seattle, Wenatchee, Yakima, Ellensburg, even Puyallup, with a sprinkling of FBI guys, ATF agents, the Mounties in their red tunics, plus the whole damned State Patrol. Well, they should be good at funerals. Richards's was the third cop funeral in eastern Washington in a year.

A familiar bleakness rose in his gut, and he drew a deep breath. Sometimes he could see himself lying beside a road someplace, as motionless as a drunk, only not drunk. Dead. He wondered if Sam ever felt that presentiment of doom, if Sam ever felt that his time was running out. Danny never asked him; talking about fear was an unwritten taboo with cops. Don't say it out loud and it won't happen.

If either of them was living on borrowed time, it would have to be Sam. Sam was forty-eight, a veteran of two departments and twenty-seven years, survivor of two marriages, and with such a thirst for alcohol that his liver should have turned to stone years ago. Booze had gotten him booted off the Seattle Police Department, out of the homicide unit. Sam had made it on the street, on the bikes, and into the rarefied air of homicide. Danny wondered how it must be for him to be back in uniform now in a county car.

But that was something else they never talked about.

He studied Sam as he bent over the report, one hand splayed on the desk, his long, skinny legs dangling next to the spitoon that had been there for forty years. Clinton looked as if he'd been born and raised in Natchitat County. His tooled boots were beat up but polished, just like every other deputy's were. His skin was as tanned and criss-crossed with frown and smile lines as any apple grower's. Danny couldn't picture him in the suit, white shirt, and striped tie he must have worn when he was a Seattle dick.

He stretched and said softly to Sam, "How's your balls? Maybe you better get home and pack them in ice."

Sam stood up painfully and grinned, showing the gap between his front teeth. "They're better than yours on a good day, Junior."

Fletcher looked up from the dispatch desk and laughed. "He's right, Clinton. You better get on back to your trailer and ice 'em down. At your age, anything that will make them keep, you better give it a shot."

"There's some things that go on forever, gentlemen," Sam said. "I may just drop in on Mary Jean on the way home, Fletch, and show her what a real stud can do—since you're stuck here playing radio."

Fletcher laughed.

"Mary Jean's working tonight, old buddy. You'll have to go over to the maternity ward and see if she can slip out to the broom closet with you, but don't hold your breath. I just talked to her and they're catching babies over there as fast as the mamas can squeeze them out."

"Full moon," Sam nodded. "You can count on it. I'll nail her next week."

"It won't be hard to catch her," Fletcher grinned. "That little woman is putting on weight. I think she weighs more than I do."

Mary Jean Sayers outweighed Fletch easily by eighty pounds, but Danny and Sam tactfully avoided agreeing with the little radio operator. Sam, in fact, envied Fletch, dreading the thought of returning to his own mobile home empty of any living thing except his old tomcat.

Sam didn't want to leave the sheriff's office; it was more home to him than anyplace else, just as all the department offices over the years had been. He belonged here, bullshitting with Fletch and Danny and the deputies who wandered in and out. He liked the smell of the place: cigar smoke, dusty files, leather, gun oil, and drifts of aroma from the jail kitchen beyond the steel mesh doors behind the waiting room. Working graveyard, he could make the work time stretch, usually delay until the sun began to creep up on the other side of the hills before he'd finished his paper work.

Everybody else had someplace to go after shift, and someone to go to. Sam had run through everyone he'd ever had waiting for him, and he tried not to think about the women who had finally had enough of him. Enough of him, and liquor, and too much overtime, too many night call-outs, and his stumblings from grace with other women.

When Sam left home at twenty to join the navy, he encountered a seemingly endless supply of girls and more-than-girls who responded both to his open acceptance of them and his profound sexual force. Somehow, he could not keep them or they could not keep him. But until he was forty, until Nina, he had emerged unscathed beyond a fleeting depression. After Nina, he still liked women but doubted that any singular love might be his again. And he blamed only himself. Even sitting here in the office, nursing his bruises, he felt no animosity toward the Indian woman who'd landed the blow. She'd been hysterical over a real or imagined rejection by the runty cowboy at the bar. She hadn't wanted to go to jail, but he couldn't blame her for that. He'd been in a lot of jails, knowing he wasn't the one to be locked in, and they still gave him the feeling that his throat was closing up, that he could not expand his lungs fully behind the iron doors.

The Indian girls bloomed and faded quickly, like the morning glories that clung to the trellis outside his trailer. Their cheekbones soon blurred with fat, their burnished skin turned putty color, and their reedlike bodies became trapped in a burgeoning cocoon of their own flesh. The Indian men buckled too under the pressures of the white man's culture, but Sam didn't feel sorry for them the way he did for the women.

Wanda Moses hadn't meant to kick him personally; he'd just been part of the enemy. Tomorrow she'd wake up in the women's section of the jail with a grinding headache, puking, and she would have no memory of how she'd gotten there.

Danny's voice pierced his reverie. "You ready to split, pard?"

Sam slid the original of the FIR into the box marked "Under-sheriff," and the carbons into the in-take file, and then limped toward Danny with the pretense of a man in excruciating pain. Danny laughed, and Sam wished for the thousandth time that there was some way to delay the moment when they'd head out on the highway in Danny's pickup. He loved Danny, as he'd loved all his partners, all the men who had stood between him and harm, all the men whose lives he, in turn, had felt responsible for.

Neither of his wives had understood the strength—the need—in that bond between males.

Penny had screamed at him once, "You care more about that god-damned Al Schmuller than you do about me! He gives you more of a hard-on than I do!"

That had been true, in a way. Not the last part. But Al knew where he lived and how he lived and what a tenuous grasp each of them had on staying alive when they worked the Tact Squad during the riots of the sixties. He and Al had faced ugly things together, and then drank together at the Greek's afterward. And three martinis barely blurred the memory of firebombs lobbed from roofs of old buildings at Twenty-third and Pine.

When he walked out, he'd thought that it would be temporary, but she'd never let him come back. Three days after the divorce, she'd married a civilian.

He'd thought Gloria would be different because she worked in the records section, and because she was a cop's widow. It had been O.K. as long as they worked the same shift. Had he loved Gloria? It was hard to remember. He'd loved her kid and had probably stayed with the mother longer because of the boy. But the marriage had started to erode from the moment he was assigned to second watch.

When it was over, he missed the kid more than Gloria.

And then there was only the job, and he was all right. He was good. He could concentrate and learn, and he went to every seminar he could sign up for: death investigation, narcotics, bomb search, even a weird demonstration of blood patterns when Englert, the expert from Oregon, showed up with the real stuff (and Lord knows where he got it) and explained how to tell from the spatters whether it was high- or low-velocity impact blood spray.

Sam found he could limit his drinking to a beer or two. When he moved into the homicide unit, it made up for a lot of his losses; it was what he was meant to do. It seemed as though he was always working, but nobody cared anymore if he was home at dawn or at noon. He had the knack. That it *was* a knack to see through the intricate puzzles of violent death did not seem strange to him. He reveled in his skill, and accepted the commendations from the brass and the respect of his peers casually.

There were women in his life again, women who wanted him, the thirty-five-year-old Sam Clinton who had it all together after the long bad time. Their faces blended into a melange of sexual satisfaction and escape. He called them all "Sweet Baby," and he was neither committed to or involved with any of them, although he tried to stay long enough so that they were not one-night-stands in their own minds, and not so long that he might inflict harm when he left. He grew adept at knowing when to leave. He could no more have done without women than he could have gone without food, but too much closeness threatened him. He'd thought he could go on forever—tasting, enjoying, and moving on when he sensed the time was right. Each parting had torn something from him, but something so subtly damaging that he'd never felt the wound.

Jake Sorensen was his homicide partner—Old Jake, who at fifty-six was long since past voluntary retirement age. Jake hung on. Sam made him strong enough to get through the six-month evaluations. Sam made him look good. Together, they made a powerful team. Clinton-and-Sorensen, never referred to singularly and they wanted it that way. They drew the more difficult cases, worked them deftly, only rarely bringing in a loser to molder in the unsolved file drawer. Jake just missed being a joke in his rumpled leisure suits dappled with cigar ashes, his gut bulging over his belt, and his eyes magnified behind thick glasses. He dithered and wasted time and energy, but with Sam he was transformed into something better, into a working dick with thirty years' experience. They filled in the chinks in each other's armor.

When Sam met Nina, she caught him to her before he could see the danger. The others had been young, so young that their personalities could not harm him. Nina was lost when he met her; she'd been lost for a long time, and yet he was drawn to her by the sheer strength of her mind.

The homicide dicks steered clear of Nina Armitage, wary of a brilliant woman, vaguely resentful of a woman in a business rightfully peopled by males. They brought cases to her in the prosecutor's office only because they had to. Nina had climbed to the position of chief criminal deputy, not through her charms—for she betrayed none—but because she was one hell of an attorney. She worked three times as hard as any man, driving her slender, awkward body beyond what seemed the point of endurance, and kept on going.

She considered all policemen, including the chief, dumb cops, and even in court, even when they were on her side, she questioned them in a patronizing way. Behind her back they called her "the titless wonder," and worse.

Still, Sam was enthralled by her presence in the courtroom, never giving ground or depending on her femaleness to curry favor with judge or jury. She was as caustic as lye, her voice so husky it seemed she fought consciously to keep any feminine modulation from it. Her long, straw-colored hair hung in her face as she bent over the yellow legal pads, scribbling constantly, and she tossed it back with the impatience that was an integral part of her. Her skin was pale and freckled. True, she appeared to have no breasts, but Sam thought her long legs were sensational.

When they carried their cases to her so carefully catalogued, so neatly sprinkled with "probable causes" and good physical evidence, she got them their arrest warrants, their search warrants, and never seemed to differentiate one cop from another. They were all "Officer" to her—never "Detective." And, for her, they seemingly had no names at all.

Jake couldn't stand the woman. "Sammy," he muttered one afternoon after a two-hour session in her crowded little office in the courthouse, "You know how all blacks and Filipinos and Japs look alike to us? Well, all cops look alike to that skinny bitch. Put you and me and Cap and Little John and Big John in a line-up, and I'll bet you she couldn't tell one from another."

Sam laughed, but half agreed. He'd never seen her smile, and she never even looked up when he tried to banter with her.

"She never leaves that building," Jake said. "She just crawls into a file drawer at night and goes to sleep. You cut her and all you'll get is dust."

Sam had been as surprised to see her on a rainy Tuesday midnight in the back booth of the Golden Gavel as if he'd run across the mayor himself sitting there with four scotches lined up in front of him.

"Hey, you! Clinton! Have a seat." she called. "I'll even move so you can face the door. You're all paranoid about your back to the door, aren't you? You've seen too many movies about Luciano and Capone."

He'd sat down, staring at her. She was drunk, but alcohol gave Nina a softer look, a gentler mien, despite her smart mouth.

"I never thought you knew my name," he said grabbing one of her scotches.

"Now I have to order another." She lifted her hand and waved languidly to the bartender who appeared with one more scotch—neat.

"I know your name. I know all your names. The titless wonder never forgets anything."

He looked down at the rings on the table top, embarrassed.

"You thought I didn't know what you guys call me? I could tell you the others, if you like?"

"No thanks. For the record, I never called you any of those names."

"A genuine gentleman. But you don't like me any better than the rest of them do. You all have wives *and* girlfriends, and you all think women are supposed to cook and fuck and stay dumb, right?"

He stared at her. Her eyes were dark brown, wide and challenging, smudged with fatigue. She smiled at him, a wry smile—but a smile.

"I don't have a wife . . . or a girlfriend." he said slowly. "I can cook, and I wash my own socks and shorts. And I think you're the best working lawyer I ever saw in my life. So now what do you want to fight about?"

"Nothing. I want to celebrate. I won today. Joseph Kekelahni. He should have been 'bitched,' you know. Third felony conviction in ten years. Rape, oral sodomy, assault with a deadly weapon . . . and, oh yeah, burglary; he took all their purses after he was done with them. You know what he got instead of the Big Bitch?"

Sam nodded. "Let me guess. Sexual psychopath?"

"You got it. They slapped his little hands and sent him down to Western State so he can get in touch with his feelings. He'll be a real good boy for six months, and then they'll give him the key and a twenty-four-hour pass anywhere he wants to go—and he'll be right back at it. If anybody needs group therapy, it's the judge." She bent her head. "Oh shit!"

He started to answer, made a half move to touch her shoulder, but she looked up quickly and smiled again. "Wanta dance?"

She stood up and held out her arms and he held her, moving slowly around the tiny parquet dance floor to music from the jukebox. They were the only people in the place besides the bartender, who polished the long wooden bar and ignored them. Sam couldn't believe it; Nina Armitage leaning her head against his shoulder.

She was almost as tall as he was and she seemed to weigh half as much. She danced well, but even intoxicated she touched him without touching him, holding back so that their thighs barely brushed. He was amused to feel that she did have breasts, and as embarrassed as a high school boy to feel his body react to her. She gave no indication that she could feel him.

They danced for two hours without talking, stopping only to empty the glasses the bartender kept filling. Sam realized that Nina had been here before, that she had a standing order.

She allowed him to drive her home. If he had pictured her living anywhere, it would not have been in the tiny houseboat at the end of the rickety boardwalk on Lake Union. She didn't ask him in, but he could see through the door, see into a rats' nest of books, plants, dirty dishes, and discarded clothing. A gray cat ducked through his legs and disappeared down the dock, and he caught a whiff of the animal's litterbox inside.

He stood, hesitantly, wanting, not wanting, to go in. She touched him lightly on the chest and pushed him into the rain.

"You can't come in tonight. But I thank you for the waltz . . . and the ride."

The door closed before he could answer. It was only as he walked unsteadily up the dock that he realized that she'd paid for all the drinks. That was a first. He grinned and ran up the steps to the road.

He meant to tell Jake about it in the morning—but he didn't. He hadn't meant to go back—but he did.

He had never been exposed to a really intelligent woman before. He had never approached a woman who seemed to care so little whether he showed up or not. And yet Sam found himself standing at Nina's door night after night, his head bent against the icy spray that whipped off the lake, feeling the boards beneath his feet creak and groan with the undulating swells of the water that cradled her floating home. The houseboat was in terrible shape, listing to port where the logs had rotted away, the eaves leaking rain on his exposed back.

She was always home, although she was slow to open the door. She admitted him with a shrug, letting him pick his way through the debris on the floor and clear his own spot on the old plush couch. She seemed to expect that he would come, but she showed neither pleasure nor annoyance at his arrival. She never fed him. Other women tried to coddle him with home cooking; he sometimes wondered if Nina cooked at all. Rather, he worried about her and brought her pizzas and greasy take-out chicken and urged her to eat. She ate pickishly, giving most of it to the gray cat, Pistol. She was never without a tumbler of scotch, laced sparingly with tap water.

Sam gradually stopped seeing other women, content to spend his evenings and nights with this intense woman who sat cross-legged on the floor with her elbows on her tender-boned knees and talked to him, listened to him. She understood the law and its intricacies in a way he had never grasped before. He had never believed that a woman might know more than he did; but he learned from her, reliving what had taken place during her long days in the courthouse, understanding for the first time the dynamics of a trial.

He asked her suddenly one night, "Why do you want me here?"

"Who says I want you?"

"You let me in. You've unbarred your doors."

"Some of them . . ."

"Do you *like* me?" He was afraid to hear her answer.

She studied him solemnly and then touched his cheek. "Sure, I like you. You're smarter than anybody else over in your little Kiddy Cop Station. You think. You even think abstractly if I push you. I like your face; it doesn't hide anything. I like the gap in your teeth, and I like your dimples." She poked a finger in the indentation next to his mouth; he moved away and rubbed his face.

"It's a wrinkle."

She shook her head. "The rest are wrinkles; that's a dimple, Officer."

"Do you miss me when I'm not here?"

"You're always here."

She stood up to fill her glass, gliding deftly through the piles of junk on the floor, effectively shutting him out.

But he worried it, following her, blocking her way from the cramped Pullman kitchen. He pinned her arms with his and forced her to look at him.

"I need to know that you give a shit whether I show up or not. I need . . . something. Hell, are you my girl or aren't you?"

She laughed. "Your *girl?* Why does that matter? Do you want to take me to the policeman's ball? Ahh, do you want me to be the policeman's ball? Is that it? You're angry because I won't sleep with you?"

He let her go. It was true; she wouldn't sleep with him, not even when she was so drunk she couldn't make her way across the room. And he wanted to sleep with no one else. He could touch her wrist and be as aroused as he'd been before with a fully naked woman beneath him, responding to him, but she refused him access to her the way a thoroughbred mare might deny a plowhorse. Sometimes she let him hold her, and she felt only of narrow bones and a heart beating in his arms.

It made him crazy.

"It's control, isn't it," he said angrily. "You have to have control over everything? You deny both of us because you need the control."

"But Samuel, I have no control. Or at least so little. Would you take that away from me?"

He left, slamming the door behind him, plunging onto the dock with such force that the houseboat deck was awash with water.

He always came back, and she showed no surprise at his reappearance.

There were some good times, enough to keep him holding on. Spring finally came—Seattle's green, water-washed spring with the sun breaking through the overcast only in late afternoon. They sat on her deck and tossed bread to the audacious ducks who ignored even Pistol. He brought her geraniums to replenish the dead foliage in the planters edging the lake, and she thanked him gravely. He painted the weathered siding and carried a pickup load of trash away.

He wanted to move in, but she was resolute that he could not.

"I need down-time. I can't have someone here all the time—not even you."

To his surprise and delight, she submitted her body to him finally, and the melding with her brought him to a place from which there was no return. Nina was as wildly responsive in bed as she was removed from him everywhere else, all mouth and hands and lips as soft as bruised roses. She sobbed and cried out and murmured obscenities, shuddering in his arms with a passion he had never encountered in more than two decades of sex.

He was never sure that he pleased her even then. When it was over, she rolled away from him and became as quiet as death. He had actually propped himself on one elbow to stare at her narrow ribcage in the dark to be sure that it still rose and fell from the force of living lungs beneath. He could not comprehend how their two bodies could move and breathe together at orgasm and only an instant later be further apart than at any other time.

He found the picture of the baby on a Saturday afternoon as he gathered still another load for the dump, a three-by-five hospital picture of a newborn infant with squinted eyes, a red face, and a tiny bow atop the thick dark hair. Beneath the swaddled baby form, there was a number and the words, "Baby Girl Armitage. 1-2-69."

Nina stepped into the room and saw him studying it, puzzled as he sat back on his heels. She took it from him and put it in a kitchen drawer wordlessly. Her skin, always milky, turned so white that the freckles seemed black in contrast.

"Whose baby is that?" he asked.

"Mine. She was mine."

"Where is she?"

"Dead. Dead these many years.

"I'm sorry."

"Don't be. It was such a long time ago. Mr. Armitage was sorry too, at first. And then, after he quit crying, he decided it was my fault. He was sure that I covered her up too tight, or not tight enough, or betrayed some other great defect in what a mother should be. I wasn't the maternal type; he always said that. He never forgave me. He took himself off and married a *very* maternal type, a real mother hen, and fathered three more babies to make up for . . . for . . . Sari."

"But you knew it wasn't your fault."

"Did I? No, I don't think I did. See?"

She pushed up the sleeves of her sweatshirt and turned her wrists over to hold them in front of his eyes. He saw the fine drawing up of skin there, almost lacy with corrugated scars. He kissed the white lines and held her wrists against his face.

"Don't pity me," she said quietly. "If you ever pity me, I'll be gone so fast your head will spin."

"Is that why you drink?"

She looked at him with no expression in her dark eyes, and shook her head.

"No. I drank before. I always drank. I have a talent for it. You'd think it would kill me, wouldn't you?"

"Do you wish it would?"

She picked up the fat gray cat and held it against her, burying her face in its fur. Then she met his eyes again, "Of course not. Don't be ridiculous."

"We could have a baby. Would you try again with me?"

"Thank you. It's a most gracious offer. But I'm too old, and you're too old, and I don't believe in babies anymore."

God, how he'd wanted to save her. He'd been so convinced that he could rescue her and he'd never wanted anything so much in his life. His track record at making women happy was somewhat muddied, but he had never loved a woman the way he loved Nina. He felt sure that if he could only love her enough, she would have to love him back and be happy.

He began to drink with her. It brought them along together through the long nights on the houseboat. Her mind—the mind that had snared him—continued to amaze him and let him think there was hope. He detested what liquor did to that intelligence and dreaded the inevitable progression to slurred words, the repetitions of half-ideas, and long silences. When he drank too, when she no longer made sense, it no longer mattered to him. They were together.

But he could not save her because she did not love him.

"Is it me?" he asked her once. "Are you ashamed of me? Downtown, you act as if I'm just another cop, someone you barely know. We could have lunch together. We could see other people together."

"No," she said. "It's me. Everything I touch turns to shit, Sammy." She cradled his head in her lap. "You'll see. You hang around here much longer and you'll see."

"You want me to go away?" He kept his eyes closed and tried to stop his ears against her answer.

"No—I don't know. But you will."

"I won't leave."

She sighed. "Yes you will."

And of course he had. Nina could handle the drinking. She could separate days and nights. She could put on day clothes and go to court clear-eyed and clear-headed and cogent. He couldn't. The change in his abilities was so subtle at first that he was the only one who perceived that he was missing details in a profession that demanded absolute attention to details.

And then one afternoon when they were working the fairly obvious suicide death of a downtown lawyer in the deceased's waterfront office, he caught Jake staring at him with a look of puzzlement.

"Why the hell did you put your cigarette out in his ashtray, Sam?"

"I didn't."

"Yes you did. You just fucked up the scene."

"Sorry." He scraped out the offending butt and slipped it in his pocket.

"Is it that woman?"

"What woman?"

"Her. Armitage."

"What do you know about that?"

"I know. I'm an old detective, but I'm a detective. You've been leaving the same number for on-call too many times. I checked the reverse directory."

"It's no secret."

"It seems to be. You seem to think it should be."

"It's private."

"Your women were never private before. How come? She too good to share with Jake? She don't sit down to pee like any other broad?"

"She sits."

"Then for God's sake, enjoy her, but don't let it mess you up. Don't let it mess me up. I know you carry me. Everybody knows you carry me. *I can't* carry you; you're my last partner. You fuck up and we both go down."

He hadn't wanted to let Jake go down. He'd tried to cut back on the booze, but he couldn't be with Nina and do that. For the first time in his life, the job was less important than the woman, and they were both sliding away from him. He showed up drunk at a homicide scene at four one morning and it was all Jake could do to push him off into the darkness and pretend Sam was gathering soil samples. Sam was so damned shit-faced that he could only rock back and forth on his hands and knees.

Sam begged Nina to marry him and she laughed and turned away. He wondered if he hated her more than he loved her, but her hold on him was just as tenacious—more so—than it had ever been. She was killing him.

But it was Jake who died.

They were called out at six on a bitterly cold January dawning to work a scene that could have waited; the victim had been dead for a week and a few more hours wouldn't have made a hell of a lot of difference. The temperature cleared Sam's head for the first time in weeks, and that night-morning it had felt almost like the old days with Jake. He'd been anxious to enter a scene for the first time in a long time and call upon his instincts and skill to winnow out what had happened. Jake had sensed it, and they'd bullshitted with each other as if nothing had happened. As if Nina hadn't happened.

The patrol officer who'd responded to the first radio call was puking in the snow when they drove up, and Jake had silently handed Sam a cigar. It was going to be a smeller, reeking of putrescence that only a body left to decay in a winter-heated apartment could cause. They'd have to burn the clothes they wore when they finished, but the strong cheap cigars would let them work without gagging.

Up three flights of stairs, past the green-tinged officer who grinned at them with embarrassment as he leaned against the stained wallpaper of the upper landing, past the manager of the old hotel who seemed more annoyed than distressed. He'd heard Jake puffing behind him, but Jake always puffed and snorted if he had to walk up more than one flight of stairs.

The room was a morass of stacked newspapers, cardboard boxes, dirty clothes, garbage, and, for some reason, a dozen blank-eyed television sets. They had had to stand for a long time before they could even see the body that lay there in the flotsam of the last few years of the victim's life. And then they saw her, a great blackened, bloated balloon of what had been a human being, her skin stretched so tautly by decomposition gases that it had cracked in places. The stab wounds in her shriveled breasts gaped apart obscenely. An old hooker, who had probably lain down for a six-pack of beer, clad in torn lace panties and high-heeled, patent leather boots that still bore a Goodwill sticker on the bottom of one sole. As they puffed determinedly on their cigars, a rat jumped from the top of a pile of boxes and ran past them.

"Oh shit." Jake said. "Why do we get all the losers?"

But they had worked together that morning, attuned to each other, measuring, recording, snapping pictures that were going to make some jury blanch (*if* it ever got to a jury), bagging evidence from a seemingly unending pile of possibles.

They hadn't talked. Talking meant breathing without a cigar to mask the miasma. Later, all the years later, Sam had wished that they had talked. He had felt *good*. Good for the first time in a long time, and never mind that a sane man should not feel good working around a body dead so long, amid trash that stank of that forlorn body. He'd been working and working well, and thinking only of the solution to the problem presented to them.

Jake had let out such a soft little sigh that Sam barely heard him, scarcely looked up. And then he'd felt the tape measure lead in his hand go slack and he'd turned to ask Jake to hold his end tighter. Jake was still hunkering down against the filthy sink, still clenching the cigar in his teeth, and his eyes were still open.

But he was dead—as dead as the prostitute who sprawled between them. Sam dragged him out into the hallway, screaming at the young cop who stood over them, transfixed by shock, to get the aid car. Sam pressed his mouth to Jakes's, willing the older man to take his breath and use it. He'd crashed his fist down over Jake's stilled heart, crushing the two cigars left in his shirt pocket; nothing changed what had happened. The Medic One paramedics with all their paraphernalia and radio-telemetry direct to the county hospital couldn't change it either.

Young men. Young men in dark blue uniforms with neat dark hair, mustaches, and flat stomachs. They worked over Jake for an hour and a half, piercing his chest with the long needle that made Sam wince, forcing air into his lungs and making him appear to breathe, letting Sam think that maybe it would be all right, that the new start they'd shared really had been another beginning after all.

They sat back on their heels finally and shook their heads, leaving Jake to lie on the frayed carpeting that jumped with fleas, his chest dotted with the white circles that held the useless defibrillator leads.

"Get him out of here," Sam said softly.

"I'm sorry," the tall young man said. "I'm really sorry."

"Get him the fuck out of here!" Sam yelled. "I don't want him here. This is no place for him to die."

They'd glanced at each other, confused by the vehemence in his voice, at the lack of professionalism. They hesitated, reaching for their gear and slowly stowing it into their Life-Paks.

"I said get him out of here! *Now!*" Sam bent over Jake and tried to pick him up himself.

"Hey, man . . . sir," the young men stood up and reached for Jake. "We'll take him."

"Then do it."

Sam stayed at the scene until noon, doing it all himself. When he finally walked down the stairway, the snow was melting, sending eddies of water down First Hill towards the Sound.

He had lost his partner. He had never lost a partner before, and he vowed it would be the last time.

He didn't go to the houseboat. Instead, he drove to the apartment he still rented, the rooms unfamiliar now, filled with dust and stale air. He shucked off his suit and coat and left them on the bathroom floor while he showered for fifteen minutes, scrubbing long after the odor should have been gone. He dressed in old jeans and a T-shirt and he carried the reeking clothes to the dumpster behind the building, throwing them in along with his shoes. When he returned to his apartment, his phone was ringing, a nagging ring that went on for fifteen shrill alarms. He looked at it without interest. It stopped, then began again. He pulled the jack from the wall and the rings ceased, leaving only the sound of dripping water from the eaves outside the windows.

All Jake had ever wanted to do was to hang in as long as he could, and then retire to his cabin on the Skykomish River with his nice, fat, dumb, and faithful wife. Sam, who had no hobbies, no avocation, had never comprehended Jake's fascination with fishing, hunting, and endless Masonic meetings. Now Jake had no time for any of it, and Sam had more time ahead than he could ever hope to fill.

He shut his eyes, and the picture of Jake—dead—came back with such force that he choked, feeling bile rise in his throat. He made it to the stool in the bathroom and vomited until his eyes hurt and the veins stood out on his neck. He pressed his face against the coolness of the toilet lid and sobbed for the man he was supposed to take care of, the man whose inadequacies had been his responsibility to cover.

Then he drank himself into unconsciousness.

When he went back to Nina three days later, he knew that it was almost finished. She didn't question him about where he'd been, and she didn't try to comfort him about Jake; she waited, knowing that her presentiments of disaster had come to pass. She was calmer than he'd ever known her to be and drank less. He drank constantly from the moment he arrived at the floating home until he fell asleep. He woke sometimes to find that she was holding him so tightly that he could not tell whose breathing he felt, but he had no stirring of passion for her any longer. She had never talked to him about anything that happened in the deepest part of her mind, and he could not talk to her now.

They gave him another partner, one of the new guys, not yet thirty, who was a stickler for procedure and who had no wish to cover Sam's lapses or absences. Sam lasted two weeks before the lieutenant called him in. After ten minutes of embarrassed platitudes from the lieutenant and stony silence from Sam, he was offered a choice: sign into the alcoholic treatment program voluntarily or transfer back to patrol.

Sam stood up and began to empty his pockets.

"Badge. I.D. Call-box key. Oh, yeah—my free bus pass. I'll keep my weapon. It belongs to me."

The lieutenant had to push it. "Clinton, don't be an asshole. Six weeks and you'll be back here and nobody will remember it. That woman is behind it, isn't she? No woman is worth it. You're going to lose it all, and you'll be lucky if you get a security job at Pay-N-Save."

Sam stared at him with eyes as dull as smoke. "You keep your college-educated baby dicks and your admirable closure rate and stuff them all. I choose to keep my woman and my bottle and *fuck you.*"

He didn't keep his woman.

Nina watched him go as placidly as she'd allowed him into her life. She sipped scotch from a smudged coffee cup and watched him pack up. She didn't ask where he was going, or if he was ever coming back. She knew. She held up dry lips for him to kiss and lifted her cup in a last salute.

"You be O.K.?" he asked, and she looked back at him with the closed, blank look he'd seen so often. Then she set down the cup and picked up the gray tomcat.

"Take him. You'll need somebody to talk to. He always liked you better anyway."

He stood for a final look at the lake, the struggling cat under one arm, and a brown paper sack under the other. The geraniums were dead, blackened in their planter boxes. If she had said one word, if she had asked him to stay, he would have. But the only sound inside the tilted floating house was her stereo, tuned to high volume. He could see the back of her head through the door's window. She stared out at the water and let him go.

His old pickup was pointed east in the parking lot. As good a direction as any. Pistol sniffed the seat covers, and then curled up next to his knee as he headed across the Floating Bridge, through the eastside bedroom communities, and up toward the pass. It began to snow beyond Issaquah, white streaks darting straight at the windshield, road ice making the truck skid on the turns.

Six hours later, the truck ran out of gas. He was in Natchitat at two in the morning, the only creature alive in the clogged street, except for the cat. He had to piss.

He set Pistol down in the snow to relieve itself, and the cat looked at him outraged. Sam watched his urine make a yellow line in the snowbank behind the truck, and then saw that the cat was peeing too. He tucked Pistol under his parka and set out on foot to find a motel, startled to hear the throaty purr begin against his chest.

They survived the rest of the winter locked into self-imposed solitary confinement in the twenty-seven-foot trailer Sam bought from a widower headed for San Diego. Sam drank, and Pistol ate, and they watched the snow melt and the apple trees bud out and blossom.

At some point, Sam realized that he had to decide whether to live or die. A thousand times, he thought he would call her, but he never picked up the phone, and it never rang. By May, it had a thick mantle of dust, and Sam knew that he was going to live.

The Natchitat County Sheriff's Office welcomed him, and few questions were asked. His record was clean, he waived medical coverage because of his age, and his former Seattle police associates were generous in their reference letters. He fit into the department as easily as he slid his service revolver into his shoulder holster.

He took Danny Lindstrom as his partner.

Off duty, Sam and Danny walked away from the office into the first light of dawn. It would be hot later, but it was cool now and the sky just above the mountains' ridges was the color of peaches and plums. They stopped silently to acknowledge the day before getting into Danny's pickup.

The town was still asleep; the guys who'd just come on watch could coast for a couple of hours. Sam leaned back and enjoyed the ride past the closed stores on Main Street, and then the neat streets lined with single-family residences, their yards square patches of green bordered with petunias and zinnias kept luxuriant by careful watering in this parched season. The citizens inside seemed safe from harm at this time of day, safe and loved and happy. He closed his eyes and let his head rest on the seat behind him, the leather cool and lightly damp from the night in the parking lot behind the jail.

Danny glanced over at him. "Tired?"

"Yeah. It's hell when you get old."

Danny laughed and pushed the gas pedal toward the floor as they neared the town limits and started up the hill where the orchards began, trees pregnant now with fruit, their branches supported by props, endless rows of them.

"You coming over for supper?"

"That would make three nights already this week. I think Joanne's getting tired of the sight of me."

"Never happen. She likes you."

"She likes all stray animals. She's a natural-born patsy for the home- less and forsaken."

"Do it for me then," Danny said. "She's in a better mood when you're there. She's antsy lately. We fight. We never used to fight. She's bored, I guess. She hates me working graveyard. And she's still not pregnant."

"Seems like you could fix that," Sam offered finally.

"Seems like I can't. What if it's my fault?"

"So what if it is? It's not like you can't get it up. It shouldn't matter whose fault it is. I hear it can be fixed."

"It matters to me," Danny said. "It matters a hell of a lot, and I don't want to find out if it's me."

Sam shifted in embarrassment; the functioning of female organs was not an area where he had any expertise or any particular interest. The vast majority of the women he'd known had been more concerned with staying un-pregnant than in conceiving.

Danny and Joanne were a happy family unit, not young enough to be his children—but almost. Their farm was a place to go when Pistol's company failed to fill the void he still lived in off duty. His partner's marriage was something to take quiet comfort in, however vicariously. There was no envy in his soul over Joanne; he found her delightful, winsomely pretty, the matured image of the cheerleaders he'd yearned for in high school. She was a nice little woman.

Danny. Danny he would kill for. Danny was his partner.

"She still running?" he asked.

"Who? Oh . . . Joanne? Yeah, she's out there running her little buns off."

"You should go with her. Get rid of that tummy."

Danny sat up straighter as he turned into the trailer park, sucking in the suggestion of fat at his waist.

"She doesn't want me to. It's her thing, and running five miles is the last thing I feel like after supper."

Sam crawled out of the truck cab and stood with his elbows leaning on the open window. "Take her on a vacation," he suggested.

"Got no time."

"You got time. Take her on a vacation, spend about three days in bed together, with no pressure. Make a baby."

Danny laughed, shifted into low, and pulled away with a wave of his hand. Sam watched the truck until it was out of sight, caught in a cloud of road dust. Then he turned and walked through the sleeping park, feeling rather than seeing Pistol's soft body against his shins.

The trailer was cool and smelled of full ashtrays; his daveno bed was rumpled from the morning before, and three days' newspapers covered the floor beside it. He caught a whiff of gas from the leaking pilot light on the chipped green stove and cracked the windows in the living room of his metal box. Pistol made hungry sounds; Sam reached automatically for a can from the stack of tins on the counter and ladled out the fishy substance. He leaned against the wall and watched the old cat eat, feeling a twinge of arthritic pain in his left hip.

Sam grabbed a can of beer for his own breakfast. Pistol leapt onto the daveno, tired from his tom-cat prowls in the night, ready to sleep the day away with him. He drained the can, crumpled it, and reached for another, watching the park outside come awake. Then he eased his body into the couch and fell into an almost dreamless sleep.

CHAPTER THREE

The entrance to the lane leading up to the Lindstrom's farmhouse was placed so exactly between the orchard rows and was so overgrown with weeds that as many times as Danny approached it he had to look carefully to spot it. He liked it that way; the spread looked like only an orchard and not a homestead. He'd deliberately mounted the mailbox a hundred feet beyond the turn-in, just as he'd vetoed Joanne's suggestion that they name the farm and put up a carved sign and arrow where the rutted lane began. He had to leave her there alone so often, and he felt easier knowing that the squat shake buildings were invisible from the county road. Townspeople knew they lived back there, just below the far rise in the lane, but strangers driving by couldn't glimpse even the peak of the roofline.

His truck jounced through the last wisps of ground fog, brushing against the dew-laden heads of wild wheat that leaned over the lane, and Danny smelled the sweetness of a recently mowed alfalfa field nearby. It was his favorite time of the day, coming home to Joanne, knowing she slept soundly in the old house. He listened for the hoarse welcome from his old dog, Frank, and then felt a keen pang of loss. Jeez. He *was* tired, and out of it. Frank wouldn't be waiting near the shed; he was buried out in back of the barn and had been for almost a year. He still missed the old Lab, especially in the early morning like this. He knew he had to bring himself to get a pup, but it was hard. Frank had been with him for half of his life, and you didn't find many dogs like that one. He'd found Frank, left behind when the migrant families moved on, when he was fourteen and Frank a pup barely able to walk. They'd looked each other in the eye and known they had the right combination. That dog had seen him through an awful lot of pain. Danny sighed, and thought of Sam's frowzy old tomcat who seemed more like a pain in the ass than a companion, but there was no accounting for taste.

The pickup hurtled over the rise in the rutted road and Danny saw the house was still there, safe and drowsy, its window-eyes closed with drapes. Joanne had left the back porch light on as always, just as his mother had when he was in high school.

He'd been itchy to get away from Joanne last night, free from her anger and depression, but it didn't seem important now. He only wanted to be with her again and hold her against him for the few hours they had to share in bed. It was no wonder they argued; they hardly ever saw each other, with his graveyard watch, and then sleeping all day. All they really had was suppertime, and he wanted those few hours to be peaceful and happy instead of a continuation of her harangue about babies, and sperm counts, and whatever the hell else Doc had been filling her head with.

Danny eased the truck into the shed, and walked stiff-legged toward the house. He tensed, alert, at the approach of the creature who waddled with wings spread warningly, from behind the sagging grape arbor. It was Billy Carter, a better watchdog than Frank had ever been. B.C. recognized Danny in mid-hiss, and lowered his wings, locking step with Danny. B.C. was Joanne's and only suffered Danny's presence grudgingly. Danny suspected that the goose didn't really sleep at night when he was on duty and was probably relieved to have him take over. The big man and the strutting fowl passed Joanne's kitchen garden, a blighted effort where only zuchinni thrived.

"She's got a brown thumb, B.C.," Danny said companiably, and then laughed when the goose darted a look of what passed for disapproval at him. "Maybe *you* can survive on zuchinni and sunflowers and worms, but she ain't no earth-mother."

The sunflowers were Joanne's triumph. Twelve-foot stalks with flowers as big as dinner plates edged the entire rear wall of the house and dwarfed the straggly petunias beneath them.

Danny paused as he always did to gaze across the now sere winter wheat field behind the house, and then to the gorge beyond where the river cut through the rocky canyon. The river was running shallow; he had to stop breathing to hear it now, but in a few months it would be filled with glacier run-off and snow from the Cascades and it would roar again.

Even in Natchitat where life moved along so languidly that changes were almost imperceptible, things did change. But not the river, nor the farmhouse where he was born. His father's going off to Korea had hardly touched him; he had his grandfather, his grandmother, and Anna, his mother. He'd only been two years old and his memory scarcely formed. When his father didn't come home, his own life went on unchanged. His mother had cried, but Danny had wept only because her tears frightened him. Like all children, he assumed that his life was blessed, that the tragedies that consumed others would not come to him. And then both his grandparents had died within a week.

Doss Crowder was fire chief then, and father to the frail little girl that Joanne had been. Doss was over at the farm a lot, helping Anna sell off some of the acreage she could no longer manage, somehow taking his granddad's place for Danny, and Danny couldn't remember if Joanne came because Doss was there or if it was the other way around. She was a pest, following Danny around like a shadow, asking stupid questions and getting in his way. It was years before he saw her as a young woman so pretty and soft that he ached to touch her, and quaked at the thought of Doss's wrath if he did. But by then, Joanne was so popular that he had to stand in line to date her.

God, he had been so jealous and so filled with frustration, secure only in athletics. Watching the river had comforted him during those years—until the day an aneurysm lying dormant in his mother's brain had burst and flooded that vital tissue with a sea of killing blood. She was dead before he could get there. She was forty-six years old and Danny was seventeen, and there was no one who could assuage his grief. He'd hated the river for continuing to flow, and the apple trees for daring to blossom that spring.

He refused to leave the farm, and he and Frank batched it while he finished high school. Joanne was the only one who could break through the anger that consumed him, and she'd given up going to college on the coast to marry him. Then the farm was a home again and after a while he even forgave the river. But he never took anything for granted after that, knowing that what seemed safe and permanent could be taken away in an instant. Doss too. But when Doss died, he had Joanne and she had him, and Danny was a man finally who could take care of his own.

Danny reached down absently to stroke B.C.'s crooked neck, felt the peck coming without seeing it, and jerked his hand away. "B.C., you're an old son of a bitch. You ever hear how easy duck soup is? Well, think about goose soup." He laughed and walked into the kitchen.

As always, he walked softly through the dim rooms to glance into the bedroom. She was there, curled on her side, her dark hair curtaining her face, her arms hugging the pillow. She lay on the edge of her

side of the bed as if she'd fallen asleep determined to be untouchable
even when he wasn't there. The room was morning cool and Joanne
was covered with a sheet. He pulled the spread up over her, but she
didn't move. He watched for a moment to see if she was really asleep,
and then relaxed to see the steady rise and fall of her ribs beneath the
quilt.

Danny shut the bedroom door gently and flipped on the kitchen
light. Except for the new stove and refrigerator, Joanne had insisted
that the kitchen stay just the way it had always been. It was a good
kitchen. Suddenly fashionable again, the old oak table with red-and-
white-checked oilcloth still stood in the middle of the room. The wood
stove, seldom used, was there too with his grandmother's rocker beside
it. Even the pitted sink with the pumphandle you had to prime to get
water. He'd put in real faucets years ago, but Joanne wouldn't let him
take the funny old pump out.

The day she'd walked into this room as his bride, she'd touched
everything in it lovingly, and then smiled at him.

"I used to come over here to get warm a long time before I thought
of you as anything more than a smelly little boy. You thought I had a
crush on you, but I came here in spite of you, old Danny. Your mom.
Your grandma. They always had time for me, and, if I got something
dirty, they didn't act like I'd just walked in with shit on my shoes. My
mother spent her whole life wiping things down with Lysol. Even me
probably. I shouldn't say that—she tries so hard."

Danny had hugged her. "She turned out a pretty good little girl,
although Doss was more than half of it. She is what she is and we'll go
have dinner with her every Sunday night and act proper."

Joanne had glanced around the kitchen and frowned. "Everything's
still here, but you and Frank have pushed it a little beyond casual
living, haven't you? Don't worry. I'll fix it."

And she had. She'd vacuumed out bushel basketsful of dog hair,
scrubbed the sticky linoleum, and made new curtains, but she hadn't
really changed anything. She'd given him his home back and loved
him.

The table was covered now with jars and jars of jam that she'd
canned while he'd been out patrolling stinking taverns with Sam. He

wondered if she hadn't plunged into a flurry of canning more out of anger than anything else; she did this sort of thing more and more lately.

"I have nothing but time on my hands," she told him flatly. "I have no one to take care of but you—and you're never here, and if you are here, you're asleep."

His sense of serenity vanished. She was changing, and he couldn't deal with her. He'd heard that women grew more and more like their mothers as they aged, and wondered if he was destined to end up with another Elizabeth Crowder instead of the wife he'd married.

Danny was more bewildered than angry; he'd wanted kids too, but he'd never thrown it up to Joanne when she didn't get pregnant. He'd never pushed her into Doc's office, and he'd gone along with her plans to go when she wanted to, but he felt sick at the idea of putting his manhood on the line, of having Doc or anyone else know if there was something wrong with him. She didn't understand what she was asking of him.

He looked under the breadbox for his note. There was always a note —something silly or sexy or teasing. He ran his hand under the tin box but came up empty. And there were no cookies or sandwiches on the counter either, nothing to indicate that she was glad he'd come home to her.

He turned on the radio on the windowsill and listened to the weather and the farm report while he ate a bowl of cold cereal. He didn't give a goddamn about the weather or the price of hogs, but the familiar drone of the announcer's voice filled the empty kitchen. He put the cereal bowl in the sink and ran water over it so the Wheaties wouldn't stick and harden, turned off the light, and walked down the hallway, unhooking his gunbelt and hanging it over the halltree. Joanne didn't like to have his service revolver in the bedroom, and it was close enough if he needed it.

She lay exactly as she had before, turned away from him, and she didn't stir as he padded through the room to the bathroom. He urinated, flushing the toilet as noisily as he could, letting the water run fullforce in the sink as he washed his face, hoping she'd wake up and reach out for him when he came to bed. And then he saw the familiar square blue cardboard carton that held her Tampax. The top was torn raggedly, and two of the white paper-wrapped cylinders were missing.

Again. Without wanting to admit his anxiety about it, he'd been counting the days crossed off on her calendar and noted that she'd been five days overdue. And now she wasn't overdue anymore, and she'd blame him. There was just a brush of dried blood on the toilet seat when he flipped it back down.

He'd laughed when Fletcher had a vasectomy and Sam kidded him about shooting with an unloaded gun. Well, he wasn't laughing now. Danny leaned on the sink with both hands and stared at himself in the mirror. O.K. O.K. Damn it to hell. He'd go and do it, but he wouldn't tell her. He didn't want her to know for certain that she'd married a eunuch.

Joanne wasn't asleep. She'd heard the truck coming up the lane, and said a prayer, as she always did—thanks for Danny's being safe. She'd sent him off in anger, and she'd gone to bed without leaving one sign for him that she cared if he got home or not. If anything had happened to him, it would have been her fault for sending him off that way.

She was barren. Barren. It was the loneliest word she'd ever heard; she'd never done anything worthwhile, been anything worthwhile, and now she never would. Danny could be proud of his job, and he had friends who understood him. He saved people, for God's sake. And she canned plums.

Without moving, she watched him through half-closed eyes. He hung his uniform shirt carefully over the chair by the dresser, creased his pants and draped them over a hanger, lined up his boots, and she thought he was beautiful. The tanned broad shoulders and back, and the white buttocks that made him look like a little boy. He wasn't the slim, perfect Danny she'd fallen in love with, but the trace of a belly only made him dearer to her. She fought the rush of love. She had to be stubborn, as stubborn as he was, because if he wouldn't do this one thing she asked of him, she knew they were lost.

No, *they* weren't lost. She was lost.

She had never wanted anything more than to be like everyone else, to be accepted, but if it hadn't been for Sonia Hanson—Sonia, square and broad-faced and stump-legged, but full of confidence and loyalty—

Joanne wouldn't have had a girlfriend in high school. Walt Kluznewski had adored Sonia ever since first grade, and if he'd looked twice at Joanne, Sonia would have blamed him and not Joanne.

She'd asked Sonia once, "Sonie, why don't they like me? I mean, they act like they like me when we're all out there leading cheers, and then they just walk away after, like I wasn't even there."

Sonia had snorted in disbelief. "Joanne, you're so *dumb!* You look like Elizabeth Taylor, and every single bitchy one of them would gladly kill to look like you. Besides, at least half of them are panting after Danny, and he's nice and polite to them, but he belongs to you. They're so jealous they almost wet their pants, so they try to make you miserable. Just ignore them."

"I can't help how I look."

Sonia laughed. "Neither can I, and I'm lucky big old Waltie doesn't mind. He likes me and I like you and Danny loves you, and high school doesn't last forever. Before long, we'll all be fat, jolly married ladies with babies and nobody will remember who did what at Natchitat High."

It worked out for Sonia. She married Walt and had three kids in three years, and Walt Kluznewski ran his Standard station with a big grin on his face in hot summer or icy winter. All the really smart girls in their class went off to college and then settled down in Seattle or Spokane. The rest of them got married and turned into housewives who seemed to accept Joanne. She ran into them at the Safeway, most of them pushing one baby in a shopping cart, and carrying another one under their belts. She was invited to baby showers and Tupperware parties, but Sonia was still her only friend.

Nobody wanted a thirty-one-year-old cheerleader. She was never the one anybody called when they needed a shoulder to cry on. She never really pleased anyone—-not even Danny. Sooner or later, he would look at her and realize how dull she was, his pretty little wife who cleaned his house and spoke sweetly to his friends, and was afraid to ask him why he cried out in his sleep. She knew it was important to him that she be in the farmhouse waiting for him when he came back from his other life, but that was only for now. Maybe not even for now; maybe there was already another woman out there who was alive and vital. And not barren.

She shifted slightly and felt a gush of warm blood between her thighs. She had tried so hard not to bleed this month, willing herself to breathe gently, to handle her body as if were breakable, not even running for a whole week of mornings and evenings—when running was all she had that belonged only to herself.

"You awake?" Danny whispered, and she lay silent. "Hey, babe, you awake? I'm home."

She was resolute, drawing her body so tightly into itself that she barely touched the sheet beneath her, breathing deeply in a semblance of full sleep. She felt the bed sink under his weight, heard him sigh, and smelled his faint male sweaty odor, and stronger than that, shaving lotion that he must have just splashed on. She had fantasized long ago about being in bed with Danny, but it had never been what she thought sex was supposed to be. If she'd ever had an orgasm, she hadn't recognized it as the powerful sensation she'd read about, or heard other women hint at. Danny was so quick, treating intercourse as an athletic event where the swiftest won. Sometimes she had a glimmer of what it might be, a curious tickling buzz, but Danny was already past her response before it could grow. He always came with a last triumphant thrust, and he dismissed her a moment later with a friendly pat on the shoulder before he turned away and fell asleep.

His beautiful hands, the hands that were so delicate in woodworking and fly-tying, were clumsy when he touched her, and he seemed to have no idea where the center of her sexual feeling lay.

"Tell him," Sonia said. "Tell him what makes you feel good. All those ex-jocks are like that. They can romance a football but they wouldn't know a clitoris if it bit them on the nose—and it should," and Sonia had dissolved into giggles.

"Oh, I couldn't. Sonia, I just couldn't. That's *awful*. It would hurt his feelings, and what if I didn't like it either?"

"Don't knock it unless you've tried it. You have to think of it as teaching braille to a blind man. De-klutzing therapy. Joanne, you keep assuming that men are more than ordinary human beings. They aren't. You have to give them some kind of roadmap."

"Doesn't Walt get angry?"

Sonia laughed. "He stomps and fumes, and once he put his fist through the wall in the bathroom, but he eventually gets the point. See, we talk to each other. He doesn't have to guess what I'm feeling or thinking, and I don't go around resenting him."

Joanne looked up sharply. "I don't resent Danny."

"No? You resent the hell out of him, but you won't admit it. You're still trying to be the Ideal Couple of 1967, but you're blowing it, kid. That was fourteen years ago. We're all grown-ups now, and you're still trying to be perfect and you're losing yourself in the process."

"Then I'll lose him too. I couldn't live without Danny."

"Oh yes you could and stop being such a wimp. Look at me. Take a good look." Sonia stood up and twirled around, displaying her ballooning figure, barely squeezed into a T-shirt and red shorts, her thick ankles rising out of black oxfords and encased in Walt's white socks. "If *I* can ask for something for myself and still keep Waltie racing home to me at night, *you* certainly can. Danny's nuts about you. Just try him."

It sounded so easy when she was listening to Sonia, but Sonia believed in Sonia, and Joanne still felt like a shadow.

She was happy that Danny was home, relieved that he lay beside her in the big bed that felt so empty when he was gone at night. She felt him roll toward her, and then his heavy arm slide across her ribs, his hand caress her breast. She stiffened.

"Joanne? Honey?"

He pulled her against him tightly, his body curving around hers, urging her silently to soften to him. His penis, half-hard already, pressed her buttocks.

"Danny, I can't. I started my damn period. I can't do anything."

"I know. I don't want that; I can't help getting excited when I touch you. I can't control that. Just let me hold you while I fall asleep. Just let me kiss you."

"I taste awful. I haven't brushed my teeth, and I'm all sweaty and yucky." She felt her body relax against his; she didn't want to be angry and alone.

"You always smell good to me, you always taste good, and I need you. We had a hell of a night, and I just kept thinking about being back here with you." His hands moved over her, as if he were gentling a flighty horse. "Sam got hurt—but he's O.K.—and your goddamn goose bit me, and you didn't even leave me a note, and I was afraid you'd run off with the milkman."

"You fool," she whispered, turning over. "We don't even have a milkman. We have a cow."

He made her laugh, and she couldn't stay angry, picturing Billy Carter attacking him. She rolled over and kissed him on the mouth, tasting cigars and toothpaste, feeling the thin sheen of perspiration on his chest, and his penis nudging her belly. He forced her hand around it, and his breathing grew harsher.

"Baby, Joanne, do it for me?"

She kept her fingers still, tried to move them away, but he held her wrist firmly. "Do it, please?"

"I hate that."

"No, no, it's O.K. Just for a little while. Just slow . . ."

She grasped him more firmly and moved her hand tentatively up and down, feeling the silky foreskin slide over the end of him. His breathing accelerated, and she felt him slip away from her, become oblivious of any part of her but her hand servicing him. She shut her eyes against it, removed herself from it.

"Faster . . . do it faster, babe." He lay supine, his back arched. "Make me come."

Something in her mind balked. She didn't want to be back in his '64 Chevy, doing what he asked of her, helping him spill useless seed. She didn't feel guilty as she had then, only tired. And alone. She took her hand away from his penis, and she heard him swear softly before he bolted out of bed and headed for the bathroom, slamming the door behind him. She couldn't hear him in there, but she knew that he was masturbating himself because she'd failed him.

She heard the rush of the faucet, and then his tall shadow walked back to their bed. He patted her on the shoulder, as if she'd been with him when he came, and then he was asleep, sprawled over most of the bed. Her eyes hurt as she watched the sun slide down the bedroom wall like hot butter, bringing with it the heat of another long day.

She couldn't sleep now, and she slid beneath his heavy arm and stood up. She stripped off her gown and panties and tossed them into the bathroom sink, sluicing cold water over them. The dark blood and water swirled together in a pink froth and eddied away. She didn't cry until she was in the shower where he couldn't hear her. She wasn't even sure what she was crying about—the blood that meant another chance gone or the man who lay asleep in the room beyond.

She shrugged into her jogging clothes and felt under the bed for her Adidas. Danny slept fitfully, fighting whatever demons haunted him. She put a hand on one heaving shoulder and he practically leapt off the bed, and then quieted as she stroked his back. She shut the bedroom door quietly and left him to his day's sleep.

It didn't matter now how hard she ran, and the road beneath her pounding feet felt resilient and supportive. The cramps in her belly eased, her muscles stretched, and she ran, leaving it all behind her.

The morning was hers, still cool but with edges of heat. Down in town, her mother would be going through her familiar morning rituals, preparing for the faculty meeting before the school year. She still taught, and she was still a model no daughter could ever hope to emulate. Elizabeth would drop by the farm after her meeting, carrying a basketful of produce, grown in her own garden, tended with gloved hands that never showed a bit of soil. Without seeming to, she would check out Joanne's housekeeping, frown at Joanne's wasted garden, and evince just the slightest disapproval because Danny slept the day away, no matter that he worked all night.

She ran harder. Slap. Slap. Remember not to flail your arms. Keep them tight against your chest. Breathe deeply. Smell the pine sap. Smell the river.

The road ahead veered away from the river bank and climbed upward through the fallow pasture-land. The muscles in her calves ached and her breath seemed to draw only from the top half of her lungs, but she couldn't slow down or rest, not at this spot. She knew the desiccated shell of the ruined barn was just to her left, and she tried not to look at it. She knew though, knew the very moment she passed it. Maybe no one else even noticed it any more, the dead fingers of silvery-black wood poking up through so many years' growth of rye grass, the agonized spears of twisted metal, all of it covered over with a funeral blanket of field daisies and Queen Anne's lace. It was a more fitting memorial to Doss than the flat bronze plaque on the firehouse wall.

What made her run this route morning and night? Penance maybe —or defiance? Danny wanted her to run in town where she'd be safe, and she was damned sick of being safe. This was the last place she'd ever seen her father alive, and while this forlorn field filled her with a wave of melancholy and dread, she felt compelled to pass it twice a day; it was her commitment to Doss.

Her running wasn't working this morning; the anxiety that she usually managed to keep just behind her crept up and paced her stride for stride. She ran faster, and it pulled at her shirttail and whispered in her ear, its voiceless message sending little balloons of fear through her veins to her gut.

I am not afraid. I am not afraid. I . . . am . . . not . . . afraid.

She raked her mind for song lyrics and couldn't remember any. Did anyone else feel this way? Was anyone else as afraid as she was, and afraid of nothing? If she could put a name to it, then she wouldn't fear it, but it was transparent, unidentifiable, impossible to ward off.

Her heart jolted in her breast at the sound from behind the grass-clogged barn skeleton, a sound she couldn't identify. Not a rabbit's panicked leap for cover, or a garter snake sliding through dry wheat. Nor a grouse flushed at the sound of her thudding feet. It was more of a whistling sigh, as if someone terribly old had called out to her from behind the pile of charred timbers.

She stopped and felt the tiny shivers ripple across her exposed neck and arms, aware that something alive was watching her.

But there was no definable presence, only the tentative wind whipping the tall grass around the jagged boards and beyond the flattened barn a stand of poplars half asleep in the early morning.

She fled, pumping her legs so violently that she was thrown off stride and tripped, catching herself awkwardly just before nearly falling headlong on the gravel road.

A dusty pickup raced from behind her, throwing up a rush of pebbles that stung her legs, and the driver leaned out his window and catcalled, "Keep 'em bouncing, Jugs!," and then fishtailed around the curve ahead.

She didn't recognize the truck, couldn't make out who the driver was, the back of his head obscured now by two rifles mounted on the gunrack behind him.

Her fear distilled to blank rage and she stood in the middle of the road and raised her middle finger at the spot where the truck had been.

"Fuck off!" Her voice echoed like a siren in the morning air. "Just fuck off, you crummy bastard!"

CHAPTER FOUR

Now that he had finally found her, it seemed as if it had happened perfectly. Duane was convinced that this time he had found the right woman. His relief that the search was over was profound enough to merit a small celebration. He had allowed himself the steak dinner—and not one of the cheap minute steaks that emerged leathery and sawdust-tasting from the microwave at the Trail's End Tavern, but a sixteen-ounce T-bone with mushrooms and onion rings at the Red Chieftain Hotel, with three martinis beforehand and Grand Marnier after.

The liquor had plunged him into a stuporous sleep despite the lumpy mattress, and he was filled with sweet dreams of the running woman, her exquisite face turning again and again to his, full of adoration and no guile, hardening his penis as he slept. The almost-forgotten sensation of oneness flowed through him. He murmured and smiled in his bed, tracing her breasts with his fingers, thrusting himself against her.

And then something woke him, a grinding of brakes from a truck outside, a drunken shout from the Trail's End maybe, and he snapped fully alert, his nerve pathways crackling with electric buzzes. The image of the running woman vanished, and he felt a jolt of apprehension he could not identify. He watched the shadow patterns on the stained wall and tried to isolate the cause of his anxiety.

And did.

The other women. They had seemed perfect too at first. Not as perfect as she was. No, they hadn't come close, and he'd realized too late that they'd been put in his path only to delay him. Most of them would be bones now, their wicked flesh melted into the earth and water where he'd hidden them. But even dead they mocked him and tried to make him doubt his selection. Sluts. They were jealous of his joy, their stupid ghosts trying to make him remember them.

He would not remember them clearly; he would only recall where they lay rotting, and remember that because he had to be aware of places where he must not return—on the off-chance that someone might have found them. Their faces were gone from his memory and gone in reality because he had been careful to obliterate them. They were no longer women, only crosses on a map. Warning signs.

He concentrated on the map in his head and fixed on the crosses.

El Paso. The one who'd gotten into his car as he headed down from Amarillo. She'd pretended to be sweet and good, and then she'd exposed her tattooed breasts in the pale moonlight that washed the Franklin Mountains, as if she were proud that other men had marked her and disfigured her. She was under the rocks in the mountains now, shut off from both the moon and the sun forever.

Niagara Falls. The American side. The college girl who thought she was a goddamned shrink, who told him he had a . . . a what? . . . yeah. An Oedipus Complex. The bitch went off the edge of Goat Island, screaming and tearing at him while the rapids swallowed her voice.

Someplace in Iowa. Council Bluffs. He couldn't remember anything more than they'd been on a train heading for Chicago, and then she wasn't on the train any longer and he was alone and happy she was gone.

Where else? He couldn't think of where because they were all alike. Wait. Yeah. L.A. So many broads got snuffed in L.A. they hardly kept count there. He remembered tearing up ice plants along a canyon road to get to the ground where he could dig a hole to plant her. And the sticky purple flowers bleeding all over his hands.

He didn't want to go through the rest, but he forced himself through the roll call. There were six. No, seven. El Paso, Niagara Falls, Council Bluffs, L.A., and . . . Klamath Falls in Oregon right off the I-5 freeway. Cut Bank, and waiting a long, long time to get a hitch that took him out of Montana. And one more . . . *Where?* He blanked on the seventh one; it was so long ago, before he was even nineteen. It was winter that time. Frozen ground and the wind pushing at him. Someplace in the north.

He lit a cigarette and went back through the litany, and it spilled into his consciousness easily, as if he was reciting a poem by rote. Bemidji! Paul Bunyan country. She was under the ice of a lake, floating with her hair like seaweed and her eyes staring up through the blue-white crypt, even though she couldn't see any more.

He had never read their names in the paper. It was probable the cops still didn't know where they were, but even if they did, they sure wouldn't connect him with any of it. He knew the value of moving on, and never going back.

Now, it was O.K. *She* was here, waiting for him. She'd be pleased when he told her about getting rid of the others, the false ones.

He'd found her, and all he needed was a plan. In an hour, he had it, a solid matrix where each component fell into place like tumblers in an intricate combination lock. Euphoria seized him. He had never experienced such a sense of rightness. He knew how he would find her again and show himself to her.

But there was no rush. There was no tearing hurry for anything.

He forced himself to go through the daily routine of the wine pick-up at the Safeway, the rebottling in the moldy bathroom of his room—not because he needed the money that badly, but because he was superstitious enough not to break the patterns that had brought him to her.

When it was done, he felt free to look for a bowling alley. The bowling alley was a good omen; every hick town in America had a bowling alley with a blue neon bowling pin instead of a glowing cross. St. Brunswick, the Divine. Come unto me all ye with bad backs, beer bellies, and empty minds. He stood on Main Street and saw the beacon calling to him above the buildings.

It was open for business. He stepped inside and walked unerringly past the counter and the smell of fresh donuts and stale hamburger grease, the sound of lumbering balls and crashing pins familiar music to his ears. There it was: the trophy case. The glass was smudged and dead flies lay parched and still on its faded velvet floor. And, of course, the framed photographs were there, recording championships wrested over long time in Natchitat, row upon row of grinning, vacuous faces.

He almost gasped out loud when he found her, saw her small wonderful image gazing directly at him. A flower shining among the ordinary. She knelt on one side of the massive trophy, one arm extended across it and touching the shoulder of a fat, red-headed woman with a foolish smile on her face. The others were grouped behind her, all of them wearing the same T-shirt she'd worn last night. His hand trembled as he traced the printing beneath the photo.

Natchitat County Sheriff's Office
Wives' Bowling League

And in smaller printing, the names. "Front row, left: Joanne Lindstrom."

She had given him the sign; there was no question about that, even if she hadn't realized it. She could have worn anything else when she ran past him, but she had chosen the shirt that would tell him where to find her.

He fumbled in his shirt pocket and pulled out the small spiral pad and his gold Cross pen. For the first time he wrote her name, printing the letters carefully. *Her* name.

He forced his eyes away from hers and scanned the rest of the group shots, carefully now. He knew he would find the other picture because it would not have been this simple to find her unless he was meant to find the next information he needed. The men's picture was bigger and on the shelf above. Two rows of cops. He could spot cops if they were walking down Main Street naked; he could smell them. They carried themselves as if they had a poker up their asses. Self-important pricks. And they went to seed and fat quicker than other men, full of the free meals and courtesy liquor.

He played a game with himself. There were nine of them in the photograph, all dressed in dark trousers and white shirts with red embroidery snaking across the right shirt pocket, broadcasting their names. He would pick the husband without checking the surnames spelled out below.

Not the old one with his bald head painstakingly covered with long hair combed across and plastered in an attempt to make it look like it grew there. Not the two fat, moon-faced ones who looked like Tweedledum and Tweedledee. Not the really young ones.

Duane leaned closer, shading his eyes with one hand to cut the glare from the bare overhead bulb, smiling a little to himself because the winnowing out process was so rudimentary. It sure wasn't the little guy in front, so short he'd never have made it in a big city department. There were two big men on each side of the dwarf, clowning for the camera with their flattened palms resting atop the head of the midget. Cocky sons of bitches.

It couldn't be the taller man with the gap-toothed grin and deep wrinkles around his eyes. He was too old. Had to go fifty—maybe more —and she could do better than that.

The other one. Yeahhh—it had to be him. Not a bad looking guy, but a stereotyped, dull kind of handsome. Brown hair cut cop-short. The regular facial features softened as they fell away to the chin that was threatening to duplicate itself in fat. He guessed there were twelve to fifteen overweight pounds padding the athlete's body, broad shoulders, thick neck, and the big thighs of a linebacker. The guy didn't look really out of shape, but on the verge. He was sucking in his gut, self-consciously, an ex-jock surely who was packing in the calories as if he was still turning out.

His eyes followed the flourish of the embroidered name on the guy's breastpocket. "Donny—no, Danny." Shit, the guy looked at least thirty, and he was still walking around with a kid's name on his chest.

He would enjoy eliminating the cop.

He glanced around to see if he had attracted attention, and was satisfied that he had not. The woman behind the counter looked hung over or bored as she made ineffective swipes at the Formica with a stained towel. The manager was smoking a cigarette and staring out of the window, as if something on the street beyond fascinated him.

Leisurely, Duane copied the deputies' names into his notebook, adding cursory descriptions to remind himself which was which. The date on the men's picture was "Fall, 1979" so there was a good chance they were all still employed by the Natchitat County Sheriff's Office. When he had filled two of the blue-lined pages, he walked over to the pay phone booth just inside the front door and turned to the front page of the thin directory.

There were three Lindstroms—Ole, Walter, and, of course, Daniel. City cops never listed their names and home addresses unless they used their kids', wives', or even their dogs' names, but the pigs in little burgs were too dumb to expect reprisal.

Dumb Danny had his address right there: 15103 Old Orchard Road. Duane noted that and the phone number, and then added the number for the Sheriff's Office. He slid the notebook back into his pocket and dialed the last number.

The voice that answered was laconic, touched with just a shadow of a drawl, "Sheriff."

Duane let his voice falter and he spoke in a thin nasal tone. "Yes sir, I was trying to locate Deputy Lindstrom."

"Not here. Anyone else help you?"

"No sir—I guess I better talk to him. Could you tell me a good time to call back?"

"Be in about 7:30. You wanta leave a number?"

"No sir. I ain't got a phone at my place. Thank you sir. I'll call him tonight."

"O.K." The phone went dead, the desk man unaware of how much help he'd been.

In fifteen minutes Duane had learned Joanne's surname, her husband's name, their address and phone number, and Danny's shift; 7:30 check-in meant third watch—which meant Danny would be gone from home from then until dawn.

Perfect.

Duane walked out into the morning sun, filled with the joyous blessing of the bowling alley; the light and the way had been pointed out to him, and he had endless corridors of time in which to develop his procedure and carry it out.

He knew the Old Orchard Road; he traversed it every day with the full wine bottles chunking together in his saddlebags. The dirt road crossed the blacktop edging the river where he had his vantage point in the woods. He had found it unerringly as if an inner voice had led him almost to her door, sensing without knowing that she would be close. He believed in no god beyond himself, but he was convinced there were forces unseeable that had propelled and buffeted him in his quest, and the sheer gift of this realization hit him now, relaxing all his taut muscles so that he almost stumbled as he walked toward his bike.

CHAPTER FIVE

Sam dreamed that he was walking across a desert wearing a fur parka, hauling his injured leg behind him. A red bird circled over his head—a vulture—screeching at him in annoying cadence, but he couldn't move fast enough to get away from its raucous cry. In his dream he fumbled with the zipper of his parka, struggling to pull the heavy garment off so that he could run.

Pistol, sprawled across his master's chest, took umbrage at the rough treatment, struck out with one unsheathed paw and caught Sam across the chin, leaving a dotted path of blood.

Sam swung and reared up in the same motion, swearing at the scarlet bird that had just attacked him, and sending Pistol off the daveno to skid against the wall. He was awake now, his mouth as parched as the desert he'd just escaped, the afternoon's ninety-five degrees threatening to bake him alive before he could stumble to the door and kick it open. Pistol spied the opening and was gone in a blur of disgruntled gray fur. The bird became a phone and continued to shrill at him.

His bad leg almost buckled under him.

"HELLO! God damn it—"

"Hello yourself, little Mary Sunshine," Danny laughed. "Did we disturb his little nappie?"

"What the hell do you want?"

"This is your wake-up service, sir. You asked the desk to call you at four so you could get the preacher's wife out of your room before vespers."

Sam relaxed against the counter, rubbing his leg with one hand and holding the black earpiece with the other. When the leg could bear his weight, he used the massaging hand to reach into the refrigerator for a cold beer. He rubbed the can over his face and chest before opening it, slowly coming back to the reality of the afternoon.

"She left at noon. Said she couldn't take anymore after the fifth go-round. They don't make women like they used to—at least *I* don't. Now could you tell me why you're calling at dawn?"

"Joanne says supper will be ready at five-thirty, quarter to six, and to get your ass out here."

"She didn't say that. She talks nice." Sam ripped the tab off the beer and took a deep draught. "You sure she wants me out there tonight?"

"I'm sure. Mother-in-law cruised by and left yesterday's harvest. There's enough to feed the whole department, but we thought we'd start with you. Corn, beans, tomatoes, and steak."

"Mother-in-law ran over a cow, did she?"

"Only the front half. You comin' out?"

Sam glanced around the trailer; it was so hot inside he could almost see heat waves emanating from the debris he'd meant to pick up when he woke up. "Oh hell yes. What can I bring?"

Danny paused for a moment and Sam heard him cover the phone with his hand and call something to Joanne. Another pause.

She says nothing—but I'll take a couple of beers if you want to stop by and get some."

"I'll stop. Mother-in-law still there. Maybe I better get a case—I know what a lush she is."

Danny laughed at the thought. "Halfway under the table already, and she's panting to see you. The woman's insatiable. Naw, really—she left after the produce run. We'll see you in a while." He hung up before Sam had a chance to change his mind.

Sam's head felt thick from his day's sleep in the heat of the aluminum trailer. He grabbed another beer on his way to the shower and enjoyed the cold spray against his chest as he opened it; it was cooler than the shower would be. He was grateful he had someplace to go. He could stand staying in the trailer just long enough to put on his uniform —but no longer.

His truck, parked for forty-eight hours with locked doors and closed windows under the tin-roofed lean-to, breathed fire when he opened the door. He held his breath as he leaned across the hot vinyl seat and rolled down the passenger window, knowing he'd have to drive five miles before enough air could circulate to make the cab bearable. Before he could suppress it, his memory tricked him and raced back to find a cool place, and he was on the deck of the houseboat again with the rain sluicing down his neck. He could feel his hand on her doorknob, see through the steamy windows to where she sat cross-legged on the floor staring out at the water.

He felt better once he was out on the blacktop, moving away from his bleak thoughts and cloying memories. He was not lost; he had someplace to go, someone who waited for him, and a job he was damned good at. It was O.K. now, and he drew a breath of air that was, if not cool, at least bearable.

Natchitat was always two different towns to him; in the morning light, the dawn light, no matter the season, it was clean, kind, almost surrealistically pure, all imperfections softened by the plum velvet shadings of summer and the blue-pink of winter skies. But late afternoons brought a harshness, an unforgiving searchlight that weathered facade and exposed an underlying ugliness. If it were possible, he would have avoided Natchitat in daylight and stayed in the hills beyond town.

Sam wheeled into the Safeway parking lot, relieved to see that the evening shopping crush hadn't begun yet in earnest. For a moment he thought about locking his truck but dismissed the precaution, unwilling to face the furnace again. He stepped into the store and felt the ice-water air piped there. His uniform pulled eyes, sparked curiosity even among the most lanquid of shoppers. When he moved easily toward the rear, nodding at the Fast-Check-Out clerk, the one with orange hair and shelflike breasts that obscured her view of the cash register, the shoppers relaxed—half-relieved, half-disappointed, that it was to be an ordinary day after all.

He grabbed a six-pack of Coors, and then realized it wouldn't look good for him to buy only beer while he was in uniform. He picked a half-gallon of Safeway Snow Sparkle Almond Crunch ice cream, and spun around toward the quick-check line. He watched the checker— Beverly—yeah, Beverly—and saw a thin trail of perspiration ooze its way toward her cleavage.

"You find everything you want, Sam?" Her breasts seemed to have a life of their own, and they vibrated as she spoke. Sam looked up, caught. She smiled.

"Seem to have it all for today, Bev. You have a special I missed— giving anything away free? I forgot my coupons." There was no desire behind his banter; it came as automatically as breathing. She was very young, and her round brown eyes reminded him of a calf's. She liked him, but, God, what was she? Twenty-three? Twenty-four? He had nothing to say to her, or she to him. Even so, he smiled back, his eyes aimed directly into hers.

"You, Sam, don't need coupons." She reached across for the beer and ice cream, leaning just off balance enough so that he knew it wasn't accidental that her breasts brushed his tan-clad arm. He kept his hand flat on the check-out counter, pretending he hadn't noticed.

"You going on duty? Or off?"

"On, sweetheart. Can't you see I'm not sweating yet? Graveyard, like always. We're ships that pass in the night. You work days; I work nights, and you'll be tucked safe in bed long before I get off. My bad luck."

She looked away from him, jabbed at the cash register with improbably long scarlet nails. Twenty years ago, he would have though about her as he rode through darkened streets. Now, she slipped from his mind like smoke before he was even through the automatic door to the parking lot.

The Harley parked next to the vapor light pole caught his interest. His own bike had been a Harley. This one had no distinguishing marks at all, just a few nicks and scrapes in its black hide, scuffed black leather saddlebags, and Oregon plates. And all alone. Harleys generally moved in herds, but this one was a maverick. Probably belonged to some businessman with a midlife crisis. Sam moved on, but the bike registered someplace deep in his mind, the cop part, a programmed chip full of vehicles, faces, distinguishing characteristics, M.O.s and peculiarities, most never needed again.

He eased the pickup through town and floored it when he hit the blacktop, passing the trailer park again without glancing at it, and a mile farther on, turning onto the dirt road that led to Danny's place.

He didn't see the black dot in his rearview mirror until it grew large enough to fill the mirror. It was the Harley, going too fast for the unstable surface—almost close enough to destruct on his rear bumper if he chanced to stop suddenly. Irritated, he tapped his brakes and the hog pulled back, controlled easily by the big man who rode it. Sam pegged him certain for a stranger; his old pickup was familiar to almost everybody in Natchitat, and no punk around town would have the balls to play games with him. He gunned the truck again and the bike pulled up closer. He tapped the brakes, watching the rider in his mirror. The bike shimmied, slid off-course a few degrees, and seemed about to tumble into the ditch before the rider rammed his booted foot into the gravel and skidded to a stop. Sam laughed and picked up speed, sashaying the old truck's rear end in a mechanical put-down. The biker's helmeted head protruded from the froth of the road dust and his silver-rimmed goggles glinted in the sun, making him ageless, unidentifiable —a disembodied, round-headed mask.

Sam lit a Marlboro from the crumpled pack on the dashboard and tasted stale tobacco flakes on his tongue, annoyed with himself because he'd forgotten to buy more at the Safeway. Now he'd have to wait until he got to the machine in the office or give in and accept one of the rotten cigars that Danny smoked occasionally.

He heard the bike roar behind him again just as he reached the lane up to the farm, where he concentrated on avoiding the weed-choked ditches on either side of the narrow entrance, his truck crawling a few miles an hour. He waited, only slightly curious, for the Harley to pass, turning his head to catch a glimpse of the black hog with its tall male rider. Jeans. A black T-shirt and the white helmet. Caucasian. The rider's right hand left the hand grip for just a moment, jutted in Sam's direction and the middle finger raised in obscene salute.

Sam debated backing the pickup out and giving chase. He would enjoy seeing the slow recognition on the Harley rider's face as he unfolded his uniformed frame from the pickup, seeing the turkey's bravado seep out of his features when he realized who he'd been playing with. He debated too long, torn between the welcome waiting up at the top of the orchard road and the satisfaction of writing a ticket for the fingerman. The hell with it; he'd have all night long to find assholes. No need to run one down now when his stomach growled for something to eat and his mouth watered for a beer. Besides, the ice cream would melt.

He pulled in behind Danny's new red GMC and headed for the back door, boots silent on the mowed lawn behind the house. He could see them inside, unaware of his presence, only a dozen feet away from him through the open window but caught in emotions that did not include him.

Danny stood, back to the refrigerator, arms folded over his chest, a closed look on his face—not angry, but cautious. Sam had seen that look a thousand times, that protective facade while his partner waited for someone else to speak, to telegraph weakness. Joanne was at the table, her hands full of silverware, her face turned toward Danny. Her shoulders, bare above the flowered sundress, were bent, almost supplicatingly, toward her husband. Sam could not let them speak because if they did, he would be able to hear every word, and they would be very private words, not to be shared with him or with anyone else.

He banged on the door, and their startled faced turned toward him, veiled almost immediately with smiles.

"Hey, can I come in before I get goosed by the goose?" He said too loudly. "He thinks he's in love."

Danny strode toward him through tension that still hung heavy in the kitchen and held the screen door open, grabbing for the Safeway sack with his free hand. "What the hell took you so long? I've been reduced to drinking lemonade."

Joanne took a beat longer to shake the dark mood, and then she laughed and brushed his cheek with a half-kiss. "He just got out of the shower, Sammie. If you'd got here any sooner, you would have had only me to talk to."

He looked at her, seized as always with pleasure at her genuine prettiness, and wondering at the same time what in hell they *would* have found to discuss without Danny in the room to share the banter.

"And that would have been my good fortune," he lied. "I have heard everything the kid here has to say too many times already. And he didn't know that much to start with."

He accepted the beer can that Danny held out to him, raised it in a mock salute to click with Danny's can, and began to relax. Even solid marriages were given to argument; he had simply blundered into the middle of one. And yet, he couldn't shake the memory of his own failed marriages. Gloria had put it bluntly, "Bad marriages need spectators, Sam. It helps you pretend for a while longer that everything's all right. I'm acting and you're acting, but if we can convince somebody else that we like each other, maybe we'll believe it ourselves."

He watched them—Danny standing close to Joanne, his big hand dwarfing her waist, holding her tight against his hip, giving her sips of beer while she struggled half-heartedly to get free.

"Let that woman go, man," Sam laughed. "Can't you see she's panting to cook, and I'm starving?"

Danny released her, and then pulled her back and gave her a resounding kiss. "So cook, woman." He turned to Sam. "You may be sorry. She's into zucchini; it's a kind of fetish. We've got zucchini bread, zucchini pickles, zucchini stuffed, fried, baked, and fricasseed, and—except for you—we'd be eating zucchini ice cream. Everything's full of little green specks."

"Don't believe him, Sam. We don't have *baked* zucchini. I didn't want to overdo it. Sit down before you faint from hunger."

He sat at the table, feeling good again, with the small rush of beer in his system, part of this little family who were now easy with each other. The table was covered with bowls of corn on the cob, sliced tomatoes, green beans, boiled potatoes, and jello. Danny forked the steaks onto each plate with a grandiose flourish. Fried steak. Nobody in Natchitat broiled steak. He shut his eyes for a moment and the aroma brought back his mother's harvest meals.

"Joanne, if I could find a woman who cooked like you do, I'd marry her in a minute."

"Liar." She looked at him accusingly. "Every woman in Natchitat County can cook like I do—and better—and I haven't seen you racing to the altar with any of them. I suppose it's my fault. If I quit feeding you, maybe they'd have a chance."

"Ahh—there you have me. It's not your cooking at all. It's your sensuous beauty that keeps me coming back. Lord knows, I've tried to fight it. . . ."

She giggled. "I can't hear you with your mouth full."

Danny sat at the head of the table, watching them with a look of pride on his face. It was a good time, with the first streams of cool evening air blown off the river stirring the ruffled window curtains, the muted lavender dusk throwing the corners of the room into shadow. Sam knew his limits with the small woman across the table. She belonged to his partner, and yet he knew Danny took some delight in watching Sam flirt with her. He felt a surge of affection for each of them, willing them to be happier.

Joanne bent over the table, slicing the brown spicy-smelling loaf with a serrated blade. A slice fell away and Sam laughed, seeing the bright green flecks in it.

"See," Danny said. "I told you. Zucchini. She spent all day grinding it up. I understand it's an aphrodisiac. Three slices of that and you'll be a frothing maniac."

Sam looked at her delicate hands on the knife, seeing the dusky blue veins that glowed beneath the skin of her wrists and pulsed in the soft places in the crooks of her arms. He could not imagine Joanne running five miles. He could not even picture her running one. She seemed to him to be the softest woman he'd ever seen—not fatty soft, but somehow crushable. Nina had been fragile on the surface, but with a resiliency that he could not find in Joanne.

"Sam? . . . Sam . . .?" He looked up, pulled out of his reverie. Danny dangled another chunk of steak over his plate and he nodded, pushing beans and jello aside to make room.

"So then, Joanne," he began. "What did you do all day while we were sleeping? Besides cooking and grinding up zucchini?"

She drew a breath, and the flowered material over her breasts expanded. She traced a line in the tablecloth with her fingernail.

"Well . . . I ran this morning, before it got so hot. Along the river road and up over the cut behind Mason's warehouse." She darted a glance at Danny who continued to cut his meat, staring down at his plate. "I guess that's about six miles going out and coming back."

"Six miles!" Sam forced a heartiness into his voice that sounded patronizing, even to him, but Joanne didn't seem to pick up on it. "Honey, you're going to have calves like Babe Zaharias!"

"Who?" She looked mischievous. "Is that one of the waitresses at the hotel? The one who's so crazy about you?"

Danny choked on a laugh and turned away from the table, coughing into his napkin.

"No. That's not a waitress at the hotel. It's—oh, forget it. I keep forgetting that we're from different generations."

"You've got it wrong," Danny cut in. "The waitress at the Chief has little skinny legs, and it's Sam who's crazy about her, but she won't give him the time of day. She likes younger men."

Sam had to work to keep the conversation light, aware that it veered dangerously close to sensitive areas, and he felt his gut began to tighten again. Joanne was talking to him, and Danny was talking to him, but neither of them was speaking to the other. As long as he kept them all together with inane humor, they might just make it through the meal without a slipping back into words that could not be easily forgiven.

He took a deep breath. "So you ran your little fanny off—and then what?"

"Then what? Not much, Sammie. There's not much for me to do

around here. I washed dishes and a load of laundry. Then I folded the laundry, and then I read another book, and then I babysat for Sonia while she took the older kids in to get vaccinated, and then I came home and cooked supper."

"Sounds like a full day to me," Sam said weakly, willing Danny to open his stubborn mouth and join the party. "I mean—all Danny and I did was sleep all day."

Joanne stood up, and began scraping her plate. Her movements were brisk, tight little sweeps of her knife across the flowered crockery.

God. How many women had he seen angry like this?

He gave it up, and joined Danny. The two of them ate silently, working through the pile of food on their plates, and he tried to pretend he didn't notice that Joanne was pissed with both of them. Danny looked at his watch and pushed his chair back. The meal was over, thank God, and Sam yearned for the freedom that beckoned beyond the screen door. The shrilling cadence of the phone broke whatever awkwardness remained. Danny picked it up on the third ring, and bellowed, "Halloo—we're on our way in, Fletch. Get off our backs, would you—"

He held the phone away from his ear, shook it, said "Hello" again, and then hung it back on the hook.

"Who was that?" Joanne asked.

"Nobody. Wrong number probably. Or our lousy phone system."

Danny hugged Joanne, kissed her averted cheek, and they were out of it, into the darkened yard with its lone circle of yellow light from the porch bulb.

Sam backed his truck out without speaking, hoping that Danny wouldn't speak either. He fumbled in his shirtpocket for a cigarette, remembered that he had none, and reached for the sun-baked pack on the dash. There was one bent white cylinder left, and he lit it without much hope; it tasted worse than he'd expected. He concentrated on the road, and Danny stared ahead too without talking.

Fletcher was pointing at the clock and grinning when they walked in.

"Fifteen minutes late, kids."

"Don't nag, Fletchie," Sam laughed.

"Wanda Moses is being a real bad girl, Sam. She threw her supper back at Nadine, and she's screaming for ciggies."

Sam bent over the cigarette machine and fed quarters into it. He pulled the knob below the Marlboro slot and waited.

"Damn it, Fletch. Is this thing fucked up again?"

"Romance it a little."

Sam whacked the machine with the flat of his hand and three packs of Marlboros let go. He slid one into his shirtpocket, one into his back pantspocket and handed the third to Fletch.

"Here, take this back to Wanda, and mind your face. She scratches. Mind your cojones too—she kicks."

"She ain't gonna be that grateful."

Sam swung the little deputy by the armpits and put him on the counter and chucked him under the chin. He was the only guy in the department who could do that and leave Fletch laughing.

"You better quit giving Wanda presents," Danny warned. "I think she's single."

"Ain't they all, pard? Ain't they all?"

CHAPTER SIX

Duane let the receiver slip softly back into its cradle, neither frustrated nor particularly annoyed that his call had failed, again, to connect. The few failures in his life were failures of patience, and he had learned from them. He was curious about the sound of her voice. He expected that it would be breathy and delicate, but he could not be sure until he actually caught her fast at the end of the phone's wire. He had got the man on the first call. Say it. Her husband. He looked at the summary in his notebook: "7:51 P.M.—male answered. 8:15—busy signal." He added "9:20—no answer."

"Hey Ace," a muted voice intruded on his thoughts. "You gonna stay in there and pick your nose or what?"

He turned to see the broad, blurred face under the cheap cowboy hat with its band trailing fake feathers. The man was half-drunk, showing off for the skinny woman who clung to his arm. Neither of them would remember him, the time of day, or their own names. He hit the fold in the door and pushed past them, catching a blast of beery breath.

"It's all yours, champ," he muttered. "Sorry about that."

"No problem. No problem. Didn't mean to hassle you."

He weaved his way through the cluster of tables that surrounded the ridiculously small dance floor, and sat at the far end of the padded red bar. The bartender wore western garb too, his belly pushing at the mother-of-pearl buttons on his red plaid shirt. Everybody wanted to be a cowboy.

"Beer?"

"No."

"So, what?"

"A Dirty Mother."

The bartender looked offended. "What the hell is that?"

"Kahlua and cream."

"You mean a White Russian."

"No. I mean a Dirty Mother. Vodka makes me vomit, and you've got such a class act crowd in here, I'd hate to disgrace myself."

He was talking too much. He looked directly at the bartender and flashed his most ingenuous smile. "No offense, friend. I've just got a bitch of a stomach problem."

The man measured him, took in his size, and gave the smile back. "Tell me about it. Stress. Makes your gut bleed if you don't let it roll off your back. Kahlua and cream. Gotcha."

"Great. I appreciate it."

"Work around here?"

"Naw. Passing through. Gotta make Spokane by tomorrow noon."

Somebody bellowed for beer from the other end of the bar, and he was left alone to observe. The Red Chieftain Hotel management had obviously redecorated in the recent past. Walls carpeted halfway up with red and orange patterned in black cattlebrands, and above that, festooned with steer skulls and horseshoes. The pretzels on the bar were offered in dried and salted bull scrotums. Nice touch.

Tacky as it was, the Totem Room was the best of all places to get a look at Danny Boy. Cops never showed up at the Trail's End Tavern unless they were summoned, but here there was always a patrol unit or two parked out in front. The pigs wandered in all day to sip free coffee and jaw with the waitresses. Short of parking across from the sheriff's office, Duane couldn't find a better vantage point. Once he had a look at the husband in the flesh, made sure he was really on duty, he had all night to check out the house.

He sipped his D.M. and watched the coffee shop door, while he made a mental inventory of his cash situation. Once he had her, they would have to hole up for awhile and that would take a thou, maybe two. Credit card slips—yeah. The marks guarded their little plastic rectangles like they were gold, but they threw away the receipts with all the magic numbers. Waste baskets were full of them, and he could get into any bank machine for all he'd need. By the time the bills came in, he and Joanne would be long gone.

He smiled, thinking of it, and the dumb barkeep smiled back, sure he was going to get a big tip.

Fat chance, turkey.

It was after ten when Joanne left Sonia's and Walt's place and headed out the blacktop for home. She dreaded driving home after dark, but she'd dreaded more the long evening alone on the empty farm.

On the last dirt road even the moon disappeared behind the trees. She would not let the dark frighten her; it was the same road she jogged along in the daylight, the trees were the same trees, grotesque and lowering only because they clawed out into the headlight cones, gnarled and crippled by shadows. If she didn't have the guts to drive home alone at night, she'd be dooming herself to isolation. Still, her heart beat too fast, responding to her thoughts. To work around it, she escaped. She was not herself; she became someone else, someone who drove along an unfamiliar road with no particular destination, safe in the Celica-cocoon.

It got her up the lane and safely into the shed. Twenty steps to the back door, with the night noises rustling behind her. Then her key found the lock and slipped in, connecting just as the darkness crept closer and shrunk the yellow sphere of the porch light.

The phone began to ring before the door was fully open, and she hurried toward it across the black kitchen. Two rings—two more. It was their line. She didn't see the chair in her path and it caught her hipbone with its oak-knobbed back, sending thrills of pain through her belly, more intense because of the cramps. It paralyzed her through three more double rings. When she finally picked up the receiver, she heard only silence and the blank buzz of nobody there.

The back door was still open, and she felt the cool draft, started back to close it, and felt something slide across her thigh, pressing insistently. Her throat closed and the back of her neck shrunk with horror. Something behind her fluttered and clicked.

There was some living presence in the room with her, and she forced herself to turn slowly to face it.

The goose eyes reflected a slice of moonlight, and even as she recognized Billy Carter, she couldn't stop the scream that rose in her throat. The gander's wings flared wide and he waddled toward the door hissing indignantly. She slammed it behind him and slid the bolt across, realizing that if the scream had been for real no one would have heard her.

Duane had been about to hang up when she answered, and she sounded just as he thought she would—soft, frightened. It was all he could do not to speak to her. He waited, letting her repeat "Hello . . . Hello . . ." a few times before he pushed the lever down gently, breaking this first link between them.

Later. Just a little while longer, Joanne.

As he turned, he saw them walking into the coffee shop. Lindstrom and the old guy, sauntering into their territory, straddling stools and leaning forward on their elbows as the waitress fluttered over.

He took his time. He added the notes: "10:27 P.M.—Heard Joanne. 10:31 P.M.—D.L. and—(he squinted to read the name pinned over the old guy's shirtpocket)—Sam Clinton, coffee break at hotel."

The fucking waitress was falling all over herself, laughing when the old guy kidded her, bringing them slices of pie, filling their cups. The dumber the broad, the more impressed by a uniform.

He left a buck-seventy-five on the bar and moved closer to the counter, but he couldn't hear what they were saying. He was close enough to see the triangles of sweat under their arms, close enough to smell them. Close enough to grab their skulls in two strides and slam them together, or to slip the .38's out of the holsters where they dangled and pull the triggers before they got their noses out of their banana cream pie. Blood and brains on the polished glass. . . .

He forced his rage inside. He had not come so far after so long to lose it. The husband was big enough but not as big as he was, and the cop was smug. You didn't see a hell of a lot of cops sitting with their backs exposed to a window. The old guy was clearly a country hick, over the hill. Duane had beaten a lot better. A lot better.

Sit there and slop up your pie, Danny. I'm gonna have your wife and teach her things you never thought of.

Her voice had turned him on; his groin still throbbed with the soft looseness he'd heard in her. She already belonged to him. She would do all the things the other women had balked at. When they were alone. When they were alone, he wanted her naked all the time so he could touch her heavy breasts and the secret, moist folds of her whenever he wanted, rub himself all over her and make her beg for it. And he would give it to her until she was so sore she couldn't walk. She'd waited long enough for him, and he would make it up to her.

The cops had finished their pie. The old guy slipped a buck into the waitress's apron and Duane heard her giggle. They ambled out the back door, toothpicks sticking out of their mouths. He watched them drive away before he took a stool at the counter.

"Miss?" She wasn't a "Miss"; she was well over forty, but the old ones loved being mistaken for young meat.

She smiled at him and bent lower, showing the dry wrinkles between her breasts. "What's yours?"

"I'll have what old Danny had. Looks like great pie."

"Oh, it is. Fresh every day." She set a conspicuously large portion in front of him. "Real whipped cream."

He ate a mouthful of the sweet mess, and signaled to her with thumb and forefinger.

"You like it, huh?" He'd got her with the first grin; she was going to watch him eat every sticky crumb of it.

"Always eat where the cops eat. Some people say truckdrivers, but it's really policemen who know where it's at." He smiled again, and let his eyes drift down the front of her as if he was hungry for her too. She liked that.

"You a cop?"

"Me?" He laughed modestly. "No such luck. I'm blind in my left eye. Vietnam. Old Danny and Sam though, they've got it made."

He could see her study his eyes to see if she could tell the difference.

"They work hard though," she offered. "You're probably better off. You a salesman?"

He shook his head slightly and gave no direct answer. "Dangerous too. They take a lot of chances, but I still envy them."

She bit. Spilled her guts, trying to keep his attention. "Danny's gonna take some time off. Old Sam talked him into it. You know how they are. Danny looks up to him, takes his advice, kind of like father and son."

The news wasn't what he wanted to hear, and he had to keep his voice calm so she wouldn't pick up on it. "Take time off?"

"You know Danny—usually just goes elk hunting in November with the guys, but he's gonna take his wife on a vacation. Old second honeymoon treatment and all."

His voice was O.K., but his pulse was spinning free. "Vacation, huh? Labor Day and all? Seems like that's their busy season."

She shrugged. "Women like Joanne—they get what they want out of men. Never have to work and go home with sore feet like I do. She wants a vacation; she gets a vacation. You aren't eating your pie. Is it really O.K.?"

He forced down two more bites and smiled at her. "The best. What time do you go home?"

"Three A.M. Pretty late, huh?"

He looked her up and down again. They all went for that; you could practically see them get wet. "For tonight. I have an appointment—business stuff. Where's Danny taking off to?"

"Didn't say. Sweetie, I wouldn't care *where* it was if somebody offered me a trip, you know? I'd go to Tacoma or Humptulips or wherever. . . ."

"Somebody told me you and Sam were pretty tight. Ask him to take you."

"Who said that?"

"Gee, I can't remember, but all I can say is he's a lucky man. You sure you two aren't engaged or something?"

She was still chuckling to herself, and trying to figure out what the old deputy could have said about her when he walked away.

In the lot behind the hotel, he slammed his fist into the Harley's leather seat. Take her away. Damn them! Never. He would not allow it, not now, not ever. He would watch her every minute of every day, and if they tried to take her, he would. . . . He sat down on the old, scarred bike and closed his eyes. In a few moments the tension drained out of him and his mind was clear again.

Run, Danny. Take her and run as far as you want, but when you stop, I'll be right there.

Joanne dreaded the sound of the phone late at night when Danny was on duty. The voiceless presence could not have been Sonia; she and Walt were on their way to bed when she left. When Danny called her, they had a signal. Two rings, hang up, and then call again so she'd know it was he who called. Maybe the first two rings had sounded as she ran from the car; maybe she hadn't heard them. She dialed the office and Fletch assured her that everything was all right, that Danny and Sam had just gone back on the air after their coffee break. She called her mother, woke her, and heard the familiar impatient little sigh as she apologized.

Joanne told herself that she was quite safe; nothing real had been taken from her. She was alone, but she was inside the farmhouse with her doors bolted. Her anxiety was familiar; she shouldn't be afraid for herself—only for Danny, riding somewhere out there in the dark, circling the county. He was a target, not she. Her rooms were safe behind drawn curtains and locked doors.

Joanne uncapped her vial of Librium, counted that there were sixteen tablets left, and allowed herself one—the first in a week. Maybe the phone call had just been a mistake.

In bed, with the drug already beginning to soften the sharpest points of worry, she drifted into a half-sleep but it was marred with echoes of Danny's words, the words cut off when Sam knocked at the back door. "Let me breathe, Joanne. . . . Sometimes I can't breathe without you wanting to know why. . . . I can't breathe. . . . You're so scared, you're making me scared."

Something—wind in the trees outside, a tapping against the house —roused her slightly and she turned over, looking for sleep on the other side of the wide bed. And remembered that she had sent him away again, puzzled and frustrated by her sullenness. A branch cracked and she heard it as a shot. She saw Danny falling dead. Again and again, his hand held out to ward off a bullet, a last agonized look on his face as he fell. She closed her eyes tight to strike the image, and another rushed in. She heard the impact as his squad car crashed and saw the brown-and-white unit reduced to crushed metal trapping her dead Danny.

Now Danny wasn't dead. He was only injured, and she was being rushed to the hospital to be with him. She would bring him back through her love and tender care. She would not leave his bedside; she would will him to be whole again and warm his skin back to life with her own.

She thought she could actually smell the hospital odor, and Danny's muscular arms were dark brown against the bandage and bedsheet white. Lying there like that, he seemed very sexy, and she felt a tickling beat in her crotch, an insistent heat there.

She was not asleep and not awake, but aware enough to glance toward the shade and see that it was not flush with the bottom of the window. She sighed and switched off the little light by the bed and then got up and pulled the shade all the way down and checked to see that the bedroom door was locked.

She lay back in bed and pictured the scene again. Danny, injured but alive, and herself sitting beside him, his hand clutching hers, holding onto her as if he would fall away forever if he lost touch. She could smell the bandages and iodine again, see his arms flex, and then, slowly, a small tent rising from the sheets where his erection pushed.

She leaned across to stroke his shoulder, and she felt his mouth nuzzling blindly against her breasts. She opened her blouse and put his mouth on her tingling nipple, cradling him as she let him suckle, knowing that she was keeping him alive.

Her fingers tugged and circled her nipple's rubbery hardness as Danny nursed at her in her mind, and she let one hand fall lightly between her legs, feeling how warm and moist she was. It wasn't bad if she didn't let her hand move; it was only daydreaming.

Danny's eyes were still closed, but his penis poked at her, fighting to get free of the knitted sheet. Still suckling his eager mouth, she pulled the cover away and saw his huge and dark hard-on trembling beneath his hospital gown, the eye of it wanting her mouth. Outside their white room, nurses and doctors were walking back and forth; they could come in any minute. She didn't care. She massaged his penis and he groaned and whimpered against her breast. She let him suck on her finger as she moved down in the bed. He tasted quite sweet where she licked him and drew the silken head into her mouth.

She wanted him so much that she felt swollen, and she couldn't stop. She mounted him, letting herself slide over his straining cock, feeling it push up. And then she rode him wildly, letting her breasts whip back and forth across his face, letting her own hand move fiercely over the pink nub between her legs.

She saw the shocked faces at the doorway, saw them raise their hands to warn her away from Danny, and still she bucked on top of him triumphantly. When the feeling grew to bursting, the lover who had been dead beneath her except for his mouth and his cock threw back his head and shouted, and his voice shimmered up through her belly and down her thighs in waves that made her legs shake.

Joanne lay back and sobbed, horrified at what she had done, and still knowing at last what had been waiting at the top of the hill she'd never managed to climb. She walked shakily to the bathroom and bent over the sink, scrubbing her hand in the dark.

Duane padded around outside the farmhouse in the dark. He knew she was in there because he heard rustles of sound—a door slamming, the floorboards or maybe the bed creaking, and, finally, a sound as if someone inside wept. Maybe. It was hard to hear through the walls. He tried each window, quietly so that no one could possibly hear him, and found them all locked. He'd expected that the doors would be and they were. He could break in, shatter the glass to get to her. But that was risky; she might have enough time to get to the phone. He couldn't cut the line; it came down from the pole and entered near the roof, too high over even his head.

He wanted to smash and force his way in, but his common sense prevailed. Tomorrow, he could find her along the road, alone, with no walls between them at all. He would have to sleep outside in a close watching place to be sure he didn't miss her—or them, if the husband took her away. His sleeping bag was already on the back of the bike, and his saddlebags were packed now and ready. He didn't even have to go back to the crummy room.

He could see into the kitchen with its single dim light glowing, but no matter how he tried, he could not see into the room where he believed she slept. Reluctantly, he turned to leave and his foot pressed against the soft feathered body.

He took the bird with him, its fractured neck flopping crazily over the saddlebags as he coasted down the long driveway.

He tossed it into the ditch below, and saw it disappear beneath the long grasses there.

She slept so soundly that she heard no sounds at all outside her window.

PART TWO
STEHEKIN
SEPTEMBER 4, 1981

CHAPTER SEVEN

The Lady of the Lake, broad-bowed and gleaming, bumped impatiently against the long, narrow dock and tugged at her lines. Beneath and around her, Lake Chelan mirrored the blue of the sky, so calm and flat that it seemed painted, the thick wash of it brilliant against the umber hills.

By 8:15 A.M., Joanne and Danny waited in line with a hundred other tourists behind the chain blocking the gangplank. Joanne saw the tension in the set of Danny's shoulders. He didn't really want to be here, and it had been Sam who'd convinced him to go, hurrying them both through immediate departure, as if their chance to leave would vanish if they didn't seize it. She'd packed in one day, wondering now what she'd forgotten to bring.

Joanne thought about the nights on the trails ahead, where she and Danny would curve around each other like spoons to shut out the cold, and was glad they had somehow managed this trip. She hooked her arm through Danny's and leaned over the rail to watch the sinuous forms in the shallows below them. Fish slid darkly beneath the surface and duck families circled, their necks craned expectantly for crumbs from above. They made her think of Billy Carter's disappearance, but she didn't want to bring that up again.

"Look honey," she pointed. "See how tame they are."

He wasn't looking. He was turned away from her, staring at the next dock where a sheriff's launch idled, spitting gray-brown smoke under the gap-planked pier. Everything in him seemed to pull away from her and he didn't notice when she released his arm. She watched him without hope, almost expecting him to walk away and start a conversation with the Chelan county deputies in the boat.

They moved into the seating area—green vinyl upholstered chairs, nine abreast, railed with white iron lattice work. She hesitated and Danny pulled her toward a window seat.

"You want a beer?"

"No. Not yet."

"I need one. How about coffee?"

"Sure. Great."

She looked up at his face bending over her, caught in bas relief by a shaft of sunlight. She could see a puffiness under his eyes, the creases in front of his ears, and a kind of fullness in his cheeks she had never noticed. With a jolt she realized she had not seen him close up in daylight for a long time, and now she saw that her husband was growing older. Not really old—not like the men she'd been watching in the line—but older. He wasn't the Danny she'd married; that one had slipped away without her knowing it. He bent his head, and she saw the sheen of his scalp through the hair at his temples. She reached out to touch his arm.

"Danny?"

"Yeah?"

"I love you."

He looked around, embarrassed, and grinned finally. "Me too."

The good moment stayed in the air even after he moved up the aisle. It was going to be O.K. They had come close to the edge of something, but they hadn't fallen over and they weren't going to now. He had come with her along the dark roads of morning, without sleep after his night's work, and they were on their way to a better place. A second chance.

The Lady of the Lake pulled out sluggishly at first, turning to port, past her sister ships, and then more smoothly as she eased past the "76" pump. Even after a hundred years of civilization, the town of Chelan here at the lake's edge looked tentative, threatened by the sere brown hills that lowered over it, muting the bright colors of houses with the sheer depth and breadth of brown, brown, brown. Close by the water, the land came alive in the rich green swaths of orchard after orchard.

Danny looked back at Joanne from his position on the deck. She was playing with a kid in the seat in front of her, hiding her eyes with her fingers and then flashing peek-a-boo. The kid was laughing and jumping up and down. She should have her own; he owed her that much because she'd never broken even one promise to him. She didn't flirt, she didn't chippy, and she tried so damn hard.

He moved forward to the prow of the boat, edging past the tall man who stared up at the hills through binoculars and who grunted at his "Excuse me." The hills seemed greener now, but the water was slate blue and smooth, deeper as they plowed ahead. A transport that looked like a weathered wood catamaran headed toward them, its deck full of cars and an antique pickup. The boatman tooted and waved as the *Lady* sluiced by.

Danny thought about Sam—Sam who had pushed him into this trip by an invitation for a tour of his pit of a trailer. Sam had wiped out all of his own illusions; he had shown him what happened to cops who fucked their badges and lost their wives. The man didn't have *anything*. Heroes weren't supposed to evaporate like that—they weren't supposed to make you bleed for them. If Sam had lost it all along the way, where the hell was *he* going? Well, Sam had made his point, made it in spades, convinced him to go into Doc's office and try for half an hour to ejaculate into a glass beaker. He'd finally managed, handed the damned jar to Doc, and escaped. He still felt like a fool about it. And worse about seeing Sam's loneliness.

Danny couldn't shake his vague depression, and something more menacing that came with it, something that should not be part of the bright morning. The mountains ahead of them fell one upon the other, triangle against triangle, and their ridges were sharp and cruel. There was no end to it; when he expected to see the lake's furthest shore ahead, there were only more of the steel blue triangles, as if the boat they rode on was chugging steadily toward the end of the world.

He walked back to where Joanne sat, pretending that he had not left her alone for half an hour. He touched her hair and she leaned toward him, smiling too intensely.

"Hey babe, come on out on the deck with me. We're coming into Manson."

She shivered. "What an ugly name for such a pretty little town."

"How much farther?" he asked. "I thought you said it was just a little boat ride, and we're already in the middle of nowhere."

She looked at her watch. "A long ways. Three hours and fifteen minutes. I told you it was the end of the world."

He had thought it, and she had said it now. Probably that's where it had come from in the first place. They were committed to the water that stretched ahead, gliding past the looming, blank-faced rock walls.

There were no more clusters of houses, only a few cottages and trailers along the lake edges. The water was olive green and opaque and the fir trees had relinquished the hills to hardier pines. The landscape was crumpled and humbled by the grinding glaciers that had formed it, and it still bled streams of rock slides, boulders big enough to crush a man. Even the last telephone lines warned of danger; the black wires across the channel were strung with orange balls to alert seaplane pilots.

Danny had not slept for almost twenty-four hours and the fatigue made his eyes grainy, filled his muscles with lead. He should have slept a day before they started out; the effort of being cheerful and interested fatigued him more. He longed to lean against Joanne's shoulder and let his eyelids drop. Instead, he bought two beers and a mammoth home-made ham sandwich from the pleasant woman in the snack bar and carried them back to where Joanne sat.

The P.A. system buzzed, and the young pilot's voice boomed out, saving them from the effort of conversation.

"Welcome aboard *The Lady of the Lake*. Lake Chelan is fifty-two miles long, the deepest lake in the continental United States, formed by glaciers many, many centuries ago. This canyon was created millions of years ago when the Cascade Mountains were formed, and the lake dropped. River gravel and sand has been analyzed and confirmed seven to eight thousand feet above the present lake. The towns of Chelan and Manson rest on a natural earth plug."

"Fascinating," Danny muttered, and Joanne poked him. "Sorry."

"Indian tribes wintered over at Bitter Creek at Stehekin almost two hundred years ago; they called the lake 'bubbling water.' With the arrival of the white settlers, the Indians were moved to the Columbia Reservation. Prospectors moved in in the late 1800s—but Holden's copper claim was the biggest. The mine was closed in 1957; four to five hundred people live in the Lutheran camp there now. Some of you folks will be getting off at Holden Village for your retreat. The camp will have a jitney there waiting for you."

"When the white man arrived here, the lake level was 1,070 feet above sea level. It was raised 21 feet in 1927, for the power plant, and the Chelan Power Station and dam was the first in the state of Washington. Forty-eight streams and one river flow into Lake Chelan at all times, and there is one million, two hundred thousand acre feet of water outflow a year. This is a cold lake, ladies and gentlemen, and a clean lake; you can see thirty feet down. Below thirty feet, bodies will not rise to the surface. Otherwise they float after three or four weeks."

"That's cheery, too," Danny commented. "At least you know you won't rot if you fall in."

She turned toward the window, wondering why Danny's response to the mention of death was always sarcastic, and then knowing—as she always knew—that it frightened him.

". . . copper, lead, zinc, gold." The speaker continued. "M.E. Fields, the postmaster of Stehekin, built the Fields Hotel where the Stehekin River ran off the lake in the late 1800s and worked a package deal with the Great Northern Railroad to have *The Belle of Chelan, The Clipper,* and *The Stehekin* bring wealthy tourists in. M.E. put in crystal chandeliers, velvet drapes, grand piano, all as grand as Chicago and San Francisco—and all brought in by barge and boat. The hotel was covered over by the lake in 1927."

Joanne shivered. Despite the scenery, nothing of human endeavor and enterprise seemed to have lasted here: the Indians uprooted from their bubbling water, the mines deserted, and the hotel covered over. She wondered if it still existed under the lake's surface, with only ghosts playing its grand pianos for the silly girls coaxed into the wilderness by rich old men who promised them lobster and champagne and nights of dancing, and then wanted payment. She told herself she read too much fiction.

The big boat nudged the decrepit dock at Holden's Camp and the Lutherans on board debarked, decimating the passenger list. And then the mountains closed in tighter. The water was deep aqua and viscous, and the sun disappeared into the rock.

Danny looked at the lake and wished they had gone to Tahoe or Vegas.

The mountains came straight down into the water with no handholds out of peril. A drowning man, his blood chilling with hypothermia in the icy lake, would have as much chance of crawling out as someone in a glass-walled pit. The rock face went up and up and disappeared into storm clouds thousands and thousands of feet above. He thought he could see a harbor in the distance and checked his watch. Less than an hour to go and all signs negative. He cursed Sam silently, closed his eyes, and fell asleep immediately.

Up on top of the boat, the red-headed man with the binoculars smiled as he focused on the moving white form high above the water and watched a mountain goat tread a clearly impossible path.

CHAPTER EIGHT

Danny woke—minutes, hours, days later?—his face pressed against Joanne's bare arm, his mouth dry and bitter tasting. Her flesh was tender now, accepting him, cradling him as she held one of his hands in hers. They would make it up—they always did. He sat up, wiping his mouth and stretching in the same movement, bringing one hand down to caress her neck.

"We here?"

She smiled at him, but her eyes were hidden from him behind her sunglasses. "We're docking now. There's the lodge."

He had expected a village, a colorful settlement cut deeply into the mountains at the lake's end, but the wilderness had given only grudgingly of itself, allowing perhaps three hundred feet from the shore to the firs and pines that loomed over the half-dozen structures. A foothold, but nothing more. The building directly in front of them was long and rectangular, its southern wing two-stories, and topped with a corrugated metal roof. In front of the lodge, a planked deck guarded with a fence made of staggered one-by-sixes was dotted with picnic tables.

He was disappointed; he'd pictured a rustic log cabin lodge, and he saw buildings that reminded him of a small-town motel built in the 1950s. There was a broad apron of concrete at dockside that appeared to be the dead end of a road that snaked along the woods to the north to accomodate, presumably, the motley vehicles parked in front of the lodge: old cars—fifties cars to match the architectural style of the lodge —and Forest Service pickups and vans, motorcycles, bicycles.

The whole settlement seemed to be temporary, nothing more than a slight irritant on the flank of the mountains, the forest so dense that it looked like a gently undulating black-green sea.

He did not want to go into that maze of trees and trails and climb straight up toward the dead blue sky. He knew it was too late to change his mind. They had come too far. Danny envied the tourists who would eat their lunches on the deck, buy souvenirs, and be back in their own beds by nightfall.

His legs still heavy from sleep that was not really sleep, he moved to the open hold door and retrieved their backpacks. The crowd milled with subdued expectancy, the bulk of them city people who seemed awed by the mountains, a few of them obviously skilled hikers who grabbed their gear and moved to wait in line for the vans that would carry them uptrail to begin their ascents. The boatmen finished unloading suitcases and packs and turned to crates of liquor, meat, produce, and clean laundry for the lodge.

Danny, seeing Joanne walk confidently toward a white Samoyed standing in the back of a Forest Service pickup, started to shout, "No!" but relaxed when the dog allowed itself to be hugged and nuzzled. She trusted too much. Damn. One day she was going to get bitten; she assumed the whole damn world would respond to love and kindness.

"Danny! Come over here and meet this fellow. Isn't he neat?"

He reached out his hand to the dog, who reared back, distrusting some scent on it, and then yelped.

The ranger grinned at him.

"He likes ladies best—and kids—but he's not too sure about men."

Danny held out his hand. "Danny Lindstrom, deputy from down in Natchitat. You guys the law around here?"

The ranger shrugged. "What there is of it. We don't have the kind of problems you guys do. Keep track of the hikers and make sure they come back or make it over the top to the North Cascades Highway. Not much crime up here—too hard to get out."

"That figures. No place to run, I guess."

The ranger laughed. "Oh, we had one poor slob—robbed the post office over in Malott and headed over here. He liked to starved to death, finally killed him a deer, but he practically threw himself into our arms when we found him wandering around in circles."

Danny smiled absently, staring beyond the buildings at the blue-gray mountains. "What if somebody gets hurt?" he asked, turning back to the ranger. "How in hell do you get somebody out in an emergency?"

"Ernie Gibson can get up here from Chelan in his float plane in twenty minutes if he pushes, and there's a landing strip towards High Bridge for a regular plane to take off in a pinch. We've been lucky though—haven't had anything we couldn't handle. The Chelan county boys have their launch docked down lake, and they can run the lake a lot faster than the *Lady*. You on vacation?"

"Yeah. The wife put her foot down. Said I was working too hard."

The ranger looked at Joanne appreciatively, and Danny put a proprietory hand on her hipbone. She nodded and smiled.

"This is your dog? He's beautiful."

"Thanks. He's called McGregor after that mountain over there." He turned back to Danny. "You going backpacking?"

"Tomorrow. The wife's got it all plotted out—up to Rainbow Lake, camp out there, and head back here probably. How's the fishing?"

"Fishing's good. Mosquitos are better. You got some insect repellant?"

"Hell, I hope so. She packed *everything*. You know women."

The men laughed, and the ranger moved toward the door of his truck. "Be sure you sign in at our office over there before you head up —so's we know where to find you if you don't come back."

"We'll do that."

Duane had a coke and a burger on the deck, watched Danny leave the Forest Service office, and waited until he'd disappeared into the lodge. He strolled over to the office, pulled the register toward himself and pretended he was about to sign it. When the ranger on duty turned away, Duane read down the list and saw "Lindstrom, Danny, Joanne: Rainbow Lake. Est. Ret: 9-7-81." He closed the book and grabbed a handful of maps and trail guides.

He knew where they were going, and he could study how to get there. Lucky he had his sleeping bag, and there was a little grocery store to stock up. He would not have to wait for them and follow them; it would be better if he went on ahead to reconnoiter. It would give him the advantage. When he walked out, he saw Joanne and Danny climbing the steps toward the lodge office, and felt the pang of knowing that she would be with the other man for one more night at the very least, closed in behind shingled walls.

It could not be helped; he would not think about it.

He caught the shuttle bus with the summer baby-ranger, jammed in with hardcore hikers eager to start up and make camp before nightfall. Three miles to the trailhead. He could have just as easily walked —and should have, damn it. Duane was out and turned away from the rig when the kid called him back, "Sir?"

He turned back, keeping his expression bland and free of the annoyance he felt, the slight apprehension.

"We need your destination, sir. If you'll sign this, put in your name, where you're headed, and when you're due back, I'll let the head ranger know."

"Sure. Fine. But I'm not coming back in. I'm going over the top and pick up the trail to the highway. What do you figure it will take me?"

"Ten hours—depending. Watch out for the rattlesnakes."

"Thanks," he scribbled on the clipboard held out to him: "David S. Dwain, Portland, Oregon. Destination: North Cascades Highway."

And it was true. That was his initial destination, a hop, skip, and a jump from the Canadian border, and once over, endless freedom. He liked the name Stehekin, liked its meaning: "The way through." He always found a way through, no matter how narrow the opening or how difficult. If the body could not insinuate itself through blocked passages, the mind always could.

His pack was light, his elation diminishing the weight on his back. He was alone, with the river rushing behind him, the empty trail ahead.

Danny watched her unpack, carefully putting away the jar of instant coffee, powdered cream, sugar, eggs, and bacon in the kitchen that was as equipped as their own at home.

"Joanne," he teased. "You call this roughing it? We've got a bathroom with a shower and a tub and a goddamned flush toilet! We've got electricity and a smoke alarm."

"Only for tonight. Tomorrow: the wilderness."

She bent over to look under the sink, and he moved behind her, his arms encircling her waist, pulling her back against him.

"He wanted you," Danny whispered into her ear.

She held her breath. "Who?"

"*Who?* That guy."

He forced her against the hard sink, one hand holding her buttocks, the other on her breasts, reassuring himself that he owned her.

"You mean the boatman? Or the kid who brought the sheets? That's who, right? The kid who brought the sheets?" She laughed but it came out hollow; she didn't really enjoy this game.

"The ranger. He thought you were some kind of woman."

"The dog liked me too."

She twisted around until she was tight against him. "Does that turn you on? Is that what it takes?"

He stepped away from her, startled. "What does that mean?"

"What if I was ugly? What if nobody else wanted me? Would you still want me?"

"Come on, Joanne. I came over here to be a little bit friendly, and you—"

"I should be enough by myself; you should be able to get turned on without seeing me reflected in some guy's eyeballs."

"That's kind of sick, Joanne."

She walked over to him and put her head on his chest, tugging his arms around her. "I'm sorry, Danny. I guess I'm nervous. It seems like a honeymoon. Remember how nervous I was the first time? I'm sorry."

"Just don't take offense at everything I say. O.K?" He brushed her hair away from her face and looked at her, and she thought that it was all right again.

"O.K. Kiss me?"

"You got it."

His hands moved down to her buttocks and he pulled her close to him, responding to her.

"Wait. Let me just take a quick shower."

"I like you the way you smell now."

She pulled free of him carefully. "Just a few minutes. Wait right here for me."

"You're not going to slip into something more comfortable, are you?"

She grinned. "I'm not going to slip into anything at all."

"That's more like it."

"Stay right there, and close your eyes."

"You close your eyes. I'll be looking."

She showered for a long time, trying to wash away the awkwardness and her feeling that she was only playing a part. Wanting to let go, and be what he seemed to want. Naked and feeling slightly foolish, she stepped out into the living room.

He was asleep, fallen on his side on the plaid couch, his legs sticking out through the maple arms, one cushion held viselike against his chest. She tried to wake him and move him into the bedroom where he would be more comfortable, but he only groaned and she gave up. He deserved to sleep undisturbed; he had to be exhausted.

The room, so recently bright with sun, had darkened and she felt cold. She wrapped herself in a blanket and crouched by the window watching the sun lose itself behind the clouds eating up the mountain peaks. Lightning darted jagged tongues into the lake, and moments later the building shook in sympathetic vibration with the thunder that followed. Danny jerked in his dreams, but slept on.

She wondered about the hikers who had headed uptrail when they docked. Were they up there now seeking shelter under a rock ledge or a mass of fir boughs? Were they frightened, sorry that they'd left the safety of the lodge down below them? No. They would be prepared for storms or they wouldn't be up there. She was grateful for the roof over their heads. She had not expected that the mountains would be so high or the forest so thick that the sun died in it.

She shivered; a rabbit had walked over her grave.

Joanne wondered if she asked Danny to stay with her in the lower valley if he would. Not likely. She'd heard him tell the ranger they were going up and maybe over the top, and his pride wouldn't allow him to change his mind even if he wanted to. They would be out there by tomorrow night, somewhere on the mountain in a place hidden now behind the clouds, beyond returning.

She turned on the kitchen light and the illumination made the room look normal and safe again: white enameled stove and refrigerator, linoleum in the same pattern as her mother's kitchen, red-and-white checked curtains, a bunch of wild sweetpeas in a water glass in the window. The light warmed her and she made coffee and a bologna sandwich, chewing and sipping in deliberate movements as she pored over the pamphlets on how to stay alive and healthy in the wilderness.

The storm drained itself of fury, leaving only a soft rain that picked at the roof and then pattered gently into the ferns and berry thickets outside. He did not wake, and she left him in the dusky living room and carried a paperback novel into the bedroom, reading in the narrow light of the bedside lamp. She was caught up easily in the story of the gothic heroine who worshipped the cruel, brooding wastrel son of a wealthy English family. The heroine came together with him every twenty pages or so, but the sex was only vaguely erotic. There was nothing for her to match herself against and come up lacking. Crashing waves and shooting stars and heaving breasts. She wished it was really so easy.

Without expecting to, she slept—through the evening and into the night, lulled by the rain. When she woke near dawn, Danny was beside her, still dressed in his T-shirt and jeans. She molded herself against him and fell softly asleep again. When she woke, it was daylight. Good strong daylight, and Danny was in the living room checking out their gear. The strangeness of yesterday had evaporated with the raindrops.

CHAPTER NINE

The shuttle bus hurtled north along the Stehekin River Road toward the High Bridge turnaround, apparently without shocks to cushion the jolting, bucking ride. The driver, a young temporary Forest Service employee, kept up a steady monologue.

"That log cabin there on the right is the grade school, fifteen students up to grade eight, and the little cabin out back—well, that's just what it looks like. They got some flush toilets in there but the ecology guys won't let them use them. The Field Hotel was over there, but it went when they dammed the lake in '27. The Golden West Museum back by the lodge still has some of the wood from it. Over on your right—that's an organic vegetable garden. The guys who run it sell to the restaurant at the lodge and they bake the pies too. Boysenberry this week. Great pies. You eat there last night?"

Danny shook his head. "We meant to, but we overslept. Have to give it a try when we come back down, unless we decide to go on over and into Okanogan County."

"Food's good. Now, look back there to the right, way back in there behind the trees there. That's all that's left of the Rainbow Falls Lodge."

They looked and saw only what looked like a pile of weathered boards and a sagging roof. Joanne had a momentary flash of the dead barn at home and heard the sighing beyond it again. She shut her eyes and it washed away.

"Old gal named Lydia George ran the Rainbow Falls Lodge in the early 1900s. Her brother—forget his name—was a miner, lived there with her. Winter of 1909–1910, it snowed and snowed and snowed. They finally had to use thirty-two lengths of stovepipe to clear the snowpack on the roof. Kind of took the heart out of Lydia's business."

"What happened to her?" Joanne asked.

"Don't know. Must be dead by now."

Danny laughed. "Unless she's 110."

Joanne looked back at the sad little pile of timber, wondering what lost dreams Lydia might have had. "Do they have a cemetery up here?"

"Someplace, but only the old-timers know where it is. People die up here now, they take them out on the boat and bury them in Chelan or Wenatchee." The boy was so young, a college boy from Indiana or Ohio, and she could see cemeteries were of little import to him. He was pointing to trees on the left of the road, hard by the river. "Notice how they're all charred black on the south side? A firestorm blew through the valley in 1889 and took out most of the timber. The ones that survived still have those burn marks on them, but they kept on growing just the same. The Indians say there'll be a forest fire every ninety years. Always has been; always will be. When it comes down the valley, it takes everything in its path."

"Then you're due for one," Danny said. "Is that why they never built up farther into the trees?"

The driver shrugged. "Might be. The only way out would be the lake."

The shuttlebus slowed and stopped, and the driver climbed on top of it and threw their packs down. He gave his instructions to Danny.

"You've got eleven miles up to Rainbow Lake. It's not easy, but it's not too rough either. Watch for the signs and be careful of rattlers and rock slides. If you go on over, it's seventeen miles to Bridge Creek. Be sure you hang your food up when you make camp. You can't just put it up a tree; the bears will shinny up and have it. You have to suspend it ten feet up and five feet between the trees on a rope—that frustrates them."

"*Are* there bears?" Joanne asked.

"They're up there. Black bears mostly. They won't bother you unless you get between a she-bear and a cub; so don't ever do that. There might be a few grizzlies left, but the last verified sighting was in 1965. We haven't seen *any* kind of bear down in the lower valley this summer, so I wouldn't worry about it. Just follow normal precaution."

They started up, with Joanne leading the way. Yesterday's rain might never have fallen; it was dry and rocky underfoot on the steadily upward trail. They passed a reservoir and she worried at leaving it behind, although their canteens were full. She tried to concentrate on the vegetation, all of it proof that living things had defied the fire and the animals and rockslides: ferns, bracken and fiddle-head, elderberry, daisies, butter-and-eggs, mock orange, salmonberry, wild sweetpeas, wild phlox, kinnikinick, and flowering moss. They moved easily as their muscles warmed and their breathing coordinated, although Danny puffed more heavily than she did. She felt happier, and then simply happy.

The trail switched back and the incline's angle was steeper now. They stopped at a knoll and looked down, seeing the tops of evergreens below and the lake, blue as cornflowers between the mountains that held it. He draped an arm lightly over her shoulders.

"You had one hell of a good idea, kid. We're on top of the world."

"Not yet. Look behind us."

He looked over at the trail still ahead and groaned, flopping down on the grass, pulling her with him.

"I'm going to tell you two secrets—if you promise never to tell anyone."

She nodded her head and realized he had never told her even one true secret.

"One. And no 'I told you so's.' I am not in very good shape. My legs hurt. My back hurts. My goddamn *butt* hurts." He held up his hand to silence her. "Two. I am afraid of snakes. I am fucking terrified of snakes. Not just your rattlers that you're exposing me to. Garter snakes. King snakes. Corn snakes. Blue racers. Rubber boas. Anything that slides through the grass or out from under rocks and sneaks up on me. Are you going to laugh?"

"No." She reached for his hand. *"No.* I wouldn't laugh. I'm glad that you felt you could admit it to me. I'm afraid of so many things, and I thought nothing frightened you. I'm glad you're afraid of snakes. Most people are."

"Are you?"

"What?"

"Afraid of snakes?"

She pondered it. "No, I don't think so. I used to have pet garter snakes when I was little; I carried them around in my sweater pockets and fed them chicken livers."

She moved closer to him, reluctant to let the moment go. "Do you want to know what I am afraid of? Really afraid of?"

"Sure. Lay a few of them on me. I earned it."

"O.K. Let me think." She looked away from him, concentrating on the lake far below. "Well, I'm afraid of being dumb—"

"You're not—"

"Let me finish. I didn't interrupt you, and if you stop me, I might lose my nerve. So, by being dumb, I mean that I was never expected to be anything but pretty and nobody has ever shared anything with me that called for a serious opinion. People talk over me and around me. It takes me longer to verbalize what I mean—and then the chance is gone. What I say is of little value."

He started to speak and then said only, "O.K. What else?"

"I'm afraid of being alone. I'm afraid of losing you. And . . . I'm afraid of ghosts."

"Ghosts? Ghosts in white sheets?"

"Are you teasing me now?"

"No."

"Ghosts that watch me. Ghosts that wait for me in old buildings and lonely places as if I owed them something—as if there was something I should have done and now it's too late."

He was quiet for a long time and their breathing was louder than the forest noises. "I felt something when we were on the boat—something like that. I wanted to turn around and go home."

"Why didn't you say something?"

"It was nothing real; it was just a feeling."

"Feelings are real. Do you want to go back now?"

"No." He rubbed her back with the palm of his hand. "It's gone now, whatever it was—probably just felt guilty leaving Sam back there working alone."

"He was the one that talked you into coming away with me, wasn't he? How did he do it?"

He could not tell her the feelings he'd had in his partner's dirty, empty trailer. It would be a betrayal.

"He said I was lucky to have you, and if I didn't watch out you'd be running away with the Fuller Brush man."

She laughed at the old joke. "He's misinformed. It's the milkman I want."

"Well, something along that line. 'You don't realize what you have until it's gone.' Sam's not one of your great philosophers. He just said to get my ass out of there and spend some time with my wife."

"I owe him."

"Yeah."

"But I *love* you," she said quietly. "And I'm greedy for all the time I can get."

He held out a hand and pulled her to her feet, holding her against him. And then they were climbing again, the high noon sun focused on their exposed skin, making them sweat with the heat of it as well as their exertion.

The trails were well marked and they made the two miles to the juncture with the Boulder Creek Trail within the hour. They detoured a half-mile to a point above the falls, hearing the roar of the endless cascade long before they saw the falls themselves tumbling for hundreds of feet down the mountainside in hypnotic continuum. Joanne moved toward the spray of suspended droplets in the air, and Danny held her back.

"No."

"But it feels so cool. I want to take off my clothes and let it touch me."

He held her still. "And I'd like to see that. But the ground could give way and you'd be part of it."

She pulled her eyes away from the plunging water and followed him back to a safer vista. "It's dangerous up here, isn't it? Everything looks so beautiful, but someplace underneath it, you know it could kill you."

He led her back to the hot trail and they hiked steadily without speaking, the big lake diminishing behind them. There were no other hikers; they might well have been the only humans on the mountainside. The trail was capricious, punishing them with a maze of switchbacks that tried the muscles of their aching legs, and then turning suddenly into meadow paths choked with valerian and daisy-mimicing fleabane, Jacob's ladder, everlasting, and creeping phlox, a vista like the fairy gardens in children's story books. They stopped in a meadow and ate the last of the bologna sandwiches, drank warmed water, and kissed like high school lovers.

Duane had traversed it all before on stronger legs, but his first night on the mountain had been miserable. The storm had drenched him in his sleeping bag, and insects rose from Rainbow Lake to sting and bite his exposed face and hands moments after the rain ceased. And in the black black just before dawn he became anxious. What if they had taken another trail? What if the storm had kept them away from the mountain?

He waited until noon, hearing the call of the loons and high wind in the pines. He headed south over his own tracks, searching for them. Up. Then sharply down past the trilling of the small falls to a place where he could see the spread of meadow. He crouched there, watching, for most of the afternoon. The sounds came before sight, laughter bouncing off trees and multiplying its vibrations back to him, before he could make out their images in his binoculars. What if they weren't alone? If a party of four or more crossed the meadows, the challenge for him would be increased ten-fold for each doubling. He held his breath as he saw them emerge from the wall of pines—the woman first, and then the man. Only two. And he knew them even before their features were clearly defined, recognized her movement from all the hours he'd watched her, graceful as only slender, fragile women are. The man moved stolidly and betrayed fatigue.

They did not see him in his watching place, secure in their belief that they were alone, their eyes cast down upon the trail as they walked toward him.

He watched for as long as he dared, reluctant to lose her in his glasses, and then he turned and ran silently back to the green lake and the hidden camp he had chosen for himself a hundred yards beyond the favored campsites. Sunset was still hours beyond. He would watch to see their exact location of encampment, and then sleep easily in his hidden blind and regain the hours he had lost to the night's anxiety, sleep with the sun orange on his shuttered eyelids, while his gear dried out and his body warmed for the things he would demand of it.

They crouched next to the fire Danny had built and battled the onslaught of mosquitos, clouds of stinging gnats. Joanne dotted 6-12 on her face and hands and then anointed her husband with the greasy liquid. The sun was gone, leaving a fluorescent glow in the western sky where the treetops were black tracings, the air as chilled as pebbles in a creek bottom. Their shirts were pulled over their hands and their pants tucked into their socks as much for warmth as to form a barrier against the mosquitos, and she moved closer to Danny to let the heat of their bodies combine, realizing that they were truly in the wilderness. They had come to the place hidden behind the storm clouds she'd watched yesterday; their legs had carried them five thousand feet above the big lake and eleven miles from the shelter of the warm rooms behind them. She was not afraid, but subdued by the way the mountain changed when the sun left it. Even the sounds were different.

On every side of them—rustling, scrabbling, a swishing as if something glided through the grasses, and somewhere, far into the trees, a crashing of brush. The birds no longer sang, but she could hear the beating of wings occasionally above them. She looked at Danny, and he seemed not to hear the hidden life around them; he gazed into the fire and puffed on a cigar, fascinated by the flames.

She was tired, exhausted really, and her legs trembled still from the day's exertion, but she was not ready yet to trust enough to crawl into her sleeping bag and sleep. Something could come for her while she slept, and she would not know her enemy until it was too late. At that moment, a woman's scream sang through the woods, leaving a silence that seemed endless. She threw both her arms around Danny's neck and buried her face into his chest, and then was startled to feel his laughter rumble against her face.

He held her against him and whispered, "Hey, babe—that's nothing that will hurt you. It's a cougar—a *lady* cougar—with the hots. She's not looking for us; she's after a mate. I hope it turns him on, because it's not doing a thing for me."

"Are you sure?"

"I'm sure. If we freak over every sound up here, they'll have to come get us and take us to the Home for the Bewildered. I thought you said you wanted to go out in the wilderness and rough it—so this is it. Too rough for you?"

She drew away and shook her head, "No, but you'll have to admit it's different. I guess we should have camped out in the backyard at home for a while to get used to it, kind of ease into it. I know what— let's sing."

"You're kidding."

"No. That's what we always did at camp around the campfire." Her voice quavered and then grew stronger. "I love to go swimming with bow-legged women and dive between their legs."

"Joanne, you didn't sing that at Girl Scout camp, did you? No wonder you grew up to be such an animal."

"We sang *terrible,* filthy songs every time we had the chance. We put rubbers in the counsellor's make-up kit, and ran Kotex up the flagpole —only nobody ever accused me because I was such a good little girl."

He sang with her while the night settled over them, obliterating first the treetops and then everything except the fire and the moon's silver quarter. "Yellow Submarine," and "Eleanor Rigby," and "Fight On for Natchitat High." He was an awful singer; she understood why he never sang in church. Their voices floated over the dark lake and drowned in it.

She sang alone for him, no longer afraid, in a high sweet soprano. "Our house is a very, very, very fine house with two cats in the yard. Life used to be so hard; now everything is easy 'cause of you—"

He moved so suddenly, his hand into his backpack and emerging with the gun, that she was singing when she heard him say, "Who's th—", with the song still in her throat and spilling out unheard. She turned from him and saw the figure loom behind the fire. The creature-thing was so large and it had crept up on them even as she sang for her husband, its face black as the night around them, the shape of it blurred and part of the night too. When it spoke, she was astounded to discover that it was human.

Danny did not relax, but stood in one fluid movement, the gun in his hand part of him, and a part of him that she had never seen. The man across the fire slowly raised his arms.

"Easy, friend. I'm no Sasquatch. Just a dummy who ran into a bear and hightailed it into the woods. Put your torch on me. I'll keep my hands up."

Danny grunted at her and she felt along the ground for the flashlight she'd used earlier and pushed the switch forward. The cone of light swept over her husband first, and she saw him holding his revolver in both hands, legs wide, his attention entirely on the man before him. She moved her wrist toward the stranger's voice and he appeared, a big man, inches taller than Danny, his eyes glowing red as a fox's in the beam. His hands were open and quite empty. Danny hesitated, and then slid the gun into his belt.

"Sorry," he said. "You startled me. We thought we were alone."

"I thought I was alone," the man answered. "Scared the shit out of me . . ." He glanced at Joanne and said, "Sorry." He lowered his hands deliberately and stood, seemingly embarrassed, waiting for an invitation to come into their space.

"How long have you been up here?" Danny asked, and she could hear his voice was normal now; the impulse to attack washed away from it.

"Hell—sorry—I don't know where I am. I came up on the boat yesterday and lit out for the hills, got caught in the storm last night, and started out for Early Winters this morning. Then I met a she-bear and two cubs on the trail. Spent half today up a tree, and the other half trying to figure out where the hell I was. When I heard singing—a woman singing—I thought I'd either died and gone to heaven or round the bend. Hey, I'm sorry to butt in."

Danny took the flashlight from Joanne and shone it into the man's face, and the last trace of tension left him. "You came up on the boat we were on—right? Saw you up top. Come on in, buddy. Joanne, give the man something to eat."

"No, thanks, ma'am." The stranger said softly. "I ate some dried stuff when I was up the tree, and frankly, I guess I've been too scared to have an appetite."

Danny added logs to the fire and the embers exploded into flames that cast yellow light over them, letting her see the man completely for the first time. He was younger than Danny and taller, a red-looking man. Coppery hair that the firelight turned magenta, red eyes, animal eyes, and the kind of skin with blood vessels close to the surface. He was quite handsome, but she did not like looking at him; his redness made her feel faint.

He held out his hand to Danny; he had barely glanced at her. "David Dwain," he said. "From Portland. How come you're carrying a .38? Most guys come up here with a rifle—if they can sneak a gun in."

"Would a plumber go camping without his plunger?" Danny laughed. "I'm a cop—feel naked without it. Almost took your head off too, creeping out of the woods like that. Name's Lindstrom, Danny— we're from Natchitat, and this is the wife, Joanne."

The stranger looked at her without interest, and slid his bedroll off his back. He grinned at Danny.

"I came up here to get away from it all, but it looks like you can't shake it. I'm a cop too. Multnomah County Sheriff's Office." He turned finally toward Joanne. "So you're pretty well protected, ma'am. You got yourself two lawmen to scare the varmints off."

He lies. The thought bloomed and then disintegrated. Of course he was a cop; he had the look. She had only just gotten Danny back, and already he was slipping into his man-man thing, urging her to wait on the stranger, pulling his pint of whiskey from their supplies. She ladled reconstituted beef stew out of the kettle and saw with some satisfaction that it was lukewarm now as she poured it on a plate for him. He took it from her with an absent nod, his whole attention fastened on his conversation with Danny.

A mosquito stung her cheek and she slapped it away dead, felt the pop of its blood-filled sac on her cheek. She moved closer to Danny, and he put his arm around her, but his mind was on the red man. He was always like this when he met another cop; they had their own language and they were like dogs sniffing each other, checking out mutual acquaintances, and then settling happily into war stories.

She stared sullenly into the flames and heard only bits of their conversation.

"You got a real antique of a jail down there, I hear," Danny was saying.

"Rocky Butte? It's better than it was—since they filled in the moat and closed the dungeon. Our offices are some better too. They moved us out of the courthouse and put us out on Glisan by the airport. Don't have any windows, but they painted it before we moved in."

"You like Checks?"

"Let's say it's a challenge. Some of those paper hangers are smarter than hell. We had one person—and I mean a really, gorgeous person. Bounced them at I. Magnin and Meier and Frank's Designer Shop so fast, she was out of town before they ever hit the bank. I picked her up in San Francisco and she was livid. Outraged dignity until she saw I was really going to put the cuffs on her. Then she flings her arms around me and starts sobbing and offering what you call sexual favors."

"You're shitting me."

"Naw. In other circumstances, I would have gone for it, but. . . . So I pull away and she's still hanging on and shaking—and her wig fell off and I like to shit. She's bald. Only it's better than that. She's not a *she*—she's a he. One of the best-looking broads I've ever seen, and it's not even female. He started to cry and kick and the motel manager says to me, 'You shouldn't be so rough with a woman;' so I grab one tit in each hand and pull and they end up around the paperpusher's hips, and you never saw such a look as that manager's face. Hell, I had to buy the guy straight clothes to bring him back on United. All he had was dresses."

Danny was loving it. Joanne had to urinate; she tried to ignore the pressure in her bladder, but it only got worse. She whispered to Danny, and he turned to her impatiently, "Well *go,* baby. You've got the whole woods out there."

"Danny." She tugged at his sleeve and felt like a child. "I'm not going out there by myself."

"We'll be right here. You don't have to go very far. Take the flashlight."

"Danny," she was embarrassed and she hated the interloper with a passion that startled her, hated Danny too. "Come with me."

"O.K." He turned toward the stranger and laughed. "The wife's got to take a whiz. Scared of the woods. We'll be back."

"Don't go too far in," he warned. "I don't think I've come that far since I ran into the bears; I've got a feeling I've been circling. Holler if you need help."

They moved away from the clearing and Danny pointed the flashlight toward a fallen log. "Go on, babe. Hurry up."

"Well don't shine it *on* me for heavens' sake. He can see me."

"He's not looking. Dammit, Joanne, go ahead and pee; it's freezing out here."

She squatted just beyond the perimeter of the circle of light and struggled to hold her jeans away from the stream of urine, her buttocks vulnerable to the cold air and whatever was beneath her. She heard a splattering sound from Danny's direction. Everything was easier for men; *they* didn't risk getting poison oak all over their private parts— all they had to do was haul it out and go. She pulled up her jeans now and felt the wet spots at the waist already turning cold and clammy. If he wasn't so damned impatient, she wouldn't have missed.

"You done?" He wasn't waiting for her; he'd already turned, ready to go back.

"Danny!" It was a hiss, furious.

"What now?"

"Come here! Stop a minute."

"What?"

"I don't like that man. I don't want to camp with him."

"Joanne. . . ." His voice was heavy with annoyance. "Joanne, we've got no choice. You want me to boot him out and send him down trail when it's pitch dark? If the animals didn't get him, he'd fall off the mountain."

"There's something wrong with him."

"What?"

"I don't know. He just sneaks up on us, and you welcome him like he's an old buddy, but he makes my skin crawl. How do you know who he is, really?"

He sighed. "Joanne, he's O.K. He knows who he's supposed to know, and he talks the language. Besides, I saw his I.D."

"When?"

"When you were cooking. You think if he was some kind of pervert he'd be up here? It's not exactly your prime stalking grounds."

"Maybe it is."

He turned away from her and then said, "I think you're mad because things aren't going just exactly the way you want. You're acting like a spoiled little girl, and you'd better learn that people have to adjust to circumstances. He'll be gone when it's daylight."

"I don't like him."

"Then don't like him. I'm going back. Are you coming with me?"

He walked away, taking the light with him, and she ran to catch up. The stranger was running her supplies and cooking gear along a rope he'd tied between two fir trees. Danny grabbed the end of the rope and held it taut as the big man positioned the canvas sack equidistant between the trunks.

"I know I'm spooky," he grinned at her. "But after today, I think we'd better be extra careful that we don't make ourselves an attractive target. I hope you don't mind?"

She shook her head, wordless, and she would not return his smile.

"This wasn't my first encounter with old Brer Bear. I was in Glacier Park in 1979, when one of the lodge girls was killed." He paused, and his voice was tight when he continued. "I was in the party that found her, and it was . . . an . . . ugly thing. Grizzly took her arm and half her head . . ."

"Hey," Danny said, jerking his head toward Joanne. "Maybe we better talk about that in the daylight."

"Sorry."

She would not let it go. "Why do you hike then, Mr. Dwain? Why don't you stay down in Portland where it's safe?"

She had asked the question, but he looked at Danny when he answered, dismissing her. "I guess I don't like to think any creature can stop me from doing what I like, don't like to be scared off. But it's made me cautious. Anyway, the girl in Glacier had a dog with her and was sleeping in a tent with her supplies. Broke all the rules."

"So she deserved what she got?" Joanne's voice was hard.

"Joanne!"

"Nobody deserved that, ma'am. I'm sorry I made you nervous. I shouldn't have brought it up."

She bent down and grabbed her bedroll, picked at the knot that held it in a tightly-packed sausage. "I'm going to sleep now. It's late." She waited for Danny to say he was coming with her, but he had turned away and was pouring whiskey for the red-headed man.

She lay six feet from them, watching their silhouettes against the fireglow, hearing fragments of conversation about guns and sex and arrests, their voices deep and rumbling and then bursting into laughter that seemed drunken. She watched the moon move across the sky. It was very, very late when Danny turned to her, fumbling at the zipper to her sleeping bag. He was singing in slurred, sibilant phrases.

"Please come down and let me in, please come down and let me in. Please come down and let me in. I'm Barnacle Bill, the Sailor—"

She turned on her side and pretended sleep, but he was persistent, sliding the zipper down slyly, letting icy air creep under her shirt and up her spine like a snake. She pushed his hand away and pulled the zipper back up.

"Baby?"

She stayed silent.

"You mad?"

"I'm asleep. Go to sleep."

"Let me in. It's cold, and I can't get my fucking bedroll untied."

"Cut it. Bite the cord in two. You're a big, strong man."

"You're mad at me. Joanne's mad at me, and it's cold out here. Come on, honey, don't fool around. Let me in."

"Go sleep with Pistol Pete from Portland."

"He smells."

She laughed. "So do you."

Even drunk, he saw that she had weakened and he played on it. "But you're used to the way I smell. Joanne . . . Joanne, remember how I said I was afraid of snakes. Well, for God's sake, let me in. I'm scared to mess around with my bedroll."

He made her remember the good time on the trail, and she let herself think that tomorrow would be better.

"O.K. But no fooling around."

"Absolutely not. It never occurred to me. I'm just so fucking cold I couldn't get it up anyway. I swear."

She let him enter her canvas capsule and felt that he was naked and hard. He was on top of her, pinning her backbone to the pine-needle-carpeted turf beneath her.

"You *lied.*"

"I know," he giggled. "I'm a rotten, filthy, stinking liar."

He pawed at her jeans, managing to slide them off her hips and down somewhere to the bottom of the sleeping bag.

"Danny, we can't. Where is he?"

He kissed her mouth and ears, gluing his face to hers as she tried to turn away from him. "Him? He's to hell and gone over by the lake. He can't see anything. Couldn't see anything anyway. We're all covered up inside here, safe as a bug in a bug, pardon me, a bug in a rug, two bugs in a rug."

"You're sure he can't see us?" She felt herself responding to him. "Be quiet for a minute. Be *still!*" He stopped moving, and they listened, hearing nothing but a few last pops and hisses from the dying fire.

"See," he whispered. "He's way over there, sound asleep, and we're not going to let him spoil our good times, are we? I'm sorry I yelled at you because you had to pee, because all God's little girls have to pee, don't they? Now, just lie there real nice and still, and nobody will know what we're doing."

She let him enter her, feeling his penis strangely cool from it's exposure to the frigid air.

"I thought you couldn't get it up if it was cold?"

"It wasn't easy."

It was quite good for her; she held him long after he had finished with a muffled groan, long after he had slipped out of her, held him like a child against her breast, his head heavy with sleep, loving him fiercely and protectively.

She opened her eyes at last to chart the passage of the moon toward dawn. And saw the big man's face above them, leaning over and staring down at them without expression. She shut her eyes in horror, and instantly opened them again to see nothing but the crescent moon and scudding fingers of cloud. A dream. A half-dream born from her suspicion and the fear of discovery. He could not have been there watching; she would have heard his feet crushing the spongy ground as he fled, and she had heard nothing.

After a long time of listening for something beyond Danny's heavy breathing, she relaxed and curled herself around her sleeping husband and dreamed with him. The she-cougar screamed again, but she didn't hear.

CHAPTER TEN

Joanne woke to sunlight, morning light—not yet full of heat, but pale lemon drifting down through the treetops, speckled with motes. Danny had been with her in the night, but he was gone. She sat up quickly, and zipped herself free of the constricting bedroll.

"Danny!" Her voice, distorted, bounced back at her from the wall of the forest. "Danny! Where are you?"

She heard crashing noises then and footsteps approaching.

"I thought you were going to sleep all day." It was Danny, and he was alone. "Don't move fast; there must have been rocks under all that moss, and it's going to hurt to stretch out."

She jumped up and laughed at him. *"One* of us was in shape, my darling, and *I* feel wonderful."

"Then I must have been on the bottom." His eyes lidded with the memory of their mating. "I didn't start out on the bottom, though."

She remembered then the fleeting glimpse of the stranger standing over them, or when she had seen him there in her mind, and remembered too that they weren't alone. "Where is he?"

"Dave? He's gone downtrail. He said he'd probably take off when it got light. Nobody's over there now, and his gear's all gone. You weren't very nice to him."

"He gave me the creeps but you were nice enough for both of us. Oh, let's forget him; I guess I was pretty bitchy. You hungry?"

"Do bears shit in the woods?"

He'd answered her that way a hundred times, a thousand times, but it jarred now. "Couldn't you have said, 'Do birds fly?' "

"I'm hungry. O.K.? I want eggs and bacon and pancakes and biscuits and gravy."

"Dream on, and shinny that pack down for me and I'll see what your choice is."

He brought water from the lake that seemed safe enough, and she made coffee with it, and mixed it with dried beef stew, fried eggs, and wrapped canned biscuit dough around a stick to bake it. They ate together, silently.

"You want to go over?"

"Over where?"

"Into the Okanogan country. If we do that, we go on up north over

Bowan Mountain, and then it's five and a half hours to the Pacific Crest Trail."

She handed him her plate to finish.

"Do we have to decide now?"

"Nope. That's the beauty of it. We're free, and we don't have to decide anything. That's finally beginning to come through to me."

He looked years younger; the puffiness under his eyes gone away, the tension lines ironed too after two good nights of sleep. She reached out to him and touched his hand. "You know something? And I think it's all right for me to say this now, and I don't know why I know it's all right. I think I might just walk off this mountain with a baby started."

He stared back at her, and seemed to be weighing something unsaid. And then he lifted her hand to his lips and kissed it, and she felt his love unfettered by desire. She leaned against him, trying to make the moment last as long as she could.

The gunshot spat out somewhere along the trail.

Danny still held her fingers to his lips but the gesture was automatic and deadened. There were two more shots. He stood up, sheltering her with his body as he gazed toward something he could not see.

"What is it?"

He answered without looking at her. "I don't know."

"Hunters?"

"No. It's out of season. Target shooting maybe. We're not the only people up here."

"Should we do something?"

When he turned toward her finally, the tension creases were there again in his face, and she saw him reach toward the pack that held his gun; it was an unfinished gesture—his hand stopped before it closed around the checkered grips.

"No. There's nothing to do; it's got nothing to do with us."

But it had.

The red stranger came back; she saw the sun glinting off his hair and turning it into a torch among the leaves as he approached. He was running, easily and fluidly, and she felt not danger *to* him, but danger *from* him. She lifted her hand in warning, but Danny wasn't looking. The big man was so close to her that she could see rivulets of sweat oozing from the auburn hair that curled around his ears, but he was shouting not at her, only to her husband.

"Grizzly! My God, it's a grizzly!"

CHAPTER ELEVEN

She waited. High in the pine tree where the men had boosted her, her arms encircling the thick trunk, slippery fingers laced together. She feared falling; her legs trembled and the limb beneath her feet bent toward the ground. With the slightest movement, it creaked and shed showers of drying pine needles to earth. The gummy sap smeared her face where she pressed against it and she thought of blood. She could not see where the men had gone, and heard only crashing far off in the woods that grew fainter each moment, leaving her as isolated as she had ever been. She had clung to her husband, pleaded with him not to go away with the stranger, but he had shaken her off as if she were only an irritant. Then both of them had lifted her with their huge hands and pushed her into the branches. Danny had said, "Climb! Damn it. Climb!" And she had cried out to him, "Come with me. Come *with* me!" even long after he had disappeared. She knew nothing of guns, but she doubted the power of the blue-black, snub-nosed gun he'd held, or of the weapon in the other man's hand. They were children's toys against the thick pelt and hide of a grizzly. Together, the three of them, they could have waited the animal out in the trees until someone came to help them. She felt frustrated rage at both men for deserting her, for risking everything in her world.

She prayed. She offered up sacrifices to God if only He would allow Danny to come back to her. Her own life. She agreed to die at fifty— then at forty—if she could have him again. She would be a better person, please God, and see that they tithed everything they had. She vacuumed all her sins up from her mind and cast them out. Gossip. Pride. Pettiness. Avarice. Jealousy. She *was* jealous; she would be no longer. *Please God—Please God—Please God—Please God.* She repeated the litany aloud, unaware, until her mouth was dry and her lips started to crack.

She did not know how long they had been gone; her watch was someplace down on the ground with their supplies. She tried to count seconds and chart minutes, but it seemed senseless anyway because she had no idea how far they had had to go or what they meant to do if they ran into . . . *it*. It seemed an hour to her since she'd settled into her perch, and there were nerve buzzes along her arms from lack of circulation. She tried to change position, but her foothold dropped farther toward the ground, and she could picture herself sliding down the limb helplessly, her hands clasping air and dry needles.

Nothing had really changed. That was the important thing to remember. Danny had gone off with his gun to do something. Danny went off with his gun every working day, and the only real difference was that now she knew the moment of his approach to danger. Their gear on the ground below her was somehow comforting, familiar possessions, the coffee pot still breathing a small geyser of steam. The tube of Danny's sleeping bag resting next to hers. The frying pan, its dregs turning hard and crusted with the last coals of their campfire. She would have to soak that or scrub it with sand to get it clean. Tonight, she could fry fish in it—if Danny caught any.

If he comes back. Don't think that! Thoughts could become real if she let them. Prayers skittered and fell away before she could hold onto them, but the fear stayed.

There was a soft rustle in the weeds below her and she looked down and saw a tiny mottled brown and white bird rise, its tail feathers clean as new snow, a ptarmigan. The birds were all around her, taking flight from their hiding places and winging to the branches high above her. But one bird flew straight to her as if she had called it aloud and settled on a branch a few feet away.

She took it for a sign of hope.

There were two men out there. Big men—with guns and branch-clubs, competent to scare off the bear; wild creatures ran from humans if they had an escape route and there was all the mountain for it to flee. The beast was probably already gone, and Danny and the stranger were waiting only to be sure it was well gone before they came back for her. She tried to picture them beyond the pale of trees that cut her off from them, resting now, lighting cigarettes or cigars, laughing at their victory.

But she did not believe it. The hopeless dread that consumed her was familiar. When Doss died and his flesh mingled with the burning barn timbers, she had watched from the gravel road. She did not know at that moment which of the canvas-jacketed men was trapped inside when the roofline sagged as if melting and then imploded on itself, could not have known that the anguished, too-late shouts of warning were for Doss. But she had felt it in her stomach and in her heart's thudding.

*Our Father who art in Heaven—Yea, though I walk through the valley of the shadow of death—*And when she could not call forth any other prayers from her numbed mind, *Bless this food, oh Lord we pray* and *Now I lay me down to sleep.*

The little birds came closer to her, almost a dozen of them waiting. If she dared unclasp her hands, she could reach out and touch the soft breasts. But with the first booming shot they lifted off their perches and left her alone. With the second shot, its blast treading on the echo of the first, she felt warm urine sluice down her legs and heard it patter on the needle carpet beneath the tree. Her hands slipped from the branch and she fought to hold on against a dark tide of dizziness.

They were not as far away from her as she had thought; the shots seemed to come from just beyond the first bend in the trail.

There was a time that was quiet again, stiller than before, or maybe it only seemed so because the shots were so loud. She held her breath and listened to nothing. And then there was a kind of thrashing sound but she was not sure if it came from where the shots had, and that was followed by something screaming that seemed neither animal nor human. A yelp that grew and grew until it split the air, and finally diminished to a choked whimper. She thought that it could not be a man's sound; a man's voice could not reach that pitch. It did not come again.

She had to go to them. She could not be safe when something awful was happening to Danny. Maybe to Danny. She prayed that the red man had screamed and not Danny. But she could not move. Her hands would not let go now; the flesh between her fingers had grown together, hand-to-hand like a vise. Vomit crept up her throat and pushed over her tongue, filling her mouth until she leaned almost lazily away from the trunk and spat it out. If she leaned just a few inches further, she would fall. She wondered if she could hope to die if she fell, or if she would need to climb higher so that she could be certain of it. And yet she could not seem to move at all.

There were no more sounds. The birds came back and the sun rose higher in the sky as if the world were still alive. Everything was the same as before Danny had walked away from her.

Any minute now, he would come back. She watched for him so steadily that she forgot to blink, and her eyes burned.

Someone was coming back to her. The faintest break of snapping twigs first, and then steady footfalls on the trail bed and crackles of underbrush. She kept her eyes on the trail and concentrated on her husband's face so that she would know him when he appeared. She thought first that she did indeed see him, and then the sun touched the red man's auburn hair, and she saw that it was not Danny at all.

He walked easily, neither hurrying toward her or away from something dangerous behind him. She would not look at him, but kept her eyes just over his left shoulder so that she could see her husband when he too rounded the trail, but he seemed to be a long way behind. The big man searched the trees quickly until he spotted her and he ran toward her in loping strides and climbed next to her, standing on the same branch and enveloping her body in his. His chest was damp against her bare back, and she remembered the red-red-red on his T-shirt that she had meant not to see while she was watching for Danny.

His mouth bent down and whispered against her hair.

"Mrs. Lind . . . Joanne . . ."

She tried to move away. "No. I don't want to talk now. I don't want to listen to you."

"It was bad, Joanne."

"No."

"I got back to you as soon as I could."

"No. I don't want you here. I want you to go back and get my husband."

He waited a long time before he spoke. "I can't do that."

"Then I'll go. Let me down. Don't hold me. Don't touch me. I'm going to get him." A voice was screaming, and she did not recognize it was her own.

She tried to slide free of him, and he held her faster, pinning her against the tree's trunk.

"You smell," she said. "And I don't want to be here."

"I'm sorry. I can't let you down because it's very dangerous and I have to keep you safe."

He was suffocating her. She pushed back hard against him with her buttocks and heard him grunt, but he still pinioned her fast.

"Let me go. Let me go, you fucking bastard!" *She never said that.* "You filthy, lousy, stinking fucking bastard. I'll kill you if you don't let me go, and I don't want to listen to you or see you or ever see you again."

She saw his hand splayed out next to her face, thick brown fingers with tiny red hairs on them, and something else that seemed bad to her —dried brown segmented streaks like broken worms that flaked away when his fingers moved. She could not remember the word for it. She turned her head and sank her teeth into the heel of his hand and he shouted and slammed her forehead into the tree, and she remembered the word was *blood.*

She bit him again and again and each time he knocked her head forward until she was exhausted and bright red blood streamed down his wrist. She leaned her cheek against the bark and closed her eyes. His voice was a buzz, full of metallic sounds that were not words.

When she finally understood him she wished she had not.

"He's gone."

"Where did he go? Where? He should have come back for me."

"No. I mean he's gone. He's dead."

"No."

"I shot the bear, but I don't think I killed her."

She was silent.

"Did you hear me? Did you understand?"

"He needs me." Her words were very careful now because if she could speak clearly, he would let her go to find Danny. But he was insane and had to be dealt with cautiously. "You see, he belongs to me and I have a right to go and help him. And then we'll let him rest and we'll all go down the mountain together and it will be all right. But you have to let me go because you're too strong for me to fight."

"He's dead, Joanne. Believe me, I checked him very carefully before I came back here. It was very quick and he doesn't feel any pain now."

"You don't understand," she tried to be patient as she would with a child or a retarded person. "We came on a vacation together and we were having a really good time until you came. I don't mean to be rude to you, but you don't belong with us. I forgive you for banging my head, but you have to let me down now."

"He's dead, and you can't go down there until I'm sure it's safe."

"No."

"He's dead."

"No."

"Dead."

"Please don't talk to me anymore." Her voice was so weak that most of it was lost in the wind that stirred the limbs around them, and then she was silent.

He waited for her to move or to say something more, but she was frozen, immobile as the tree itself. It was an hour before she began to weep, softly at first and then with ugly retching sobs that were more animal than human. He held her tenderly high up in their green-blue thicket of pine needles; she seemed unaware of his erection, his groin pressing against her buttocks. When she had cried her throat raw, he told her that it was finally safe for them to climb down to earth. He steadied her and helped her place her nerveless feet and hands and then lowered her to the ground as gently as a leaf's dropping, dangling her with one hand. She seemed weightless. She sagged and rocked quietly while he gathered up their gear.

She knew, finally, that there was no place she could go where she might find Danny, and there was no use to fight the big man, and no use not to. There was simply no use for anything. She was tired, more tired than she knew a human could be, and she was amazed that she could stand and move when he signaled to her that it was time for them to go. Her legs had no strength but they obeyed her brain's command to move forward.

She had forgotten his name. There was something. What was it? Something she had to ask him. "Stop," she called. "Stop, please."

He turned his large head to her, waiting, "What?"

"Do you know me?"

He seemed not truly surprised, but a bit off balance. "What do you mean?"

"Do you know me?"

"I met you last night, remember?"

"Oh—yes. Last night, we . . ."

"Is that what you meant?"

The tree-green kept coming at her in waves, and then pulling back and it was hard to focus on anything and keep it bracketed in her vision. She was confused. She looked down at her own body and was surprised to see that she was a woman and not a child.

"I don't know why—" She stopped and tried to find words that fit together correctly. "When I was little . . . you know, when I was a little girl, I always needed to know that. There were so many tall people, but that's only because I was so small, and they talked to me as if they knew who I was—probably because of Doss. But you don't know Doss, do you? Never mind about that. The thing is I had to know if they knew who I was because I was frightened. I'm very frightened now, you know, and you're very large and you don't know me and I'm afraid you are going to hurt me."

"No." He was talking to the child, very softly. "No, I wouldn't do that."

"Is Danny really—oh, I don't want to say it. Is he really?"

"I'm sorry."

But he wasn't sorry; the edges in his voice told her that. He was glad.

"You killed him, didn't you?"

He walked back to her and knelt on the ground in front of her, taking her chin in one hand. "Of course not. But you can't understand now. You mustn't think about it. You're very tired now, and you're in shock and I need to take care of you."

The tree-green and the color of his eyes blended together and spun around like a kaleidoscope picking up black particles until there was only black on black on black. An instant before she fainted, a little door in her mind shut tight and locked the horror behind it because it could not be dealt with. She did not feel him as he picked her up in his arms and carried her farther into the woods. She breathed and her heart beat on, but her mind was hiding somewhere back in the black.

He looked down at the white face bouncing against his chest, at the delicate, veined eyelids, and the mouth with the vestige of vomit dried in the corners. He smiled tenderly. He had told her all that she would have to know.

Her husband was garbage now, and she belonged to him, and they were all alone in the woods. He couldn't have planned it better if he had set out to have it this way. He'd had to tie up some of the others and gag them and rough them up, and even when their bonds were loosened, they'd cried and fought him.

She wasn't fighting him now. Maybe she already knew who he was. Maybe she only realized that she had no way out without him. It didn't really matter because he would have her with him when it was dark, and she would do anything he wanted. This time, she wasn't going to go away and leave him.

He smiled down at her. This part, the first part, was almost his favorite part of the game.

CHAPTER TWELVE

Joanne had lost all measure of time and place; she was only vaguely aware of being carried. She could feel her arms around a strong neck, and feel the slight shock as step, step, step hit the earth. For the briefest moment she thought she *was* a little girl again, back in Doss's arms being carried from the old '47 Studebaker to her warm little bed. Then the picture disappeared. That was wrong. She was someplace else, moving through the fading light of another day. Was it still Sunday, still the endless day she clung to the tree? Or was it a long time after? She seemed to remember following the big man through the forest for a long time, and then waking from a drowsy shock-sleep from time to time after that to find that he was carrying her, not through the trees but along a lake shore edged with thin ice. It was dusk now, but which dusk? And which meadow was this?

She caught a whiff of a metallic smell, and saw his shirt against her cheek, its hardened, crackling surface stiffened by something dark red. She moved in his arms and looked up into his shadowed face. She closed her eyes and opened them quickly so she could see clearly. He looked exhausted. She thought it was good of him to carry her because she must have been injured by something she couldn't recall. Danny should carry her for awhile and let the other policeman rest. She remembered that Danny couldn't do that but the fuzziness in her head prevented her from understanding why. It was peculiar, this blankness where she lost whole segments of recent memory and yet still sensed something just beyond her thoughts, something better not pursued. She would think of it later.

"You can set me down. I can stand."

He lowered her carefully to her feet, but she couldn't stand; her knees buckled and she knelt in the long grass and alpine asters, surprised to find the ground still warm below the chilled air. He shrugged off the backpack he had carried for all her lost time. He kneaded his cramped shoulders and swung them in arcs to bring back circulation, grunting.

"Do your arms hurt?" she asked finally. "Did you carry me a long way?"

"Not that far. You're not that heavy anyway."

"Are we going back to the lodge?"

He shook his head.

"We must be. I think I remember this meadow. I think this is where we sat yesterday."

He stared over her head, sweeping the forest beyond them with his eyes. "We can't go back to Stehekin. I couldn't risk it."

"No, you see . . ." It was so difficult to talk to him. She was so tired. "No, it wasn't that steep; the trail was safe."

"I didn't mean the trail."

"Then, why?"

"She might still be waiting—the grizzly. Some of those animals are cunning. They set their own traps."

Her mind focused on the terrible knowledge. She moaned.

"Where's Danny?"

"You remember. We had to leave him."

"But I didn't want to."

"But we had to. You musn't cry again. You cried for a long time this morning, and it made you sick."

"Did I talk to you after? I remember the tree and then the woods."

"We're safe here for awhile. Tomorrow, we'll go up over Bowan Mountain and then down toward the Pacific Trail."

"Danny said that was what we were going to do; so that's good, isn't it? That's what he'd want me to do. He always knows what to do."

Her constant harping on the other man irritated him, and he had to remind himself that it had only been eight hours, that she would forget soon enough. He turned away from her to unroll the sleeping bags.

"What's your name?"

"Have you forgotten again? It's Duane. Duane Demich."

"Why did I think it was David?"

"Beats me. They both start with D."

"So does—did—Danny. Which is it?"

"That *was* his name."

She hadn't moved from her kneeling position, and she swayed as if she had lost her center of balance.

"Why couldn't you have saved him? Did you really try to save him?"

He moved to her and let her rest her head again on his shoulder, feeling her whole body vibrate with fatigue and shock. Then he held his right arm up for her to see the long deep scratches that ran from his wrist to his arm pit.

"I almost had him free of her. She like to took my arm off and I had to back off. Somebody had to come back for you. You would have been all alone up here and you couldn't have survived. I had to make the choice between letting her kill both of us and your survival. He would have wanted me to take care of you."

She nodded against him.

"Can you eat?"

She gagged and turned away from him at the thought, and then slowly stood up. Her bladder was bursting, and she wondered how bodily functions could go on when nothing mattered any longer. What was she going to do? She was terrified of going into the dark trees alone, but she couldn't urinate with the stranger nearby.

"I have to go to the bathroom," she said softly.

"Do you want me to go with you?"

"Oh no!"

"Then go on over there behind those larch trees. You'll have your privacy and you won't have to go far in."

She walked carefully away from him, aware that his eyes followed her, and she went deeper into the blind of trees than she wanted to to get away from his watching. It was so dark now, and she could make out only pillars of black as if the sun had never penetrated the spaces between them at all. She wondered how far he had carried her away from Danny. Maybe only a little way. There was still a chance she could get back to him, find him waiting for her to come and help him because it was not possible for him to be truly dead. Danny was too strong to die in a few minutes.

But there were no trails; if she tried to find the way back, she would be lost forever on the mountain and ferns would grow through her skull when spring came. She crouched and emptied herself. Something nearby scuttled through the dry leaves, but she couldn't tell if it was coming toward her or going away from her. She held her breath and listened for its breathing. The creature too had suspended breathing, waiting as she was.

She had hated the big man before—yesterday? Today? And she wished herself away from him forever. She wasn't strong enough. There was fear here and fear ahead of her and fear back with him, all around her, waiting for her in the darkness. He seemed the least of it.

He held the sleeping bag for her to crawl into it, and she was so cold, deep into the insides of her bones, dead cold where sleep might promise no awakening. She did sleep, almost immediately, tumbling into a pit of nothingness where even dreams had no substance and spun themselves out before she could catch them.

When she woke, her eyes snapped open and she felt her heart beating too fast. She had forgotten again where she was, but the image of death consumed her and she reached above her head to touch the cover of her casket to see if she had been buried alive. Her hands rose high, touching air, and she could see stars and an opaque slice of moon behind clouds. She heard a man breathing next to her. Thankful that the nightmare was over, she reached out to touch Danny.

Then her hand froze in mid-air as she remembered.

My husband is dead.

She accepted it with complete lucidity, with such a pang of hopeless loss that she felt her heart break.

The man—the stranger—David?—no, Duane—caught her hand and held it fast. She thought he had done it in his sleep, and she tried to pull free, but he would not let her go.

"What is it?"

He didn't answer.

"Please let go."

She could not tell if he was awake or asleep still, but his breathing was different, faster. She tugged at her trapped hand, and his whole body rose up and he rolled on top of her. She tried to squirm out from under him, and he drove the lower half of himself against her and pinned her to the ground.

His eyes were wide open, light and luminous as a fox's. Crazy eyes.

"What" She whispered. "What's wrong?"

But she knew.

"No!"

"You're belong to me now."

"Please—"

It was no good talking to him. She began to cry because she couldn't help it.

"Don't do that. You're going to enjoy this. You're going to like being fucked. Say it."

"What?"

"Say 'I want you to fuck me.' "

"No."

"I want you to say it."

"No—"

He hit her in the face so swiftly that her head twisted and smashed into the ground. She tasted blood in her mouth.

"Say it."

She spat at him and he smiled while her spittle ran down his cheek.

Then he slapped her again, holding her chin with one hand so that she couldn't roll away from the force of the blow.

"Say it."

"I . . . want . . ."

"That's good. I knew you wanted it. Say it real nice for me."

"I want you . . . to . . . fuck . . . me."

"That's better. Now, I'm going to touch you all over, and I want you to keep telling me how much you like it. See, like this—"

He rolled off her, lay beside her, and unzipped her sleeping bag. Freed to run, she scrambled away from him, but he caught her with one leg and held her in a scissors hold.

"Don't try to fight me. It only makes me angry. I don't want you to make me angry. If you do, we'll have to start all over again or something bad might happen to you. Can't you understand that?"

"I'm so cold. My teeth are chattering."

"I'll make you warm. See? Doesn't that feel good?"

His hand moved over her skull first, and she thought he could crush it if he chose to. Massaging fingers poked into her ears and around the edges, and then over her eyes, her nose, and into her mouth. He did not kiss her; his fingers touching her teeth, her tongue, were worse than his mouth somehow.

She stiffened as he trailed over her throat with his huge hand, encircling it and squeezing, testing to see how much pressure it took to make her cough.

"Your air even belongs to me. Say that. You can't breathe unless I say so."

"My air belongs to you."

"Let me see your breasts. I want you to show me."

"Oh . . . Please—"

He pressed her throat and took away her air. "Show them to me."

She could not feel her own fingers, but somehow she managed to unbutton her shirt, her eyes closed so she could not see his own glitter above her.

The hand on her throat moved down and yanked at her brassiere. She felt it rip and fall away, and then the hand circling and massaging her nipples, kneading, flattening, playing with her. He buried his face between her breasts and wallowed there, licking her with his tongue so that the air chilled his saliva. She shivered.

"You like that, don't you?"

She shook her head, but he wasn't paying attention; his control was sliding away, and he nibbled at her in a frenzy, hands and mouth moving over her breasts and down her belly. He crooned and growled and sighed. He was going to devour her.

"Do you feel me, Joanne?"

". . . yes."

"See how hard you make me? See what I've been saving for you? You must be so happy. Touch me." He released her to expose himself.

She lay still, her hands across her breasts.

"Touch me."

She couldn't do that. She could not touch him.

"I said touch me. See how big I am. Put your hands on my dick."

She rolled and managed to get on her hands and knees and crawl before he snaked out a hand and grabbed her ankle. He flipped her like a wrestler would and nailed her hands to the ground, his weight on her wrists so that she could no longer move at all. She thought he would kill her now, but he only smiled at her as if she had somehow pleased him.

He seemed to enjoy playing with her, letting her crawl just far enough away so that she thought she might be able to run into the trees, and then drawing her back to him and laughing. There was no way to escape him.

She could not fight him. She could not run. She felt bruised in all the places where he'd caught onto her to drag her back. He was going to do it anyway. She watched him, panting, submissive and only wanting it over with.

"That's better. Now say it again. 'I want you to fuck me.'"

"Iwantyoutofuckme."

"That's not good enough. You have to sound like you really mean it. You sound like you're doing me a favor, and I don't like that. You're not ready yet, are you?"

He stood above her and shucked his jeans, preening for her. The first fingers of dawn light had crept from behind the trees, and she could see his pale solid flesh and the terrible jutting penis. He was immense. Monstrous. He would split her cleanly in two with it and leave her bleeding in the meadow to rot in the sunlight, just as Danny lay rotting somewhere behind them in the shadows. Danny had died with more dignity. She was a thing now, something for the red man to play with.

She shut her eyes tightly and waited for him to do it to her. She felt him turning her body as if she were a doll. He was taking too long, folding her clothing carefully and laying her things in the weeds. She felt him looking at her.

He was touching her again with his thick fingers.

"You're sweating. You're getting hot."

A finger moved beneath her breasts, sliding across the cold perspiration and then down, circling her navel and poking into it. Over the flare of her hipbones. She felt him turning her over and panicked.

"No . . . please—"

His hands cupped the cheeks of her buttocks, and then the awful tracing started again. There was no part of her that would belong to her when he was finished. Nothing. The finger moved deeply along the crease and prodded, trying to enter there. She held her breath, too terrified even to pray.

Finally, the hands turned her onto her back again, and she thought that now—

"You're not wet enough. You're holding back from me."

" . . . no."

"Don't lie!"

He was between her legs, his hands almost lazy. Touching, rubbing. He stopped for a moment and she opened her eyes and saw that he was staring down at her crotch, his mouth open and slack. He caught her looking at him and smiled.

"You like this. You love it, don't you?"

She shut her eyes.

"I'll bet you taste sweet."

"No . . . "

"Oh yes, you do." She felt his lips and tongue violate what had been her private center. Danny had never done this to her. The red man made some noise, some humming growl against her most vulnerable flesh. He seemed about to bite into her and leave her bleeding. "You do taste sweet. Taste."

He plunged one finger deep into her and withdrew it, bringing it up to her lips. She clenched her teeth.

"I said *taste it!*"

His finger forced its way in, past her lips, cutting her teeth, and she tasted blood and a muskiness that must have come from herself.

"See?"

"Yes. Just do it if you're going to. Please."

"Beg me."

"Please . . . "

"Say, 'I'm begging you to fuck me.' "

"I'm begging you . . . "

"To fuck me."

" . . . to fuck me."

"On your knees."

"I can't move."

He yanked her by the hair and her body rose up to its knees. She repeated whatever he wanted to hear.

"Where do you want it?"

"What?"

"Where? In the mouth. In the ass? In the pussy?"

" . . . in the . . . pussy."

He hurt her more than she had ever been hurt, at first a tearing pain in her pelvis, and then something shattered inside, and she could no longer tell where the damage was centered. She heard him gasping out words against her ear, but could not grasp their meaning and did not want to know. It went on for a very long time, until she was sure that he was killing her; all she knew for certain was the pain.

He drove himself into her rhythymically and then faster and faster, his face a set mask—so red from the sun that shone directly into her own eyes—and there was finally no sound except for the slap, slap, slap of his thighs against hers and the screaming in her head. Suddenly, he whimpered and gasped, and stopped, rolling off her in flopping motion.

She did not turn her head. She could see the sky and a hawk sliding on the wind above her, could feel some insect creeping in the sweaty furrows of her neck. The red man gulped for air and sighed to himself.

She knew that she would kill him. She would find some way to smash him and smash him until he was no longer recognizable. And then she would go to Danny and lie down beside him and wait for death to cleanse her.

He leaned over her and she flinched, but he only kissed her cheek and patted her shoulder. Did all men do that, even rapists? She felt hysterical laughter bubble up, but it emerged a sob. He let her crawl away now without protesting or grabbing for her and she searched through the grass until she found her clothes. She dressed with her back to him, but he said nothing.

She saw that he was asleep, his face soft and open. He was not afraid of her, and he didn't move at all when she walked away. If he woke, she would tell him she had to go into the woods to pee, and he would believe that. She had to find a weapon. His guns were somewhere in the pack underneath his head, and even if she could get to them without waking him, she didn't know how guns worked. Danny had tried to show her so many times. Why hadn't she paid attention? She could not kill him with her bare hands. It had to be with something that would stun him as he slept. If he was conscious, he would kill her. He was going to kill her anyway when he was done with her.

She couldn't find a club. The fallen boughs were either too big for her to carry, or so rotten that they crumbled in her hands as she lifted them.

The rocks were too round, with no true cutting edges, and they were covered with moss. After a half hour she found one rock, heavy—but liftable—and chipped cleanly on one side, sharp enough perhaps to sever an artery. She cradled it against her breasts and carried it back toward the treacherous meadow. Killing him might possibly wash him out of her body and her mind. She could still smell him; his semen drained out of her and she shuddered. She would not be clean if she bathed for days.

The rock was warm and solid and the feel of it calmed her and her rage calmed her, but her legs trembled.

He was still asleep, on his back now, one arm flung across the place where she had lain. He did not hear her approach, or perhaps he only seemed not to hear her and was listening. Animals did that and he was only an animal. He was ugly.

She looked down at him and wondered which part of the head must be smashed. She assumed the forehead, but if she missed, the thudding stone would alert him. Her preference was the face itself. She wanted to see his eyes and mouth lost in bone chips and blood. But she knew he would still be able to rise and strangle her, even with his ruined face and blinded eyes.

She would have to chance the forehead, crack the skullplate hard enough so that the brain beneath would bruise and bleed. Danny had told her people died like that, quite easily. The brain bounced around inside the skull like a balloon as it crushed itself on every unyielding plane of bone it hit. And brains controlled life—not hearts or lungs. She should have paid more attention to Danny's stories of murder. She had never killed even a spider or a mouse; she had avoided hearing about the killing of humans.

He stirred in his sleep, and she raised the rock higher, casting its shadow over his face. She could not do it, hesitating not from mercy but because she was afraid. Life was no longer important to her, so she should not fear dying. But she feared more pain. She dreaded the violence that would fall upon her if she could not render him helpless with her first blow. And she was ashamed. If she could be assured that she too would die in an instant, she would not be afraid, but she could not endure another long time of hurting.

Her arms ached from supporting the rock over his face, but her hands could not let it go, any more than she could put it down. If she let him live, he would rape her again—and probably worse. That was one choice. If she succeeded in destroying him, she would die, but at a leisurely pace in the wilderness. She did not know which way they had come and therefore knew no route out. Either way, she was dependent on him. Living or dead, he controlled her existence.

There was God to consider. If she killed the red man first, would God forgive her—or was murder murder, no matter?

Her hands shook and bits of dirt broke free from the rock and bounced off his sleeping face. She willed herself to let go of the weapon, but she could not. Then she saw his eyes flutter and open. He watched her for a moment. She had expected fear in him, but there was only a flicker of surprise. She raised her arms higher and he moved like a mongoose, the side of his hand catching her behind the knees so that she fell heavily across him. She still clutched the rock and it crushed her fingers against the ground. There was an instant of numbness, and then her hands flamed with pain.

He was on his feet, and all her tenuous advantage was lost. She waited for him to hit her. Instead he crouched beside her and took her hands in his, turning them to see where she was cut.

"What were you doing?" He seemed genuinely puzzled.

"I was going to kill you."

"Why?"

She pulled her hands away from him and sidled back into a sitting position against a stump. "Because you raped me. You had no right to touch me. You told me you were going to help me."

"I am going to help you."

"You hurt me."

"I didn't hurt you. You fought me. You may have hurt yourself."

"You raped me. You destroyed something that was very precious to me."

"I don't understand you. You need me."

"I didn't need rape. I didn't need . . . what you did to me."

"You were slipping away. I had to warm you. I had to make you part of me so that I could give you some of my life."

"You're a pervert—"

His hand covered her mouth. "You don't understand, but you will. You'll remember why I'm here and you'll be sorry you talked like this. You have to live. You will have to eat and sleep and walk when I tell you to because I'm the only one who can save you."

He took her cut hand in his and watched her blood seep into the marks her teeth had left in his palm. They were part of each other now.

"Will you promise not to—not to touch me that way again?"

"I don't have to promise anything. You don't know what sex is. You don't understand at all. I will show you that sex is a way to keep from dying. I gave you life when you were trying to throw it away. You were allowing yourself to die. You didn't want me, but you will."

"Never. I will never want you, not like that. Not in any way, and I will kill you the first chance I get."

He stood up and gathered their gear, ignoring her. When he had shouldered it, he turned back to her. "It's daylight, and the days are growing very short up here. We have to get over the mountain summit while we have the sun. You can come with me or not. If you stay here, you're going to die and there won't be anyone to help you. If you think that she-bear has given up, you're mistaken. She's out there right now tracking us. She can smell exactly where we've been when the ground fog lifts. I had to kill her cub, and she won't forgive me for that. She's big. Bigger than you can imagine; she could take your whole head in her mouth and crush it until nobody would ever recognize you. Is that what you want? To be nothing but pieces of bloody meat?"

She covered her head with her arms to shut him out.

"I'm going now. Are you coming with me?"

"Go away."

He sighed, and she heard him throw one of the backpacks down, and then the sounds of his feet moving away from her through the meadow. When she looked up finally, she could see only the back of his head and his shoulders disappearing fifty yards beyond where she sat, heading down into the apricot haze of larch, and then she couldn't see him at all, only the meadow itself and the walls of trees on every side. She could hear far-off noises behind her, something moving through the way that they had taken, and she knew she wasn't brave enough to die alone.

He turned and looked back toward the meadow. He could see her weaving through the weeds, looking for his trail. He could shout to her and tell her the way, but he stayed silent and let her fumble her way along. She had been ungrateful and hostile to him. She needed humbling.

He leaned against a boulder, shutting himself off from her sight, and lit a cigarette.

She would come.

CHAPTER THIRTEEN

It was almost noon when he stopped in the shade of a rock cliff, and handed her two protein bars. "Eat them," he said. He had not acknowledged her at all when she'd caught up with him, had pretended she wasn't walking behind him.

She forced them down, chewing with jaws clenched unconsciously for too long. She felt leached of any kind of feeling at all, save a stubborn resolve. He would pay, and she would be free of him.

He reached to take her pack, and she shook her head; she wanted nothing from him except escape and the satisfaction of seeing him arrested. And she asked nothing of herself beyond the physical stamina to maintain his pace along the trails. She thought she could do that. All the hours of running had prepared her to climb and hike and cling to the narrow trail with an efficiency of effort that few women—few men—could match. She could not think of Danny or ponder why he was dead and the red man lived.

There was an awful thought that she'd tried to block before it bloomed fully. Was it possible that Danny was dead because of her, because this crazy stranger had wanted her and knew that the only way to have her was to kill her husband? If that was true, and if she had only suspected that, she would have lain down for him. Anything to keep Danny safe.

She hadn't flirted with the stranger; she hadn't even liked the stranger. She'd been bundled up in layers of shirts and jeans, without make-up and with greasy, tangled hair. She could not be the cause of it. She had to push that explanation away each time it crept toward her, or it would mean that she had killed Danny. No, he had raped her as an afterthought, because she was female and helpless and *there*.

They were climbing toward a summit, and she tried to gauge their direction from the sun. It seemed that they were heading north, but she wasn't sure of it and she would not ask him. His self-control seemed erratic, as if his surface calm might splinter at any moment and catch them both in the madness beneath. As long as they kept moving, she felt safer. For the moment, she was more afraid of the mountain, revealing itself now as bare rock, deeper and deeper hues of stone where nothing could survive beyond the clinging lichen, a few tenacious bellflowers, and the thickening larch trees, evergreens that were not evergreens but stunted, burning bushes caught in a last fiery display before winter left them naked. Another time, she would have been awed by their splendor, but now they looked like the flames of hell.

She thought they had been moving steadily upward for almost a mile, and that his leg muscles must be screaming in pain as hers did.

It was a clean pain and she almost welcomed it. He betrayed not the slightest slackening of effort. She followed him six paces behind, her boots slipping on the rocky scrabble that scaled off the boulders. His sweat soaked his armpits and formed a wet V on his shirt from his shoulders to the lower point of his spine. It was a different shirt; she wondered what he had done with the bloodied green shirt.

It was odd how her mind jumped as if it had to skitter away from dark places where it would be trapped. She tried to dull its sharp edges with safe thoughts, the way she did at home when she couldn't sleep, when she built a little house in her mind, with her own safe room where rain danced on the roof and she lay swaddled in soft blankets. She could create the exterior of that cottage now, but she could not find the safe room. The stairs leading to it became the mountain trail with nothing certain at its end.

Just as she knew she could climb no farther, they reached the top of the pass. He stopped and waited for her.

"There. Look."

She gazed where he pointed and felt sharp disappointment; there was only more wilderness below them, nothing that promised freedom. The trail down was so steep that she gasped aloud. Dropping, dropping, and snaking around a sheer rock face. One misstep and death waited just out of sight, over the edge.

"Rest here," he panted. "Then down through that forest, into the meadows, and out to the trail. Five hours. Six maybe."

She didn't speak, but accepted the canteen he passed to her and drank until he took it from her.

He gazed down into the meadow. From this angle he looked boylike and, when he closed his eyes and leaned back against the rockface, almost angelic. Lucifer. Fallen angel.

Sometimes all men looked like boys—in sleep, or in grief, or in moments of exuberance when they dropped their armor. He sensed her watching him, even with his eyes closed, and he turned to her and smiled, the first open smile she had seen on his face. It transformed him, making it almost impossible for her to believe that he had raped her. She felt suddenly dizzy.

He stood up and stripped off his soaked shirt, his back to her, and she saw the scar that flashed brilliant on his shoulders. At sometime he had been terribly burned. She spoke without intending to. "How did you get that?"

"What?"

"That burn scar on your back."

"That? I was just a little kid, and I pulled a coffee pot down on me. I was screaming, I guess, and the old lady in the next trailer put lard on it and wrapped it in a sheet—wasn't supposed to do that. Some nurse had to peel it off and my skin came with it."

"Where was your mother?"

"Working. My father took a hike before I was born."

"Does it hurt?"

"Nothing hurts anymore. You ready?"

He didn't wait for her answer, and she had to scramble to catch him. They worked their way down trail now, the brunt of the pull on different muscles, making her ankles ache and strain against the laces of her hiking boots. The larch trees were close, but not close enough to stop her if she began to slip. Then the forest pulled back and there was only the rock shoulder of the mountain. She slid often and felt a thrill of fear erupt from her stomach and tingle in her arms and legs. He held out his hand and she took it instinctively, letting his power steady her.

We're dropping a thousand feet in a mile," he said. "Put your feet sideways if you start to slide. Don't panic. I can stop you."

Halfway down the slope he paused, so suddenly that she could not keep from bumping into him. He put one hand back and propped her against him. She followed his eyes and saw the avalanche meadow far below them. She could see the short grass and forest edging it. Some of the great trees had been wrenched from their hold on the earth by avalanche, their roots dead or dying in the cold air, but she could see no way out. No trails at all. She turned to ask him which way they would go, but the waterfall spewing out of Bowan Mountain filled the air with a roaring din that absorbed human sound.

She trusted that he knew and trusted him in that way only. She followed him again through a forest that expanded from stunted, struggling fir, pine, spruce, and the changed larches to tall trees that blocked the meadow view. Miles and miles of it, closing her in with him. She was close enough to smell his odor, to see the jagged scar stretched even tauter by the movement of his free skin, and the barely healing scratches along his arm. She saw that he had bite marks on his hand, purple indentations too small to have come from the huge bear teeth he'd described. She wondered about them, wondered who—or what— could have bitten him.

Halfway down the damned mountain, he should have been able to spot the trail, but he hadn't seen anything ringing the meadowland but trees. He was more annoyed than alarmed. He had studied the relief model in the ranger's office and read the guide book they sold for three bucks. The route was clear from both those sources. But the trail wasn't there. He couldn't find it when they were in the meadow either. The book said to look for cut-ends of deadfall trees, but there were so many of the giant pick-up sticks, and none of them pointed the way out.

But he had *her,* and that was good. She was already depending on him to save her. Just like Lureen, unsure of herself, looking for a man to rescue her. She was only acting mad because she was scared—just like Lureen did when she had her temper tantrums. She was physically stronger than Lureen, but even so she was slowing them down. It was midafternoon. If he didn't find the trail in an hour or so, they would be trapped by night. He paced the perimeters of the grassy plateau, searching for a channel through the trees while she sat in the meadow plucking the little daisies that grew around her.

Her chin lifted defiantly at his approach and her eyes were dark with fatigue and indecision.

"You're not a policeman, are you?"

"No."

"And you're not from Oregon either, are you?"

"No."

"And you're going to kill me, aren't you?"

He dropped beside her and slowly unbuttoned her blouse, letting his fingertips touch her breasts lightly. "Why would I kill you?" He pressed his lips to the vein that beat frantically between her breasts and felt her breathing stop. "I won't kill you. I love you. You've always belonged to me. You belong to me now. You're my possession."

She realized then that he was quite insane.

She didn't fight him or beg. She lay back and let him touch her. She felt his penis slide over her eyelids and circle her mouth, poke into her ears, and move over her body as if he was anointing her with it, and heard him chanting "Your eyes belong to me, and your mouth, and your breasts. It all belongs to me—all of you." It was all a dream, and she was not really part of it. She was no longer inside of her own skin, but stood somewhere away from it, watching but not feeling. She moaned when the red man told her to, and she parted her legs when he burrowed between them. When it began to hurt, she let the woman on the ground absorb the pain.

He held her afterward, rocking her in his arms, stroking her as if she were a rabbit until her breathing quieted. When she tried to pull away, he pressed his thumbs against her throat and choked her again, and she made herself be still. He seemed pleased with her.

She tested him later, pulling away just an inch or so at a time, and he allowed her to slip away from him. She put on her clothes and he watched her.

"You are the most beautiful, most perfect woman in the world. I will protect you and keep you safe. I didn't hurt you. You didn't fight me. It was the way it should be. You're part of me now."

She walked away from him, toward the edge of the wood. He made no move to stop her, but he watched her while she pushed into the foliage. She tried several places, willing the trail to be there. When she found it, she would run and if he caught up with her, she would find someplace to jump off. Some high place.

She looked for a long time, but she could find nothing that looked like a trail; it was all choked with woods and underbrush. After a while she walked back to the meadow and lay down, curling herself into the smallest possible ball. He walked over to her, but he didn't touch her; he only cast his shadow over her and then he went away and she slept.

CHAPTER FOURTEEN

Sam turned his pickup into the lane and headed up to the farmhouse; it was raining again and the weeds seemed to have grown a foot in four days, his fenders catching them wetly and then flopping them back away in a shower of water. No one had answered when he called at seven, but that was cutting it close. Their boat should have come into

Chelan at six, and the drive south would take a good hour, barring Labor Day traffic. 7:45 now, they should be back. He was disappointed when he pulled into the yard and saw that Danny's truck was not in the shed. He lit a cigarette and waited for Billy Carter to waddle up in full attack, but the gander didn't appear. The farmhouse had that lost look of all empty houses. The grass was tall here too, and Joanne's sunflowers bent like old women's heads from their weight of water. He finished the smoke, lit another, and listened for the distant throttle of Danny's truck coming up the hill. He heard occasional tire-on-gravel sounds from the road itself, but nothing nearer.

It occurred to him a little before eight that Danny might have left him a note. But the little cedar house with a notepad attached hadn't been opened for a long time; there was an old cobweb across the latch. If Danny was really running late, he'd probably taken Joanne to her mother's and gone straight to work; he had a spare uniform in his locker. Sam felt for the key they always kept under a loose shingle over the porch. It seemed important to go in to the house—just to see if there was some sign that they had been home at all.

He walked into the silent kitchen. The ticking of the old grade-school clock on the wall the only sound except for his own steps. The room smelled stale—cigar smoke, dust, and a faint trace of garbage—two plates left sitting in the sink with moldered toast and hard yellow egg bits. A row of canning jars sat on the counter, and he ran his finger along one and he saw the mark left in the thin veneer of dust. They were labeled in Joanne's neat hand: Peaches—September 3, 1981. He smiled; she'd been canning right up to the last minute. It must have bothered her to have to leave dirty plates behind.

He walked to the phone and dialed the office. "Fletch?"

"You better get your ass in here, Sammy."

"Danny show up there?"

"Negative."

"I'm out at his place, and they're not back here yet."

"Probably got held up in traffic. Everybody waiting until the last minute to head home."

"Yeah, well—I'm coming in. Tell him to wait for me if he comes in before I get there."

The trip out to Danny's place had fouled up Sam's timing, placing him in the squad room with the under-sheriff, Walker Fewell—or, more likely, Fewell had cooled his heels waiting for a deliberate confrontation. Fewell was a short, well-muscled martinet of a man who looked like a Marine DI shrunken and preserved—which he was. He'd squeaked into the Natchitat County Sheriff's Office through a loophole in the civil service qualifications list. Everything he knew about police work could fit into a shotglass with room left over; perhaps worse, he realized it. So he made up for his inadequacies by demanding absolute respect, spit-polished boots, and perfectly creased, spotless uniforms. He brown-nosed the press, and he nit-picked everything Sam did because he couldn't stand a deputy who simply refused to acknowledge his existence. Sam always stared somewhere over Fewell's right shoulder when the under-sheriff addressed him.

Walker Fewell sat now in his little office with walls plastered with certificates and awards for work not done, behind his clean desk, and worked over Sam's field reports from last night, marking out and changing Sam's round printing with the prissiness of a school teacher.

Sam eased past his door, and signaled to Fletch to toss him the keys to his unit, but Fewell called out in his high, nasal voice.

"Deputy. Deputy Clinton. Would you step in here before you leave?"

"He's gonna check to see if your shorts are ironed, Sam," Fletch whispered.

"Hell, I'm not wearing any."

"Then Lord help you. Sam—don't get him riled up. He's been going over the time sheets and he saw you were late three times last week. He'll have you sweeping up the jail if he can work it."

Sam leaned into Fewell's office, his hands splayed on either side of the doorjamb, dwarfing the under-sheriff where he sat in his little chair at his huge desk. His expression was respectful, but Fewell either recognized or imagined mockery in Sam's eyes.

"Clinton, you're not indispensable."

"No sir."

"You were tardy several shifts last week, and you're seven minutes late this evening. Is punctuality a problem?"

"No sir. I've had some trouble with my truck."

"Then you should make other arrangements."

"Yes sir. Is that all, sir?"

"We're a small department, but our standards are as high as any in the state. You know the pride I take in running an efficient, productive organization?"

"Yes sir."

"This follow-up on the incident last night with—er—a Mrs. Alma Pavko." He tapped the yellow sheet in front of him with the bowl of his unlit pipe. "Deputy Clinton, this comes across as a very crude comedy routine. We do not use the word 'shit' to refer to human excrement. They'll read your FIRs and follow-ups into the record in the courtroom, you know, and 'shit' and 'bare-assed' show an appalling lack of taste."

"I have testified in court a few times, sir. I am aware of the use of the reporting officer's follow-ups. I doubt that Mrs. Pavko's case will go into litigation. I would expect she's somewhat embarrassed today."

"Perhaps it won't—but I think you take my point."

"Yes sir."

"Where's your partner? Is he late too?"

"He took some comp time, sir. The Lindstroms have evidently been held up in traffic. I'm sure he will check in the moment he gets to town."

"That's all. You're dismissed—but I want to see Lindstrom when he shows up."

"Thank you sir." Sam moved out of the doorway, and then leaned in quickly, catching Fewell picking his nose. "And have a good evening, sir."

He called Fletch so many times during the shift, checking to see if Danny had checked in that even Fletch got exasperated. "If he calls, dammit, I'll let you know. Now get off the air and earn your salary."

CHAPTER FIFTEEN

She woke slowly, surfacing through layers of tension, and when she broke through the top of her sleep, her terror was as bright as the sun that stabbed into her eyes. She knew now that Danny was truly gone, and that there was no going back to save him. That tomorrow and next month and Christmas and next year, and all the years of her life lay ahead without him. The knowledge was more than she could bear.

She turned her face into the crushed grass and tried to shut the world out. She was alone.

She was not alone.

He crouched above her, pulling at her shoulder. She moaned and burrowed herself more deeply into the carpet of grass, deep enough to feel the grave-cold earth beneath it. There was no comfort there; there was no comfort left anywhere. She stood and began to pace with tight little steps, wringing her hands. That spot of meadow seemed safer. No, this spot. No, the terror was inside of her; there was no place to run to.

"What time is it? What time is it? Time? Time—" Her voice was a chant.

"Almost five."

"Morning five? Night five? We have to go. I have to get away from here. Hurry. Hurry. Show me which way."

"It's afternoon. You slept a long time. I let you sleep because you were worn out. The meadow is soft, isn't it?"

"It's cold. The ground is cold. We have to leave. We have to go down the mountain and tell someone to come and get Danny and take care of him."

"He's dead."

"I know—I know—I know. But he has to be in a clean room, a place where—oh my God—nothing can get at him. We have to tell someone."

"We can't go tonight. It's too late and the forest is too dark. Things in the woods—at night—they follow you and find you and you don't see them. You don't have any warning. They come for you."

"You did, didn't you? You came in the night and you crept up on us and you changed everything. You killed everything."

"No. I warned you. I came and warned you of the danger. God put me there so that I could save you. You believe in God, don't you?"

"I did." She had forgotten God the moment He failed her.

"You still do. Nothing happens without a reason."

"What reason?" She was screaming at him. "What reason for my husband to die instead of you?"

"I don't know. I only know that I'm here for you, and that you must trust me."

"Why?"

"Because you don't have anyone else."

He was mixing her up. He was not God's emissary; he was Lucifer, using God's name to confuse her. But what if she was wrong? He hadn't killed her yet, and she had expected that he would. He was probably crazy but she was not sure now if he was bad-crazy or good-crazy. She was quite sure that he had raped her, but whenever one memory segment became clearly defined, other recollections blurred. Was she remembering sex with Danny or with him?

She watched him bend over the fire to stir something, and she smelled food.

He smiled at her. "You have to eat. You must be strong because I've found the trail. It was right there behind those deadfalls; I found it while you were sleeping. In the morning, after you've eaten and slept, we will follow the way out. I promise you."

"Why did you rape me?"

He smiled at her again. "Is that the way you remember it?"

"Of course that's the way I remember it."

But in fact she only remembered their bodies moving together and the moon above or the sun—and then his face. No, that was with Danny. What did she remember?

"Do you read the Bible?"

"I used to read it a lot."

"Then you know that a man is responsible for his dead brother's wife; it is given to him to care for her and to hold her in love because his brother cannot."

"It was too soon . . ."

"The time is not important. It was inevitable that we should be together in love."

She was so frightened of him. He spun words around and around her so rapidly that she had no point of balance. He was capable of killing her in so many ways. She could not argue with his madness. Perhaps she was crazy too. That thought made her dizzy again.

"Look around us." His voice was low and steady. There was something wrong with her heart. Too fast. Staggered beats that dragged and then tumbled out of sync.

"We are in paradise. We have been through hell, and we have been rewarded with paradise. God created the world in six days—the whole world. Were those six days of our time or six days that each lasted a century? Do we know what time it is? Can we believe absolutely that there is still a world beyond what we know now, today, this minute, this place? Is there anything on the other side of those trees and behind those hills? Maybe there's nothing more—maybe the rest of the world has died."

"But you said you'd take me out tomorrow. You promised me."

"I did, and I will. But you must not grieve for anything or anyone while we still have all this. We can only know that we have been blessed."

"I can't be certain of anything. It is very, very difficult for me to think."

"I will think for you."

"I have no choice, have I?"

"You can leave me at any time."

She did not believe him, but she had no strength to argue. She was so tired. She could not form long sentences and her thoughts fragmented before they came together.

"You can leave me. But it isn't going to happen. You would die without me. We've come through the worst of it. Eat this."

She stared suspiciously at the brownish lumps and liquid he held out to her in the bisected metal pan. It tasted of tin and cheap TV dinners and she ate it mechanically.

The meadow was already darkening, closing her in with him for another night. She shuddered and he noted her movement although he seemed to be looking away from her.

"You're cold."

"A little."

He moved to drape a sleeping bag around her shoulders, his hands touching her impersonally. What did she remember about his hands?

She did not want to talk to him, but having no one at all to talk to was the worst thing; the quiet let her mind rove freely to pick at fragments of the horror. She saw Danny's face, his dead eyes beseeching her, his dead mouth calling to her before it filled with a fountain of blood. And she fought to keep the food she'd just eaten from rising in her gorge.

"I have to go into the woods again," she said faintly.

"I'll go with you."

She didn't argue. Her body and all of its functions didn't matter any longer. He had taken it, erasing something she had guarded carefully all her life.

She squatted near a stump and turned her head away, but she felt him watch her. He turned back toward the clearing, their little camp visible now only by the molehill of yellow embers lighting the black.

He tossed more logs on the fire and it billowed high, a circle of warmth against the true cold around them. The smoke choked the air on the downwind side of the flames and she was forced to sit beside him, but she held her sleeping bag around her like armor, dreading his hands.

He had raped her; she was sure of that now, but she could not remember how many times. He was like an animal in rut. She had heard Doss say that a ram could do it dozens of times in a single day, and there was that kind of energy about the red man.

She spoke very carefully. "I need to know what happened to my husband. I think—if you could tell me everything—that I could cope with it. I am having a great deal of difficulty. I imagine things. I see terrible pictures because I don't know what really happened."

He was quiet for a long time. "If I thought it would help you, I would tell you, but it wouldn't help you. I told you that it was sudden, that he didn't feel pain, and that's enough for now. When it's time, and when there isn't so much danger around us, I will answer everything you ask. Not now. And we won't have sex tonight . . ."

She felt a wave of relief. No. It was probably one of his tricks.

"We can talk, but there are rules. You have to take the part of life that cannot be dealt with and shut it off. Talk about anything that happened before we came together, or talk about what will happen tomorrow or next week. But we will not talk of anything in between."

"That's impossible."

"No. Think this: that you and I are riding on a train through the night. We're going somewhere we want to go, and you're a nice pretty woman, and I'm not such a bad guy, and we have a long way to go together. So we talk to each other and we pass the time, and we leave behind us everything that we don't want to think about, and everything ahead of us is under my control."

"But nobody can control the future."

"*Yes.* Yes, it can be shaped and painted the way we choose. Now, look at the fire and keep staring at it. See the lights in the houses along the track? Hear the whistle blowing? Hear how the wheels go clackety-clackety-clackety underneath us, bumping over the tracks."

"No. I hear a loon crying."

His hand grasped her arm so tightly that his fingers hurt. "That's *not* a loon; that's a whistle. You have to listen."

"I'll try."

"Clackety-clackety-clackety-clack." His voice was so deep that it vibrated oddly in her bones. She shifted so that her arm slipped away from his hand and he let her go easily.

"How old are you?"

"That doesn't matter. That's only part of time."

"I don't know how to talk. I'll break your rules."

"You're soft and gentle, like my mother was. You even look like her."

"Where is she now?"

"Gone."

She waited for him to say more, but he fell silent, staring into the fire.

"I remember everything, you know. Do you believe that I can?"

"Yes." She would not disagree, afraid to set off some spark that would trigger his crazy side.

"We weren't town people like you were. We were with the carnivals —because that was the only thing she knew. My mother was very young, but everything she did was for me, and she was with me every minute she could be."

He paused as if he expected her to deny that, but she said nothing.

"She danced and she was good; she could have danced anywhere, but she was afraid to try. I remember she wore this little pink costume with shiny things on it, little beads—whatchacallit—sequins. She looked like a princess. And her hair was like yours, but longer." His voice changed, anger sliding into it; she tensed, but he talked on, remembering. "We never had shit. Nothing. We lived in a crummy little bus-trailer thing, cold in winter, an oven in the summer, and the tires always blowing. I'd wake up in the night and we'd be stopped somewhere along some road and she'd be crying because we'd been left behind and she couldn't find anyone to get us going. Unless you've lived like that, you don't understand. Town kids used to laugh at me when I tried to play with them. Their mothers would come out and tell me to go away.

"So, anyway, I always wanted a bicycle. Fuck, she couldn't afford to feed us. She had these silver shoes with different colored bows to match her costumes, and they were all cracked on the sides and so thin on the bottom that she got slivers from the stage, and she couldn't afford new ones because she was trying to feed me. I'll bet you've never been hungry in your life, have you? Did you ever eat cornmeal mush and boiled potatoes for a whole month running?

"No."

"So a bicycle was out of the question. I could ride one when I was four. Some bratty town kid came by and he had his bright red bike and I got on it and I rode that sucker and he started screaming and crying and saying I stole it. I just got on it and rode it. First time. That was *free*. The wind swishing by my ears and my legs pumping and I knew I could go anywhere I wanted, only his daddy comes running up and grabs the handlebars and says, 'Give it back, you little bastard,' and the kid's standing there and grinning like a monkey and sticking his tongue out.

"Lureen, she tried to explain I was only trying it out, and I remember that prick town-daddy reached out and patted her on the breast as though she didn't deserve any respect, and he said, 'You keep your little bastard-trash kid off my son's bike.' "

"You must have hated him."

"I showed them. They were sorry."

"You were just a little boy. How could you—"

"Oh, I was a smart little fucker. I watched them go back to their car once, and they had their stupid dog with them—shut up in the car with the windows rolled down a little bit because it was hot. I just waited until they went back on the midway, and then I tried the doors. They weren't locked, so I rolled up every window really tight. They had a nasty surprise when they found it."

She felt a wave of nausea and fought not to let him know. But he kept talking.

"I got a bike later. Some kid left it with a flat tire, and I took it before he got back. The geek patched the tire and it was good as new."

"What's a geek?"

"Some old alky that bites the heads off live chickens."

". . . why?"

"Because it brings the rubes in. They go for sick stuff, like pickled babies."

"You don't like people."

"Some. Most of the time there's not much to like. Everybody's out for himself."

He was so violent. Every subject that came up seemed to draw some awful story from him, as if there was nothing inside him beyond hate. She tried to think of something gentler to talk about. "Where is your mother—Lureen?"

"Haven't you figured that out yet?"

"No."

"She died. That's the only way she ever would have left me, the only way. She was going into town one night in—hell, it doesn't matter—Texas, Oklahoma maybe. This cowboy was driving and she was sitting in the front seat, and he ran his convertible right up the back of a truck loaded with telephone poles. He saw it coming—damn him—and he ducked, but one of the poles came through the windshield and it took her head off."

"Oh!" It hit her bluntly and she could not stop the gasp, although his voice remained steady and matter of fact.

"I was about five, and I waited and waited for her to come back. They put me in the fat lady's truck and they just moved on out of town. I used to worry that she wouldn't be able to find us when she came back. I used to go write my name on the outside of that truck, so she'd know I was in there. Then I started writing it on billboards in different towns and putting down where we were headed next. So finally they told me she wouldn't be back. They just said she had gone away, but I heard them talking about the poles one night, and what happened to her head, and I knew she was gone for good and I quit leaving messages for her."

"Didn't your father try to find you?"

He laughed harshly. "We have to sleep. I've got to get you down the mountain tomorrow."

She picked up her sleeping bag and started to spread it out on the other side of the failing embers.

"No. Over here."

She was afraid. "Why?"

"Because I have to know where you are."

He led her to a spot beside his sleeping pallet and drew a length of rope from his pack.

"Lie down, but don't zip up your bag."

"I'll freeze."

"You can zip it part way. Hold out your right ankle."

He looped the rope around her calf and then cinched it around her ankle, tight enough so that she couldn't get it off, but not so tightly that it cut off her circulation. He tied the other end around his own leg, binding them together with the foot-long hobble.

"You don't have to do that," she protested. "There's nowhere I can go at night. I promise I won't try to get away. Don't you trust me?"

"Why should I?" His voice was close, so soft that she could barely hear its muted whisper, but she could not see his face. "You tried to kill me this morning. You were going to splatter my brains with a boulder."

She could scarcely remember it, but if it had happened—if she had held the stone above his face—it had been a long time ago, a week, maybe more. They had been in the meadow for days. She was quite sure of that.

CHAPTER SIXTEEN

On Wednesday Sam called the farm phone six times in an hour, had the operator check the line, found it in working order, and then forced himself to stay off his own phone so that it wouldn't be busy when Danny called. If they'd taken an extra day, they'd be in soon.

Waiting, he confronted the possibility that Danny's constraint during their last conversation in his trailer had been more than embarrassment over his own confessions of loneliness. He had blundered into Danny's personal boundaries, intruded into a marriage, and Danny had begun to shut him out. Their travel plans were their own business. Let them stay away on their private journey. Let them come back when they damn well pleased. It was Danny's responsibility if he failed to show up for shift tonight. It was *his* night off, and let Danny cover his own ass.

He switched on the five o'clock news and watched it without interest as he lit one cigarette after another. After an hour, he grabbed the phone again and dialed information and asked for the number for the North Cascades Lodge in Stehekin.

"The only listing we have, sir, is a number in Chelan."

"Give me that, then."

After a dozen rings, a young man's voice answered. No, there were no passenger lists. No reservations on *The Lady of the Lake*—you bought your ticket, you rode up, you rode back, nobody checked you in or out.

He hung up, dialed Walt Kluznewski's number and that too rang empty. He called the Chelan number back.

"Son," he said, pushing authority into his words. "This is Deputy Clinton at the Natchitat County Sheriff's Office. You have a parking lot up there for your passengers?"

"Yessir—for the overnighters and longer."

"Give it a quick look-see and tell me if there's a 1979 GMC pickup —red with Natchitat County plates—lemme see—here: TLL–687 or 876 still parked there. No. I'll wait."

He heard Willie Nelson wailing over the boat office radio. Twenty seconds later, the phone was picked up again.

"Deputy?"

"Yes."

"It's here. Looks like it hasn't been moved for a long time. Can't see through the windshield for dust."

"Don't touch it. Leave it alone until I get up there. You got a boat to Stehekin tonight?"

"No sir. One trip up everyday at 8:30 A.M. One trip back."

"Any other way to go uplake?"

"Yessir. Ernie Gibson'll fly you up in his seaplane. He can make Stehekin in about twenty or twenty-five minutes—been doin' it every day for over thirty years except in deep winter. Or you got you a power boat, they go up. Chelan County's got a sheriff's boat out there. Why don'tcha call them?"

Sam hung up without thanking the kid and sat staring at the phone.

If he were to go charging up to Stehekin to find Danny and Joanne enjoying themselves, safe, they'd be pissed. More than pissed; he'd interfered enough in their lives.

He cracked a beer and turned the television up, trying to quash the niggle of alarm that wouldn't go away. When the phone rang, he jerked so forcibly that he splashed beer over his coffee table, and cracked his shin in his leap toward the ringing.

But the voice was a woman's voice, familiar and faintly querulous. "Mr. Clinton?"

"Yes, ma'am." It registered: Elizabeth Crowder, Joanne's mother. He tried to keep the disappointment out of his voice.

"I'm feeling some concern, Mr. Clinton. I have heard nothing from my daughter and son-in-law. They were to be back Monday night. Did you know that?"

"Yes, ma'am, I know they intended that, but I wouldn't worry if I were you. I'm sure they'll be in this evening."

Mrs. Crowder began to weep. "I drove out there, and nobody's home, and I drove over to Sonia's—Mrs. Kluznewski's—and they haven't heard anything either. I'm so concerned, Mr. Clinton. Joanne is the type of person who always calls, even if she's only going to be fifteen minutes late—"

He felt sweat bead the back of his neck. "There's no telephones up there ma'am. She wouldn't be able to call you."

"I didn't want her to go."

"I'm sure everything is just fine. I'll tell you what, if they call me first, I'll get right back to you, and if they call you, you give me a jingle. How about that?"

"Yes, yes. We'd better keep the lines clear. It's just—Mr. Clinton—it's just that they're all I have—"

He stripped as he walked through the trailer, pulled on jeans and an old flannel shirt, dug through the dust under the bed in the back room for the fatigue boots they'd issued him for the Tact Squad in the riots in Seattle, and cursed the rotting laces when they snapped. He was on his way out the door when he remembered Pistol. He opened five cans of cat food and set them on the counter, dumped some dry food in the sink; the cat always drank out of the toilet anyway. He propped open the bedroom window above the wall marked with a trail of claw marks, and saw that Pistol had eaten his way through one tin of shrimp and tuna already and was working on another.

"Make it last, kid, or you'll have to work for a living. And keep your eyes on the valuables."

He didn't bother calling the office. If he wasn't back, he wasn't back. And Fewell could like it or lump it.

They lifted off the south end of the lake at dawn in one of Ernie Gibson's seaplanes, the DeHaviland left over from World War II. Sam, riding copilot in the six-seater, noted there was still a knob marked *bomb release* on the instrument panel, and speculated on the craft's history. He saw himself at eighteen, the gung-ho sailor who never saw anything of the war outside of Great Lakes Naval Station. Ernie Gibson had. You could tell by the way he flew, as easily as if he and the plane had welded into one form four decades before. He glanced sideways and saw the pilot, ageless—but he had to go sixty or more. Tight weathered skin over aquiline features, his concentration focused on whatever tune played through his earphones, his whole mien so relaxed he seemed to be napping. That was O.K. Sam wasn't up to small talk.

They flew over orchards, farm houses, and bright aqua swimming pools, and then over the lake itself, between the dark mountains. Twenty-five minutes later, the DeHaviland settled on the water in front of the lodge as gracefully as a gull pouncing on a bit of bread, and Gibson was out and tying them up before Sam could react. They walked up the creaking dock toward the smell of coffee and bacon from the lodge, and Sam felt a moment of regret that he had no time to talk to Gibson or know him. Another time, another place, they would have been friends. Now Ernie headed toward the restaurant's steamed-up glass door and Sam walked toward the ranger's office, grateful that he'd worn his down jacket; the air here whispered of frost even while the zinnias and petunias still bloomed along the walkway. What had been summer here was gone, and the feeling was one of closing up and closing in.

The Forest Service Office was warm and comfortably familiar, and the ranger in charge smiled broadly and held out his hand. "Deputy. Glad to know you. Must have been one of your guys through here last week."

"That's why I'm here. My partner and his wife were headed up here, and they're late getting home. Thought I'd check in with you and see what's up."

The ranger frowned slightly and pulled a ledger toward him. "That so? Let's see what they wrote down here. We keep track of people— follow some of them all up and down the Pacific Trail. Lindstrom? Right?"

"Right."

The ranger ran his finger down a column of names, turned the page, and repeated the motion, stopping halfway down the list. "Here it is. I talked to them last Friday; they stayed that night in the lodge. They signed out for Rainbow Lake, and your buddy talked about going on over to pick up the North Cascades Highway instead of coming back here. When they weren't back Monday, we figured that's what they'd done. Seemed to be experienced hikers—had plenty of gear."

"Yeah. Well—he hasn't called in. How far would it be for them to go over the other side?"

"From the lake? Ohh, five, six hours. Once they got out to the North Cascades Highway, they wouldn't have had any trouble getting to a phone. We figured they'd decided to go over Bowan Mountain, and pick up the highway and catch a bus from Winthrop back to pick up their vehicle in Chelan."

Sam shook his head. "Their truck's still back there at the boat dock. If you'll point out the trail to me—the one up to Rainbow Lake—I'll hike on up there and have a look. They're probably just having such a good time they decided to stretch out their vacation."

"You want me to come along?"

"Thanks, but I'll be fine."

"Grade's fairly steep. You in shape?"

The ranger was nudging fifty too, and Sam grinned. "As much as any of us old guys. Do me good to sweat a little."

"O.K. Here's your map—pretty basic."

"Do you want me to leave crumbs behind so you can find me?"

"Just stay on the trails. You'll probably bump into them coming down."

"Most likely."

For half an hour, Sam climbed without stopping on a surge of false energy, but it could not last. His hip sent first a twinge of pain when he put his right foot down too solidly, and then it sprouted a steady ache that was like a girdle radiating from his lower back. He tried to ignore it, but it would not go away. His muscles knotted in spasm until his entire back was rigid. Too many years of sitting. Too many years period. He tried to pace himself, stopping and resting too often. His lungs would not expand the way they had—how many years ago? Ten? Twenty? Thirty, probably. He panted and grunted like an old woman.

At the first meadow he eased his treacherous body down and lay on his back, feeling his right leg twitch by itself. He could see why they shuffled most cops off the street before they were fifty; he couldn't chase a one-legged blind man and expect to catch him.

He stretched, and the spasms lessened their hold, but only partially. He knew if he lay too long, he'd never walk again, and if he started climbing too soon, they'd have to come get him with a litter.

He was sure he'd made three miles, but when he checked the map, he found he'd gone just under two. He wanted a cold beer more than he'd ever wanted anything, and he remembered the perfect rows of Olympia that waited back in his trailer. It hadn't occurred to him to bring any. He'd thrown two cans of franks and beans into his jacket pockets and bought some beef jerky at a 7–11 in Chelan. What the hell could you expect from a city cop?

He groaned and hit it again. The trail was obviously designed for mountain goats. The switchbacks were a maze. Once he was on the zig-zag path that led higher and higher, there was no stopping, no place to sit, and sure as hell no place to lie down.

His tension—the steady hum of concern that had seen him through the night's drive where nothing existed beyond the two yellow funnels of his headlights—shaded gradually until it became anger. Anger at himself because he was a fool. Anger at Danny for somehow summoning him to this mountainside, and, only slightly diminished, anger at Joanne for thinking of the whole fucking mess in the first place.

He crossed the creek on the plank bridge and lay on his belly to drink the icy water that, miraculously, tasted better than beer. The air was warm now, and the sun deceived him into thinking he had found summer. With the heat, a faint suggestion of well-being crept over him.

A mile further on, at least by his shirttail reckoning, he came to a camping area. Five campsites, and none with the look of recent occupancy. A scrabbly, blighted area with no view of anything. The little can of franks and beans opened with a tab that made him think of beer. He had had no supper or breakfast, and the food, cold and gelatinous as it was, restored his energy.

He lit a cigarette and sensed at the moment he slipped his lighter back into his shirtpocket that he wasn't alone. The presence was to his left, and he turned his head slowly—ready to speak until his eyes met the flat lidded yellow orbs staring at him with lazy interest. The rattler, thick as his wrist, lay stretched across the rock pile three feet away.

Sam blew out the smoke that swelled forgotten in his throat and lowered his hand very slowly. The snake watched him but made no attempt to coil. Its forked tongue flashed and the wedged head followed his movements. He inhaled again, trying to match his arm motion to the snake's torpor.

"Want a puff?"

The eyes blinked; the tongue shot out.

"No? Nasty habit, anyway. Get much traffic through here?"

Gone fucking crazy. Talking to rattlers.

He'd be damned if he was going to move first—not until he'd finished the cigarette. He took his time, watching for a sudden change in the serpent's position, but it moved nothing but its head. He searched the ground where he sat for other snakes, but there were none; then he ground the butt out under his heel. He wouldn't know until he tried just how much agility remained in his bad hip. He rolled to his right, away from the rattler, balanced for an instant on his boots and fingertips, and then was on his feet and out of striking range. When he looked back at the rock pile, the snake was gone.

CHAPTER SEVENTEEN

She knew that they had been in the same meadow for a long time, but she was not sure how long. She forgot things very quickly and it was so hard to call them back. One morning—it might have been the second or the third, she wasn't sure—they couldn't leave because a thick fog made the trees vanish and he'd said they would fall off the mountain if they tried to move down. Remembering the drop so dangerous even in clear air, she knew he was right. The next day, or maybe some other day, there was a reason to stay. What was it? She couldn't remember. Sometimes it seemed as if the light lasted so long that night would never come, and at other times, the periods between day and night and day again flittered by in minutes. He liked it when she sat quietly and listened to him talk, but there was often a sudden panic that demanded that she move. When that happened, she found she could lessen the terror by action. She circled the meadow's boundaries then, hurrying faster and faster to leave the crawling feeling behind. He always made her stop before she was entirely free of it and led her back to their little camp. She tried not to cry because it seemed to annoy him, no—infuriate him. Sometimes in the night she had to cry because her tears choked up in her throat and she couldn't breathe, but she learned to do it softly. Even so, he caught her at it, his thick fingers finding the tears on her face.

And once he had touched her he would not let her go until he had touched her all over, exciting himself and finally plunging into her. She had learned to lie still and accept him passively so that he wouldn't hurt her, and afterward he was nicer and calmer and left her alone. In the blackness and especially in the fog—when she thought she had died —his hands defining her were proof that she was still alive. When she didn't fight him, he was almost gentle with her. He let her breathe, and he allowed her to live.

In the daytime, when she could see his face, he looked at her so strangely sometimes as if there were something she should know. Once in a while, when he came, he cried out some name or some word that sounded like "Reen" or "Reenee," but she didn't know what it meant.

When he talked, she didn't have to think or remember and she could let her mind rest. And when he talked, he would not fondle her—as long as she responded correctly. When his voice made her drowsy with the deep buzzing cadence it could have, she had to balance her answers carefully. Most of the time, he only wanted her to listen and to look at him.

". . . some souls never die." He was staring at her again with his questioning look.

"No. They go to be with God."

"There is no God. There is only a continuum of particular, special souls. Special people—the rest are only reflections of the best and they die like cows. I am a special one. So are you. We will never die."

Hadn't he talked about God? She was sure it was the red man who was talking about God a long time ago.

"What cannot be seen by fools is truth. Do you agree?"

"Yes."

"She died when you were ten years old and became part of you. Do you remember?" He asked.

"I—"

"Say you remember!" He was angry, demanding an answer.

"I remember."

"I always knew you. All the times we were together, you always needed me. When I had to leave you, you died. But when you left me, I was stronger. I was always stronger because you belonged to me, and I possessed your soul. I never let it go, but you hurt me when you went away."

"I'm sorry." His stories were so confusing. They made her feel dreamy, tumbling along the tunnels he formed, trying to understand.

"I forgave you. I always forgave you because you were weak. Do you remember who we were?"

"I don't understand—"

"Don't make me angry. You said you remembered when you started to be Lureen."

". . . oh, yes." Maybe she did remember. He was so sure of it, and she was no longer positive of who it was that she was now. There were no mirrors here, only his eyes, and he seemed to recognize her.

"I went to libraries and I saw our pictures in old books. We had different names, but our eyes stay the same. That's how you can be sure —by the eyes. I knew you when I saw your eyes. Did you know me?"

"I—yes, I knew you." She couldn't seem to pull her gaze away from his, and she could truly see her image in them. She finally looked away because they made her so dizzy.

"Would you like to sing?"

"What?"

"You always liked to sing—Elvis' songs. Love me tender. . . ."

She joined in because it seemed important to him. They had sung at their other camp. . . . No. Not with him. She had sung with someone. With Danny, maybe, but she couldn't remember.

All she could remember was that she had been safe then—and happy—and the thought of it made her want to cry again. But she sang with the red man for a long time because it seemed to calm him. When he was calm, because she pleased him, he seemed almost nice. He didn't frighten her then. She only had to remember not to talk about things that bothered him. There were so many things she had to keep track of. To keep from dying.

They had stayed in the meadow far too long, and he railed at himself for that. It had been so perfect, having her with him, belonging so totally to him, that he had not wanted to end it. But the days had run on, and they had only come four miles from the lake. He had seen no one, but there could conceivably be searchers. He couldn't be sure because she didn't remember when her vacation was supposed to end. When he asked her, she would say "Monday" one time, and another time she said "In time for graduation." He should have questioned her earlier. He was pleased by the vague hazy way her mind was—it made her sweeter. Physically, she was doing well; she ate and slept when he told her to, and she complained only rarely of nausea. She let him make love to her, and she allowed him to hold her at night and fit himself around her to keep her warm.

But they had to leave now, and he was ill; his body had suddenly betrayed him. He was certain it would pass, but his mind was dulled by a stubborn fever. His body responded slowly to what he asked of it. He could work his way around the pain by blocking it out, but his swollen arm got in his way, and the burning in his head expanded and made it impossible to concentrate.

The damned arm had wakened him Monday night. He thought at first that she had pulled on her hobble and was trying to leave him, but she lay asleep beside him. It was not his leg, but the arm that felt oddly tight as if its skin had shrunk and could no longer accommodate his flesh and muscle. He could not tell what it was then, not by the quartering moon and the remnants of fire. It itched and hurt when he scratched it and was full of unhealthy heat.

He finally found sleep again just before dawn by letting the swollen arm rest outside his sleeping bag and pretending it was not part of him. When he awoke, he saw the arm swollen from his wrist to his armpit where the lymph nodes bulged like walnuts. The scratches and the marks left by her teeth gleamed a bright, unnatural color.

She didn't know. He'd kept his sleeves rolled down, and the new coldness in the air made that seem reasonable. But the arm seemed almost alien now, a heavy, throbbing weight. He tried to throw it out in a wide gesture to end the song, and she looked at him sharply when he could not.

"What's the matter with you? What's wrong with your arm?"

"Nothing. I got scratched when—you remember, I told you. The grizzly ripped up my arm some. It's kind of sore."

"Let me see it." She reached for his arm and he drew back.

"It's nothing. It's beginning to feel better now."

"You're moving funny, and you've been dropping things."

He shrugged and rolled up his sleeve, holding the arm out.

"Oh my God!"

He followed her stare and was startled to see the arm, swollen and darkened so that it looked sausagelike. The tracks were spread apart and oozing pus. Her teeth marks looked worse. He shivered.

"Why didn't you tell me you were hurt? You've let it get infected. What happened to you? What did this?"

"You've forgotten again."

She turned his hand in hers, gently pressed the tooth marks. "What's this? What bit you?"

"You did."

"I couldn't have!"

"When we were in the tree."

Her face was stricken. "I'm sorry. I'm so sorry. You were hitting my head—"

"You were hysterical; I had to keep you from slipping down. You didn't mean to. It doesn't matter now."

"No. I wouldn't have done that to anyone deliberately." She turned away and started pawing through her pack. She looked back at him, "Are you allergic to penicillin?"

"I don't know. I never had it."

"What about when you were a child? You never had it for a sore throat? You must have."

He stared back at her, wondering at the vast blank spaces in her recollection. She seemed truly to have forgotten.

"No. Never. I always got better eventually—even that time with my ears."

She dug a brown plastic tube out of her pack and shook two round white tablets out. "Take these. I'll get the canteen. Just take them. I have enough for four days—that should help. I always bring them just in case."

"What if I'm allergic?"

"We can't think about that; we don't have a choice. You're not allergic to bee stings, are you?"

"No."

"Then it will be all right, I think." She carried a silver tube with a paper label with her and reached for his arm. "Neosporin. We'll put that on too. You should have told me before, though."

And it had helped some. His arm still bothered him, but the infection seemed static, neither retreating nor accelerating, only smouldering with chronic pain. He liked having her take care of him, and what he had viewed as a setback seemed actually to be a blessing. During the time she fussed over him, she seemed serene; nurturing seemed a comfortable role for her. It was only when she had nothing to do that she grew restive.

She was afraid he was going to die, and that she would have caused it. She could not remember that she had tried to kill him before; she only knew that if he died, she would be all alone. He told her that often, reminding her that it was her teeth that had sent the deadly spores into his blood stream, and then he cried when he talked about what would happen to her without him. He slept, or seemed to sleep, much of the time, and she had to keep the fire going and fix food to make him stronger. But he would not eat, and he grew weaker.

He had promised her he would take care of her and he had done that. She didn't know where Danny had gone, but Danny had left her on the mountain and something bad had happened to her. But she couldn't recall what it was. She could not remember beyond yesterday. When he touched her, he had given her life; he had willed her to live. She remembered that. Alone, even standing alone in the meadow, she was afraid. She needed some human thing to touch and hold on to because the air around her was empty. Caring for him was the most important thing. Women took care.

Sometime, sometime when there were walls to lean against and secure space with a roof and doors, she would sort it out. Unless he died and left her behind even though he had assured her he wouldn't. If he died, there would be no one left to see her. She would not belong to anyone, and she would cease to exist.

She had misjudged him, thought he had deliberately kept her in the meadow. And that was wrong. As sick as he was, he kept rousing from his delirium and telling her they had to leave. Of course, she could not let him do that. When she pushed him carefully back to his sleeping pallet, his muscles were still as heavy and strong but they seemed not to be able to work efficiently. He looked at her, but he seemed not to see her, and still he let her gentle him.

Someone—or something—had frightened her but she did not know who it was. She belonged to the sick man, and she knew that because he had explained it to her so many times. If she belonged to him and let him die, nobody would forgive her.

She watched him. He moaned in his sleep, but he would not talk to her, no matter how often she called out to him.

When he opened his eyes and saw her and she knew he knew her, she was grateful. He seemed to be in terrible pain still, but she thought her medicine was helping.

"Tell me the stories," she pleaded, and he talked to her again, in a voice not so deep, but steady.

"You won't leave me, will you?" she asked.

"I will never leave you. I possess you. I am part of you."

And she felt alive again.

"I have to know how protected we are," he explained. "You must go out into the woods and show me. I have to know if something could sneak up on us. Try to surprise me. Go far enough away so that I can't see you, and then try to fool me. I'll close my eyes. When I hear you, I'll shout 'Bingo.'"

She was rather good at it, but he always heard her; she betrayed herself with a crackling branch or a rustle of leaves when she was closer to him than a hundred yards or so. Even when he drowsed in his fever, he heard her. It made her feel safe.

When she was finished with her games, she came back to him and lay down beside him. He was far too ill and weak to make love to her, but he felt her against him. The tension that had been there was gone. She lay beside him as easily as a lover, no longer a captive. He had sent her out of his sight deliberately, and she had come back. He was too sick to hobble her, but it didn't matter. She would not leave.

CHAPTER EIGHTEEN

The fork in the trail was clearly marked, and Sam could see the arrow to the left reading Rainbow Lake and the one to the right indicating Mc Alester Pass. Five and a half miles to go now until he found them. The trail seemed easier for the moment, deceiving him into believing he had conquered the worst of it, falling downward beneath his feet to Rainbow Creek. He crossed a jerry-built bridge and filled his canteen, feeling more confident. The old man wasn't doing so bad after all.

But beyond the creek the trail became a maze of switchbacks, steeper than those he'd already climbed, and his lungs sucked up dusted air. At the top of each ramp of dry ground there was another and another—a labyrinth—as he trudged 1200 feet higher on the sere breast of the mountain. He could not imagine anyone's deliberately seeking out such agony for recreation.

Five miles. He drank the last of his water grimly and started up one more switchback. His throat was dry as baked gravel as soon as he turned the corner.

And then there was water again, and the trail grudgingly flattened to negotiable planes. He mistrusted the mountain now and the mirage of meadowland sheltered by peaks on every side, but the hike was easy for more than a mile, the land lush and bespeckled with flowers again. His breathing eased and his body ached less. With the slackening of physical pain his sense of isolation grew strong and made him eager for the moment he would walk into their camp. Danny was going to whoop and clap him on the back for surviving this ordeal.

And he was starving. He hallucinated food odors on the wind. Steak and fish frying, whatever else Joanne might be cooking up only a mile ahead. Danny was going to devil him about being out of shape. Joanne would smile and tell her husband to shut up, and the three of them would sit around the campfire and fill each other in on their days spent apart. Where they waited was as fixed in his mind as if he really could see beyond the top of the trail; he held the picture as the path started upward again—not fooling him this time, but made bearable by the waterfall close by. What the hell. So he'd missed them; that was no crime.

He looked at his watch. Almost six thirty. The ranger had said five and a half hours to the lake. It had taken him a little more than six, not too bad for an old man fueled on beans and water and no sleep.

He saw the lake, green water surrounded by a horseshoe of crags and spires, looking like a goddamned picture post card. They would be down there hidden in the trees. He shouted an "Halloooo!" that startled him as it burst from his throat. He waited.

There was no answer.

He was probably beyond shouting distance; he would continue calling as he drew closer until he reached a spot where the woods wouldn't swallow his voice. He would not sneak up on them. He knew better than to surprise a cop. He kept shouting at regular intervals, stopping each time to listen. If they were in there screwing, he was going to feel like an ass.

"Come out, come out wherever you are . . . Uncle Sammy's come for supper . . ."

He listened. There was some answer. And then he realized it was his own echo mimicking him. Tree limbs sighed and groaned around him too, and a flight of tiny birds rose from the ground and circled over his head before they disappeared deep in the forest.

The smell at first was only a trickle of an odor. The rancid sweetness resembled the skunk cabbage stench that lay over sodden lowlands around Seattle in March. Cloying perfumed air, urging the unitiated to pick an armful of the greenish-yellow hooded lilies. Once in drunken romanticism, he'd picked Nina a mass of them, and then been sorry;

at the first bruise, they'd bled their pungent stink over everything.

But he knew what the smell really was; he had encountered it more than most men. He would not acknowledge it.

It grew stronger with every step toward the lake, and he held his breath. When he opened his lips to shout again, it rushed in and filled his lungs. Rotten air. He lit a cigarette and gulped the smoke, but the miasma choked out burning tobacco.

It was decaying flesh, something long dead that surely rested off the right side of the trail, close by now, fouling the air. He did not want to walk toward the slope of land that sheltered the dead thing.

But his feet took him to the edge and he bent his head slowly to look down through the underbrush and narrow-trunked saplings. There was a roaring in his head and then no sound at all as if he had slammed full-tilt into a wall and died. And yet, there was no surprise. He had known it for a long time, days—all those days of pretending and manufacturing explanations while the man below him had never moved at all.

The corpse lay on its face next to a deadfall, one dead hand lightly curled around a rock, its knees drawn under the swollen belly. There was no life in it; even its hair looked spiked and false, the scalp beneath it dull white.

Sam stared down for a long time before he could unlock his knees and side-step through the underbrush, down and down and down. He began to slide and saw the previously hidden ravine twenty feet beyond the corpse. He did not will himself to stop or make any effort at all to stop. He thought for a moment that it would be easy to go with the momentum and drop heavily on the rocks below—easier than greeting the dead man.

He did not go over; the ground cropped out just at the end of his descent and held him fast. A great lassitude filled him, and he lay alongside the precipice for a time and looked up and back now at the body, trying to make it unfamiliar.

Something or someone had dragged the corpse downhill by its boots; the arms reached back toward the trail, the plaid shirt was bunched up beneath the armpits, exposing a wide band of visible flesh, striated with purpling lividity along the belly portion and leached of blood on the back. He could see no blood stains on the jeans or the flannel shirt, nothing on the back of the head. He could not see the face at all.

He did not want to see the face. He longed to run away, back down the eleven miles of mountain to Stehekin. If he had not come, he would have had what? Maybe three or four more days of not knowing. It seemed an important block of time to hang onto, but it was too late; he had rushed to this place to find what he could not endure.

He gulped air and found that the smell was not as awful as it had been up above. The dog men always said that and he'd never believed them—that death odor rises in the woods, leaving the corpse oddly pure of scent. He'd seen dogs circling and howling at treetops and still hadn't believed it, but it was true.

His legs could not support him. He crawled on his hands and knees until he was four feet from the faceless, ruined man. The boots were nondescript, the jeans were Levi's, the shirt looked like all plaid shirts.

It could be any man.

His damn teeth were chattering. He crawled closer and allowed himself to look more carefully. He reached out and touched the left hand, finding it cold, its skin slippage already begun. The first layer would slip off like a glove if the skin was severed at the wrist. He unbuttoned the taut band of flannel with his own dead fingers and tugged the material back.

The tattoo—Danny's dumb home-made heart—crept into view, expanded now, stretched along with the bloated arm until it spread out grotesquely like something in a funhouse mirror. The D and J were there in the center of it, distorted too.

"Oh pard, oh pard, oh pard, oh pard," he was not aware that he spoke out loud. "What happened to you, Danny?"

He could not keep a partner; it was as simple as that. He sat back on his heels and let out a sound, a howl. Rage and grief, a primitive lament common to all tongues. It sent a hundred wild creatures scuttling for shelter, terrorized.

And then he worked rapidly with some icy deftness, racing the sun that had begun to sink toward the western ridges. He felt a curiosity, an obsession to know, coupled with a dull conviction that knowing would change nothing.

Danny was heavier than anything he'd ever tried to lift, and he struggled to turn the corpse over. Rigor had come and gone; what had happened had occurred days before. All that time. Danny had lain moldering through sunrise and sunset and sunrise again, unattended. An unattended death had to be the loneliest death of all.

He fought to think objectively. This was just another dead body, like the dozens of others he'd worked over. He could manage it in time-sets. For fifteen minutes he would not remember that this was Danny. He checked his watch and saw that it was only seven o'clock, not hours since he'd slid toward the rocky edge.

The eyes rolled into view, open and staring, their pupils clouded over with opaque circles. He did not recognize them. He did not recognize the face either. Purple as wine. He noted what he was supposed to note; the body had lain prone since death—it had not been moved or the lividity pattern would not be so classic.

Sam jotted findings on an imaginary pad. Cause of death?

The right cheek was scratched deeply with four parallel lacerations —bloodless. Why bloodless? An animal's claws maybe, but why bloodless? Post mortem. Mutilated after death. But why?

The blood was along the shirt front, pints of it spilled there, staining the blue and white plaid so completely that only black lines remained, framing neat squares of red now. The gore had sluiced down over the blue jeans and left them stiff. He lifted the shirt and saw puncture wounds, sucking wounds, over the heart and lungs, the skin around them already putrescent, green going black. Stab wounds? Bite wounds?

Eleven minutes to go.

Danny's—*no, the corpse's*—right arm flopped loosely, its humerus wrenched from the shoulder socket. Oh God, the power. What power? What creature?

The gun was there, lying in the crushed foliage where Danny's body had been. Danny's battered .38 that had belonged to the old man, to Doss. Sam picked it up by the checkered grips where fingerprints never clung, released the cylinder cautiously, and saw that every chamber was full. Danny had not fired it. He had carried it with him to this dying place, but why had he waited too long to use it? Neither of them had ever had to shoot bullets into a human being; they both knew what all cops knew—that any cop forced to shoot a man is himself maimed by the experience. Seattle P.D. or Natchitat County Sheriff's Office—the

officers forced to shoot had all retired early on "mentals" that were
called other things. It was one of the silent axioms of law enforcement:
don't shoot or the bullet will eventually hurt you worse.

But killing an animal was different. Danny hunted; most cops fished
and hunted, perhaps to find some acceptable channel for the hours of
required marksmanship. Danny should have fired, emptied the damn
cylinder. Sam shuddered and lay the weapon down, terribly puzzled.

He was not thinking well. There was something else he should be
remembering, something of vital importance. He was not afraid; that
wasn't it, although he visualized some animal, a bear probably. They
were six feet, eight feet, when erect. Razor teeth. Five hundred pounds,
a thousand—maybe more. He would relish the sight of the creature and
the chance to destroy it. His pistol would be a pea-shooter—unless he
could put out its eyes, but it scarcely mattered. There was nobody left
to grieve over him. He could die up here and be absolved of guilt for
having killed yet another partner.

Then he remembered. *Joanne. Where was Joanne?*

He scrambled through the saplings to the trail, shouting her name.
He called until he was hoarse, listening each time for her answer, and
then unable to stand the mocking quiet, shouted again.

He thought he heard something near the lake, a woman crying,
some muted sobbing. When he reached the water, a dark jade now in
the gloaming, the sound stopped. He could hear it again, this time
behind him on the left of the trail—wailing and pleading—but when
he pushed deep into the trees there, the sound had moved back into the
meadow from where he'd just come.

"Joanne! It's Sam," he shouted. "Wait for me. Stay where you are—
I'm coming!"

Now the crying woman seemed to answer from high in the trees. He
wondered if he really heard her at all.

He grew frantic in his search; she would be so frightened, perhaps
even afraid to come out where *he* could see her. She had waited far too
long for help, all alone. Danny had lain dead beside this lonely trail for
at least three days, and she had been alone all that time. Frightened?
God no, she would be terrified.

If it occurred to him that she too might be dead, he never let the
thought bubble up. The worst had happened. There could be nothing

more. He talked to himself unaware, "I'll find her, pard—don't worry, I'll find her and take care of her. She's in here someplace, pard, and she'll be O.K. Don't you worry about that."

He saw her then, her back to him, leaning against a log in the small clearing near the lake, motionless.

He ran now, unconscious of the pain in his back and thighs. Closer, he could see their little camp, the burned-out fire with the coffee pot resting on grey ashes, but even as he reached out to touch her, he saw that the figure he had been so sure was a woman with lowered head was only a sleeping bag, left propped against a log. Danny's old surplus khaki sleeping bag.

They had camped here, but there was no one here now, nothing but shadows. He looked up and saw something suspended from the trees and felt sick, afraid to go nearer and find that she had hanged herself in despair. When he drew near the swinging thing, he saw that it was only a duffel bag of spoiled food twisting in the wind and bumping against the pine.

The tree's bark was scuffed and he could see the broken branches where someone had crawled frantically upward. He saw even the crusted mounds of dried vomit on the ground. Someone *had* hidden here, someone in the grip of nauseous horror. He expected to find blood on the ground. She was no longer in the tree, so she had either come down of her own volition or she had been dragged down.

He was relieved to find no blood, no claw marks on the foodbag, nothing at all in the abandoned camp itself that indicated the bear had found her. Her sleeping bag was not here nor was her backpack, although he found Danny's pack behind a log. She had to be alive, but he could not imagine where in this morass of wilderness she crouched hidden—or how much longer she could survive.

The cold came with sunset, and he was aware of his body again. He gathered wood mechanically and lit the fire, but only for her, a signal she could see and know that it was safe to come out from her hiding place. He watched it burn and tried to work through the complexities of what had happened.

She had been in this camp, and she had tried to hide from . . . something . . . in the tree. There was physical evidence of that. Danny had been a few hundred yards away, but for what fucking purpose? He wasn't hunting; he wasn't armed for hunting. If he'd been fishing, he'd have gone toward the lake—not the trail out. If he'd forseen trouble, he wouldn't have left Joanne alone.

Danny's death scene spun around in his head, a film reel playing over and over, but he could never get a fix on a frame that made sense. He could not keep the two separate: the dead man with the livid, swollen face and the live Danny—laughing, waving goodbye to him.

And he grasped only one thought. Nothing would ever be the way it had been again.

He had not meant to sleep, but exhaustion crept over him where he sat and his head dropped on his chest.

When he woke, it was dawn and nothing had changed. No one had come seeking the fire's warmth. He called for her for hours, until the answering silence was so heavy with futility that he knew he had to seek help.

He took nothing with him but his canteen as he headed downtrail. He looked straight ahead as he caught the corpse odor from below the path, and concentrated on putting one foot ahead of the other until the air grew fresh again. He called out to her occasionally, knowing that the chance she could hear him grew less and less as he neared the fork in the trail and turned down the last route to the ranger's station. She would surely understand when he came back with help that he had not been able to find her by himself, alone.

He drove himself without let-up, feeling no jolt or shock when he slid and fell with the loose shale on the downward inclines, unaware of the tears that coursed through the deep crevices of his face.

CHAPTER NINETEEN

He was not sleeping well. She thought that he was recovering, but almost as soon as the sun disappeared, he had stopped answering her questions and slept, his bad arm held gingerly away from him. She was careful not to bump it; even the wind across it made him whimper in his sleep. She tried to sleep too, but his groaning and tossing woke her again and again. During the stealthy games he had been all right, but now he was delirious.

She wanted to say his name to comfort him and found it so odd that she did not know what it was. She had known his name, and now she didn't. She wet a rag from her canteen and stroked his forehead, and his eyes opened but they would not look at her.

"Are you O.K.?"

His good hand darted out and gripped her shoulder, hurting her.

"Damn it, Damn it, you bitch. You're trying to kill me."

"No . . . oh no—you're sick."

"Open the window. There's no air in here."

"We're outside. There are no windows. You have a fever."

"I said open the window or I'll—"

His head dropped back and he seemed to sleep again, but his hand held her shoulder fast and she could not pry herself loose of him. She touched his face and his skin was hot, taut, and papery.

She didn't know what to do.

"Listen!"

"What?"

"They're coming to kill us again. Lock the door, Reenie."

"There is no door . . ."

"I said *lock it!*"

"All right."

"You brought them here on purpose. You've been fucking around with all of them and I told you and told you—"

"No. I didn't—"

"You lying bitch." His sick arm rose up, and then fell back onto the ground and he cried out. "You're so fucking dumb, Reenie. Now, you've gone and killed us."

His fingers slipped to her breast and clutched there and she thought she would faint from the pain. She began to cry.

"Don't cry, Reenie. I forgive you. I always forgave you. I won't let you die forever. I'll find you. You belong to me. I own you."

She could not remember what she had done that had to be forgiven, or why he called her the other name, but she knew she had done something despicable, and that she had killed him—them. No, just him.

She poked at the fire, trying to make it warmer; he thought he was burning up, but it was really so cold.

And she tried to think. It was like building a bridge without enough lumber to go across, but she searched her mind for the pieces she was sure of. She knew they were on a mountain, but she did not know where it was. She had come up here with someone, not him, but someone else. *Who?* Danny. Thinking about Danny made her feel sad, because Danny had left her. Then *he* had come to take care of her. Because she belonged to him, because he knew her, because they were meant to be together. He could have killed her. *Why?* Why would he kill her? She couldn't remember why she had been afraid that he would. But he hadn't. She was grateful for that. Since she knew he possessed her life and that he had chosen to allow her to breathe and to live, she was very grateful.

He knew that she was someplace near him, but the fever drugged him and kept him in his deep sleep where the nightbirds' cries echoed down fiery corridors and he could not hold onto her. It took tremendous concentration to waken. He was weaker than he thought possible, his blood clattering through his veins, hot as steam pipes, his infected arm throbbing almost rhythmically.

He closed his eyes and dove under the pain again, asleep but not resting.

She caressed him awake, her hands cool on his penis. Too late. She had come to him of her own accord just as he had known that she would, asking for it without any prompting, and it was too late. He was too goddamned sick.

He watched her, naked over him in the first daylight. Her breasts swung close to his mouth, and her fingers were insistent on his cock. He was incapable of any response beyond his hard-on.

"What should I do? Tell me what to do."

"Kiss it."

He had ordered her to kiss his cock before, and she'd turned away, gagging. She'd told him she'd never gone down on a man. Now she bent over him eagerly and took him deep into her mouth. He was the first. She was his.

He could trust her completely now. She would not jar his arm or humiliate him or leave him behind. She mounted him and slid herself so gently onto him. He could feel that she was like oiled silk, so moist and cool where he burned. She moved herself back and forth over him, and he possessed her, this butterfly caught on his shaft.

He left the pain behind, or perhaps it vanished inside her. He rose to meet her climax and clutched at her shoulders with both of his hands, pressing her down against him so that her breasts and belly flattened on his chest.

He came in a shattering spasm that submerged everything else, and he did not feel the bursting in his hand, the stretched skin opening over its thinnest points. Neither of them felt the viscous stuff that poured out.

A long time later, they looked at his hand and saw that it had spilled its poison, leaving a pale torn glove of a hand, but no longer deadly. She brought water and washed herself and then him. She watched over him while he slept the morning away, his face serene.

She heard nothing, not the slightest fragmented sound in the thin air washing down from the other side of the peak. She heard no one call her name.

CHAPTER TWENTY

The head ranger, his brother who ran the lodge, and both their wives sat with Sam in the restaurant section of the bigger building at a table next to the window, their coffee cups on the red checked oilcloth sending plumes of steam onto the glass and obscuring the view of the dock beyond. One of the women was cooking behind the counter, cooking for him because he needed to eat, although he wondered if he could. They were all nice people, really nice people, quiet now in shock and sympathy for him, but Sam found it impossible to speak more than an occasional word now and then, and they were silent too. Waiting. Waiting for the Explorer Scouts and the Chelan County Sheriff's deputies, and Ernie Gibson, who was flying dogs in as soon as he could locate containers. Hopefully, too, a helicopter from Chelan County. All of them summoned via solar-powered radio to deal with disaster in paradise. From time to time, the door opened and someone stepped in and whispered to the ranger or his brother, the college kids in their last week of temporary forest service, or one of the pretty girls who cleaned the cabins.

Sam sensed they found him inappropriately cold and contained in the face of the loss of his best friend. He had barked out his orders of who to send for, what he wanted done, and when—"immediately." He had accepted coffee, a shower, a change of clothing from the tall, lanky college boy from Indiana, and a shot of whiskey from the ranger's brother but he discouraged any sympathy or small talk. His face and neck ached from the strain of remaining expressionless.

He reached for a cigarette and found the pack empty already. Before he could move to the counter to buy another, the ranger's wife placed a pack in front of him.

"Thanks." He looked at the blank window and rubbed at it with his hand, exposing a circle of view. The boardwalks were empty of people, the lake and the mountains beyond all the same metal gray, the show for the tourists over and the serious business of winter begun. Sam tried to remember the heat in Natchitat only—when? Yesterday. The day before maybe. He hated it, but now he wished it existed here; it would help to keep Joanne alive until they found her.

He spoke to no one in particular. "Saw a rattler yesterday."

"That so." The ranger looked up, obviously eager to encourage any thread of conversation to lift the pall. "Big one?"

"Maybe four, five feet. Maybe he just seemed that big."

"Pacific rattlers don't usually run much over three feet. It takes them a while to coil. They can't jump and they strike less than their own length."

"The guy seemed amiable enough."

The ranger chuckled, a strange sound in their long quiet wait. "I wouldn't call any snake amiable. Probably getting too cold for him to feel frisky. I still wouldn't try to shake hands with one."

"The bear—" Sam said it aloud for the first time in an hour. He plunged on. "You think it could have been a grizzly?"

"I won't say absolutely that it couldn't be—but, like I said, the last verified sighting around here was in 1965. It's not like Glacier Park. Grizzlies were wiped out here a long time ago. It's possible that one could have come down from Canada, but I can't figure it, nobody catching even a peek of one all summer. We had thousands of hikers this year."

"They didn't see any bears?"

"Sure, some black bear in the upper valley. The usual stuff—trying to make off with food, pestering. One sighting of a she-bear and her cub up by High Bridge at Coon Lake in July. Woman tripped over the cub and the she-bear reared up and growled, but she didn't attack; she let the hiker take off and she skedaddled up the trail. You just about have to corner them before they'll attack."

"It had to have been something huge. He didn't shoot. His wounds were . . . terrible."

"It was pretty dark last night. You might not have seen everything clearly."

"No, I saw."

The ranger reddened and looked away. "You'd know best."

For the first time, Sam could identify with the "220s" he'd hauled in to Harborview Hospital in Seattle to be locked away on the fifth floor. The woman who lived in her car with twelve cats, the old men who refused to be moved from condemned buildings, the black girl who screamed obscenities on the corner of Third and James, and Herbert Pyms and his daughter, Violet, who crashed every society party in Seattle in their matching outfits Violet sewed of funeral ribbons and T-shirts. In their world, in their minds, they made perfect sense. Well, he had seen what he had seen, and it didn't compute with what was supposed to be. He was going to raise hell until he found out what was wrong.

He thought of Joanne's little hands and the way she hunched her shoulders when she felt threatened, remembered her kitchen and the jars of jam waiting for her to put away, and felt a stab of pain behind his eyes.

"How the hell long does it take them to get up here?" he demanded.

The ranger looked at his watch. "An hour and a half. They'll be rounding that last bend in the lake any minute. The kids here have got a crew started up already, and Ernie's bringing in two bloodhounds."

"I want the helicopter. I want to bring her down right away and get her to Wenatchee to the hospital."

The ranger looked down.

"What's the matter?"

"Deputy—Sam—you've got to be prepared that . . . she might have . . ."

"What?"

"If we've got a renegade bear up there . . ."

"You do! Dammit. I told you it killed my partner."

"She might be gone, too, Sam. She may be dead."

"No. I'm going to bring her down."

"You're exhausted. Let the search party go up."

"I'm going with them."

"O.K. But eat that. It's going to be a long night."

He looked at the plate before him. Steak and eggs and hashbrowns, the meat rare and bleeding into yellow yolk. His stomach balked, but he dug into it, wanting to ask for beer instead. They wouldn't let him pay for the meal.

The food hit the bottom of his stomach and bounced, but it stayed down. He didn't feel exhausted; he felt steely anger and frustration at the wait for the Chelan County deputies who seemed to be taking their sweet time responding. By noon he had made up his mind to head up alone when he heard the distant buzz of a motor, growing louder until the launch appeared. Just behind it, Ernie Gibson's DeHaviland dropped gracefully from the leaden sky and touched down.

The deputies were young, kids in their twenties. He had grown impatient with young men. They either knew nothing and pretended to know something, or they knew unnecessary things and flaunted their superfluous knowledge. They moved too slowly now and point-lessly, tying their cruiser up with agonizing care. They listened to the ranger explain something out of Sam's hearing, nodded, looked back at him, nodded again. He watched them from the dock as they shrugged on coveralls.

The tall kid walked towards him first, empty handed, and Sam frowned. "Where's your gear?"

"Sir?"

"Not sir—Sam Clinton, deputy from Natchitat. You'll need your death kit.

"Ranger said it was a bear attack."

"That's hearsay. *I* said it. You assume that everything you hear is true? How many deaths have you investigated? You always just write down what somebody tells you?"

The kid turned on his heel and walked back to his boat. Sam could see him whisper to the other deputy, a stocky man not more than a year or two older. They rolled their eyes and laughed, quickly turning away from him. The stocky man reached into the launch and brought out a small attache case. Sam relaxed for the moment, still doubting that they had any idea at all what they were doing. When they walked back toward him, their faces were bland and watchful.

The older man stuck out his hand. "Dean McKay. Sergeant out of Chelan. Pleased to meet you, sir."

Sergeant? He wasn't thirty yet. Sam shook his hand and felt no confidence. "Clinton."

"This is Rusty Blais. You goin' up with us?"

"Let's go."

Yesterday's empty trail was crowded now, full of men and dogs, all of them more fleet of foot and gifted with stamina that left Sam and the ranger far behind. The older men climbed with stoicism, stopping by tacit agreement when their lungs were pumped out. They could hear shouts and bursts of laughter far ahead of them, but they seldom caught a glimpse of the young, disappearing backs.

At the last meadow, the ranger stopped and sat down, panting. "Wait up, Clinton. We made it. Sit for a minute."

Begrudging the delay, Sam rested.

"Don't mind when they laugh. They mean no disrespect."

"Hell, I know that. I've done it. The M.E.'s deputies dropped a corpse once—over in Seattle. Didn't belt it tight enough and it kind of bounced down the steps. Thank God, the widow was over at the neighbors and didn't see it, because it struck us funny—weird funny. My partner started to laugh, and then I did, and then the M.E.'s guys caught it and there we were, four grown men, giggling like maniacs while the deceased sits on the bottom step looking confused. You can't cry over every stranger's tragedy or you crack up—but—"

"I know. When it's one of your own people—You gonna be O.K.?"

"Hell. I don't know. Maybe not. I loved that man."

"He was a nice guy. Her too. She was—she seemed like a nice person."

"She *is* a nice person. Scared of the dark though." He stood up. "I've got to go. We have to find her before the sun goes down again."

"They're looking now. It's a good crew. They grid search, using the dogs. Ernie's up there flying over. If she's in there, we'll find her. What color were their backpacks? I can't remember."

"Khaki, damn it. 'Chubby and Tubby'—surplus specials. His is still up by the lake. I guess I told you that. Of course, she's in there. Where else could she be?"

The ranger shook his head and then drew his breath in sharply as he caught a whiff of death. The two men were silent as they left the trail and slid down to where Blais and McKay stood, nostrils pinched, lips tight together.

"What do you think?" Sam asked, not caring what they thought.

"Seems like a bear."

"*Seems* like? He's a brother. You owe him the full treatment." They weren't going to like him. He didn't care about that either. "Give me some of your baggies. You have baggies, haven't you?"

"Yessir." They handed him several and stood back, watching him suspiciously.

He worked alone, dismissing them, barely aware of their presence. He filled the plastic envelopes with blood stained leaves, dirt, a broken button, and labeled each with a grease pencil, marking his initials and the date. He had trouble for a moment remembering the date. September 11. Friday. One week since he had seen Danny and Joanne alive and smiling and happy and—

He thought he smelled cigar smoke, and turned his head, half-expecting to see Danny sitting up, alive, the joke on Sam. McKay, the sergeant, sat on a log twenty feet away, puffing on the brown stub. Blais teetered back and forth on his heels, hands in his back pocket. Even as he hated them, he was aware that they had done nothing really to pull his rage; they were guilty only of easy assumption. If they weren't cops, it could be forgiven.

He could not forgive them. Respect must be paid.

He lifted one of Danny's softened hands and slipped a baggy over it, held his own hand out like a surgeons's and was only slightly gratified to feel McKay slip a wide rubber band into it. He secured the plastic covering and repeated the process with Danny's other hand.

McKay hunkered next to him. "Fingernail scrapings? You think there might be any?"

"I don't know. I want to know why he didn't fire his gun. I want to know why he didn't fight back."

"He didn't fire?" McKay whistled in amazement. "Shit, I would have emptied it into that mother."

"The gun's there. *Don't touch it!* Cylinder's full, chamber too."

"Maybe she jumped him from behind?"

"Not him."

He finished his work. He longed to be done with this ruined Danny who was no part of the real Danny. He would not be until after the post mortem was accomplished. And he could not now conceive how he would manage that process. He turned to McKay. "Who'll be doing the post?"

McKay looked surprised again. "The post?"

Sam spoke evenly. "The autopsy. You do autopsies up here in the toolies, don't you?"

"Hey, man . . ." McKay reddened with irritation, but checked himself.

"Who'll be doing it?"

"If they have one, it will probably be Doc Hastings. Albro's on vacation."

"You have a suspicious death here, deputy. You don't really know what happened, and neither do I. You have sucking chest wounds; you have deep facial lacerations; you have an unfired weapon, and you fucking well better be scheduling an autopsy."

"It's not up to me."

"That's a relief."

Blais muttered something, and Sam heard a faint "asshole."

"You got something to say, kid?"

"No sir."

"Then shut your fucking mouth." He turned away, and crawled up the bank, carrying his baggies full of evidence with him. He had no time for inept idiots.

Sam clung to his anger, warming himself with it; it was vital that he keep it aglow. Without it, the icy core inside him would expand and immobilize him. It was no longer necessary that anybody like him or find him a good old boy.

The helicopter settled over the meadow, its backwash flooding the long grass with air. Blais and McKay emerged from the brush with the same apparently deliberate lanquor and strolled toward the craft. Sam watched them silently and wondered why the whole world seemed to move in slow motion, heedless of the lowering sun and the terrible necessity for action. By conscious force of will he kept himself from directing the removal of Danny's body. He had worked Danny's death scene and worked it as meticulously as any he had encountered. They wouldn't be able to goof it up now—unless they dumped the bird in Lake Chelan.

Blais and McKay disappeared into the woods with the rubberized body bag and struggled up finally, carrying Danny's shrouded body. He watched them strap the bag onto the helicopter and wave it away as the plane rose up and disappeared into the clouds. He felt his throat close up on him and walked quickly away toward the deserted camp. When they followed him, they saw him scrape the vomit beneath the tree into a baggie and nodded at each other.

The old cop *was* crazy and best left alone.

CHAPTER TWENTY-ONE

Sam did not pretend to be a woodsman; all his searching skill had been honed in cities. Spin him around three times in Seattle and send him into an alley full of human rejects, and he could find his man nine times out of ten. He knew the wilderness of the city, all the dark, inaccessible places that gave shelter to derelicts and innocents and predators. But he was no use at all up on this mountain and he knew it. If he plunged into the brush beyond the green lake to call Joanne out, he too would be lost.

He waited alone near the fire, ignored by the occasional pair of searchers who broke off from the pack to warm themselves by the flames he kept replenished. He caught something in their manner, something he recognized. Like the deputies, none of them moved with the purpose or energy that suggested urgency. They did not expect to find her—or, they assumed, if they found her, she would be dead too.

He moved into the brush to take a leak, and heard voices carrying clearly through the chill air.

"Whatta you think?"

He stood and slowly buttoned his fly, listening.

"Negative."

"How long did they say the man's been dead?"

"Five . . . six days."

"Then I don't know what the hell we're breaking our butts for; them dogs are just circling around like turkeys. Can't find their own ass-holes."

"You think the bear got her too?"

"No. I think a bunny rabbit ate her. The guy was armed and look what happened to him. *Shit.*"

"I never heard of a bear actually attacking anyone up here."

"Happens every twenty years or so, and then people forget about it. They get to thinking they're just big teddy bears and they go and try to feed them. Tourists. You can have 'em."

Sam froze, breathing shallowly, feeling rage fill his chest again. The older man was enjoying himself, playing big-shot for the young guy.

"They messed with a she-bear. Grizzly maybe. The only choice you got when you meet you a grizzly is to lie down and play dead. If you're lucky, they'll only chaw on you a little. We ain't never gonna find nothing of that woman but some left-over pieces. That sow's probably dragged her off somewheres to eat off her slow . . ."

Sam's figure rose out of the brush and loomed over them, his face a contorted mask in the firelight. The bloodhounds leapt at him, snarling, and then reached the end of their leashes and gagged.

The dog men stared at him open-mouthed. The dogs howled, their hoarse baying bringing more men into the firelight, all of them watching Sam cautiously.

"If that was your wife out there, you wouldn't be so quick to find her a pile of bloody lumps," his voice shook.

The dog man studied him, realized who he was, and sat back, stroking his hound self-consciously. "Didn't see you out there."

"I guess not."

"Hey—I'm sorry. We get to talking rough sometimes. Don't mean nothing."

Sam's shoulders sagged and he felt weak as the adrenalin dissipated. He moved to his watching place by the fire, chilled from even the short foray into the brush. "Nothing?" he asked.

"She might be up a tree out there," the younger man said quickly, glancing back at his partner. "It's easier for our dogs at night. Be better now. The skin 'rafts'—sweat and bacteria—come up with night moisture. Bloodhounds' old ears just sweep smells up like brooms—right into their snouts. Dogs are amazing. We'll find her."

The old guy held out a flask. "Have a hummer?"

The liquor went down with a jolt and sang in him. He took a second hit and then a third before he handed it back. He wanted to believe the young man, but the conversation overheard smacked more of truth.

"What's the longest you ever looked for somebody up here—and found them—O.K.?"

Lies came, and he swallowed them whole because he needed them.

"Oh, lessee. Three weeks, probably. Two—three weeks. People can be resourceful when they get pushed to it." He turned to the young man. "Remember that guy from Wenatchee back in '72—'73? Must have been missing that long. Right?"

"Right. Yeah, at least that. Kind of skinny when we come on him—but O.K." He lied glibly. Not mean men, either of them.

Sam slept again, his second night huddled against the logs that defined Danny's and Joanne's last camp. He heard only faintly the shouts in the woods and the heavy feet of men who filled the circle of bodies around the fire. The dogs snuffled and groaned in the night, twisting and turning on their leashes, and the searchers talked in voices so deep that their words were only rumbles. He dreamed of her, that she had come back through the trees alone and stood outside the cluster of sleeping men crying to be let in to the warmth. When he held out his hand and reached for her, she disappeared.

It snowed in the night, dainty flakes at first, and then fat snow that dropped on his cheek and melted there. His hip pressed against the ground and ached, but he slept on, unaware of the white mantle that covered all of them. When he woke finally, he found them up before him and he felt guilty that he could have given in to the warmth of the sleeping bag so easily, when she still waited somewhere alone for help to come for her.

It was barely seven and daylight only beginning to wash over the shallow snow pack. He felt stronger, less likely to go off half-cocked at the men around him. They were doing their jobs, unfettered by personal involvement—just as he always had.

He forced himself to make small talk with the searchers as they sipped coffee. He could not hurry them.

"Don't let the snow scare you." The ranger was talking to him.

"It looks bad to me. Will it just keep on piling on now until spring?"

"Naw. It's only fake winter. We always have snow above 4,000 feet the first week or so of September. I guess the mountain wants to warn us of what's coming. It'll melt off in a day or two and then we'll get three, maybe four weeks of Indian Summer. The snow might make it easier—give us tracks to follow."

But what if the tracks were only their own? Sam didn't press him.

"Did anybody find anything last night?" He knew no one had, or the ranger would have mentioned it.

"No—but they got started late. None of her gear's turned up—and that's good, I think. She did have a pack *and* a sleeping bag? You're sure?"

"Positive. I saw them packing up their truck."

"Good. That's a good sign."

How many times had he placated families with such empty words? He was tainted by his own experience, and he had no guile to fool himself.

But she lived. Just as he had known that Danny no longer lived—long before that awful instant of discovery—he knew that Joanne was alive.

There was something about the tree. When they left him alone again, he walked around and around it, studying the broken limbs, the bare spots where pine needles had been skinned off. The scuff along the trunk had come from something wide and flat—a human shoe, not claws. Someone had climbed, fifteen to twenty feet high, and clung there.

And then come down. Not fallen down. Sidled down with handholds of needles, sliding feet cracking branches, sliding further.

He found a place to start and climbed upward through the trunks and limbs slippery with wet snow. He had not climbed a tree in forty years, but he inched higher until he found a place where the marks on the pine stopped. He looked down and saw the spot where he'd retrieved the vomitus, a straight line below. He knew that it had been Joanne who had hidden here, terrorized into nausea.

It was an old technique. You put yourself in the victim's place and tried to see. He'd never gone as far as the dick in Seattle who talked to corpses in a conversational tone all the while he did a crime scene —but it was a way of going to the source. She had stood here. What was happening when she did?

He turned his head to look downtrail to where Danny had been, everything blanketed with white now. But the spot was hidden by a jutting back of the path. She might have heard the struggle, but she could not have seen it.

He turned too quickly the other way and felt a stinging scratch against his neck. A sharp little nubbin of forked wood and, in it— *caught in it,*—two long strands of fine dark hair. It was hers; he knew he could put it under a scanning electron microscope and isolate it almost absolutely as hers. The top of her head would have extended to the twig that scratched him. Her head came exactly to the point of his shoulder.

He leaned back against the thicker spur of the bisected "school marm" tree and tried to think. The branches directly in front of him blurred as he focused beyond them into the woods, catching a glimpse now and then of the searchers moving arms' length apart, their feet shuffling for something that might lie beneath the snow.

He blinked and his focus changed to close up. And he saw it. Green and black, so close to the tree's color that it was almost lost in protective coloration. An impaled triangle of fabric, checked, its threads drifting lazily in the wind.

He reached for it, mesmerized. He had never seen it before. That was the important thing. *He had never seen it before.* He had never seen the garment it had come from. Danny would not wear green; he found it unlucky. And it was a man's fabric, nothing that Joanne would have worn.

She had not been in this tree alone.

The baggies were below on the ground, stashed in his gear. He braced his back against the trunk so that both his hands were freed, and slid his pack of Marlboros loose from his inside pocket. He slipped the green plaid between the cellophane and paper pack on one side, and the strands of her hair on the other, and climbed down.

She wasn't here any longer, nowhere within the range of the men who searched, but if he told them that, they wouldn't believe him. He was not sure himself how he knew, so how could he convince them with a few strands of hair and a bit of rag?

Danny knew the answer. Somewhere in his disintegrating flesh lay the key to the puzzle.

Sam did not want to leave the mountain, but he could not stay. Danny lay waiting for him. He had no use here; he was the only observer who would know what to look for when they cut into Danny, and how to sort out the false truths.

Sam went down with the ranger in the helicopter, and the snow beneath them disappeared as they left the high elevations, making the winter wilderness scene seem something he had only imagined.

While he waited for Ernie to pick him up in the seaplane, Sam paced the Forest Service office.

"You talked to them the day they hiked in?" he asked the ranger, although he suspected he had asked it before.

"Not that morning. The day before when they got off the boat."

"You talk to anyone else that day?"

"A lot of people. Let's see—that was the fourth. Right?"

"Yeah—the Friday before the Labor Day weekend. How many people hiked in that day? No, let's look at the whole week before and through the weekend."

The ranger slid the ledger across the counter and Sam studied it, pages of unfamiliar names scrawled in a variety of handwriting, some of it almost illegible. The routes varied: Purple Creek Trail, Boulder

Creek, War Creek, Rainbow Creek *via* Mc Alester, Rainbow Lake, and next to all but a very few of them, the check mark to show that the hiking parties had returned and signed in.

"What if somebody just took off and didn't sign in?"

"That happens. We don't like that because if somebody got into trouble, they'd be out of luck."

"But it happens?"

"I'm sure it does. We can't stand by the trailheads and stamp their hands."

"Can I have a sheet of paper?"

The ranger handed him a tablet, and looked at him sharply. "What are you looking for?"

"I don't know." He ran his finger down the pages and copied the names with no check beside them. "Vincent party?"

"Oh—them. Let's see. Went up Boulder, transversed south and came back down Purple—over here. They come up once a month maybe."

"O.K. Dr. Bonathan and son? No check here."

"I know them too. They came back in Sunday night. Had dinner in the Lodge. Forgot to check in."

"Steven Curry?"

"He was going over to pick up the Pacific Trail. Young fellow, hippie type, looked like he could do it easily. Working his way up from California to Canada."

"What did he look like?"

"Little guy. Blond beard. Stocky. Smelled like a horse barn."

"David Dwain?"

"I don't know. What does it say?"

"Rainbow Lake. Did you sign him in?"

"Lemme see. No, that's Ralph Boston's writing. One of the summer hires."

"Can I talk to him?"

"He left Wednesday to go back east to start school."

"You never saw Dwain?"

"Nope. What are you thinking about?"

Sam equivocated. "He went up there Friday night. My friends went up on Saturday. He might have seen them—might know something."

"He probably went on over Bridge Creek and into Twisp before they got there. You have a party leaving here even a half hour ahead of another party and they never see each other."

"I suppose so." Sam folded the sheet from the tablet and slipped it into his jacket pocket. "I'm going down to Wenatchee. Will you let me know the minute they find her? If you hear anything from Curry or Dwain or—anything—would you give a holler down to the sheriff's office in Wenatchee? I don't know where I'll be staying but I'll leave word there. You've got radio contact with them?"

"Yes." The ranger paused. "Is there anyone else I should notify? Any family of—of the Lindstroms?"

Shit. He'd forgotten Elizabeth Crowder. Waiting by her phone in Natchitat, pacing and calling and calling and calling for three days. He hadn't thought of her. He hadn't even thought of calling the office.

"He's got nobody. She's got a mother. I'll call her from Wenatchee."

CHAPTER TWENTY-TWO

Joanne heard the thick lub-lub-lub of the helicopter's rotor blades long before Duane did. Submerged in his dense, healing sleep, he had seemed to drift in and out of awareness for most of the day, and she had watched over him. She was concerned that he might chill again; he slept so deeply, scarcely moving. She covered him with her own sleeping bag and fashioned a kind of windbreak of their packs between the boulders that already sheltered him. She was awkward with fires, not able to bring back the coals that had guttered and died during the long, long time they had made love, but it wouldn't matter until dusk. The sun was a steady heat in the pewter sky.

She could not get enough of touching him, and she found reasons to place her hands on him; she stroked his forehead free of wrinkles, and held his uninjured hand, her own so small by comparison, so pale against his calloused brown palm. She was quite content to stay quietly beside him oblivious of the passage of hours, although she longed to have him waken again and respond to her. The time between dawn and full morning had seemed only minutes as they rolled and heaved together, moving without any definite stopping place from the first climax to the second and, for her, a third. She was tender inside from his thrusting, but hardly satiated. Her desire had seemed to grow with each consummation of the act, and she would have kept him inside her all of the day and into the night if she could have.

She had walked along the narrowed precipice over death, felt it actually crumbling beneath her feet, and he had pulled her back. And now she had saved him, and she would keep him safe. She could not imagine that she had doubted him. He had almost died for her. *He had almost died for her.*

She rubbed his chest gently, but he didn't wake. She rolled on her side and moved her thigh until it covered his. He smiled in his sleep and she traced his mouth with her finger. She couldn't tell if he was awake or gone someplace away from her; she was jealous, even of his sleeping, and lonely. She touched him and felt his penis flaccid and defenseless, a soft tube of flesh in her curled hand. She wanted him again. She stroked him, kneaded him, and felt him swell in her hand. He groaned, but his eyes were still shut away from her.

The sound of the helicopter brought her back to the present. She listened with stopped breath until she recognized what the noise was. He had never told her exactly what it was that threatened their existence. But there was something. Some reason that he'd trained her to crawl on her belly through the weeds, something that demanded their stealth and cunning. Something evil intent on destroying them. He'd promised he would teach her how to shoot the guns. That would make her feel safer, and it proved that he had forgiven her and that he trusted her.

She thought that she didn't deserve to be trusted, but it was only a feeling. Because she could not remember what she could not remember (and on and on into the black vortex), she had to move very carefully around the edges of it and ask no questions. He would insulate her from any memory that might torment her. He always had, but sometimes—and so queerly too—when she was the happiest, the most greedy in tasting of him, she was afraid and had to pull away from him until her terror eased.

There were several things that she could be totally sure of now. No one else had ever loved her this much. No one else would ever love her this much. He would never leave her. He had told her those truths over and over and over until his words made a little rhyming hum, and she could hear melody behind them.

And whenever she grew frightened, he told her again.

She could not, of course, allow any harm to come to him.

She lay beside him and heard the enemy in the sky looking for them. She put her hand over his mouth so that he could not cry out and give them away before he was fully awake, and then she placed her lips against his ear.

"Wake up."

His eyes snapped open and she felt his lungs expand and hold open against her breast.

"What is it?" His words were so muted that she read his lips more than heard.

"Something. A helicopter, I think. Listen."

"Did you see it?"

No. The clouds came over just before I heard it. I think it's back on the other side—where we were—before."

"We'll have to leave. We've stayed too long here."

"Yes."

"We'll have to be in the forest again when it's dark; we can't wait until tomorrow. Are you afraid?"

She kept her mouth against his ear. "I am never afraid with you. Are *you* O.K.? Do you feel strong enough to hike out now?"

He lifted her on top of him effortlessly, and she felt him still erect against her as he kissed her mouth. He *was* strong again, reassuring her with his penis and his hands and his mouth of his capacity to survive all things. They made love in the shadows of the rocks and clouds, their coverings blended into the landscape, the dead fire incapable of signaling their location to the intruders who walked the forest on the other side of the pass.

When they had finished and lay, still joined, they heard the craft again, its rotors roaring through the thin air miles away. They could not see it lifting off into the clouds, but they knew it would come again. He explained the new heaviness in the sky meant the clouds were full of snow. They had no choice but to head down away from the threats behind and above them.

Within fifteen minutes they had packed everything, and their meadow was as it had been before, save for the ashes of their fire which could have been left behind by any camper.

"Where will we go?" She looked so small under her burden of gear.

"Does it matter?"

"No, not really. We're together."

"We'll stay together. We have always been together, and we will always be together. Do you realize that?"

"Yes—but I—get afraid—not for myself—but for you. I get afraid that they'll try to separate us, that they might hurt you."

"Why should they hurt me?"

"I don't know. The—the people who are looking for you. You've never told me why they're following us. The games we play—wasn't that because someone's looking for us?"

"You don't have to worry about that. I will take care of you. All you have to do is obey me. If I tell you to do something, you will have to do it without question."

"Yes."

"Come here."

She walked over to him, and he took her hand. He slipped his cat's eye ring from his own finger and held it out to her. She saw there was a wedding ring still on her left hand and was surprised. She twisted it off so that her finger would be ready for his ring. His eyes reflected the bleeding sun on the horizon.

"With this ring, I thee wed. I did not exist before you and you did not exist before me. Separated, we no longer live. Do you believe that?"

"I believe that."

"If I die, you will no longer exist. If you should die, I would not exist. We are entwined, flesh together, blood together, bone together, throughout eternity."

"Together."

"I would kill for you. And you would kill for me."

She shivered.

"You would kill for me."

". . . and I would kill for you."

"And if we should die together, here on this mountain, we would be glad."

She bent her head against his chest, and he could see the slenderness of her neck, tender and fair where her hair fell away. "We would be very glad."

"Very, very glad."

She looked up at him, and he saw himself in her pupils. He regretted that they had to leave.

"I want to say a few words for him," he said finally.

"For who?"

"For Danny."

"Oh." She looked away, back toward the mountain behind them, and he could sense that she seemed distracted. He spoke quickly. "Give me the ring—the one you took off."

She handed it to him absently and watched as he snapped three white daisies from the ground and slipped the wedding band over their stems. He lay the flowered ring on the large boulder and bent his head, his eyes open and watching her, "In memory of Daniel—was it Daniel or Danny?"

"Either. But he hated *Daniel.* Say *Danny.*"

"In memory of Danny Lindstrom. Ashes to ashes . . . dust to dust."

He could see that she no longer really remembered who Danny was.

The rock turned black as the sun sank lower and they shouldered their packs again and walked away into the forest. The trees closed in behind them as the trail fell away, down steeply. She kept her hand hooked into his belt, afraid of losing him.

CHAPTER TWENTY-THREE

"I know who you are. What puzzles the hell out of me is what you were doing messing around one of *my* scenes? You really threw your weight on my men. You're not going to sit on me, buster."

Captain Rex Moutscher glared at Sam, letting him stand at the counter like a citizen making a lost dog complaint, obviously unwelcome in the Chelan County Sheriff's Office.

"Can I come in?"

"You're asking permission now? That's a pleasant change. Clinton, the big shot. This is my county. This is my office. I don't care if you're governor of Washington. You don't fuck up my scenes. And you don't order my men around. If you've got any ideas about playing God, here, you can turn your ass around and find the door out."

"I lost my partner. I needed to know why."

Moutscher softened only slightly. "I'm aware of that. And I'm sorry. But that's no license for what you did—not in my book. What do you want here?"

Sam leaned his elbows on the counter, monumentally fatigued. "I've been up in the mountains for three days. I flew down in a little-bitty plane through a snow storm, and then I drove from Chelan here. And I'm out of cigarettes."

Moutscher held out a pack and Sam took one, waiting.

"That all you want? A smoke?"

"I came for the post. I want to attend the post."

"I haven't decided if we need one."

Sam fought to hold his tongue.

"Come on in." Moutscher held the pass-through door open. "Sit down there and keep your hands in your lap."

"I'm not here to grab your follow-ups and run."

"You bet your sweet ass you're not. You used to be with Seattle, didn't you?"

Sam sighed. "Seventeen years, until 1977."

"How come you vested with three years to go?"

"Personal reasons."

"I heard you blew it over there. I know a lot of those guys."

"What did they say?"

Moutscher looked away. "Said you hit the sauce."

"That was nice of them. You got on the phone right away, didn't you?"

"Look, Clinton. You were up there doing a very, very accurate impersonation of a 220. I expected you to show up here—why else do you think I'd be sitting here on Saturday night? I wanted to know what to expect."

"And here I am. Two heads. Breathing fire. Loony-Tunes."

Moutscher grunted. "Why do you want an autopsy?"

"I don't believe grizzly now. I don't believe any kind of bear. I don't believe any of it."

"You're fighting the obvious. Why?"

"I knew him. I knew how he reacted, and he reacted fast and he wouldn't go down without tearing up the landscape and himself. Not with her up there too."

"They find any sign of her?"

"They didn't call down here yet?"

Moutscher shook his head. "They won't find her alive. Face it."

"You're a real bleeding-heart, aren't you, Captain?"

"I'm a realist." Moutscher looked away from Sam and stared out over the trees that surrounded the old courthouse down toward the Wenatchee River. "You're wrong about no bear. The way Lindstrom looked—I saw him, and I don't agree with you. Have you ever seen somebody a bear was into?"

Sam shook his head slightly.

"Well, I have. And he looked familiar. I'll tell you what—I'll make you a deal so's we both come out of this with our feathers battened down. You turn over all that physical evidence you withheld from my team, and I'll have Doc Hastings meet us tomorrow morning at seven. You can have your post."

"I thought we might give Doc Reay a call in Seattle. I know him; he'd fly over. You've got a coroner system here. I want a medical examiner."

"Clinton, if you think the coast is the only part of the state of Washington able to handle for-en-sic sci-ence, why didn't you stay there? You see this file? You see here? We've had eight homicides this year. And we've had eight convictions. They match that over there? Not on their butts they can't. They're lucky if they do 75 percent. So don't you go sticking your nose up at us. I've been to Louisville. I've been to the FBI Academy in Quantico. And I've been around. Take it or leave it."

Sam knew better than to remind Moutscher that his 100 percent on eight had undoubtedly been Mama-Kills-Papa or Papa-Kills-Mama-and-Mama's-Lover homicides—messy to mop up, but easy to solve. The dicks on the coast had strangers killing strangers, nut cases killing strangers, druggies killing each other with no mourners, and murderers with a lot more room to hide. Given that, 75 percent was damn good. He looked at Moutscher and let the argument go.

"I'll take it."

"Where's my baggies full of stuff?"

"In my car."

"Then you go get them now—as security—and I'll call Hastings."

"Where's Albro?"

"In Dallas."

Moutscher had him by the short hairs, and Moutscher didn't like him. He had broken all the rules of getting along with a fellow officer, and Moutscher was never going to like him even if he reached across the desk and gave him a kiss and a hug. Fuck it.

He turned over the baggies, but he kept the long, dark hairs and the green plaid. They didn't know about that, and they weren't going to; they'd probably throw them away.

Sam left his truck where it was, lonely on the street behind the looming courthouse, and walked downhill to the Cascadian Hotel where he lost himself in the lounge full of Saturday night cowboys and their girls.

He sat at the bar and listened to the jukebox. He ordered Glenlivit and had downed three doubles before he realized someone was playing the same damn song over and over and over: "Woman" by John Lennon. After three hours of Lennon and drinking, listening to a dead man sing of improbable, impossible, true love, the bartender pulled the plug and the jukebox blinked off and died too. The woman at the jukebox turned to Sam and tried to focus on his face.

"Doesn't that just want to make you puke it's so sad?"

"Almost everything does, ma'am."

"You want to go upstairs with me?"

He considered it and remembered with a dull jolt where he would be in less than five hours. He lifted her hand, turned it over, and kissed her palm. "No thank you, Ma'am—I'm driving."

It seemed to make sense to her. She got up gravely and maneuvered her way to the exit, still wiping her eyes. The bartender washed her glass and winked at Sam. "Don't blame you. She's a pig."

"So am I."

"Have it your way, ace."

He remembered that he hadn't called Elizabeth Crowder or Fletch, or Fewell, or anyone. Maybe Moutscher had. There was no point in getting a room; he couldn't remember when he'd slept in a bed. He couldn't remember when he'd slept.

He threw twenty dollars on the bar and walked out into the cold air of Wenatchee. He slept in the back of his truck with Lennon's song going round in his head.

He woke with an unbelievable pain behind his eyes and a pounding in his ears. Moutscher was banging on his truck and Hastings was waiting for him.

Sam washed up in the lavatory on the first floor of the courthouse, the cavernous, high-ceilinged room unchanged since the building went up decades before, grandiose with marble floors and golden oak cubicles. He wondered idly where they'd gotten the money for such a fancy outhouse. The radiators buzzed on and filled the room with the smell of layers of baking paint, but there was no hot water and he sluiced his face with cold water in the vain hope he could wash away the scotch that still fogged his brain. Moutscher watched him silently, puffing on a pipe.

Sam turned with a grin that didn't work. "You got a breath mint?"

"Don't bother. You smell like a distillery. I smelled you when you crawled out of your truck, and Doc Hastings can't smell anything but formaldehyde. Fewell puts up with your kind of drinking?"

"I don't drink with Walker; I don't socialize with Walker, and Walker has no jurisdiction over what I do off-duty."

Moutscher said nothing; maybe he knew Walker Fewell.

Sam stared into the mirror and had difficulty recognizing the image he hadn't seen in five days. An old man looked back at him, the pouches around his eyes creased with dark new gouges, the eyes themselves sunk in their sockets and branched with red. He had needed a shave for days, and his beard was gray. He had never seen it gray before. He brushed his sandy hair back with his hands in lieu of a comb. No wonder Moutscher thought he was a derelict. He was a derelict.

But Hastings, as it turned out, was older. "This is Dr. Wilfred Hastings. Sam Clinton, Doctor."

Sam took the pathologist's veined hand and felt the bones beneath the thin skin, the tremor there. Hastings looked at him from behind trifocals, his pale blue eyes huge and vague. Sam guessed seventy-five —no, eighty-five.

"Doc Hastings was coroner here—when was it, Doc? 1945?"

"1936 to 1962."

God. It was a joke.

It wasn't a joke.

The room was too bright, the slick tiled walls reflecting the lights that dangled over the sheeted mound in the middle of the room. Sam inhaled formaldehyde and refrigerated death, and the floor slid downhill beneath his feet. He shut his eyes, aware that they were staring at him—the fat detective captain in his white socks and the old man. He concentrated then on the framed sign on the wall:

> All Who Lay Here Before You Were Once Loved;
> Respect and Dignity For the Dead
> Will Be Maintained At All Times.
> As He Is, You Will Be—As You Are, He Was.

And beneath the words in very small print, "Courtesy, East Wenatchee Sign Co." The thing was printed, apparently mass printed. How much call would there be for such homilies? Every home should have one?

A flash of light pierced the brightness, and Sam turned to see Moutscher winding the film sprocket of his Yashica. The first frame would show Danny's shrouded body, awaiting Dr. Hasting's ministrations.

The sheet was whipped off and it began.

As he is, you will be; as you are, he was. I hope the hell not, Sam thought, staring at the felt pen scrawl on Danny's thigh—the coroner's reference number.

Something on the body moved. Maggots, tumbling over themselves, gray-white and fat in the black chest wounds. Sam's hand darted out and closed around the container of ether. He sprayed the parasites and saw them stiffen and roll onto the table, dead. His gorge rose and he swallowed the acid that had been expensive scotch, turning his head toward Moutscher.

"The container. Give me the container."

"Let them be! Knock them on the floor!"

"I want the goddamned box."

Moutscher passed a thin plastic vial over, and Sam scraped a clot of maggots into it, capped it, labeled it, and finally was able to breathe.

"I want to know when he died. The flies come and they lay their dirty little eggs and they hatch and they crawl and they fly and they lay eggs and they never change their timetable. Those goddam grubs can tell us something."

Moutscher seemed about to argue, and then his face changed. Sam recognized the expression. *Don't argue with a maniac.*

"You ready to go ahead?" Hastings was ignoring Sam completely, looking to Moutscher for permission to cut. Moutscher took four angles in his lens, snapped, again, again, and then nodded.

"Wait," Sam blurted.

"Now what?"

"Could you cover his face?"

"Why don't you wait outside?"

"I have to be here. Could you cover his face?"

Moutscher turned to the old man. "Put a drape over his face." And to Sam. "It's not going to hurt him any more." Sam could not isolate the emphasis in the words. Sympathy? Empathy? Scorn? The words lay flat.

With Danny's blackened features hidden, it was not all right, but it was bearable. He concentrated on the old doctor's hand, saw it pick up the scalpel, saw the hand and cutting tool shake, and then plunge with remembered deftness across the chest, leaving the skin flayed open from armpit to armpit. Again, down the body from sternum to pubis, finishing the huge T.

Sam roared, and the old man jumped back with alarm.

"You cut through one of the fucking wounds! Can't you see what the hell you're doing?"

"Shut up!" Moutscher bellowed so loud that his words bounced off the tiled walls. "You say anything else and your ass is going to be out in the hall! Go ahead, Doc."

Apparently oblivious that he had just contaminated much of what he had to work with, Hastings bumbled ahead. Rib snips cut through the chest cage, and Sam heard the snap of bones giving. The ribs and flesh folded back like wings, and the soggy lungs and dull red heart came into view.

Sam could see the damage, a familiar destruction. There were two —perhaps three—penetrating wounds that had gone through the chest wall, through the third intercostal space, perforating the lingula of the upper lobe of the left lung, the pericardial sac, and on into the heart at the left ventricular wall. The wounds seemed directed left to right, front to back, and angulated slightly downward, administered certainly by someone taller than Danny—and Danny had stood six feet, two. The track was at least four inches deep, but the width of the weapon would be impossible to determine now, given the extent of decomposition. One thing was clear; it *had* been a weapon, a knife, a dagger even—but never a tooth. The wounds were separate things that he could concentrate on without personal involvement. Sam glanced at Hastings, who seemed confused.

"Bear, you say?" Hastings focused obtusely on Moutscher, who nodded.

"Looks like a bear, sure as hell."

Hastings nodded. Sam turned to Moutscher to protest, and then looked back into the open body cavity. Before he could prevent it, Hastings had lifted the heart out and was cutting throught he pericardial sac *into*—NO!—*into* the heart, exposing the valves with their leaflets. *The damn old fool had destroyed the tracks of two more wounds!*

"You didn't even put a probe in, you idiot! Will you open your eyes and look before you cut any more? You've just fucked up all three wounds."

Hastings looked to Moutscher for assistance, stricken.

"He knows what he's doing, Clinton. You open your mouth one more time and I personally will take you out."

"He *doesn't* know what he's doing."

"You going to shut up?"

It was too late to save it. He was dealing with incompetents; there was no way to put it back together. He felt vaguely sorry for the old man and knew that Hastings was too late aware of what he had done. He sighed and waved him on, this parody of a post mortem. "Go ahead."

The room was choked with death stink, clouds of it bursting from the decaying organs. He ignored them, his right hand skimming incessantly over his yellow pad, recording only his own observations, denying most of what Hastings perceived. Even as he wrote, he knew that his view had no credence, would never have credence—but it was all he had left.

He saw Hastings's hand emerge holding Danny's stomach, saw the scalpel flick it open. Hastings sniffed. The old man might have been good in his day; he seemed to slip in and out of proper procedure. Sharp now. Fading away again.

"Stomach contents." Hastings's voice was reedy, high as an adolescent boy's. "Undigested eggs, vegetable matter, probably potato. Animal protein, perhaps ham or bacon. Subject succumbed within fifteen minutes, half hour of eating."

Good, doctor. Really important. Now that you've obliterated the vital wounds. Sam wrote it down anyway.

One by one the organs that had kept Danny alive were lifted out: liver, lungs, heart, spleen, kidneys, bladder. Each was sliced and examined. All normal. *Danny, if you hadn't died, you would have lived to be one hundred.*

Sam could feel a presence in the room. The two of them were together, laughing at the travesty. He could almost feel Danny nudge him and say, "Pard, they don't know any better." He chuckled, and the other living men in the chamber looked up startled. Then they looked at each other and shrugged knowingly. He let it go.

Hastings piled the lacerated organs back in the body cavity willy-nilly. Later, somebody would stitch up the gaping T with thick black thread. No fine surgeon's hand needed now.

Sam felt as if he watched from a distance, curious. When he spoke, his voice echoed from the vantage point where he observed. Good. He was handling it.

Even when the drape was tugged off the corpse's face, it was still O.K. The face wasn't Danny's.

"Looks like bear all right," Hastings mouthed from a long way off. "See where the claws ripped down. Bear."

Moutscher's face nodded. It was hard to hear his voice; he shrunk in his distant perspective.

"It didn't bleed." Sam's own voice seemed too loud.

"Post mortem. She must have mauled at the body some. Won't bleed after you're dead."

Hastings's scalpel scored the skin at the back of the neck, and then he loosened the scalp from its moorings and peeled it back until the face was hidden again by the inverted scalp. The saw burred along the skull and the hot smell of burning bone rose into the air. Sam watched the skull cap lift off with wonderful detachment.

"You want a stool?" Moutscher's voice was almost too faint to understand.

Sam was not aware that he had answered, but felt the solidness of a wooden stool beneath him, and thought it remarkable that it was there just as his knees declined to bear his weight. There was a continuous buzzing in his head. He assumed Hastings was still sawing away at the skull, but when he looked, the freckled, blue-veined hands were empty.

"Brain's liquid," Hastings muttered.

"Let it go then." Moutscher's voice, coming back down the tunnel where it had been.

Sam meant to say no, but his own voice eluded him.

"You O.K.?"

"Who?"

The voice, much louder now. *"You O.K.? Clinton?"*

His head snapped up and the room spun.

"Get out of here for a while." Moutscher again.

He made the door, walking uphill along the floor that had suddenly tilted up at him, and he was grateful that the heavy metal door pushed outward. The air was better—not good air, but better, full of dust and floor wax and no death. The alley exit was a long way down, and his stomach betrayed him even as his head cleared. He vomited up the scotch, oblivious to the stares of a Sunday morning cleaning crew unloading their van. It came up for a long time, seeming to strip some of his stomach lining with it. But when he was done retching, he felt better. Not good. It was unlikely he would ever feel good again, but the red foam behind his eyes had dissipated and he could think.

Moutscher looked up, surprised, when Sam walked back into the tile room and reclaimed his perch on the stool.

"Everything fits, Clinton. The right humerus has got a spiral break, pulled completely out of the socket. It's a bear kind of injury. I'm satisfied."

"I'm not."

"Then it was a Sasquatch. You try to convince somebody of that. Our prosecutor will laugh you out of his office. You don't need that. You've had enough. Give it up. Go home. Let it go."

Danny's hands still rested in their plastic casings. Sam turned away from Moutscher and loosened the bindings from the left hand. Danny's wedding ring shone under the lights, its tracing of entwined hearts grotesque against the loosened flesh. Moutscher assumed it was the ring he wanted.

"Take it. You might as well take that and the watch while you're here."

"I want nail scrapings."

"Shit. Go ahead. Take it all. I'll give you your other stuff back too, but I can't see that any of it will be any use. I'm clearing it accidental."

Sam said nothing, bending to his work, sliding an orange stick beneath the long, ridged nails, loosened now on their beds. The other men watched him, looked at each other, and shook their heads.

It was over. When he walked away from Moutscher, he carried his gleanings from the mountainside, the envelopes and tubes and vials from the autopsy—all of it jammed into a cardboard box that said "Friskies" on the side. The sum total of what was left of four years with Danny. Danny wasn't the body that awaited delivery to the double rear doors of Phelps's Funeral Home in Natchitat. Danny was in the Friskies box.

Sam got a motel room, but only after producing every piece of identification he had; the clerk studied the neat cards with their official seals, looked at Sam suspiciously, and finally agreed to take his fifteen bucks.

The physical evidence that Moutscher had believed in so little that he had given it away was still cold, straight from the morgue's refrigeration. It was not as perishable as ice cream—but close, its useful life wholly dependent on time and temperature. Sam set the white box full of vials and bags in the square refrigerator that other motel guests utilized for beer and headed out to find a Fred Meyer store. He was startled to find that he had no more cash, but his MasterCharge bought him styrofoam pellets and cotton batting, brown paper, and strapping tape.

Back in his room he arranged his bits and pieces as tenderly as a mother sending cookies to her son in college, finally satisfied that nothing would break or roll or crush in the journey ahead.

He had, of course, no proper forms for lab requests, but he knew the language. The motel stationery featured the Holiday Inn logo, and he crossed it out, and printed, "Natchitat County Sheriff's Office" below it. Beneath that, his listed exhibits: twenty-seven samples; twenty-seven questions. Not professional in appearance, but correct. The answers would come back to him neatly typed on thin yellow and pink and green sheets. With great good luck, they might neutralize the damage done by Hastings and Moutscher. He figured he had four hours safe time before all of it disintegrated. Not a prayer of getting it to D.C. and the FBI Lab, or to Rockville, Maryland and the ATF Lab, but they were not his first choice anyway. They would leave his treasures to wait their turn. He wanted the Western Washington Crime Lab to ferret out what lay hidden among the white pellets.

He debated how to send it and settled for Greyhound. The dog-bus would get it to Seattle as quick as a plane would by the time you considered all the messing around at the airport.

He ducked into a phone booth at the bus station, took a deep breath, and hoped his voice was going to come out official and uncrazy. He dialed the Crime Lab, charged the call to Natchitat County, and asked for the director.

"The director doesn't come in on Sunday," a woman's voice replied.

Sunday. How the hell did it get to be Sunday?

"This is Detective Sam Clinton of Natchitat County. Our office is sending a package of evidence via Greyhound. It should arrive at the Eighth and Stewart Station in Seattle at—let's see—at 4:02 P.M. I'll need a police courier to pick it up. It's very important. Can you do that?"

"Well—" She sounded annoyed.

"Very important. Perishable material. Must be refrigerated by 5 P.M."

"All right. I'll send someone."

"Tell the director I'll phone him tomorrow morning."

"O.K."

"You've got that?"

The phone was dead. He had no more change, not even enough to dial the operator.

He thought of his motel room, and he thought of driving home and neither seemed possible. He thought of Moutscher home watching football on his television, drinking beer and surrounded by his family. He could not think of Joanne and the mountain and whoever had worn the plaid shirt. He understood now why street people crawled under their cardboard blankets and shut out the world. Without his magic plastic card, he would do the same. With it, he could walk into the Cascadian and find Nirvana in a glass.

He stared at the antique apple crate labels displayed behind the bar as he downed the first double and realized with dread that it had lost its power. It took three before he felt the warmth. After six doubles, he found the lounge as comforting and soft as a mother's breast. After eight, he didn't have to think about anything at all.

Sam dreamed of Moutscher's voice shouting in his ear. He smelled disinfectant and urine, and a harsh fabric scratched his face. Something tugged at his shoulder and shook him like a rag doll baby. He opened his eyes a slit and saw Moutscher's florid face bending over him and yelling so loud that spittle spattered on Sam's cheek. *Go away Moutscher.*

Moutscher would not go away, and Sam painfully separated his eye lids from one another and saw where he was. In jail. Not his own, but jail; it was unfamiliar-familiar. He looked beyond the Chelan County captain and saw that the yellow-painted metal squares in the door didn't match up, that the cell door wasn't closed.

"If you weren't a cop, you'd be in here for a month, you damned fool." Moutscher's words fell into place and made a sentence. "It's Monday morning; you've slept it off. We don't owe you anything else. Now get your ass off that bunk and take it home."

". . . It's Monday?"

"Eleven in the morning. You drank up the bar at the hotel, you tried to deck the bartender, and you vomited all over our patrol unit. Clinton, you are a fuck-up and I don't care to spend the whole day baby-sitting you."

"Go to hell."

"He hated Moutscher, and it felt amazingly good, this strong, cleansing rage. If Moutscher wasn't the enemy, he would do for the moment. Sam got up, folded the army-green blanket neatly, hitched up his pants and headed for the opening in the cell door. By the time he was in the corridor, he remembered where his truck was, waiting for him parked beneath the maple trees.

"I called Fewell and told him where you were. He wants to see you —pronto."

Moutscher had little tiny piggy eyes; Sam wondered that he hadn't noticed that before. And hairs growing out of his nostrils. And a gut that hung over his silver belt buckle.

Sam turned to leave, turned back, and severed all good will.

"And you sir, my good captain, have a brain as tiny as your pecker."

CHAPTER TWENTY-FOUR

It was dusk on their second Sunday together when Duane looked at the forest and then at the slope of the land and knew he had made a mistake. The route down below Bowan Mountain had appeared the easiest of all those he'd considered. If he had not been so sure of it, he would never have let them linger so long in the meadow. But he had been weak, and it had been too easy to feel secure knowing that they were only a few miles from the highway that could carry them swiftly to the Canadian border, to the beginning of their new life.

While his arm hampered him from other movement, he had worked over the Forest Service map for hours and found it rudimentary; the Pacific Crest Trail would lead them in two—or at the most, three—days to Slate Peak, and then into the Pasayten Wilderness where no motor-ized rig could venture. Their food would last a week or even two without supplement from his hunting and fishing. He could build them shelter before the heavy snows came.

He had planned to tell her where they were going when they actu-ally crossed over into the Pasayten, and he was annoyed that she broke his concentration with questions as he focused on leading them down the mountain. It was neither cold—they had left the thin snow layer behind them—nor was it dark; the moon had swollen now to three-quarters of its face. Once their eyes adjusted to the dim light, they could maneuver the trail. But what would have taken them four hours in daylight required double that at night. Even draining of its poison, his arm still ached and the aching distracted too. Her hand hooked in his belt did not seem enough to assure her that he would not leave her behind. She talked to him continually.

"Are you there?"

"You're touching me. You know I'm here."

"Talk to me."

"I'm trying to find the way."

"Then tell me what you're thinking. Think out loud so I can hear your voice."

"I can't think out loud."

"Then sing."

"If we sing, we can't hear . . . things."

That frightened her. "Then talk to me."

He made no reply.

They reached Bridge Creek at dawn, but he allowed them to rest for only a few minutes. They were an hour's walk from the highway, too exposed to other hikers. She started to protest when he ordered her to follow him again, but she obeyed.

An hour later, he missed the turn-off at Fireweed Camp. They had gone on for almost two hours before he felt the first niggling of doubt, so involved in hiding them that he had misjudged the simplest turn they came upon. When he put his finger on the pleated map, he saw the problem at once—but it was not easily corrected. He had gone east at Fireweed instead of obliquely north. If he backtracked, she would know that they were lost. It was a matter of pride and he continued, thinking that they could rest in the meadow he saw ahead and then go back on a circuitous route she would not detect.

One fly and then a dozen of them landed on his seeping hand and he batted them away, hurrying further along to a place where he could rethink their route.

He was very tired now, and the flies that buzzed and stung at him aggravated the pain in his arm until he found it almost to heavy to carry. When he held it over his chest, it threw his balance askew; when he let it hang down, the blood fell into it and pressed his nerves.

They climbed north along rock cairns to a ridge, and then the trail was clearer. There had been a look-out site, but he relaxed when he saw that it seemed long deserted—only weather-scored, broken timbers remained of whatever building men had tried to place here. No one had come here recently.

He led her along a scrabble trail that seemed to be easterly and was rewarded. A splendid, tiny plateau of meadow lay below and beyond that he could see a lake and a few narrow streams—A place meant for them, surrounded by flaming larches, protected by rocky peaks.

She was enthralled. He pretended that he had meant to bring her here all along. When he was really well, he would find their way into the Pasayten, but until then, he was quite content to stay where they were. He was sure that they had been led here by some design.

"Where are we?" She lay on her back in the grass and spread her arms, tumbling in the greenness of it. "It's wonderful. How did you find it?"

He looked at his map. "Stiletto Meadows. I chose it for you."

"I never want to leave. Can we stay here forever?"

"Forever," he lied.

CHAPTER TWENTY-FIVE

Sam let the dusty truck decide, allowed the steering wheel to whirl lightly in his open hands, and it headed for the barn: Natchitat. There was no reason to go back, but there was nowhere else to go. He was not welcome in Wenatchee. Alone, he was of no earthly use in Stehekin. He still coaxed the delusion that Danny and Joanne somehow lived in Natchitat, a crazy hope that he had endured a terrible alcoholic nightmare that would dissipate in daylight. It allowed him to maneuver his vehicle through the traffic on this bright blue and yellow Wenatchee noon, despite the steady thumping in his head. He would have preferred to simply cut and run to a place where memory could not follow him, but he'd already exercised that option when he bolted from Seattle. A man could do that only once in his lifetime. A second blind flight would stamp him a bum for whom there could be no redemption. He had no plan, but he trusted that one would take form as his head cleared because there was a powerful urgency in him. Wherever she was, Joanne waited for rescue.

He drove faster, although he had no good reason for going home. *Home.* Home meant dealing with Fewell, explaining what could not be explained to Elizabeth Crowder, and a starving cat. He passed his hand across his forehead and felt cold sweat.

The taverns beside the road, their windows shuttered but their blue neon "Open" signs beckoning, called to him seductively. He longed to let the truck turn in, to find shelter himself inside one of the bars where the air was icy and the sunshine was lost behind thick walls and translucent colored glass.

He could not run. He could not hide. He apparently was not going to die; his heart had got him up the mountain and down and up again, and he could not depend on a medium-grade hangover to kill him.

He crossed the Natchitat County line, still forty miles from town, the highway skirting the reservation, and rounded the long curve past the quarry. Two lean hogs dashed across the center line, stopped and gazed placidly at his approaching truck. He hit the brake and slid onto the shoulder, swearing.

He had seen the sign a thousand times: Max Ling's faded totem pole beside a tree studded with advertisements for himself. It drove Walker Fewell into quiet rage because he had no dominion over Max's enterprises, protected as he was by treaties drawn in another era.

In descending order, the signs read:

Puppies: Bird dogs. Watch dogs. Pets.
Cigarettes: No tax—all brands.
Dahlias—Cut Flowers for Weddings, Funerals. Tubers.
Honey.
Used Cars: Classics
Antique Bottles
SEARCH

and a new sign, bigger than all the rest, its paint so fresh that it appeared still wet: DMSO HERE NOW!

Sam and Danny had been at Max's place a time or two, sent out by Fewell to confiscate cigarettes, and to sniff for untaxed liquor. They'd always had to return the cigarettes because Max had an attorney who knew tribal law and federal treaties a hell of a lot better than Walker Fewell did—and Sam had been delighted to bring back the evidence. He liked Ling, although he had always found it a little hard to believe in a blue-eyed Indian.

His eyes ran down the signs again, and stopped at "SEARCH," and he could hear Danny's voice laughing, "That little blue-eyed chief can track anything—if it interests him. Runs circles around dogs and white men and any goddamned scientific gear you can name."

At this moment Sam could not remember anything that Max had found, could not be sure that Danny hadn't been pulling his leg, teasing the old flatlander cop. One thing was clear; almost anybody could track better than Sam himself could.

He wheeled his rig through the opening in the poplar trees that cut Ling's operation off from the highway, into a jungle of Max's peculiar collectibles.

The field on the right side of the dirt lane was full of vehicles, heat devils shimmering from their baked metal. Packards, Terraplanes, an Edsel, a half dozen Hudson Hornets, and the overturned-bathtub Nashes of the early fifties. What Ling considered "classic" had always amused Sam. Max never seemed to sell any of the rusting hulks, only added to his graveyard of Detroit's embarrassments.

Dahlias dominated the left side of the property, in full bloom now, their red, yellow, white, maroon, and salmon flowers so brilliant that they hurt Sam's eyes. Between the dahlia patch and the three-storied, asbestos-shingled house, bees hovered and soared over their white hives, fifty, sixty of the square bee-homes, lined up with precision.

The dogs, the ugliest dogs Sam had ever seen—liver-colored dogs of no particular lineage—ran beside his truck and barked in hoarse whoops. There were a dozen of them. He could not imagine that anyone ever bought "Puppies," and assumed that Max must breed them only to add to the guard that protected his empire from unfriendly visitors. He braked the truck and they sat back on their haunches, waiting for him to make a move.

He waited for someone to emerge from the house, although it was impossible to tell if anyone was inside, the front of the residence was so camouflaged with trellises, awnings, honeysuckle, wisteria, and the odd piece of auto body left there when its intended purpose was forgotten. The dogs had always liked Danny—but Danny had liked and trusted dogs. Sam was a cat man and he wondered if they knew that. He hit the horn and listened; the house remained silent while the dogs smiled at him with their teeth bared and their tongues lolling. A bee flew in his side window and danced over his nose. Something was going to bite him or sting him no matter what he did.

He slid out of the cab and headed for the door that looked most likely of the four fronting on the long porch, the killer dogs jostling each other for a chance to lick his hand. They waited with him as he rang a bell that didn't ring and then knocked. When there was no response, he sheltered his eyes with his hand and peered through the screen. He could see a woman inside the living room, a space so aqua from its shades that it appeared to be under water. She sat with her back to him, watching a huge, tavern-sized television screen.

He knocked again and she didn't move. He pounded on the wall beside the door and she flinched, looked around, and strode like a graceful dancer towards him. She held open the screen door and smiled at him; he found her one of the most beautiful women he had ever seen in his life. An Indian, surely, but not a Northwest Indian, her features delicate and Caucasian, her skin the color of almonds. She was at least six feet tall, full breasts suspended in a white lace halter, long brown legs emerging from denim cut-offs. She turned away from him and looked back toward a darkened area beyond the living room and her straight black hair, which reached to the top of her thighs, brushed his hand. He felt the slightest surge of masculine appreciation for her excellence. A small thing but wondrous in its displacement of nothingness. He spoke to her as she was looking away from him.

"Max here?"

She didn't answer.

"I said, is Max at home?"

She turned back toward him and stared at his mouth, waiting. And then her hands moved across each other like brown birds. He saw instantly that she could not speak or hear.

He enunciated slowly and she read his lips, nodding and smiling. She moved her hands again, her fingers so rapid that they blurred.

He shook his head and touched her shoulder lightly, then pointed at his own lips, "I don't understand. I cannot speak the language."

She took his hand lightly and led him through the shadowed room. Ling's house was a series of additions, each one built either a little higher than the next, or sunken—so that no threshhold matched another. Sam stepped carefully, his pupils still contracted from his long drive in the sun. One room was lined with narrow shelves full of bottles —blue, aqua, amethyst, white—their glass flawed and thickened, lips applied awkwardly, bases marked with pottles where some glass blower had sealed off their melted substance before the century turned. All of them valuable now, when they had once been somebody's garbage.

The next room was clearly the woman's studio. Canvasses with paintings of wild flowers and studies of hands. Hands folded; hands held out in supplication; some graceful; some gnarled. Hands would be important to her. He touched her elbow and inclined his head toward the paintings and smiled. She nodded.

They moved into the last room, the kitchen. Max Ling, bare to the waist above painters' pants, siphoned clear liquid from a gallon container into what looked like mayonnaise jars. He recognized Sam and grimaced, but his hands were steady at his task. He spoke not to Sam, but to the woman—in her tongue—when he had finished pouring. His hands moved and she answered, their eyes catching one another's. Max pointed to Sam and said something in finger talk. Her face grew solemn and she looked at Sam, alarmed.

"Tell her I come in peace."

Max laughed. "You don't have to talk Indian. She can't hear you."

"I know. Tell her I'm not here officially."

Max put his arm on Sam's shoulder in a gesture of friendship and the tall woman relaxed. "Sam, this is Marcella, my wife. Marcella (he spoke directly to her and she studied his lips gravely) This is Sam Clinton, a good friend of mine. He says he didn't come from the Sheriff. Not today. It's O.K."

She smiled again, her face magical, forgiving him for whatever she had assumed, and walked away, leaving them alone.

"Damn it Sam. I've got a right to sell this stuff. They've been selling it for months down on the Nisqually Reservation. I just put that sign up yesterday. Your undersheriff must have smelled it."

The jars had plain black and white labels: "DMSO, Solvent" and Sam was confused; he had no idea what Max was talking about.

"You've lost me. What is it?"

"What *is* it? This is an elixir to cure all the ills of mankind. Bruises, cuts, sprains, arthritis, rheumatism, sore throat, burns—probably even herpes. Some M.D. down in Portland was on 'Sixty Minutes' talking about it, and he's got patients lined up all the way across the Columbia River Bridge, fighting to get some. And here it is, $11.95 a pint. Cheaper than aspirin."

"Solvent?"

"To appease the law, my friend. What my customers do with it is not my concern. They buy it as solvent. That's O.K. with me, and it should be enough to placate your Mr. Fewell. It comes from the trees, all those trees that belonged to my blood brothers and stolen by yours. A heretofore useless by-product. A natural remedy." Max looked sharply at Sam. "Which it would appear you are in need of. You look like something no tom cat would piss on."

"Thanks."

"Seriously. Let me give you a sample. You have any spots that hurt, any arthritis due to your advanced age and life of excess?"

"Pick a spot. Name it; it hurts."

"Lower back. Lower back is the first to go. Turn around and lift up your shirt."

"Come on, Max. I didn't come to arrest you or haul off your merchandise—or to see the medicine man."

"Lift your shirt."

Sam let Max daub some of the oily, clear liquid along his spine. It burned within seconds and he jumped away. He tasted garlic and oysters in his mouth and spat. "What the hell is that?"

"DMSO. Put that on three times a day and you'll walk again."

"God. But nobody is likely to kiss me. That's disgusting!"

"Taste it? That shows how quickly it moves through your system. The big drug companies are fighting it. It's too effective and too cheap. Scares the shit out of them—but all the big leagues use it. Whole damn Kingdome stinks of it, but those athletes stop hurting."

"I hope it sells better than your fleet of classy cars. They don't seem to be moving."

"They will," Max's clear blue eyes leveled on Sam's. "Where's your partner? Where's old Danny?"

He could not say it again. Not yet. He tucked his shirt into his jeans, feeling the sandpaper burn of the solvent on his back. "I still don't believe you're an Indian, Max. I think your name's really Abraham Stein, and you're hiding here on the reservation from three previous wives in New Jersey."

"My father's name was Blum. Morris Blum. Ahh, but my mother was Mary Toohoolzote Ling, a Coeur d'Alene, once removed. That's enough. An eighth, a sixteenth, is enough. You've decimated us. The Jews don't need me; the tribe does. Now, Marcella's a Tuscarora. Niagara Falls. Beautiful people."

"She is that."

Max Ling was a good six inches shorter than his wife, compact to the point of squareness, muscled like a wrestler. Sam had no idea how old he was. He could be anywhere from twenty to forty, and his hair was Indian black and fine in startling contrast to the pale eyes. "A lot prettier than you are."

"Where's Danny?" Max would not allow him to change the subject again.

"Dead."

Max screwed the top on the jar of solvent and did not speak for so long that the word hung on the air, bounced around the room, and came back to Sam full-blown. Finally, the little Indian looked up, his face quite bland but his eyes darkening.

"Was *that* him? There was something on the radio this morning, but I only caught part of it—something about some deputy who died up at Stehekin. I figured it was somebody from Chelan County."

"That was him."

"He was O.K. I always like him better than . . . the rest of you."

"Everybody did."

"What happened?"

"I can tell you what I think happened, and I can tell you what the searchers and the rangers and the Chelan County Sheriff's Office said happened, but I don't believe that either version is completely accurate. I'm prejudiced in favor of mine."

"So tell."

"What makes you think she's alive?" Ling's voice betrayed no doubt, only listening.

"I've answered that before and nobody believed my reasoning."

"But what?"

"Some things I can explain—some I can't. Danny was stabbed. I saw the wounds before the coroner destroyed them. Joanne's gone, and so are her sleeping bag and her backpack. And . . . she's not alone. I found the piece of a shirt in a tree up there that wasn't hers and wasn't Danny's. Somebody's got her. There was no damned bear, except in some fools' imaginations."

Ling looked thoughtful. "So what do you want with me?"

"Your sign says, SEARCH." Danny said you could find things. And frankly, you're about my last chance. Chelan County ran me out this morning on a rail. I'm probably going to get canned here because I took off without permission. I'm what you call a person with very low credibility, and I am strictly no-talent in the wilderness. I cannot find my way from Point A to Point B."

"I believe *that.*"

"I want you to go with me."

"You got any money?"

Sam looked up sharply. "You don't strike me as a mercenary."

Ling laughed. "Look around you. Look at everything for sale and tell me I'm not a mercenary."

"Are you?"

"In this case, no, but you just told me you are not exactly sanctioned by your fellow piggies. That means that it's unlikely that any county is going to loan you a helicopter or any other gear we might need. So have you got any money?"

"I've got about two thousand dollars in savings."

"You'll put that up?"

"Hell yes, I'll put that up."

"Do you believe that I can find her?"

"I'm not sure."

Ling slapped his hand on the table in front of Sam, the splat of it making Sam jump back. "For that, I'm charging you my standard rate as an Indian guide, $100 a day, payable when we find her. You know why my fee just went up? Because if I don't charge you an arm and a leg, you're not gonna believe in me. If you have to pay me, you'll think you got somebody *exceptional.*"

Sam winced. "I believe in you."

"Too late. Doubting me cost you. You bet your ass you believe in me. Every time you get all wishy-washy, my price goes up another $25 a day. Dragging you along isn't going to be easy. You are not exactly what I call fit."

"I'll hack it. If I die going uphill, you can cover me with pine cones and call the meat wagon—or the meat sled, or whatever. And sue my estate, you little fucker, for your consulting fee."

"You can't drink up there."

"What makes you think I drink?"

"When you came in you smelled like a week of firewater; now you smell like stale booze, garlic, and oysters."

"That's so you won't keep trying to hug me."

"It's even possible you have a few cogs missing."

"Several."

"Marcella's not going to like it. She doesn't like to have me leave her."

"And you aren't going to like to leave her. Will she be safe here by herself?"

"The dogs won't let anybody close to her."

"They let me in."

"Sheriff Sam. Believe it or not, that's one of the main reasons I'm throwing in with you. Those hounds like about one sucker out of a hundred. They evidently saw something in you that your own mother wouldn't recognize anymore. I was watching you when you drove up, and I saw those dogs laughing and bouncing and licking your hand. I trust dogs."

"Then you've never had your ass bit."

Max stood up. "Nope. When did you eat?"

"What day is it?"

"Monday."

"Friday. Maybe Saturday. I can't remember."

"Then you're going to eat and you're going to keep eating." He strode to the stove and lifted the lid on a pot simmering there. "Voila! Chicken soup."

"You're kidding."

Max laughed. "It's really lamb stew."

"I have to make some phone calls."

"After you eat. I'm going to tell Marcella that we're taking off this afternoon. She may not forgive you soon, but she'll forgive you."

While Sam spooned up food, he could see them together, through the several doorways, framed silently in the underwater parlor. Max leaned over the couch where she sat, his hands tender on her face, soothing. She shook her head and Max lay one finger on her lips. Then he spoke to her with both his hands. After what seemed a long time of mute conversation, she nodded and bent her head.

Marcella rose and walked down the corridor of doorways toward him, and Sam looked up and smiled at her. She did not acknowledge him. Her face was troubled as she turned into her studio. When he walked past her room toward the phone in the living room a few minutes later, he saw her at her easel, filling the canvas with white daisies against a purple-black sweep of rugged peaks. It jarred him in its familiarity. She must have begun it long before he came into her house; she could not have painted so much in a few minutes.

Fletch's voice on the other end of the line was chastened with shock and sorrow with no hint of his raucous humor and Sam felt a somber returning of loss. He listened to Fletch's disbelief, to his questions that had no clean answers, and tried not to let the emotions touch him. He had called Fletch at home, allowing himself harbor for a while longer from Fewell's wrath, and he could hear Mary Jean in the background, whispering questions for Fletch to pass on. Then shushing, quiet, and more questions.

"They brought him back here this morning," Fletch said in the same hushed tone. "Mrs. Crowder's taking care of the arrangements. Then she's going up to that place—the lodge place in Stehekin—with Sonia Kluznewski."

"She can't do any good up there!" He was angry, and then softened. Elizabeth Crowder deserved her own chance at futile vigil.

"We're not going to set the date for the services—until, until—they find Joanne."

"Yeah, that's good. She'd want to be there."

There was a painful pause on the other end of the line.

"Geez, Sam. I thought she was de—, er, gone too."

"We don't know that, Fletch. There is no evidence at all that she's not going to be found alive."

He could not convince Fletch of something he could not truly convince himself of.

"Fletch, there are some things I want you to do for me. And I don't want anyone else to know about it—nobody—especially not Fewell. Have you got a piece of paper?"

Fletcher sounded better, given something to do. "Gotcha. No problem with confidentiality. Shoot."

"First, I sent some evidence over to Seattle, to the Crime Lab. I want you to watch for any response on that. When it comes, you take it home and keep it. I'll check in with you. Second, I've got two names here— let's see—I want you to run them on the computers—NCIC, WASIC, and SEA-KING. Whatever hits you get, clear the machine after you write down the info. Then, I want you to take these two names and— this is a little tedious, Fletch—I want you to go through all the FIRS in the county since August first and look for a match. If you don't get an exact match on names or vehicles, I want you to look for 'sounds like,' or similarities. Make me a packet of anything you find. Don't even tell Mary Jean."

Fletcher was transparent as cellophane; his voice lowered confidentially as he whispered, "O.K. Our secret." Immediately Mary Jean's voice rose suspiciously behind him. He could hear Fletch cover the receiver and say something to placate her. Then he was back on the line.

"Fewell say anything about me?"

"Oh, Sam—he's raving. He's frothing. Your butt is in a sling; he wants you like a baby wants milk. Some brass from Chelan got him on the horn. What'd you do up there?"

"Nothing important. I'll tell you when I see you."

"Where are you?"

"No place where I'll be for long. You ready for the names?"

"Lay them on me."

"O.K. Number one: Steven or Stephen Curry. Birthdate roughly 1958 to 1963. White male adult. Five feet six to nine. Blonde. No eye color. Possible birthplace, California."

"The computer won't do much with no firm birthdate."

"It can scan a couple of years in either direction. Give it a shot. Next: David Dwain. No birthdate. Address, Portland, Oregon."

"Shit, Sam. You're dreaming."

"Try it. Try the FIR's. Maybe you'll get more that you can put into the computer."

"O.K. What do you want this for?"

"I'm not sure I can tell you. A hunch. Maybe nothing."

"Good luck. You want anything else?"

"Yeah. Feed my cat."

CHAPTER TWENTY-SIX

Duane had never expected to be angry with her. In their perfect companionship, there were to have been no negative emotions. No anger, no jealousy, no doubt, no rejection, no annoyance. She had opened up her mind finally and allowed him to slip into it. And he had drawn her back into his. She was in him and of him and part of him.

But she had lost the goddamned map.

It had to have been her fault. It had been next to his hand. He could still place it there in his memory, feel it rustling against his wrist when he fell asleep. And now, it was gone.

"Don't cry. Try to think. Try to remember what you did with it."

"I can't. I didn't have it." She began to cry again.

"But you saw what it looked like? It was a big sheet, all folded up, blue and green and red."

"I remember that, but I don't know what happened to it."

"You can remember anything if you clear your mind and concentrate. Close your eyes and try to picture it."

She closed her eyes. "I can't see it."

"Think. Dammit!"

"You're mad at me."

She was a child. She had always been a child-woman. He reached out to touch her shoulder and she flinched and pulled away from him. He should not have trusted anything important with her. But he was still so easily fatigued, slipping suddenly into naps, each of which he expected to reward him with the return of his usual vigor. Any renewals were shortlived. He had slept most of the day away, his blood sluggish in his veins and seeming to carry no oxygen. And they had made love again all during the night until he finally slept only fitfully toward dawn. She was draining the life out of him.

"Are we lost?" She sounded like some other woman now.

"No."

"Are you sure? I look back and it looks the same as any other direction. Everything looks the same. Rocks and mountains and trees. It would be easy to get lost up here."

"We're not lost. I simply need the map to pick the best way out."

"I feel lost."

"You're with me. You cannot be lost."

He closed his eyes and saw the map in his mind, all the trails spread across its face, arteries and veins of escape. He remembered Copper Pass, and Stiletto Peak, and Twisp, and something else—McAlester Pass. But they would not fall into place; they twisted like snakes, doubling back into a maze. Without the map he would have to make forays himself and construct a new one.

She moved close to him and massaged his neck, her finger tips sliding gently around the cartilage of his ear, her breasts pressing against his shoulder. She made it difficult for him to think.

"I made the fire," she whispered. "I didn't want you to wake up and be cold. It's so warm and sunny all day. And then it gets cold all of a sudden."

"That's nic—" Before the words were out, he felt a terrible premonition. He sat up, tumbling her away from him, and strode to the fire that licked blue and orange around blackened limbs. He stared at its edges and drew his breath in sharply. There was a small triangle of paper caught under the uncharred end of a branch. It had white borders and what he could see of the rest was blue shaded to green.

She cried out as he kicked the fire apart, sending chunks of flaming wood spinning into the grass. He was on his hands and knees then, pawing through what could be touched without searing his flesh. Finally he turned to her with a look she had never seen before, the man vanished, the boy gone, both of them destroyed by the twisted animal rage on his face. She thought, "red man," could not remember who that was, and waited, hopelessly, to see what she had done that was so awful.

"You burned the map. You burned the goddam map."

She deserved punishment. He left her beside the ruined fire and crashed into the woods while she wailed behind him, begging him not to leave her alone. *She* had left him enough times. Let her get a taste of what alone could be. He knew she wouldn't follow him; she was too frightened of the woods at night.

The way out might be quite obvious; he could do it without the map, but he had to hurry before the sun went down again. He would stand on the ridge and look down and find the way. Then he might forgive her. The scrabbly trail fought his foothold and mosquitos settled over him in clouds so thick that their drone maddened him and shut out her distant voice.

He became aware of something watching him, although he could hear no sound above the bugs. He stopped and looked behind him. She had not followed him; there was only the dark trail that seemed to disappear in the sky. Ahead it was the same. He was suspended on a thin wall of rock with no beginning and no end except air. Still, something prickled the back of his neck and the feel of it made him so dizzy that he dropped to one knee to stop himself from catapulting into space.

He saw them then—first their eyes, eight orbs of fluorescent gold, unblinking. Big cats. Cougars. Their faces were as gentle as kittens' faces, but their tails wound down and around, six feet long and as thick as his arm, their shoulders muscled thickly. They stared at him with interest and he knew they could be upon him in two, maybe three, bounds. He waited in his half-crouch for minutes and the cats never moved.

He should not have left her. After what seemed a very long time, his shaking legs steadied and he stood cautiously. The cougars seemed stuffed and lifeless. And then he saw pale membranes slide over yellow eyes. They were real.

When he turned and made his way back toward where he'd left her, he thought he heard them padding behind him, imagined their breath on his neck. He reached the end of the ridge and turned back, ready to shoot if he had to—and there was nothing. The rocks where the yellow cats had perched were empty.

He would kill her himself before he let an animal have her. He would kill her himself before he let anything or anyone else have her. She was his own possession, and neither cats nor men would take her. He could see her near the rebuilt fire, huddled in misery, long before she heard him approach. Waiting for him.

The thought of killing her seemed to be part of him, the last exchange between them. Not like with the others. They had died because they were false, because they had proved early on that they didn't recognize him. He was quite sure that she knew him now, but even as she proved herself, memories came back to him. Bad things. If they had time and freedom, he might be able to forgive her. He wished passionately that she didn't have to die. She had pledged to kill for him and he for her, but she had not understood what that might mean.

CHAPTER TWENTY-SEVEN

The chartered copter circled over Rainbow Lake and Sam peered down, seeing again the green expanse whose color seemed to change like a lying woman's eyes. Today, it was an innocent bright green, reflecting the sun, and the scene of searchers huddled in the cold was only a dull memory. The weather and the landscape changed continually up here and he trusted none of it.

He glanced at Ling's profile and wondered why he trusted Ling, or perhaps more puzzling, why Ling had thrown in with *him*. Hell, he was having a hard enough time convincing himself. Neither "Curry" nor "Dwain" had drawn a hit on the computers, and Fletch seemed lackadaisical about searching through the FIR's for something more. Sam wondered what Moutscher had insinuated when he called Fewell. If he'd hinted that Sam had cracked up, that would be enough to scare

Fletch. If there was one thing that alienated cops, it was craziness. *Because we're all half-sure that we'll catch it from being exposed so often.*

He hated helicopters. Once in Seattle, he'd been sent out to photograph the decapitated uniformed bodies and burned fuselage of a crashed police helicopter. Air I all in ashes. He breathed easier as the rotors lowered the pod they sat in onto the ground and he could feel solid land beneath his feet.

"Watch your head!" Ling shouted above the cyclone of noise and Sam bent double as he trotted clear.

The pilot promised to fly over areas designated by Ling each afternoon until they signaled him they were read to be picked up. Sam doubted that Joanne would be able to walk out when they found her.

It was very quiet when the craft's rotors faded in the distance, all of the searchers dissipated. They had left their mark, bright ribbons on trees and bushes where they'd shown sections already combed, electric blue plastic streamers flowing in the wind, mocking and empty.

Ling paced back and forth along the lake edge, lost in a reverie of his own. Sam watched him silently, smoked a cigarette, put it out, smoked another, and was lighting a third when Ling padded back toward him.

"They're not here now," he said finally.

"I'd say that was taken for granted."

"They might have come back—after the searchers left. But they didn't."

"You're saying 'they.' Why? Because of what I told you? Forget what I told you."

"I have." Ling squatted in front of him and his nostrils twitched. "I smell two people."

"Come off it, Max. How can you *smell* anyone?"

"Because if I said 'feel,' you'd go all antsy on me. Nobody understands my methods. You'll have to trust me. We've got layers of human spoor through here. Men and dogs clomping around and smashing hell out of everything. Right?"

"Right. Is it too late?"

Ling shook his head and started pacing again, his head cocked in a listening stance. "The search team showed us where they've been, so we toss that out. We go deeper. You tell me the woman had never been up here before. Say, she was alone—she's scared shitless. She would never have made it farther than the perimeter of those ribbons. And they didn't find diddley. So we assume she did go farther, but not alone. You with me?"

"I always assumed that."

"If she'd gone downtrail, you would have met up with her."

"Yes."

"So she went uptrail. I can't see her running into the brush of her own accord and no matter what those guys told you, bears don't drag their victims very far from the point of attack. They lose interest when the essence leaves after death. Bears kill for the same reasons humans do—out of fear, frustration, to protect their young, or because they think they're trapped."

"But not out of jealousy or for financial gain."

Ling grinned. "Bears are a little nicer than your average man on the street. Your woman wouldn't have been much of a threat to any bear."

"No."

"Tell me what she looks like."

"Why?"

"It helps if I have a picture of who I'm looking for. Just tell me about her."

Sam sighed. "Shit. Ling, I never could describe women."

"Give it a shot. How tall?"

"Little. Not real little, but—maybe five foot, two or three, hundred-fifteen maybe. Dark hair, blue eyes."

"Pretty?"

"I guess so. Yeah, she's a real pretty woman."

"What color is she?"

"She's Caucasian."

Ling snorted. "I don't want a cop description. I'm trying to get a total picture. Everybody gives off a color. You—you're kind of a burnt sienna. I'm dark green. Marcella's pale lavender . . ."

"Ling . . ." Sam's exasperation burgeoned.

"We're playing by my rules. What color?"

". . . rose, very pale rose."

Ling looked at him and whistled. "You have the hots for her, don't you?"

"No! Damn it, Ling. You asked a ridiculous question. I come up with an equally ridiculous answer—to pacify you—and you start playing Dr. Freud. She's my partner's wife."

"Whatever you say." Ling walked to the hiding tree, although Sam had not told him where it was, and circled it. "Look at it this way, deputy. You have certain talents; I have certain talents. You don't believe in my hocus-pocus, which, by the way, is only part of what I'm good at. But you've told me there are at least three dozen sensible men who don't agree with your assumptions. Part of what's burning a hole in you comes from what you've picked out of the air. You've got vibrations too. You combine that with physical evidence. Isn't that the way it goes on TV?"

"Yeah."

"And in real black and white life too?"

"I guess so."

"O.K. Pretty soon I'm going to show you what I can see in dirt and leaves and broken branches. That's my physical evidence. The other is my gut stuff. We put those together with yours, and we'll find your rosy little woman." He looked up into the pine boughs. "She was up here, wasn't she?"

"I think she was. I think she was up there with someone—not Danny."

"A man. A big man. Twice as big as I am. Bigger than you are."

"How do you know that?"

"I can't tell you. I just know."

Sam laughed without humor. "What color is he?"

But Ling took him seriously and reached out to touch the tree trunk. "Hot. A hot color."

"Ling," Sam said suddenly. "Where's your weapon? You brought a gun, didn't you? You're talking the Incredible Hulk here, and . . ."

"I don't own a gun," Ling said quietly. "I couldn't shoot one if I had one. I'm what you call nonviolent."

"*Shit.*"

"Let's start with the part we can see, Deputy. Give me your foot."

"What for?"

Ling pulled a buck knife out of his belt and bent over Sam's boot sole. "I'm gonna mark you, Sam." He cut a diagonal line across one heel, reached for the other foot and marked that. "If I'm following somebody, I don't want it to turn out to be you. This way, I'll know you. Now, do mine."

Sam took the knife and scored tattoos on the tracker's boots. That made a lot more sense to him than personal colors. He relaxed a little.

"Whose stuff is this around the campsite?"

"The coffee pot and skillet and junk was theirs—Danny's and Joanne's. The beer bottles—I don't know."

"Where'd you find him?"

"Down trail."

"Can I see it?"

"There's nothing there now."

"*You* say."

"Hell, come on."

They walked along the trail so dry that it was impossible to remember that snow had covered everything only three days before; it had evaporated like seafoam under the sun as hot as August's. The blue plastic banners were tangled in the trees where Danny had lain, slim snippets of color there too. The leaves that had been crushed under Danny's body had all blown away, leaving the forest floor unmarked— at least to Sam. Ling, however, walked immediately to the body perimeters next to the fallen log, an outline emblazoned in Sam's mind if not in his sight now. Ling noted tiny bony twigs still pressed into the moldering mulch of other seasons, flattened leaves from this autumn pressed too tightly to the earth.

"He was here?" It was more a statement than a question, and Sam's estimation of the little tracker's expertise was enhanced again.

"Right there."

Ling padded over the body site, touching, listening, searching—but he found nothing more.

"You were right, deputy. You do know what you're doing. There's nothing left here except for the place he fell."

They walked back to the lake camp in silence. Ling seemed given to spells of introspection—or perhaps concentration—where he shut out all conversation. He would not respond to Sam's agitation to do *something*. Despite the deceptive heat of the day, twilight was closer than he had thought.

"The trail's gone; isn't it?" Ling had reassured him before that it was not, but he took Ling's taciturnity for the same lack of purpose he'd sensed in the first searchers. "They blew it for us, didn't they?"

Ling looked at him, annoyed at his distraction. "I am trying to find my starting point. I'd rather search the right ten feet perfectly than crash all over to hell and gone half-assed. Nobody ever has the smarts to bring a tracker in first. I'm used to working with a whole bunch of shit that has to be eliminated before I can move. I'm a sign-cutter; you know what that means?"

Sam shook his head.

That means that we're going to pick out the most likely direction, and then we're going to find our signs on the ground that make us believe we picked right. Isn't that what you detectives do?"

"Yeah. Like the green plaid I found."

"Exactly. Sam, you're already trained for this. Just close off your blind side and question more. Look at everything twice and when something doesn't look quite right, give a holler. Deputy, I think you're a natural. You wheeze some, and you've got a hitch in your getalong, but I'm going to consider you a blood brother. I'm even getting to like you." Ling grinned. "Although I'm not known for my taste. You're going to look for signs until your eyeballs get dusty. If I say go back and do it again, you're going to do it. Don't expect to find footprints leading us right to her. We don't have snow, and we don't have sand, and we don't have mud. We'll be lucky if we find a piece of a print anywhere. Pick a trail."

Sam sighed and stared into the jungle of trees and vegatation. "O.K. I'll start rudimentary. She didn't—I *think* she didn't—double back, so that means she, or they, went ahead."

"Seems fair."

"So what the hell constitutes *ahead?* It all looks the same to me."

Ling unfolded the map from the National Park Service. On one side it carried a banner headline, "Touch the Wilderness Gently," and the other was swirled in concentric circles that reminded Sam of the whorls and ridges of fingerprints—all of it a far cry from the Texaco maps he was accustomed to. Max ran his finger along a thin red line of ink and stopped, tapping.

"Over Bowan Mountain—here. That's maybe six miles to the Pacific Crest Trail or on out to the North Cascades Highway. And there ain't no way we're going to make it before dark. I'm good, but not that good.

"We'll lose them"

"That's another twenty-five bucks a day." Ling folded the map. "If you feel that way, we've already lost them. They have—what?—nine days start on us? But they didn't come out the other side yet, did they? And if *I* can't move in the dark, they can't move in the dark. And if you keep pissing and moaning, you aren't going to see what you're supposed to see. We pack our butts out of here at dawn. In between, we eat; we sleep a little. You with me?"

"I better be—I can't afford your rate hikes. You know, Ling, you must be really insecure, you don't handle rejection well." Sam laughed.

"My mother abandoned me. I was raised by wolves in Spokane and they never understood me. Go build me a fire."

Sam woke in the deepest part of the night, used now to having to orient himself to where he was. He had slept in the woods, in his truck, in jail, in Ling's house, and—he remembered—now in the woods again. He lay unmoving, trying to figure out what had wakened him; he listened to the sound of Ling's snoring next to him, a shudder of wind in the quaking aspens, an owl—and something more. There was another presence.

He listened and tried to see into the darkness beyond their own outlines without moving his head. The sound came again, a stealthy murmur that seemed human and then not human. A soft whistling of air drawn into heavy lungs, followed by a grunt of displeasure. It was not Max's labored snoring; the snores continued in a counterpoint to the alien noises.

It scared the hell out of Sam as he realized that something moved fifteen or twenty feet away, some live thing watching him while he lay swaddled and damn near helpless. He eased one arm free, and then the other, still unable to see what thing had come upon them as they slept.

The thing was heavy. A padding, thudding noise—feet, booted feet, stomping on the turf—emanated from somewhere near the pine tree where Ling had hung their food.

Sam felt his pistol in his hand and he cocked it and pointed it toward the coal black nothing in front of him, waiting for his pupils to adjust so that he could see some outline. And even as he did, he was sure he heard something coming up from behind, through the line of trees. His shoulders tensed and he braced for the blow.

It did not come. The thing was still in front of him as his eyes adjusted to the dark and the moon's cloud cover shifted.

He saw the pack jounce on its rope and then begin to swing back and forth as if something batted it. And then he saw the animal on its hind legs, one foreleg outstretched. A dark pelted mound of muscle. He moved slightly and a twig cracked beneath him. The creature froze and turned its head toward where they lay. He saw its eye-whites and a yellow blob that was its nose. And in that instant, saw that he had been wrong. All wrong. A damn, stubborn fool. There *was* a bear.

He nudged Ling who came awake immediately and made no sound at all. He turned Ling's head with his hand, and Ling's breathing seemed to stop when he saw the bear. The little man's hand snaked out of his sleeping bag and Sam heard the whisper of the zipper, loud in the night.

And then, before he realized what Ling was about to do, the tracker was on his feet, grabbing for the mess kit that lay beside the dead embers of their recent fire. The clang of metal beaten against metal was louder than a gunshot as Ling ran suicidally toward the bear.

Sam's zipper stuck and he tugged at it frantically, finally giving it up and shucking himself out like a corn cob. When he was finally on his feet in the frosted air, he heard a new sound: Ling laughing.

The Indian walked toward him and Sam saw that the tree space was empty, the pack still swinging lazily on its ropes.

"Old bear liked to peed himself," Ling chuckled.

"You're nuts," Sam muttered. "I could have gotten a shot off if you hadn't spooked him."

"No, my friend," Ling said. "I thought *you* were nuts. I swear I wasn't really positive about you. Thought maybe there really was a grizzly up here. You know what that was? That was a plain old, soft-living, beggar black bear. Not even full-growed. Ain't no man—or small girl for that matter—couldn't have scared him off by shouting."

"How did you know that when you started out after it?"

"I could see it was only a yearling or so bear."

"It looked big to me."

"White man is chicken, ain't he? Woods full of varmints and all. Sam, that little black bear wouldn't come in here if there was a mammoth grizzly around."

"So now you believe me. What'd you come up here for if you didn't believe me, you little fucker?"

Ling slid into his sleeping bag, "Because you're so damned pretty, deputy. I couldn't resist you. Go to sleep. In the morning I'm going to make a sign cutter out of you."

CHAPTER TWENTY-EIGHT

He had not had any penicillin for days, and each morning he felt another layer of fever, a thin hotness that weakened him and made him sweat inside his sleeping bag. His hand and arm had ceased to heal, the wounds once again edged in pus. He bathed them often, sinking his arm in the tiny lake they had found, letting the frigid water numb and cleanse it, but the throbbing always came back as his injured arm warmed. He was at first impatient with it, annoyed that it had defied him and would not mend itself—and then frightened when he counted the days that he had not recovered but had only grown steadily weaker. He thought of being in a clean bed in a clean motel room, safe between ironed white sheets that would cool him. And at night when the air became icy and he could not get warm, he dreamed of a fireplace full of solid logs that would not burn out. He had been uncomfortable many times in his life, sleeping in fields and airports and bus stations, but he had always come to it with a strong body and a clear mind to find a solution. Now he felt trapped.

The more the woman clung to him physically, the more her attention struck him as sticky and cloying, and the thread of communication between their minds slowly unraveled. She talked at him when she should be listening.

He could not build anything in this meadow. The first serious winds would whip any shelter off the mountain and into the chasms beneath them, and most of the trees were dwarfs, blighted by the altitude, able to give only minimal shelter from storms. Worse, they were isolated but not safe from intruders. He could not be confident that some party of climbers wasn't going to stumble upon them.

And there were the cougars. He had gone downtrail three times to search for the passage through into the Pasayten Wilderness and each time the big cats had blocked him. Sometimes one or two of them, and once half a dozen. They watched him boldly and he had even heard them purr.

He was phobic about cats, all cats. Lureen had left him alone in the trailer one summer day with a big old tom cat she'd picked up off the road. And the thing had gone wild as the trailer heated up, snarling and hissing and leaping from counter to ice box, and ending, finally and horribly, a frothing monster in his crib. He could not remember if it had bitten him, but he did remember screaming until he was mute, alone with it for hours before anyone came and took the thing away. Somebody with greasy, hairy hands had strangled the cat right in the doorway of their trailer while he watched, still fighting for breath himself. After that, he had always skirted the cage full of bobcats although he'd been unafraid of the rest of the mangy menagerie that was part of the Hungarian's gig. In his adult life he seldom encountered cats of any kind but when he did, the old terror came back.

He knew the cougars smelled his fear and that they rejoiced in it.

He argued with her on Wednesday morning.

"What did you just do?" He asked her sharply, and saw her too-familiar look of alarm.

"What?"

"You just poured half a day's food away. We could have eaten it later."

"It's hot out—the sun would have spoiled it. Besides, you haven't eaten anything since yesterday. You don't like anything I fix."

"We don't have endless supplies. We can't run down to the supermarket. You've wasted more than we've eaten." He plunged his hands into his pack and came up with only four envelopes, staring at them in shock. "Where's the rest of it?"

"That's all that's left. Some of them were torn and I thought they might have gone bad, so I threw them away. You said you could hunt." She smiled. "I found some berries—a whole lot of berries."

He said nothing.

"I'm sorry, but I'm so tired of powdered food. Couldn't you find us a fish or a wild turkey or something?"

He mimicked her sarcastically. "Couldn't you find us a wild turkey or something? I'm tired, and there aren't any wild turkeys." *Shut up. Shut up. Shut up.*

"You're sick again, aren't you? Why didn't you tell me you were sick?"

"I'm not sick; I'm only tired." He forced himself to hold out his arms, and she moved into them and let herself be petted and stroked. "You make things so difficult."

She shook her head against his chest and he held it still with one spread hand so that she couldn't move.

"You have to listen to me. You remember how it was—a long, long time ago when you were my mother? You made things difficult then because you never could understand anything. You tried to do it your way and it didn't work out and they took you away from me."

She managed to pull away from him and she stared back at him without comprehension. "I don't know what you mean. I never knew you. I wasn't your mo—"

"You remember. Tell me you remember."

"You're scaring me."

"You knew me when you saw me. I know you recognized me. You were afraid to say anything, but you knew me."

She couldn't remember the first time she had seen him. She thought that she had been with him for several months, and she loved him, but he made no sense to her. His games were so bewildering, but he was so urgent about them.

"You did know me, didn't you?" His hand around hers had begun to hurt her, the vise tightening.

"Yes," she lied. "I knew you."

He relaxed and let her go. "That's better. You must never tease me like that.

"I'm trying to be what you want me to be." She thought she perceived an opening, a calm place where she could tell him what she had been thinking of continually. She massaged his thigh, making circles with her fingernail. "You know what?"

"What?"

"I want to go home."

He froze; she felt the muscles beneath the jeans tense. "We can't go home. We have no home."

"I want to be in a house. I want a roof and walls."

"You're trying to get away from me. You always tried to get away from me."

"No!" She tried to pull his head onto her shoulder and felt his rigid neck. "No. I want to be with you. You said we could have a place for us and that's what I want too, but I'm cold and I'm getting hungry, and I need a bath, and people to talk to."

"You have me to talk to. You don't need anyone else."

"That's true, but wouldn't you like a warm place to sleep? Couldn't we go down the mountain now, and find some place? We've never made love in a bed. We could make love all day and all night, and I would bring you food when you were hungry and we could take a shower together. Would you like that?"

She had not changed. He felt his heart a cold stone beneath his ribs and his throat constrict with the horror of it. She had let him think she believed, weakened him with her constant craving for sex, and all the time she'd been planning how she could abandon him again. He had always known that he would find her some day. He had found her. *And she did not love him.*

"Honey?"

He turned to look at her, his green eyes quite calm.

"What?"

"Do it to me now."

"It's too hot."

"In the lake. It's cool in the lake."

"Whatever you say. Whatever makes you happy."

He followed her to the pebbly edge of the water, and she laughed because she thought she had won. He let her undress him and toss his shirt and jeans into the shallows where tiny fish nibbled at them. She nibbled at him and drew blood into his penis, wizened and soft in the cold water and then engorged when he looked down and saw how wantonly she serviced him. They stood in the water further out, waist deep, and he lifted her onto him. Their hips' undulating changed the lake's wave pattern, and he felt exultation when she was impaled on his penis. But with his ejaculation, he lost the sense of power. Even before he slipped out of her, he remembered that he could not trust her any longer, that she mated with him simply because there was no one else. If another male came, she would betray him. She had always betrayed him. If he allowed her to live, she would turn on him.

She followed him back to their camp, unaware that he had seen through her. She chattered at him while she cooked the last of their food. When the sun began to slide down the sky, he knew that it had to be their last night together. The fever was suffocating him, blunting his strength until he knew he could not keep her if someone came to take her away. He would much prefer to have her dead. Dead, she would still belong to him, and he could find her again when he was well. This time, she had been almost perfect, but she had slipped back into being a slut, just as all the others had.

"Dance for me," he ordered.

"I'm tired. I'll dance for you tomorrow."

"I said I wanted you to dance—like you used to for the others."

"I don't understand you—"

"Damn you. You do understand. Don't make me angry."

She moved slowly near the fire, swaying awkwardly, teasing him.

"Not that way. Take your clothes off."

"I'm cold."

He didn't believe her, but he wouldn't argue with her. "Take your damned clothes off and do it for me—just for me this time."

She slipped out of her jeans and shirt and waited for him to tell her what to do, pretending that she had forgotten.

"You need music, don't you? I'll hum it for you so you can shake it up." He hummed "The Steel Guitar Rag" and beat a stick against the log with his good hand to give her the rhythm. "Dance."

But she only shuffled her feet and her hands covered her breasts.

"Let me see them. You sure as hell showed them to everybody else. Roll them like you used to, and wiggle your ass. Come on now. Da da-da *dah*. Da da-da-da *dah!*"

She seemed to get it then, slipping back into the old nasty bumps and grinds, thrusting her pussy at him and then snapping it back.

"Roll them."

"Roll what?"

"Your tits. They're standing up real nice. Roll them for me."

She jiggled and bounced them, but she wouldn't roll them the way she once had, making them seem as if they were alive. She was deliberately holding back and it made him angry.

He sang faster, beat the rhythm faster, and she whirled and stomped, but she had grown clumsy, or more likely, she was being deliberately clumsy. She wanted the whole damned bunch of rubes out there, panting and clapping for her. He wasn't enough. His tentative hard-on shrunk, reversed by his rage.

"How many of those cops did you sleep with, you filthy cunt?"

She stopped moving and covered herself with her arms. *"What?"*

"All those horny cops back there in town. You slept with all of them, didn't you? The young ones, and the fat ones, and even the tall one— the old one, that Sam—didn't you?"

"That's ugly. Don't say that."

"You did, didn't you?"

"I only slept with my husband. You know that. I only slept with you."

"Liar. Put your clothes on. I don't want to see you dance any longer. You make me want to puke."

She cried and cried, long after the sun was gone. She begged him for forgiveness, and a long time later he let her creep next to him, although he lay rigid and unbending while she tried to fit herself into the spaces around his body.

"I love you. You know I love you. I don't know what I did that made you angry."

There would be no more nights, and only part of tomorrow. His arm was dead already. He could feel the infection where it crept into his chest and the nodes of his neck. She had drained him, well-nigh killed him, and he would be almost relieved to be rid of her.

The control he had left, the only choice that remained to him, was to pick which hour of the day he would destroy her. He thought that he might go with her this time and disappear from the treacherous sun that promised life and gave no life. They could fall together into the black void that had to be traversed before they could begin again.

CHAPTER TWENTY-NINE

Sam found Ling an undemanding teacher. Like most men of special skill, Ling required perfection of himself, but he was confident enough of his own ability that he had no need to criticize other men. Sam could sense a certain impatience when he bumbled, but that was quickly quelled. And he realized that it was his own inner screaming to make haste that caused him to plunge ahead too rapidly. He had managed to keep a fragile lid over his anxiety for days, simply because there had been so many steps to take and so many miles to retrace before he could expect to find Joanne. Now that they were relatively close, with the possibility of coming upon her with each turn along the trail, the shackled foreboding had broken free. He remembered all the searches of his life where discovery had been barely—but effectively—too late. Children crumpled in abandoned refrigerators with air only just exhausted. Old men who had lain too long under bushes and died a scant fifty feet from busy thoroughfares; old women in sad little rooms who could not call for help while their hearts beat more and more faintly. Young women, their veins full of killing dope. All of them salvageable —if someone had come in time. He could not remember his rescues; he wondered if there had been any rescues, and recalled only those he had lost. In retrospect, it was clear that he should have found them, and he had not.

"Patience. Patience," Ling was muttering at him. "You must allow your conscious mind to focus clearly on what your eyes already see."

"But how the fuck do I know what's right and what's not?"

"O.K. Start with what you are trained to look for—cigarette butts, paper, buttons, old shoelaces, anything that people throw away or that falls off of them. That should be easier up here because this is wild land. They blocked this whole area off to hikers during the search, so nobody's gone beyond those blue streamers except the ones we're looking for. If they dropped something, it will be fresh. Right?"

"Right, I guess."

"That's fifty dollars extra a day, dep."

"O.K. Dammit. Right. Right. Right. You are all-seeing and all-knowing, you little bastard."

"So we look for little pieces of them."

"You could phrase it a little better, Ling. But I take your meaning."

"After that, we look for what the mountain shows us, where twigs are snapped, where leaves are crushed, where grass is flattened . . ."

"How are we going to know if it's been people or animals?"

"If it was deer or goats, you can hardly see where they've been—their hooves are cleft; they don't smash the way humans do." He walked along a sandy spot of trail and then into the brush, demonstrating. "Look now. See the positives? See those little segments of prints where you can spot where you cut my boot? See the angle where the buck brush gave and didn't quite snap back up? We're going to be working this in no more than fifteen foot segments. If you go more than fifteen feet and you don't see a positive, you've lost it, and you back up and hit it again."

"Fifteen feet! They're miles ahead of us!"

"Fifteen feet at a time, but if we work it well, we can do it at a trot."

"You trot—I'll walk."

"Make up your mind." Ling grinned. "You're not as stove-in as you pretend, dep. You've even got roses in your cheeks. When we get going, you're going to cut—you're going ahead, and I'll be behind you with my nose in the ground and my ass to heaven. When we run out of positives, that will mean we've either lost them or we've got them boxed in. Now, leave me for a couple of minutes. I need to meditate."

Ling turned his face up to the sun and closed his eyes, as if he was drawing from some psychic source, pulling something from the air that was completely incomprehensible to Sam.

What the hell.

The climb was rugged and Sam envied Ling his close-to-the-ground construction, the low center of gravity that let him climb so easily, and yet his own endurance seemed to have extended itself, and he experienced little of the fatigue and muscle ache he'd noticed before. He didn't deserve it; he had treated his body as a vessel to be filled with poison: booze and cigarettes. But the booze was gone; Ling allowed him little time to smoke and made him eat.

They were rewarded early on with many signs, so many that the task ahead seemed child's play. The green plaid shirt, its front full of old blood lay scarcely hidden between two rocks on the way up. Sam folded it carefully and dropped it into an empty pocket of his pack.

The cigarette butt and the crumpled wrapper from a protein bar marked the summit for them, and they slid down and down again through the pines and larch forest. Ling shouted to him regularly as he sign-cut, finding something here—and here—and here that validated their direction.

The meadow itself confirmed the presence, only recently, of more than one person. Wrappings and food packages rested there where the wind had tossed them against a circle of rocks, dried-food pouches, bandages—which made Sam's heart beat faster, although these blood stains seemed not to indicate serious hemorrhage. The ash of the campfires was deep; many fires had been built on the coals of previous fires.

He turned to Ling. "They were here for days."

"A long time. They might still be here."

They looked into the blank circle of woods ahead and saw nothing. Sam felt exposed, wished that Ling wasn't such a purist about weapons, and his skin erupted with goose pimples. He looked quickly around, framing consecutive sections of forest in his vision, and still saw no movement beyond wind ripple.

Something bright caught the sun. Probably mica embedded in the boulders or fool's gold. He gazed into the rocks' joining.

"What is it?" Ling said.

"I don't know. Something. Beer tab maybe."

The ring came out of the stone crevice in his reaching hand, the limp daisies still trapped in its circle, and he stared at it, amazed. It was Joanne's; it was the diminutive of the other ring that rested in his shirt pocket along with Danny's watch, forgotten since the moment Moutscher had given them to him. Ling walked over and studied the gold band and the dead flowers.

"Hers?"

"Yeah. Just like his. Sam fished the bigger ring from his pocket and set it beside Joanne's, wondering heavily why he should be in this lost place holding two wedding rings not his. "She must have left it as a marker to let someone know that she was here."

Ling held the flowers in his hand, studying them.

"How long?" Sam asked. "How long?"

"They were picked—maybe three, four days ago. Not longer, Whoever picked them isn't here now, and hasn't been since last weekend. Sam, they could be to hell and gone or to Spokane by now."

"What does your gut tell you?"

"Give me the rings. Let me hold them."

Sam dropped them into Ling's open palm and watched the tracker close his fingers over them, slow his breathing, and disappear someplace into his head. Minutes later, Ling handed the rings back.

"So?"

"His ring is cold—but we know that. Hers is still warm, and she's not far away. Not close, but between here and where the trees end before the highway. And . . ."

"What?"

Ling was silent.

"Say it anyway."

Ling looked into the woods until he spotted the trail. He shouldered his pack. "Her ring is getting cold, and I didn't want to hold it any longer because it made me sick. She's in trouble."

The positives were hard to find, but Ling found them. When they broke out of the trees and into the avalanche slopes, it was still early afternoon. True to his word, the copter pilot found them, circling low until Max waved his arms and signaled with thumb and forefinger. The bird slid sideways along its air channel and disappeared over the woods behind them.

Full dark trapped them at Fireweed Camp. Sam paced the campsite, filled with tension that had no energy behind it. Ling left him alone. It was a drab camp, offering nothing beyond water and wood for their fire.

After a supper of jerky and hardtack, Ling fell asleep at once and left Sam gazing into the fire for what seemed like hours. He tried to calculate what day it was, or even what time. There were no days in the wilderness and no time except for day and night. When he could fight it no longer, he slept so solidly that he did not hear Ling's snores or the fire crackling—or even the cougar screams that began an hour after midnight and continued until dawn.

The two men headed out while the sky was still gentian, only slightly streaked with pink, and Sam found Ling strangely subdued as he moved ahead, hurrying more than he had before, but still marking positive signs.

The boot markings that had become familiar appeared on the trail with regularity, and Max Ling turned onto the Stiletto Trail with no hesitation at all. Neither of them spoke. They made the ridge beyond the rock cairns and Max pointed to a pile of feces.

"Cougar."

When Sam's voice finally broke free, it was gravelly. "They attack?"

Ling shook his head. "Naw. Old-time stories about cougars carrying off babies. Never found one that wasn't a made-up scare yarn." He lowered himself onto the rough trail. "Used to be an old look-out here. Burned or blew away, or both. Sam . . ."

"Yeah?" He reached automatically for a cigarette.

"Don't smoke."

"Why?"

"We're close to whatever we're looking for. There were two people going in. Then there are prints of one person—big boots—going out, going in again. But he didn't come all the way out, and she didn't come out at all."

Sam's blood slowed down. He reached for a smoke again, and

remembered he could not light it. His hand stayed still in front of him. "What does that mean?"

"I don't know. They're probably still in there."

"Then let's go."

The worst was she was dead, lying ahead of them in some farther meadow. At least he would know. The best? She was alive—injured perhaps, captive possibly—probably—held by a faceless man who'd worn a bloody green shirt, who was strong enough to tear Danny's arm from its socket, whose boot print measured fourteen inches. He was a cop and he always expected the worst. Danny was dead. He'd known that all along. And Joanne's body was probably waiting for them now.

Ling moved in a crouched trot along a fresh field of green, and Sam tried to bend his own length into a semblance of the Indian's stealth. He did not want to see her body; seeing Danny had been enough. He held his breath unconsciously, fearing the sickly sweet odor that would soon rise up and meet them.

Ling dropped to his belly, and they both crawled then to the stone notch where the larch trees gave a measure of concealment. Then Max looked down onto the plateau below and grunted with astonishment.

"What is it?"

The tracker grunted again, and Sam could make nothing of it. Ling's left hand moved along the ground, signaling Sam to slide up next to him. The last three feet of their search seemed to take him longer than all the rest of it.

He saw, and looked away, stung with a mixture of shock, embarrassment, and disappointment that they had followed the wrong trail, stalked—not Joanne and her captor, but the naked lovers below. Ling had taken him on a wild-goose chase, tracked the wrong quarry.

Ling grunted again, and Sam heard, "Goddamm . . ."

Sam looked again. The woman was naked, tanned so darkly that Sam wondered if she were a black. There were no white lines; she had obviously been naked for days. She seemed wild, a wild woman whose hair fell down her back and over her shoulders, full of snarls and electricity and stuck with flowers. She was young and her body was quite good, all of it except her breasts solid with smooth muscle, graceful in a primitive way. He could not see the man except for his shoulders that protruded from the sleeping bag and the back of his head.

Sam turned to Ling and failed to recognize whatever emotion was written on the Indian's face. "Hell of a long hike for them just to get laid."

Ling only grunted and continued to gaze down.

The brown woman bent over the man on the ground, her breasts swinging free and heavy. While they watched, the man's hand rose up and clasped one breast, stroking it and pinching the nipple. The woman threw her head back and her face was heavy with sensuous pleasure. And then he recognized her.

"Oh my God. Oh my God, Ling . . ."

"Sam?"

Sam pushed his shoulders up, ready to scramble down toward the couple and Ling's fist pounded him flat again, driving his chin into the sharp pebbles that dotted the rock face.

"That bitch!"

"It's *her?*"

"I can't believe it. It can't be her. Look at her. . . ."

"Shut up. Shut your stupid mouth, Sam. They'll hear you."

"That bitch."

"Be quiet. You know him?"

The man peeled out of the sleeping bag and stood up, the light flashing off his red hair. His head swung in their direction and he sniffed the air like an animal sensing danger. But his eyes were blank; he had not seen them.

"You know him?"

Sam looked closely and saw nothing familiar about the tall man, saw that he was huge, so tall that he would not be easily forgotten once seen.

"No. I don't know him. I never saw him before. I'm going down."

He was on his knees and then on his feet before Ling could stop him, sliding on the baked gravel of the path, still shuttered off from them by the trees. He was unaware of the gun in his hand. He had no plan. He had forgotten everything he'd ever known about stealthy approach. He did not hear Max behind him; he was aware only of the man and the woman who stood naked, their eyes turning toward him with a swiftness that seemed lazy because of the roaring in his head.

Joanne recognized him. He could see her eyes widen and the open ring of her mouth. She raised a hand toward him, the palm flattened, and then she fell sidelong, swimming in the grass, away from his line of vision.

He saw the rifle, cradled in the red-haired man's arms and rejoiced that he now had a reason to shoot. The man hesitated. He lowered the .22 and swung it away, pointing down into the grass at her, and hesitating again as Sam thudded toward him. All of their movements were in slow motion. Sam was amazed that he had so much time to think, to decide. When the big man turned again toward him and raised the rifle, Sam was crouched in a shooting stance. He could see the flat green eyes, even a thread of spittle on the bastard's lip, and he chose his spot leisurely, unafraid of the barrel of the rifle pointing at his own heart. When he squeezed the .38's trigger, it gave so smoothly that it seemed inoperable.

Noise deafened him. Two reports, then a third, echoing off the rock walls around them. Still in a crouch, he prepared to pull the trigger back again and make it function, and found that his target had disappeared from his view. He swung right and left, and could not find the naked man.

But he saw Joanne and was incredulous. The gun—he registered .38 —was completely foreign in her small hands. She could not shoot; she had never picked up a weapon. On her knees, she pointed it toward him with one hand and reached toward the ground with the other.

"No!" It was his own voice roaring. "Joanne! No!"

He knocked her sprawling and the gun slid out of her hand. She came up clawing and kicking, and he struggled to be free of her before the big man had a chance to fire, but she clung to his back and he could not dump her off.

"You've killed him!" Her screams became words that could be understood. "You've killed him."

She tore at his eyes, but her hands were wet with something and slid off his face. With her hand grip gone, her scissored legs let go of him. She came at him again, and he wondered how he had recognized her before. She wasn't Joanne; she was some crazed animal, her mouth distorted by screaming. She hit him in the gut with her head, and tried to drive her shoulder into his genitals, but she was weakening, her screams hoarse whispers now.

"You shot him, you bastard. He saved my life. He was trying to help me—and you shot him. You filthy pervert."

He tried to hold her off him with his palms against her shoulders, but she twisted and clawed at him again. He grabbed one wrist and spun her around, pinioning her against him while she sobbed and twisted, spitting out obscenities. When he felt her sag, he let her go and she fell onto the grass, gasping for air.

"You son of a bitch. You lousy, fucking murderer."

She was either unaware that she was naked, that she sprawled in front of him wantonly, or she didn't care. He turned away, prepared to deck her if she came at him again, but she stayed quiet.

He looked for the tall, red-haired man, actually sensed someone just behind him, spun around, and saw no one but Joanne.

"Where is he? Where did he go?"

She began to sob again.

"Where the hell is he?"

"Over there. He's over there. Go see what you did."

He moved behind the boulder that was as high as his waist and saw the prone figure in the long grass. He did not trust it.

"Get up."

The man played possum, keeping his face buried in the turf.

"Get up you asshole!" Sam nudged the knee raised where the red-haired man had stopped crawling. "Game's over."

There was no response and Sam saw that a thin line of ants disappeared into the red hair and then emerged over the visible ear and descended into the hidden face. The guy had a lot of control—they must itch like hell. He touched the knee with his foot again, harder, and the man rose up and rolled over on his back.

There was a red furrow along his skull, disappearing behind the right ear. The green eyes stared half-closed into the sun without blinking. The mouth smiled slightly, and the ants dampened their legs in blood that drained into a pool in the ear. The man's left arm was purple and swollen, streaked with gaping peninsulas of pus.

"What's the matter with his arm?"

She didn't answer. She seemed unable to walk, and crawled to the body on her hands and knees, and flung herself on it. He watched her breasts flatten the red, curling hairs on the body's chest and overcame a terrible compulsion to pick her up and throw her off the precipice just beyond them.

"Get dressed," he said finally. "Go put some goddamn clothes on."

Sam walked slowly back to where Max waited, ashamed that Ling had had to see what Joanne was. He could not see the sleek black head on the rock where they'd waited. When he shouted, there was no reply.

"Ling! It's over. You can come down now."

Sam called again and waited for the crackling in the trees where Max hid.

He thought first that the little gurgling sound had come from her, but the source of it was too close for that. He looked down and was surprised to see how small Ling really was, all curled up with his hands clasped around his knees, made into a ball so that he could not be seen.

Ling breathed very badly, taking in air and some liquid so that his breaths were bubbles and whistles. Sam knelt beside him and carefully pried arms and legs apart, expecting blood again, feeling that every human he came in contact with had begun to leak red fluid, burst from veins where it belonged.

He found no blood. There seemed to be no wound. He loosened the shirt buttons one at a time, letting Ling rest between, talking steadily and with some reassurance—enough so that Ling's eyes followed him without doubt.

He could not understand where the hole in Max's armpit had come from—from which gun. It didn't bleed externally, but it sucked in air when the Indian's chest flared, and Sam clapped his hand over it automatically, shutting out the sound. Closed, the hole was not as formidable, and Ling breathed easier.

"You're O.K., kid. You're going to be fine."

Ling's eyes closed and he shook his head.

"Hardly a scratch," Sam lied.

". . . scratch."

"Does it hurt?"

Ling grinned faintly. "It smarts."

"I'll get you down."

". . . bird coming."

Sam looked up, expecting to see some mythic winged creature, and remembered the helicopter. If it could find them, and if it came in time, and if Max wasn't drowning in blood quietly and efficiently, he might be able to keep his promise to Marcella. He had kept no other promises.

He carried Max, as light as a woman, all muscle slackened by shock, down into the flat. She looked at them without interest or compassion. She sat next to the corpse and held its good hand. Clothed, she resembled Joanne more—but she no longer smelled of flowers and soap; she smelled warm and musky—unhealthy, like the hookers on Pike Street who bathed less than they perfumed.

He could not take his hand from Max's axillary; if he kept it there, he could form a barrier of his own flesh, sealing the air out, forbidding the wound to suck and flatten the lung. She watched him listlessly.

"Sam?"

He turned to stare at her, surprised that she had remembered his name. "What?"

"He's dead."

"So is Danny. You're not very concerned over Danny, are you?"

"Danny's dead." It was not a question, and it was not a statement. "Is Danny dead?" That was not really a question either, because her voice dropped, and her eyes slid out of focus.

"Does it matter?"

"Don't tell Danny."

"Don't tell him what? How could I tell him anything?"

"Just don't tell him."

She's crazy, he thought.

"Are you mad at me?"

There was no way to give an answer with dignity. He stopped his ears to her and watched Ling's face, gray green under the dark first layer of skin. Sam thought he heard the rotors buppering a long way off, and he watched the clouds, willing the helicopter to find them.

Sam was not sure how long they waited. He watched to see if Max still breathed, and he concentrated on willing the brown chest to rise and fall. She moved somewhere behind him. He heard her pacing the grass shelf. She wasn't a threat; her gun rested where he'd flung it, lost in the weeds. The dead man's weapon was beneath his leg; she could not lift her red-haired lover and roll him off it. She talked to herself, nonsense words, from which Sam could draw nothing. He preferred not to look at her.

Her movement stopped and he heard her whisper so faintly that he barely heard her. He held his palm tighter over Max's wound.

Something touched his shoulder, a light touch he easily shrugged off. And then it touched again.

"Go away, Joanne. Just go away."

He heard her say something, sounding far back in the meadow, the sound all out of sync because of the altitude. He spoke again without turning to look at her. "Please stay away. Just be quiet and leave me alone."

The rifle butt caught him just at the base of his skull and threw him sideways, tearing his hand from Ling's wound. Sam looked up, prepared to knock her away from them again, not yet connected to the pain in his head. And saw . . .

The green eyes were wide open and the dead man towered over him, his face a twisted mask of rage and blood.

Sam rolled away from Max, felt thundering noise in his own head, and focused on the man above him. One arm hung dead, and he realized his attacker could not shoot; there was a fogging, a blindness in the eyes.

The rifle butt swung down at him again, and he ducked and rolled away, closer to the edge of the precipice. Too close. He detected a lack of balance in the giant, but the rifle swung again and thudded against his shoulder. He grabbed it with both hands before it could be pulled back, and put his weight behind it.

The red-headed man seemed about to fall heavily on top of him and he braced for the impact, and then saw that the big man was going over him. The bloody face was above his for a second and then gone. His attacker made no cry as his face and useful arm slid into the rocks above the ravine, as the purple arm was crushed under him, no last roar of protest or fear as he slid slowly and then faster down the meadow's lip and disappeared into the air beyond it. It seemed an inordinately long time before Sam heard the sharp clatter of the .22 on the rocks below, and then a heavier, hollow thud.

He did not look down. His head still jangled with pain and dizziness as he fought to find a handhold to stop himself from going over too. He caught something and held on. He pulled up a little, found another safe thickness of weeds, and used them like rope to crawl farther from the edge. He remembered now that if he could not get back to Max, Max would have no air.

Sam's head began to clear, and he saw that Max still breathed very lightly, and that his eyelids still fluttered. The big man had not been dead, only an ox felled with a stunning blow—but he was sure as hell dead now. Sam sealed Ling's wound again, even knowing it had been uncovered too long.

He watched Joanne now because he did not trust her. She had seen her lover creep up on him, and she had made no cry to warn Sam. If he let her get behind them, she might try to kill him herself.

She seemed not to be aware of anyone beyond the dead man below. She paced along the ravine's edge, trying to find some way to climb down—testing here and there and only pulling away when her movements sent showers of rocks plummeting down.

"Come away from there. You'll fall."

She didn't answer him. When she found no way down, she stretched herself along the edge on her stomach, and held out one arm—crazily, as if she could somehow grasp her dead lover and pull him up to her.

She would not move from that spot. She would not respond to his warnings that she would fall. She gave no sign that she heard his voice at all. He let her be.

Max died so quietly that Sam did not hear him slip away; his breathing had only slowed and gentled until there was no breath at all. Sam heard a heartbeat when he pressed his ear to Max's chest, but it was only his own drumming in his ear. He could not bring himself to pound the little Indian's chest or to force breath into the slack mouth. Ling had spoken of essence, of soul and spirit, and he knew that Max had gone away, so much more swiftly than Jake or Danny had. There was no use to try. And still, Sam held the shell that had been Max, his hand tight over the bloodless wound.

When the helicopter found them, he carried Ling to it, so used to his burden that he felt strangely light when he let go of it. The pilot looked at Max, shook his head at Sam futilely, but strapped the little Indian into the seat when Sam insisted.

When the pilot held his hand out to Joanne, all of her lanquor and madness seemed to vanish. She turned toward Sam, and when she spoke her voice was cold and rational and utterly calm.

"Killer. You killed for no reason. I saw it all, and I will see that you pay. I hate you and I will always hate you. Murderer. . . ."

PART THREE
WENATCHEE
SEPTEMBER 17, 1981

CHAPTER THIRTY

CHELAN COUNTY SHERIFF'S OFFICE

FORM #27

CSS 21-87 REV 5-78

INCIDENT NUMBER
81-1157

DATE 9-20-81   **TIME** 0930 Hrs   **PLACE** Deaconess Hospital

STATEMENT OF: Joanne C. Lindstrom

My name is Joanne Crowder Lindstrom. I live at 15103 Old Orchard Road, Natchitat, Washington. My date of birth is January 29, 1949.
 On Friday, September 4, 1981, my husband, Daniel, and I arrived in Stehekin, Washington to begin a four day hiking vacation. On Saturday evening, September 5, we were camped at Rainbow Lake. We were joined by David Duane Demich who was also hiking. He informed us of the presence of a grizzly bear in the area, and we made camp together that night. Mr. Demich hiked out the next morning, but returned to tell us that the animal had threatened him. My husband and Mr. Demich helped me climb a tree, and they went to see about the bear. Within a short period—about ten minutes—I heard the sounds of a struggle and a shot. I think several shots. I looked toward the area where they had gone and saw a very large animal in the brush. I heard a scream. I think it was my husband. Mr. Demich was wrestling with the bear. Mr. Demich returned to where I was and told me that my husband was dead. He told me that he would take care of me and see that I got off the mountain safely. We waited in the tree for several hours, and then Mr. Demich led me over a mountain pass. Because he had been injured in his arm, we had to stay in a meadow for several days. After we left the meadow, we became lost. Mr. Demich was quite ill. We were planning to try to find our way out. On the last morning. I'm sorry—I cannot tell you the date—a man I know as Sam Clinton burst into our camp. I told him that Mr. Demich had saved me and I screamed at him not to shoot, but he shot Mr. Demich. At no time did Mr. Demich threaten Sam Clinton or me with a weapon. Mr. Demich was unconscious for a while, and, during that time, Sam Clinton attempted to rape me. I would like to say that Sam Clinton has made suggestive remarks to me in the past and that, on two occasions has attempted to put his hands on my body. (I had told my husband about this and he said he would speak to Mr. Clinton.) I attempted to aid Mr. Demich, and he did regain consciousness. When Sam saw that Mr. Demich was alive, he struggled with him and threw him off a cliff. There was a man with Sam Clinton, a man I do not know. He was injured but I don't know how. Mr. Clinton continued to make suggestive remarks to me until the helicopter came to rescue us. I fear for my safety if Sam Clinton should be released on bail. I will testify to the above in a court of law. The above is true to the best of my recollection. No promises or inducements have been made to me.

STATEMENT TAKEN BY: *Capt. Rex Nkutscher, #9271*   **SIGNED:** *Joanne Lindstrom*

WITNESS: *Lenore Skato*   **WITNESS:**

PAGE 1 OF 1

Sam read the Xeroxed sheets for the third time and then turned them face down and stared at the tan wall of the interview room. The public defender shuffled papers and sighed. He was a kid, a kid dressed in what had to be his daddy's Sunday suit.

"They autopsied him, I suppose?" Sam spoke without looking at the young lawyer. He came free; that was about all you could say for him —provided by the public's taxes for indigent defendants.

The lawyer pawed through his papers and drew forth a sheaf of yellow sheets stapled together. He seemed not to be familiar with the contents. "Yeah. It took them three days to bring him out of the canyon. Let's see—'Bullet entered just above the right ear, traveled beneath the skin transversely along the skull without penetration and exited above the occiput two centimeters right of midline. Bullet not retrieved. Nonfatal wound.' "

"Lucky bastard. It should have blown his brain apart."

"Mr. Clinton—I hope you won't make a comment like that to anyone other than me?"

"I wasn't thinking of calling the papers. What killed him?"

"Broken neck—at the—ah—C–3 and C–4."

"They think I did that too?"

"No. Dr. Albro attributed that to the fall."

"Albro? Where was he when I needed him? A guy falls sixty feet on his head, and even Hastings could have figured it out."

The public defender cleared his throat. "It's Mrs. Lindstrom's statement that disturbs me the most . . ."

"Disturbs *you?*" Sam stood and paced the six feet to the other wall, back and forth, back and forth, and fought the impulse to put his fist through the wall. "It bothers me just a jot too. That woman is nuts, and she's a liar. She was up there playing kissy-face—and worse—with Demich. They were getting ready to screw when we walked in on them."

Sam did not want to ask about Ling's post mortem, but he had to know. "What was the scoop on Max?"

The shuffling of paper again. The lack of emotion. "Hemopneumothorax. Both lungs. The bullet tore out—"

"O.K. That's enough. I know what it means." The wall in front of him blurred. "What's your name again?"

"Mark Nelson. You ask me every time I come in here."

"I think somebody better get another statement from Joanne—because you could walk out of here, find your nearest asylum, go up to the first patient you ran into, ask him—or her—to give you a statement, and you'd have something just as relevant as hers is. He pulled the rifle on me. He was ready to fire. I shot in self-defense. I shot in *her* defense. Check the bullet that came out of —out of Max, and you'll see what Demich was up to—"

Nelson squirmed in his chair. "The bullet that killed Ling was a .38 —it shattered on impact and the fragments indicate jacketed, probably hollow point—110 grains."

"That's what I use."

". . . yeah." Nelson brightened slightly. "But the .38 you said she had —they found that down in the canyon. Same kind of ammo."

Sam shook his head, disturbed. "No .22 bullet at all?"

"They didn't find it. But they found the rifle down on a ledge. It had been fired recently."

"That's no help. I fired. He fired. She fi—. Naw, I can't remember if she fired. I can't imagine that she would."

"The thing is," Nelson said quietly, "it's your word against hers. There's no way to show that the debris in their guns didn't come from a couple of days earlier. Without a .22 bullet at the scene, there's no way to prove he fired at you. And everybody's believing her statement."

"I suppose they think I deliberately shot Ling too?"

"Moutscher's willing to stipulate that Ling got caught in the crossfire. Your gun had three empty cylinders; hers had only one."

"I don't know *how* many times I fired. Somebody's got all the marbles, and it sure ain't me. Have you followed up on checking for a rap sheet on Demich?"

"I'll get right on that—"

"I told you to do it yesterday."

"Sam—even if he's got a rap sheet as thick as a brick, it won't change the charge against you. There are plenty of guys in Walla Walla who went up for shooting one of their felon buddies."

"I still want to know who he was."

"I've got a case load that simply isn't workable, and . . ."

"If I'm keeping you, I apologize. You probably have other clients who are more grateful. Kindly shoplifters and maybe a rapist or two who needs a little understanding?"

Sam watched the pink flush turn red and creep up Nelson's neck and over his ears; he knew he'd better shut up. He didn't dislike Nelson. Hell, maybe he did—but not Nelson himself. He was only one of the junior boy scouts who seemed to have taken over law enforcement and the legal process, all of them inexperienced and inept, posturing little devils, and Nelson the worst because he was dealing with a charity case.

"This statement. Where she says you made advances to her. Made obscene suggestions?"

"Where does it say *obscene?*"

"Well, suggestive remarks. Did you ever—ever—kind of kid her, or anything? Did you ever touch her?"

"Sure. Of course I did. Just like you're always messing with your partner's wife—or do you have a partner? Every chance I got, I whispered filth at her while my partner wasn't listening. Damn it, Nelson. Use your head. I've got almost twenty years on the woman. I liked her; I respected her, but I was never so hard up that I'd go sniffing around my own partner's wife. She said she'd see that I paid because Demich died. She's crazy like a fox. *I* don't know what happened. I have lain here night after night trying to figure out why she went off with that man, whether she had it all planned out before, why she was running around bare-assed with him like they were Adam and Eve—and I can't come up with any explanation at all. I've been a cop for over twenty-five years, and I have never, never, *never* come across anything that left me pole-axed like this. If I didn't know better, I'd begin to think *I* was crazy . . ."

"That's one way," Nelson cut in quickly.

"What's one way?"

"You could plead diminished capacity—only temporary insanity . . . shock over your partner's de—" The moment the words were out, Nelson saw his mistake. "It would be difficult—under M'Naughton. It's just one way . . . to consider . . ."

"Get the fuck out of here!" Sam's right hand smacked the wall.

Nelson picked up the brown accordion file and clutched it to his chest, expecting that he was about to be hit. Backing toward the door, he forced confidence into his voice. "We're looking at second degree murder. We're looking at twenty years. We've got an appealing prosecution witness who says you're guilty as hell, and the state will make the physical evidence substantiate what she says. I'm just trying to find a way—"

"Just get out of here, Nelson. If I weren't so angry, I'd laugh. Even a raving loonie can't beat M'Naughton. You know that, and I know that. Don't come back unless you can generate the tiniest spark of belief in your client's integrity and defend me on the facts."

Nelson looked longingly at the closed door, but stood resolute. "Mr. Clinton, I cannot help you if you refuse to cooperate with me. I am not an errand boy. I am a member of the bar of this state. I'll come back when you send for me, and you're not so combative. In the meantime, I will do whatever I can on your behalf."

"Go away, kid. Just go away."

"If that's what you want."

"What I want seems to have ceased to matter. Go get your shoplifters off. Give'em hell."

Sam found his box of a cell vaguely comforting. He was alone of course; put an ex-cop in the general jail population and you have a dead ex-cop. His likeness had graced the pages of the *Wenatchee Daily World* and the *Natchitat Eagle-Observer,* even the *Seattle Times* and *Post-Intelligencer,* and the Spokane *Spokesman-Review* every day for a week. The most illiterate felon who shared space in the Chelan County Jail knew who he was. They called to him in the night, hooting and laughing until the jailers came to shut them up. If he went to prison—and he could not conceive of it despite Mark Nelson's dire warnings—they would have to give him a new name and send him to a federal joint. He'd known of rogue cops who'd been convicted and vanished into anonymity in prisons in Indiana or Illinois, and who'd been scared shitless that one day somebody would blow their cover.

He had felt such desperation for haste while he searched for Joanne, and he had found her, only to realize in one blinding instant that she needed no saving. With that shock he had been rendered powerless. He was glad Demich was dead. Whatever came next, Danny at least was avenged and had been spared the awful vision he himself had witnessed. What Joanne had come to was his own burden.

He tried not to think of Max or of the way Marcella had stared at him when he took her husband away. Cossetted in the hot, airless cell, he slept or read the dog-eared western adventure paperbacks the jailers brought him. Sometimes he thought about Pistol and longed for the heaviness of fur purring against his chest, the only creature who might now miss him.

In the time after lights-out, a woman in the female section sang jail songs—"Detour" and "500 Miles From My Home" in a rough, sad-sweet voice, and then it was quiet except for coughing and the occasional muffled sound of crying that was neither male nor female.

And then he slept again.

CHAPTER THIRTY-ONE

They told her she had been in the hospital for nine days, but she was not convinced it had been that long at time, or that short a time. They told her there was nothing really wrong with her—only shock and exhaustion and a too rapid weight loss—and that she would be fine. She did not believe them because their smiles were painted on and they whispered to one another outside her room, but she ate because they insisted and because they called her "a good girl" and stopped nagging at her. When she tried to sit up or walk to the bathroom, the room spun, probably from all the little blue and yellow pills they made her take.

They told her he was dead. She could not bear to remember that. It made her cry and turn her face into the pillow so that she couldn't hear them. They would not let her read the newspapers; they would only bring her vases and vases of mums and carnations that suffocated her with their fragrance. But she smiled and said thank you. And that made them smile their false smiles again.

Her mother was there, sitting beside her bed everytime she woke. So strong. Just like the nurses. Solid, thick women with strong heavy legs in white stockings. All of them seemed so large, and she felt so small and weak, as if she were an infant resting in a huge bed.

The policeman was big too, with a great belly. When he pulled up a chair and sat close to her, the smell of pipe tobacco that clung to him made her nauseous. She did not want to have him near her, but she wanted to tell him what had happened. She owed that much to the man who was dead, to the man who had loved her so much that he had died for her.

Rex Moutscher blamed himself. He had misjudged just how crazy Clinton was. It had never occurred to him that the damn fool was going to go back uplake and take matters into his own hands. He should have seen how obsessed Clinton was with the woman. She was a pretty little thing but nobody to drive a man around the bend. But then you couldn't figure sex. He'd seen men go crazy over women too many times; they stalked and waited and eventually managed to strangle or shoot or burn up women who didn't want them anymore. Or didn't want them in the first place. Clinton had had a thing for Lindstrom's wife—but he'd sure managed to cover it up.

He asked her again, "Clinton bothered you before, Mrs. Lindstrom?"

"Sam?" She picked at the spread over her and looked out the window. "Yes. Yes. All the time. I was afraid to be alone with him."

"He knew you were going up to Stehekin?"

"It was his idea. My husband didn't want to go."

"Had you ever seen Duane Demich before?"

"Who?"

Moutscher waited a long time for her to answer.

"He said—that . . . No, I don't think so. He was just there, and he saved my life and he was kind to me and he said that nothing bad would happen to me because he wouldn't allow it to happen to me and he was going to take me out to a safe place that morning but he was sick."

She spoke with no expression and Moutscher figured it had to be the tranquilizers they gave her.

"Sam killed him, you know. Just came up there and shot him and threw him over the edge and I tried to get to him and he was dead way way down below."

She started to sob, and Moutscher had to wait for her. The nurse, Lenore Skabo, made a sound of disapproval. He'd forgotten she was there, witnessing. He hoped she would keep her mouth shut. Some of these nurses worked faster than Western Union with gossip.

"Now, tell me again, Mrs. Lindstrom. When did you first see Sam Clinton. Where was it?"

"Up there. In the meadow. In the trees. Coming at us with a gun."

"Which meadow? The one where the helicopter found you?"

"Yes."

"Or the one when you camped with your husband?"

"Yes."

"Your husband was already . . . dead when Sam went up there, wasn't he?"

"I'm sorry. Of course. I didn't understand your question. It was in that last meadow, the one with the big cliff. I'm very tired, Mr. Moutscher. Could we—"

"Of course. You get some rest."

It occurred to Moutscher as he rode down in the elevator that Clinton might have killed Lindstrom too. Wanted the wife. Sent them up there. He called down to Fewell's office, but Fewell said that Clinton had been on duty in Natchitat the whole weekend, seen by good witnesses day and night. Trust Walker to think of checking. It was a long shot anyway.

Ling had no record of violence. The guys in the Natchitat office were sure that he and Clinton hadn't buddied up before. The wife said that too, after Moutscher got a finger-talker to ask her. Ling was just a patsy who ended up dead.

He fed the info on Demich into the NCIC computer, going through WASIC first, and waited for the dull green screen to come alive.

Demich, Duane Elvis . . . D.O.B. 5–23–57
832 Larrabee, L.A., Cal. DL8X30P2-EXP5 23 83
WMA [White Male Adult] Rd-Gr., 6-5, 220.

That was him, all right. He waited and another paragraph appeared, a warrant number: WASP–D00012–789633, 6-13-82.

He checked Seattle P.D.—Illegal use of bank card machine. No more information. No contact with suspect.

The FBI rap sheet was on his desk, and he tore open the yellow envelope from the Bureau.

PD, Denver, Colo.	Demich, Duane E. #27081	1–19–81	Fraud	Dism.
SO, Alameda Co., Cal.	Davis, Darryl E. AKA Demich, D. E. #11143	3–11–81	Bunco	6 mo.C.J. dism.
PD, Salem, Ore.	Demich, Darin E. #62191	9–2–81	Vag. Narc. GL 1st	Disch.

Demich was no angel, a conman with a lot of luck—until now. But all of it was Mickey Mouse stuff, and no convictions. No morals arrests, nothing in the crimes-against-persons area. A traveling man and slippery, but not violent. Seeing the woman, how helpless she was, Moutscher could understand why Demich would have wanted to help her off the mountain, and knowing Stehekin, he could see why they'd gotten lost.

Given a choice between Clinton's story and Joanne Lindstrom's version, it was no contest. Clinton was lying in his teeth.

Moutscher slipped the rap sheet back in its envelope, punched three holes in it, and slipped it into the case file. He was a little nervous, remembering that he'd let Clinton take away physical evidence from the Lindstrom scene. If that came out, he would look bad. But the stuff was basically only shit that Clinton had picked up himself and had no intrinsic value. He still had the autopsy report and Blais and McKay's follow-ups. If push came to shove, he would go on record that Clinton had taken the stuff without his permission or knowledge. Hastings would back him up because Clinton had made the old man look like a fool and the doc hadn't appreciated it.

Put Joanne Lindstrom and Rex Moutscher up against an alcoholic cop and ask anybody who a jury would believe.

Joanne lay in her bedroom at home, the shades pulled down so tightly that they made a dim twilight of the afternoon. She was awake after sleeping a long time, but if she needed to sleep again, she had only to cry out and they would bring her the little bottle of smooth blue pills, talking to her all the time in hushed voices. Her mother was somewhere in the house and so was Sonia. Who was taking care of Sonia's children? Everyone was so kind. Everyone took care of her. They brought her trays of food with fresh flowers in little vases, and begged her to eat. Yesterday—was it yesterday?—Sonia had bathed her face with cool water and helped her change into a clean gown. Sonia was so subdued and quiet now; before she had always been boisterous and sure of everything. Sonia careful in choosing her words—it frightened Joanne.

She knew that a great deal of time had passed since she had last lain in this room, but she was not sure how much and she was afraid to ask. What month was it? The light seemed weaker, but that might be the shades. She was surprised to find that the songs on the radio in the kitchen were the same songs that she had liked in August.

A certain instinct told her she must not talk to any of them about the things that mattered. They spoke to her, but very cautiously, about Danny and of what "Danny would have wanted." That confused her. Danny had been dead for such a long time that she thought they should not mention him so much. They barely mentioned *him*, David—no, Duane—at all. When she thought about him, she sobbed quietly into her pillow, so muffling her tears that the women who waited in the kitchen could not hear her.

She remembered the time at the cemetery strangely. Color. Blue and red lights flashing on top of a line of cars. A whole sea of red that turned out to be the tunics on the mounties who came down from Vancouver. Why? Black stripes across silver badges. White faces and flushed faces and gray faces bending down to speak to her. She had no idea which of her lovers had been hidden inside the coffin. No one had told her and she had not asked. She thought it was probably Duane. Of course, it was Duane. But then why had there been so many policemen? Duane hadn't liked policemen, but he'd had good reason; policemen had made most of his life miserable. Maybe the police escort had been for her—because she'd been married to Danny once. She had wanted

287

to throw herself into the grave with Duane.

Sometimes she could close her eyes and smell the way his skin was when the sun had baked it all day. Sometimes she could see him above her, and the way his mouth changed—softened—when he was just about to make love to her. She tried to hold onto that image and always found it swept away by the terrible image on the mountain. She saw Duane struggling to save her from Sam, the odd slowness of movement as he moved behind Sam—as if his arms and legs could not move smoothly together—and then Sam's face looking around when Duane hit him with the rifle. She had tried to scream a warning to Duane and been completely voiceless. Duane had floated off the mountain; he hadn't even called out a farewell to her. Maybe he had been voiceless too.

One thing she could not forgive herself. That she had not gone over with him. It should have been so easy, but she couldn't do it. She had been unable to follow him down through the air between the rocks, even though she willed her body to go over. Just as her voice wouldn't work, her body had failed to obey her mind's commands. She had only reached out to him as if she could summon him back up from the pale rocks that glistened red with his blood, as if she could lift and touch him and make him whole.

He had been so strong—so powerful that she still could not really believe that he was finally and utterly dead. Sometimes in the night when the wind made the forsythia's branches scratch against the bedroom windows, she thought it was Duane. She believed—if only for a little while—that he had come back for her, that she could slip away with him through her window before her mother or Sonia could stop her.

Without him there was no point in eating, or sleeping, or getting well. If he was dead, she did not exist. He had told her that so many times. "Separated, we no longer live . . . Entwined. Flesh together. Blood together. Bone together. Throughout eternity . . ." If he did not come back for her, she would evaporate. They would come to wake her one morning and find no one.

The food did her no good. It only exacerbated the nausea that seemed to grow in intensity with each day. It was worse in the mornings, coming piggyback on the anxiety that shook her awake. She vomited then until she had nothing more to bring up, her retching sounds masked because she always had the cunning to turn on the shower before she bent over the stool. The workings of her body, its refusal to exist without Duane, without Duane's body to make it live, were no business of her mothers's or of Sonia's. Now that she was away from the hospital, no one could force her to live. She welcomed the nausea; she took it for a sign that she would not live. No matter how much nourishment they coaxed her to ingest, she could get rid of it and they would never know until it was too late.

She didn't blame her mother and Sonia. It was more that she was on a plane that they could not imagine. They were part of her old life, part of the time when she had lived with Danny. They had never known the absolute, final, and convincing joy that she had known with Duane. Since they could not conceive of that rapture, they could not understand. She had loved them once, and she still did, but in a far-off way, in a time that was gone.

When she slept, she dreamed continually. She dreamed on different levels, and her dreams bewildered her. The top layer of dreaming was about Duane. He was there beside her again and he made love to her. His touch was so insistent and real that she came close to orgasm but never actually climaxed. She woke too soon, and she wept because she had not.

Deep, deep in the soundness of her drugged sleep, she dreamed of Danny. Those were not dreams but nightmares. She heard a man scream—so loudly and terribly that she thought the whole house would wake. She woke drenched in sweat, her heart beating chaotically, and knew only that something in the dark had terrorized her and she could not name it.

Joanne came to dread the moon. When she was a child, she had believed that the moon belonged to her alone. Because it followed her everywhere, she thought it was her moon—that all children had their own moons. When she was very small, warm in the back seat of Doss's old car, she had watched the moon through the little triangle window next to her. No matter how far they drove, even over to Seattle, the moon—*her* moon—had tagged along. It was friendly then, protective, its man-face smiling down at her.

That moon had died. The one that had emerged to take its place was evil, staring down at her while she slept. Her mother or Sonia—one of them—crept into her bedroom while she slept and raised the shades, opened the window to let in air, and exposed her to the flat, dead-white moon with its craters and mountains forming a malevolent presence. She had no idea why it watched her.

The night air was cold. It smelled of no season. The wind came at night too, whipping the sunflower heads so that they thumped and woke her. The soft breeze before had come, somehow, from *him*. The shaking vicious wind—cold as if it had whistled down through ice tunnels—was something else. Some*one* else—trying to make her remember what she would not.

At first, she had taken more pills when she woke in the night, but then they must have counted them and found her out. Her mother took the pills into the kitchen and now she had to ask for them.

So in the dying hours of the morning, long before daylight, Joanne lay awake and shook with an unremembered fear. She always fell asleep before dawn to wake to new terror. She could not tell them about it. She did not know why. They told her she was being very brave, for Danny, and they left her alone.

Joanne wanted only one thing before she died. She wanted to see Sam Clinton punished. She had told the fat detective in Wenatchee exactly what had happened, told him how Sam murdered Duane, let him tape her words, write down her words, and she had signed the paper. No matter what happened to her, that paper existed.

Duane would be proud of her.

She kept no track of time. She thought it might be March. Sometimes she looked at her hands to see if they had blue veins and wrinkles, thinking she might have grown old and not known it. They looked smooth and taut, and they had small white lines where her scratches had healed.

She could not remember when she had last had a period. She didn't think of her body except to hope that it was dying. When her breasts seemed heavier and when the nipples grew tender, she thought that it must be because she had been in bed so long that she had crushed her breasts into the mattress and irritated them.

CHAPTER THIRTY-TWO

On the few occasions when Mark Nelson arrived at the jail to talk with him, Sam was led past the single clear window prisoners ever had access to. He was startled to look down upon Wenatchee and see that the season had changed, the old trees lining the courthouse lawn gone golden and russet now, the light slanted differently, hurting his eyes. He hungered to be one of the vagrants who drowsed in the midday glow that turned the fading grass bright again, a dozen of them lounging on the benches below and desultorily watching those who had business in the courthouse. He had always felt sorry for bums before because they seemed to have no purpose and no joy—but he envied them now. They were free.

He was not—nor was he likely to be. The chance that he might walk away from the tower that held him captive seemed more and more remote. Whatever Nelson did on his behalf was done with excruciating slowness and with veiled petulance. He had not gone down to Natchitat and contacted Fletch until the first week in October, and when he came back with the crime lab reports, he looked grim.

"Here're your reports, but I can't see where they'll help us. And I might as well tell you that Moutscher's got into them too. Your little friend got intimidated by your undersheriff. The lab sent a follow-up letter about something; it came in on Fletcher's day off. Fewell saw it and started sniffing around. Fletcher had to turn the stuff over to him —but he made copies first."

"That was considerate."

"Look, Sam. His job was on the line. That little man was scared. It took a lot for him to sneak copies out."

Sam sighed. "I guess you're right. Let's see what you got."

Nelson handed over a thin stack of white sheets, the printed material barely readable. The copy machine wasn't very good.

"Blood samples. Lindstrom's blood was O positive. The blood on all the clothing samples was O positive. A small sample found on the leaves was from a human, AB negative."

"That's what Demich was. Right?"

"Yeah. But she said he was wounded in the fight with the bear . . ."

"*There was no bear!*"

"All right. She said his arm was hurt when he came back for her. So it fits with their theory that he was wounded and he bled some."

"Where's your animal blood? She says he told her he knifed the bear. Where's your bear blood? That big hero said he spilled bear blood, and there isn't any, is there?"

"No."

"What's the time table on the maggots?"

Davis thumbed through the thin sheets. "Here. Life-cycle projection is eggs were laid six days before autopsy."

"Shit."

"Yeah. Just like she said. Lindstrom died either Sunday or early Monday. Just corroborates what the prosecution says again."

"Danny's fingernail scrapings? What's the poop on those?"

"That's kind of interesting."

"What?"

"Epidermis . . . human. Traces of AB negative, not enough blood to reduce to enzyme characteristics . . ."

"There! Try to tell me there were twenty-seven guys up there with AB negative blood—twenty-seven guys who got scratched in a fight. You know how rare that blood is? Maybe 5 to 7 percent of the population. If Demich was trying to help Danny, how come Danny scratched him deep enough to take off a layer of skin?"

"You're reaching. You know what the state will do with that? They'll paint a picture of two guys fighting off a bear, arms and legs all entangled, say Lindstrom was hitting out at the grizzly and Demich got in the way."

"Let's see the rest of that." Sam reached for the remaining blurred copies and flipped through them. He paused finally and looked up triumphantly at Nelson.

"Got him! Try to explain this away. Three cigarette butts. Benson and Hedges. Found—*I* found them beside Danny's body. Saliva traces from an AB negative secretor. Danny never smoked cigarettes, and he sure as hell didn't puff away on one while he was fighting your mythical grizzly. Besides he's O—not AB negative. So you got your hero—hurrying back to save the damsel in the tree. Only he lets her stay there scared to death while he has him three cigarettes. He's done what he set out to do. He's stabbed Danny—killed him—and he wants her good and scared; so he takes his time. He sits there and he has him several smokes. He's so damned terrified of that bear coming back and he waits around and smokes? No way."

"That is kind of peculiar. It might be of some help."

"Some? It gives you the whole picture."

"I don't know."

"Well then, what can you do about her testimony? How come she remembers so clearly what she couldn't have seen? She doesn't remember. She's lying."   ˎ

"It would seem so, but she's convincing everybody."

"Why don't you go on down to Natchitat and talk to her?"

"I tried, but her mother won't let anybody close to her, and her doctor says she can't talk to me."

"So every door we knock on get's slammed in our faces—and you won't pound to get let in?"

"For the moment. It won't look too good if we push a sick woman."

"I'm going to trial the week after Thanksgiving. You remember that? I'd like to go in there with more than three cigarette butts and my good reputation which ain't so shiny anymore. Did Fletch find anything in the FIR's in Natchitat—anything that shows Demich was down there? They had to have known each other before. I can't believe she'd lie down so easy for a stranger. She wasn't that kind of woman."

"Maybe you didn't know her."

"It there's anything I know, it's women. I may not have been so good at keeping a relationship going with one myself, but I understand them. Something's hinky. She didn't chippy on Danny—at least almost until the last, if she did. They were arguing some before they took off."

"About what?"

"It doesn't seem to matter now. If it looks like it might, I'll tell you. I don't want to have to unless it's absolutely necessary."

"You don't owe her anything, for God's sake—and it won't matter to him anymore."

"It does to me."

"Anybody ever tell you you had a self destructive streak?"

"Often." Sam stood up and signaled to the jail guard watching through the small window in the door. "I'll take these sheets if you don't mind. You can come get them in a day or two. It'll give you time to work your case load without thinking about me."

CHAPTER THIRTY-THREE

Sometime in the night a revelation came to Joanne, wrenching her out of sleep violently. It was a truth so awful that she could not share it with anyone. As reality rushed back, she wished that she had remained mad.

She remembered the red man.

His name was Duane. His eyes were green and smoldering and they had no bottom to them at all and they never blinked. He was the worst thing . . . yes . . . thing—not person—she had ever known. She had been so terribly afraid of him.

She gagged and the rest of the memory came tumbling out of her brain like vomit from her throat. Unstoppable and putrid. She was not imagining this. My God. OhmyGod. She had let him touch her. No— not just touch her. She had allowed him into her body with his penis and his fingers and his tongue. Wait, that was a lie she was telling herself. Not just allowed him. She had begged him to do it. All soft, she had been, and burning for him.

It had happened. She did not know why.

Her skin crawled, remembering, and she looked to see if her flesh was truly black and scaled from his touch. It felt so defiled. The red man. The hideous, disgusting red man.

Shame rolled over her and she was consumed by it. She had crept to him on her knees and her belly and asked him to do those things to her. Worse. It kept getting worse, no matter how hard she tried to stop remembering. She had done things to him too.

She needed to scream, but she dared not do that. She shuddered and lifted her shaking hands to her mouth so that she would make no sound. She forced herself to breathe slowly. She remembered hating him. And she remembered wanting to kill him. She had *tried* to kill him and failed because she was a coward. She remembered terror and revulsion. But she could not grasp why she had come to accept him and desire him . . . *lust* for him.

It was incomprehensible, and it was too much for her to face without going crazy again. Crazy was safer than where she was now, but she could not guarantee where she would go if she slipped back. It could be worse. If there was more to remember, she did not want to know.

She switched on the bedside light and saw that her room was the same. She paced quietly, afraid of waking her mother. When she was exhausted, she read and when she could not read any longer, she counted the holes in the ceiling tile and prayed—although she did not deserve to be heard by a Higher Presence.

And then she slept, and her deepest dreams burst forth full-blown with horror. *Danny.* Danny came back to her, his hands held out, his face so sweet and good, and so full of shock at her betrayal. Danny was mute. She begged him to shout at her and damn her with his rage, but he would not. He only stared at her beseechingly and his dead lips mouthed "Why?"

She didn't know why. She tried to tell him that and woke saying it aloud. But he would not listen.

She had pictured Danny dead. She had imagined him injured so she could care for him. And then he was dead.

In this bed, to turn herself on, she had done it. And she had killed him.

And then she had clung to another man, had rolled and rutted with a stranger when Danny was scarcely cold. When Danny was not even buried. It was so awful because she didn't know where Danny was now, or if he was buried at all. She could not ask, because she could not tell. *If anyone knew* . . . If anyone ever found out what she was, what she had done . . . She could not tell.

She had lied to everyone. She was a bad woman, a worthless woman, a whore, and a liar.

When the truth came, it was demanding, sucking up every particle of knowledge that she had buried within herself. She prayed for dawn to come but the night hours stretched and widened.

She had refused to acknowledge something else too—her nausea, and the darkening nipples that ached like boils. She crept into the bathroom and flipped the calendar back and found no mark after the middle of August. Even though she had no idea what month it was now, she knew it was not August. She hadn't bled at all, not even a spotting. What a cruel practical joke God had played on her.

She had no clue whose child it was. If it was Danny's baby, she did not deserve it. She had betrayed him in as many ways as a woman could, and she would surely betray his child, come to a day when it would ask about its father and look at her with clear, trusting eyes— Danny's eyes. If it was *his,* then part of the devil—a fetal demon—even now pulled her blood into itself. She did not want it; she would not bear it, and she would not suckle it. She would dash out its brains before she would raise the child of the red man.

She would run. That would jar it loose from her. She would run until her heart began to falter, and take her blood away from the monster inside, pound and pound with her feet until it could no longer cling to her womb.

When they woke in the morning and brought her her pills and her breakfast, she did not let them know what she had remembered. They were fooled and thought that she was better because she said she wanted to get dressed and come out into the other rooms and be with them. She could no longer bear to be alone.

The days were shorter than the nights, and she bought time, day by day, allowing herself more of it when she truly wanted none of it. She sat with Sonia while her mother taught—or rushed to find something to can, paring and dicing and blanching to keep her hands from shaking. She sat with her mother through the evenings and she did not scream out loud. She let them take her to see Doc because she had no more excuses, but she lied and gave false dates of periods that had never been. She let him examine her and asked no questions about what he found. When he tried to talk with her, she turned away and said, "I think perhaps I would not like to talk about anything until next week."

She saw something in his face, and then it was quickly replaced by a professional mask. He knew about the fetus; he had to know—but he said nothing.

There seemed to be something about her that stopped them all from confronting her, as if they expected that she would fly into a thousand fragments if they pushed her too far. They did not know that she was leaden, too diminished and tight to explode. She saw that people were born with a certain portion of hope that belonged to them. Life took hope and goodness away like cupfuls of flour from a bin. If you were lucky, you still had some left when you were old. If you weren't, there was no reason to go on after your bin was empty. There was no way to replace hope. When it was gone, it was gone—and her luck had dwindled to a thin layer of white, so few grains that no amount of yeast could make it double and redouble again. A breeze could blow it away.

She had harmed Sam, but he was strong. She had no strength or courage left to save him. She wished that she could, but it always came down to the fact that she could not tell. She *could* not tell.

It was the last thought she held before she finally slept from sheer exhaustion. The bad dreams came immediately, and she woke with the same terrible mazes to be worked through until she came to the final question. And knew not what the solution was.

CHAPTER THIRTY-FOUR

Sam heard footsteps approaching, and then the face of Noteboom, the day shift jailer, loomed beyond the bars of his cell.

"Lawyer's here, Sam." Noteboom grinned as if he had a secret.

Noteboom stopped outside the interview room and gestured grandly with one beefy arm. "I'll be back in half an hour to see if you're finished."

Sam walked into the little room, expecting to see Mark Nelson. Instead, a woman stood there, her back to him, her head bent toward the file folder on the table. The scent of her filled the room, a scent so familiar that his stomach turned over. Yardley soap and linen and English cigarettes. Nina's smell.

He absorbed her image in a second; the long hair was gone, replaced by a rough shag cut. The suit—beige and well cut, the long slender legs in low-heeled, plain brown leather pumps. Nina.

He turned and tried the door. Locked, of course. No way to get out without buzzing for a jailer.

He had thought he would never see her again. For five years, he had done without her. Done badly, done so-so, and finally, done well. He had thought of her and dreamed of her and gone without loving anyone but her.

Until this moment.

She turned and stared at him without smiling, searching silently with her brown eyes. She held out her hand and he stepped forward and took it; there was nothing else he could do.

"Sam."

"Nina."

"Sit down. Talk to me."

The five years had not been particularly kind to her. She had been a youngish woman, a woman who could have been anywhere between thirty and forty. She was not youngish now. Her skin stretched too tightly across her cheek bones, thin dry skin that ages badly. There were tiny lines around her eyes and the corners of her mouth, and her neck was no longer the taut smooth column he remembered. Still, she was lovely.

She watched him watching her and picked up on his thoughts as if he had spoken them out loud.

"Time got to the old broad, huh?"

Caught, he stammered. "You look well. You look wealthy and successful—like a rich lady lawyer."

"I am. Rich and successful—and well. You won't believe this, but I haven't had a drink of anything stronger than tea for four years. But I know how I look. My dance card is empty. The men I meet are old fools and young guys who could be my sons. How about you?"

"Me?" He grinned slowly and reached for her hand again. "Old fools and young guys too. None of them come on to me. I guess I've lost my charm."

"I meant do you still drink like it's going out of style?"

"Not lately. They don't serve much in here. Not that much before—before it happened. Beer mostly. What are you doing here?"

"You fucked up, Sammie."

"That depends on how you look at it. You didn't answer my question."

"I came because I read about you in the papers. I saw you on the six o'clock news and the eleven o'clock news. After awhile, it occurred to me that you needed a good attorney, and you always said I was the best working lawyer you knew."

"This embarrasses the hell out of me. I suppose you know that. Anyway, I've got an attorney."

"I met your attorney. When his ears dry out, in about ten years, he might make a criminal defense attorney. You deserve better than that."

"Maybe, but I'm broke babe. I spent my entire life savings renting helicopters and a peerless Indian guide—who I managed to get killed. I am what you legal types refer to as indigent."

She looked away. He felt her hand cold in his.

"I'm not for hire. You're a famous defendant, and we big-time criminal defense attorneys thrive on patsies like you. Me and F. Lee and Melvin B. lust after defendants who'll bring us headlines. You're money in the bank."

"That's not why you're here."

"You haven't seen me for five years. How could you know why I do things? You didn't even know me then."

"I tried."

"You did that. Like they say, Sammie—if only I'd met you ten years earlier." She pulled her hand away from him, and opened her file. "I dismissed Nelson."

"The hell you did."

"He was glad to go. He told me he was 'terribly overloaded.' Actually, I think you frightened him. I assume you didn't want a defense attorney who could be scared off so easily. In your situation, you need a tough guy."

"You're a tough guy, are you?"

"You bet your sweet ass I am. I'm the Iron Maiden—well, maybe the Iron Matron now—and you're stuck with me representing you. Unless you say no."

"How could I say no to such a proposition?"

"How's Pistol? Did he survive the exodus as well as you have or has he gone to the great kittyland in the sky?"

"He's fine—the last I heard. He asked for you often."

"He never. He used to sit at the window and watch for you to come ho—. . . to show up." She stuffed her handful of papers back into the brown file, and reached for the handsome attaché case beside her on the floor. "Let's go see him. We can work over these later."

"They got real funny about prisoners walking out of here—something about maximum security. And we're having macaroni and cheese for lunch. It's my favorite."

She laughed, an unnatural sound. "You'll have to forego that. I bailed you out."

"You're kidding."

"I never kid. I never, never kid. You should know that."

"That's $5,000 on the barrelhead. You have that kind of money?"

"That—and more. I'm very good at what I do. I told you that. You're not going to skip on me, are you? I'll get it back. You can pay me 18 percent interest if you like, and we'll be square. Why don't you push that buzzer and go and pack your gear? I'll wait for you outside. I'll be the lady in the silver Mazda. The sun is shining; the leaves are what they call a riot of fall color. We'll go get a steak and you can tell me what really happened. Then we'll go see Pistol and Joanne Lindstrom and we'll rearrange the pieces of this odd puzzle until they fit the way they're supposed to."

"I don't have to tell you that's the best offer I've had today."

"No."

". . . and how grateful I am."

"Wait until you have something to be grateful about." She held the file and briefcase against her chest. "And Sam . . ."

"Yeah."

"Nothing's changed. I'm in a comfortable place now. I don't want to lose hold of it. I like my life. Do you understand?"

"Gotcha."

He rang, and Noteboom let them out.

The air outside smelled wonderful.

Nina drove well, if too fast. The wind through the driver's side window picked at her hair and ruffled it, and he wished that she had not cut it, wanting to see it whipping behind her as he remembered it. He was too aware of the movement of her right thigh as she accelerated and braked, of her elbow inches from his hand as she shifted down. He had not thought of sex in jail, where all men are said to be obsessed with it, but she brought all of his libido back.

The silver car left Wenatchee behind, skirting the rolling bare hills and plunging past miles and miles of orchards and their windbreaks of poplars, the fruit trees so pregnant now that they seemed to creak under their burden of red and yellow delicious apples.

Sam experienced again the sense that the seasons had accelerated and telescoped upon themselves—heat and then frost and then snow, and heat, and now it was fall again. The apple smell filled the wind and drifted into her car.

She turned south and the Mazda took the foothills approaching Blewett Pass, its engine a throaty purr. He remembered his truck and wondered idly what had become of it. He'd left it in the cruise ships' parking lot in Chelan during one of the spells of summer, and it probably waited someplace in an impound lot, had, perhaps, even been sold at auction by now. She picked up on his thoughts as she always had.

"What do you think of my jalopy? Beats your truck, huh?"

"Anything would. What happened to your Volkswagen? I always liked your bug."

"Somebody pushed it into Lake Union in—oh, probably 1978. I found it sitting there underwater one morning. We had a funeral for it and a dock party, threw flowers in, and said words over it. It's still there. The crawfish use it for a condo."

He shivered involuntarily, remembering cars with bodies in them that he'd seen winched out of Puget Sound. He thought often of death now, dismissing calm memories and going straight for the macabre. She looked younger—not young, but younger; the fluorescent lights of the interview room had not been kind.

"Are you happy?" He hadn't meant to ask it and was surprised to hear himself speak the words.

"Was I ever?" There was neither gloom nor lightness in her inflection.

"I guess I meant to ask how things were going with you—beyond the obvious. Private practice has certainly raised your standard of living."

"Sammie, you'd pee your pants if you saw my houseboat now. Nothing's left but the flotation. Cedar shakes, skylights, a greenhouse window, a sleeping loft—it's two stories now, honest to God. I've even got a cleaning lady. I drive her nuts."

He smiled. "I would imagine she'd find you confusing. You *seem* happy."

"That was always so important to you—being happy. Hardly anybody is. I finally found the formula for—what would I call it? Equilibrium. No big highs; no more excruciating lows. I juggle. I've got my career. I've made some friends on the dock. No lie. You may not believe it, but I have. And I have young lovers . . . "

She looked quickly at him, saw nothing on his face, and looked back at the road. "Nothing heavy. Their bodies are nice, and they're enthusiastic in bed and they haven't grown up enough to think deeply enough to interest me. When one leaves, there's always another one. All of it is like walking barefoot on a hot sidewalk. When one foot starts to burn, you jump onto the other one. If one part of my life disappoints me, I concentrate on another part. I never dwell on the hurting part, so I don't feel it."

"What if you run out of places to jump to? Your anesthesia might wear off."

"I'll find something else. When I told you I was comfortable, I meant it. I'm O.K."

"Am I someplace you jumped to because your sidewalk got too hot?"

She was quiet for a full minute, shifting into lower gear as the incline rose ahead of them. "Not you yourself, although I do care what happens to you, even if you find it hard to believe. What you are, *where* you are, and what they're trying to do to you represents a challenge."

"Maybe you should have left me where I was—like your bug. The challenge may get sticky."

"No." She laughed her mirthless laugh. "The bug will stay down, and it's quite content underwater. You're such a stubborn bastard, you'll always try to surface. Now reach into my purse and light me a cigarette and let's get down to business. Tell me what happened . . . every little detail you can remember. When you've finished, I'm going to want to hear it again—and again—and again, until you get so sick of going over it that you'll want to strangle me."

"What about your young man? Won't he get tired of waiting while you play nursemaid to an impossible defense?"

"If he does, I can always find another."

Before they rolled into Natchitat, he had told her all of it three times over.

He could not tell if she believed him.

Sam watched Nina, saw her sitting on his couch in his trailer, her stockinged feet tucked under her, her thin arms bare in her sleeveless blouse. He had visualized her in the little trailer a million times the first year, twenty thousand the next, and finally, not at all. He was thankful he'd cleaned up the hulk and bought furniture after he'd seen Danny's shock at the mess that last day; she looked out of place enough as it was, too rich for his blood, his salary, his taste. All of her energy was channeled into listening to him. He felt glad to be able to talk freely to someone he not only trusted in the ways of the law, but someone who might be able to grasp and understand what he could not.

Pistol clung to him, a matted lump of gray fur, scrawny but not starved, purring ferociously. The old cat had forgotten to be sullen and full of rebuke and had leapt at him the moment he crawled out of her car. Only after he had licked Sam's face had the cat allowed Nina to hold him. She looked at them now, man and cat, and said solemnly. "See, he always liked you best."

"Tomcats cling together."

"No they don't. They walk by themselves. You're both pussycats. Make me another cup of that disgusting stale tea and get me a sheet of paper and a pen. Let's see what we have."

He moved to refill her cup, still carrying the cat draped on his shoulder.

"This time dust the cup out."

When he passed the window over the sink, he felt rather than saw the eyes outside watching them. He knew Rhodes, the manager, and probably half of the park were out there beyond in the cold dark, staring from darkened mobile homes so that they wouldn't be seen. He suspected that Rhodes was plotting at this very moment how to break his lease. Killers in the park certainly were even less desirable than sick old men who didn't mow their grass or haul their garbage. Sam raised his right hand, the middle finger extended and waved it toward Rhodes's triple-wide. He pulled another beer from the refrigerator—

only his second; it didn't taste as good as he'd imagined.

"So what do you think? We gonna blow them out of the courtroom and leave it a disaster area?"

She grimaced and ran her hand through her hair, revealing her pale, high forehead, unfreckled like the rest of her skin was. "We might only make them a little nervous with what we have here. There's nothing that will make the prosecutor foul his trousers."

"She said she saw the bear attack Danny."

"So . . . "

"She couldn't have. She was in the tree. She admits that. I was in the same tree. You can't see from there to where she says the struggle happened, to where I found Danny. The trail turns back on itself there; there's no visibility at all from where she was—all you can see is rock wall."

"Then why would she say that?"

"Nina, it's obvious. She had something going with Demich right here in Natchitat. She coaxes and pleads with Danny to go off someplace where her lover boy can fake a death. Then she covers for him."

"From what you've told me about her—and your perceptions were always reasonable, even when you weren't—I can't see her participating in that kind of treachery. She doesn't sound devious. She sounds like a rather simple, naive, dependent woman."

"I thought she was."

She lit another cigarette. "Suppose she didn't know Demich before . . . "

Then she wouldn't have been so willing to kill me to save him, would she? She wouldn't have been rolling around in the grass naked with him when I found them. Even sluts have loyalty, and she wasn't a slut. She loved Danny. Shit, Nina, I used to envy him she loved him so much."

"Did you now?"

"Not her—just the situation. Why would any woman change partners so easily? I *saw* her. She was nuts about Demich."

"What? Say that again."

"She was nuts about Demich."

"Again."

"Come on, Nina. All right. *She was nuts about Demich.*"

She stood up and paced, hampered by the confines of the narrow trailer.

"That's all we have, Sam. A mind."

"A *mind?*"

"You've been concentrating on physical evidence. That's what you do best, and God knows, we need all of it we can get our hands on. You know where I think our real evidence is? It's locked up in a mind that's not working the way it should. I think what we need is inside her head. She may not even know it's there . . . "

"I must have made your tea too strong. Look, she's lying, so I guess that means that she holds the key to why it happened. If you want to get fancy and say it's inside her head, that's fine with me."

She stopped walking and pulled the hassock up so close to him that her knees touched his.

"Let me tell you a story. We had a case. I went to court with it. The victim was a hitchhiker—seventeen, maybe eighteen, kind of a plain stubby little girl. A runaway. Nobody wanted her. Mother took off with stepdaddy number four. Father was supposed to be in California; so she figures she'll hitch a ride and go find him and say, 'Hi there. I'm your long-lost kid.' She started out from Bellingham, and she made it to the southern limits of Seattle when this creep picked her up. He had no intention of taking her to Portland. He got off the freeway someplace south of Tukwila and drove into a gravel pit. The usual stuff. He screwed her. He made her blow him. And then he screwed her again. That tired him out; so he tied her up and put her in the back seat while he slept. In the morning, he repeated the whole process."

"That's almost your average American rape scene—"

"Shut up. O.K., you're right. A nice average rape. Well, it went on for three days. Forced sex. Bondage. Isolation. No hope of surviving for her—at least in her mind. On the fourth day, he finishes with her, and he remembers he's supposed to be in Vancouver, and what's he going to do with her? So he shoots her. Not once. Not twice. He shoots her three times, and any reasonable victim would have lain down and died. She certainly seemed to be dead. Blood all over, eyes closed, breathing so shallow he thinks he's gotten rid of a complaining witness. He takes off."

"I can't see how . . . "

"Please shut up. O.K. This little girl is made of tough stuff. She's got a .22 slug in her arm, and one in her hip, and one in her neck, only—get this—the one in her neck is stuck neatly in her carotid artery. If it had gone through, she would have died right away. If it stays there, her brain will die. *But,* if they take it out proper, they can stop the bleeding and she might live. She can't know that, of course. Her organism only wants to live. She comes to, and lover boy is gone, and she's hurting like hell; so she crawls, *crawls,* up to the road and lies down there. She probably crawled three hundred yards a little bit at a time, and she leaves a trail of red behind her. Somebody comes along, sees her, scoops her up, and gets her into Harborview Emergency. They operate, see that slug that stopped her from bleeding to death, and didn't quite kill her, and they take it out and sew the carotid together neat as you please. She lives. She not only lives, she eventually walks and talks."

"Babe, if you just want to trade war stories, I can match you horror for horror. I can invite the neighbors in and make popcorn."

Nina shook her head impatiently. "She gives a statement when she's in the hospital, while she's maybe not quite rational—but the county dicks figure out what happened to her; they find a gas credit slip with his license number on it, and they pick him up in Camas and charge him attempted murder, rape, sodomy, kidnapping. They match the gun he had with the slugs that came out of her. They find somebody who saw her get in his car, but you know what happens when they go to see her about testifying against him?"

"What?"

"She starts to cry. She refuses to testify against him. She says she wants to marry him."

Sam stared at Nina. "She what?"

"She loves him. There was nothing the dicks could do, nothing *I* could do. That girl was totally entranced, totally in love with the bastard who almost killed her, who left her bleeding inside and out. He went to prison—but without her testimony. *She married him* before he went to Walla Walla."

"Why?"

"Right. *Why?"*

"She must have been nuts."

"Right again. No particular argument on that. Which brings us back to where we started. There's something here, I think—something that matches what I just told you. The shrinks kept mumbling about isolation . . . and fear. Let's think about it over night and see where Joanne fits into it."

Nina moved toward the couch where her suit jacket lay, and he stepped aside, too conscious of the small space with only the two of them in it. She bent over to pick up the jacket, poised in mid-movement without moving at all, and then she turned back to him, her hands empty.

"Oh, hell Sam. I'm not going. I have a forty-five-dollar motel room downtown, all reserved and paid for, and I can't go."

He thought he knew what she was saying, but he stuttered like a schoolboy. *"You want me to go through it again?"*

"No."

"What then?"

"I want you to fuck me." She would not lift her eyes to his face, but kept them focused at his chest level. "I want to be here with you tonight when the wind out there picks up and rocks this trailer, and feel Pistol on the bed between us, scratching fleas and being annoying. I want to feel your old bones next to my old bones."

His arms were awkward, but she moved into them easily, fitting against him just as she always had.

"You think it won't get too hot, too uncomfortable?" he whispered. "You won't have to find a cool place, some stalwart young man who doesn't have one foot on a banana peel and the other in the joint?"

"Not tonight. All I want is tonight."

"All you ever wanted was tonight."

"Don't talk. Don't ask for a goddamn commitment."

He heard her undressing behind him while he unfolded his new hideabed. And remembered he was a loser. Maybe he would fail at this too.

She was thinner; her expensive suit had hidden a new boniness, flesh gone from her hips and breasts. It didn't seem to matter. Even knowing the risk, he responded to her completely, recalling in his loins their exceeding joy in one another. The ache went out of him when he was at last inside of her, and just before he came, he thought that it was quite wonderful that he should be here, locked with her, instead of lying on his jail bunk in Wenatchee.

He fell asleep on top of her, too exhausted and too consumed to move away from her. He kissed the damp hair at her temples, and remembered nothing more all night long.

She was gone when he woke, chilled under the single blanket, the cat purring against his chest. He thought that he had dreamed her there. And then he saw the sheet of paper pinned to the hideabed arm, a yellow legal sheet with her square printing on it.

S.—

Will call later. Gone to see Joanne.

N.

CHAPTER THIRTY-FIVE

Nina had found the element of surprise wise in her first contact with Sam in five years; she now considered it essential in getting close to Joanne Lindstrom. Mark Nelson had tried the proper channels and had been rebuffed by Elizabeth Crowder, and the welcome wouldn't be any warmer for her. None of them were going to give anything to Sam. She had no doubt that they had been warned to avoid the defense, told they did not have to face Sam Clinton outside the courtroom. Well, Mark Nelson was forthright to a fault—at least a fault in a defense attorney —gifted with no slyness and precious little ingenuity. Nina imagined him, hat in hand, announcing who and what he was and asking to see Joanne.

She had left Sam's bed at six and driven to the Holiday Inn to claim her suite, take a shower, and dress again in something that did not label her "professional woman." In jeans and a red-checked shirt, boots that had cost three hundred dollars but didn't look it, she could have been the wife of a well-to-do Natchitat rancher.

She found the Lindstrom farm easily enough. She was good at directions, and she was lucky. She was invariably lucky for other people—

unless they depended on her for something more than she could give. Just before she drew up to the lane to the farm, she saw a perfectly maintained 1972 Plymouth emerge from the narrow road and turn toward town. The driver had to be Elizabeth Crowder, an older woman sitting bolt upright behind the wheel. Nina slowed and satisfied herself that the Plymouth had disappeared around the first curve in the gravel road before she turned her Mazda toward the farm. Bumping over the last rutted hillock, she saw that there were no vehicles parked in the yard or in the shed, that the curtained windows shut any occupant off from a view of her.

She rapped sharply on the back door and waited. There was no answer. She rapped again and heard some sound in the house beyond, but no one came. A door slammed inside; music rose and then stopped as if someone had turned the volume knob of a radio or television up when they'd meant to turn it off. She knocked again, and called, "Joanne!"

No answer.

"Joanne! I have to talk to you."

A figure moved toward her from the far end of the kitchen, and she thought at first that it was an old woman, the movement so tentative. The woman inside peered at Nina at a disadvantage as her eyes tried to focus into the sunlight of the back yard.

"Joanne?" Nina called loud enough to be heard through the glass.

The door opened slowly and Joanne Lindstrom stood before her, so pale that her skin seemed translucent.

"Yes."

"I came to talk with you."

"There's no one here."

Nina stepped inside as if she had been invited, and Joanne moved aside, her back against the edge of the counter. "There's no one here now."

Nina smiled and drew no response. "You're here. You're the one I want to see."

"I'm afraid I don't remember you. I . . . "

"We haven't met."

"Then I don't understand. I've been ill."

"I know, and I'm sorry for the trouble you've been through. My name is Nina Armitage." She held out her hand and saw that Joanne was confused, only belatedly lifting her own fingers. "I'm a friend of Sam Clinton's."

The reaction was immediate and full of panic. Joanne slid around her and moved frantically to the other side of the room, using the long table as protection. "No. No, I can't talk to you. I'm not supposed to talk to anyone who . . . "

"Who what?"

"Anyone who knows Sam. Anything like that."

"Sam bears you no ill will. He asked me to tell you that. He wondered how you were."

"I'm . . . I'm all right."

"You look upset. Does my coming here upset you?"

"No! Yes. It's only that I haven't seen anyone. I've had to rest, and my mother has talked to—people."

Nina studied Joanne without seeming to do so, and she noted her sunken eyes, the lines in her face that had not been there—at least not in the pictures she'd seen. Joanne Lindstrom's hands trembled; she looked down at them, saw the tremor, and grasped the back of a chair to quiet them. She looked near collapse. Her arms were thin as sticks and her jeans bagged around her hips, the line of her jaw so bony that it had the harshness older women who diet obsessively attain.

But there was something else. Joanne Lindstrom wore a T-shirt that hung over her jeans, and the flesh beneath it was not wasted as the rest of her body was. Her waistline had thickened and the material over her breasts was drawn taut. Joanne saw Nina studying her, and stood up straighter, sucking her stomach in. But the thickness remained, and Nina recognized it for what it was.

Joanne Lindstrom was pregnant.

"Could I sit down?" Nina asked quietly. "Could we have a cup of coffee and talk?"

"But there's no one here."

"You're here. We'll be talking in the courtroom in a little over three weeks now. It might be easier for all of us if we could talk now instead."

"What do you mean? What do you mean about the courtroom?"

"I'm Sam's friend, but I'm also his lawyer. I came over from Seattle to represent him."

"You lied to me!" Joanne was poised for flight, but she seemed not to know where to go or how to get Nina out of her kitchen. "You lied."

"No. I didn't tell you all of the truth, but I didn't lie. Are you positive —absolutely positive—that you want to go on with this? Do you really want Sam to go to prison?"

"I want you to leave. I shouldn't be talking to you. Could you please go away?"

"You didn't answer my question. Do you really believe that Sam did you any harm?"

"He made you come here to get me all confused."

"He didn't know I was coming here. He's too kind for that. I came on my own."

"How is he? Is he terribly unhappy in jail?"

"He's all right. He's not happy, and he's not in jail anymore. He's back home."

"Oh." Joanne smiled, but it was not a real smile, only a vague mimicry. "That's good. Tell him 'Hi' for me?"

"Tell him Hi? *Tell him Hi?* You could do a lot more for him. You could tell the truth, Joanne, and there wouldn't be any trial. Peoples' lives are involved. Your life is involved. Joanne, do you know what the truth is? Do you realize what you're about to do to that man? What you've already done?"

The bright kitchen was quiet. Joanne moved one hand slowly and brushed a strand of dull hair away from her face. She looked at Nina as if she could not remember who she was or why she was there. Then her eyes shifted and she was panicked again. "Go away."

"I'll go away now, but I will have to come back again. Will you talk to me again?" She started to go and then asked suddenly, "Do you have bad dreams?"

"I don't know . . . just please go away."

Joanne disappeared down the hall. Nina waited to see if she would come back and heard the sound of a television blare from somewhere far back in the farmhouse. The kitchen phone rang but no one answered it.

As Nina drove back toward town, she knew what it would come down to. If Sam was to survive, Joanne would have to be driven into the ground, all her deceptions exposed, broken so badly that she might never again function with any degree of sanity. Nina wasn't sorry. The strong survive and the weak perish. That was the first law. All the others came after.

CHAPTER THIRTY-SIX

Joanne stayed in her bedroom for two hours, afraid to look into the kitchen to see if the woman was gone. She had been foolish to open the door. Her mother would be angry with her, and so would Mr. Moutscher and the lawyers. She stared at the portable TV without seeing anything but a jumble of color, and she scarcely heard the sound. She was afraid to pull the shades aside to see if the thin woman's car was gone. She was afraid to answer the phone. Her mother should not have left her alone.

After a long time, she turned the volume knob down and listened. There was nothing. She heard only crows calling outside her window. It took all she had to raise the blind and look. She saw no vehicle, no one at all outside except for the big black birds that perched in the elm tree and stared down at her. One of them broke away and flew toward her with its clumsy, jagged wings barely moving. At the last moment, it veered off and avoided her window. She could hear claws scratching on the roof overhang above the window and knew it was waiting for her.

She took the black bird for a sign.

The thin, sure woman *knew.* Joanne had expected the day would come when someone would accuse her, but she had also expected more time, tender forgetful time—a long tunnel of it—through which she might miraculously emerge with a solution to what was insoluble. She had contrived to put the trial out of her mind as an event that was far, far in the future. Rex Moutscher had told her that long trials—and Sam's promised to be protracted—were almost invariably postponed when they were scheduled during the holidays. She had managed not to ask, "What holiday?" Her mother talked about getting a turkey and who would make the pies and she knew that it must be either Thanksgiving or Christmas. There was a calendar in the kitchen but that was for 1981—the year Danny died—so that was no use to her. She looked at the calendar in her bathroom, and saw with amazement that it was a 1981 calendar too. She had only looked at the days before. Was it possible that time had stood still—that so much had happened in a matter of three months? Moutscher had dictated the dates when she made her statement to him, but she had not been listening.

That woman—Nina—had seen that she was pregnant; Joanne had caught it in her cool glance.

They weren't going to leave her anyplace to hide. And they'd seen to it that she couldn't run away. Both the truck and her car were gone. Where were they parked? She could ask Sonia. No. Sonia would tell her mother. They were all lost to her now. Every single person she used to count on. Danny. Sam. Sonia. Her mother. Doss. It made her cry to think about Doss. He would have helped her. Would he? Or would he be as disgusted with her as everyone else would? Nobody left. Nobodynobodynobodynobody . . .

Fletch had retrieved Sam's truck from the impound lot—possibly an act of contrition—and parked it behind the sheriff's office, but Nina refused to ride in it. They took her car again, although Sam would have much preferred to drive. He arranged his bony knees beneath the Mazda's dashboard as Nina headed back toward town.

"Did you see Joanne?"

"I saw her."

"Well, *what?* How is she?"

"Have you eaten?"

He felt his stomach growl. "I guess I haven't."

"I saw a Cakes-N-Steak place down the road. Let's have a cup of coffee and talk it over."

"How are you this morning?" Sam glanced at Nina as he spoke and thought she looked, again, younger—dressed in jeans and a shirt, sunglasses covering any wrinkles around her eyes, wrinkles that he might only have imagined. "You look chipper."

"I'm fine."

He waited to see if she would say more, acknowledge in some way what had happened between them in the night.

She didn't.

He would have chosen to talk to her in a private place, away from the frank stares of Saturday diners. He appeared to be a most recognizable commodity, so much so that he almost expected that they would be asked to leave, but the young waitress slapped placemats and silverware down in front of them, her jaws busy with chewing gum and her eyes blank behind her smile.

When the girl left, he repeated the same question he'd asked before. "You did see her?"

"Easy as pie. She was alone out there. Mama Hen passed me going into town."

"So how was she?"

"Funny. She asked the same thing about you. She said to say 'Hi.' "

"You're not serious."

"Quite. I, of course, didn't know her before, but the woman I saw this morning is not playing with a full deck. I could have been talking to a child, somebody who wasn't supposed to answer the door while her mother was gone. Very, very frightened. So full of denial that you couldn't believe her if she said the sky was blue and the grass was green. She was terrified when I told her who I was. And she looks like hell."

Sam sighed and made grooves in the place mat with his fork.

"Don't act like it's your fault, Sam. For God's sake, the woman is trying to destroy you. You can be such an ass."

"What do you want me to say? That I'm happy she's cracking up?

"Joanne's pregnant. You should have mentioned that. A widow on the witness stand is bad enough—but a pregnant widow . . ."

"No."

"No what?"

"She couldn't be pregnant."

"She looked fecund enough to me, perfect maternal soil. What makes you think she couldn't be pregnant?"

"Well. Well, she had a period just before they left. They were trying to have a baby."

"She really shared everything with you, didn't she?"

"She didn't; he did." Sam stopped talking while the waitress put their food down, her eyes sliding toward him now; someone in the kitchen had apparently filled her in on his notoriety. When she walked away, his voice lowered to a whisper. "Shit, Nina, they were spending half their time down at Doc's, having tests, taking their temperatures. I don't know what all."

"And what were the results?"

"I don't know. I never wanted to get involved in it in the first place. I hate to talk about it now." He sighed. "O.K. Danny said he was going to have to take a semen sample in to the Doc to have a sperm count or something. He was planning to do that just before they took off. He didn't tell her because he was—shit, he was worried that something was wrong with him."

"Maybe there was. How long were they married?"

"Thirteen, fourteen years, I guess."

"And she never got knocked up before?"

"You still talk as delicately as ever, don't you babe? I guess not. It seemed to be what they both wanted. They weren't holding back on a family on purpose."

"And now she's pregnant. Isn't that a coincidence? She said she was only 'good friends' with Demich, never even held hands probably. It must have been something in the wind."

Sam looked at the stack of hotcakes in front of him and knew he had no appetite. "What's she going to do? Are you sure? It seems awfully soon to tell."

Nina shook her head. "You are a constant puzzle to me, Clinton. No, I guess you're not. What she's going to do is not your concern, and nobody declared you the White Knight. She is definitely pregnant. She's one of those dainty, short-waisted women who blow up like a balloon the minute the seed's planted—or almost. I would say she's about ten weeks gone. Due date would be about the first of June. They'll put your trial off until the middle of January because of Christmas, and you'll have a witness sitting up there with her round little tummy under a smock and you'll look like the meanest son-of-a-bitching defendant a jury ever saw. Unless we can show it's Demich's, not Lindstrom's."

"Isn't there another way?"

"Not that I can see now. Look, if it bothers you, think about something else. Think about spending the rest of your life in jail."

He looked down at his plate again and pushed it away.

The primary medical care personnel in Natchitat itself included three osteopaths, two chiropractors, a podiatrist, and Doctor Will Massie, Jr. Massie, the son of a doctor, had grown up in Natchitat and was known as Little Doc from the time he was ten. When Big Doc retired, he became plain Doc, and at thirty-eight was treated with all the respect the only M.D. in town reserved. A burly, competent man, given to practical jokes when he was away from the office, he stood four inches taller than Sam.

His staff of two slim, blonde nurses looked at Sam with surprise, but passed him back to Doc's office ahead of the full waiting room.

Massie's handshake was firm, and his smile seemed sincere. Sam wondered if he would spend the rest of his days wondering what people really thought of him, if there would be no final vindication—ever. He appreciated the doctor's tact in asking nothing and offering no regrets. Even "Nice to see you back" would have hit a nerve.

"Sit down, Sam." Massie waved one fat forearm. "Take a load off."

"You're busy. I won't stay long."

"I'm always busy. I need a break. You don't look sick. Are you?"

"Probably should be—but I'm not. I've been eating all that balanced, nutritious jail food—"

Doc Massie looked down, and Sam detected embarrassment. That was it. He either embarrassed or annoyed with his presence. He hurried ahead and damned Nina for forcing him to do what he was about to do.

"Doc, I've spent a lot of time lately asking for information that doesn't seem easy to get, and isn't easy to ask for. This may be the worst."

"Shoot."

"I have been charged with the murder of a man whom the prosecution paints as a kindly stranger, a veritable Samaritan. I have reason to believe the guy was a good deal less than that. Joanne Lindstrom's statement makes him look like a saint and makes me look like a monster. Her perceptions may be less than accurate."

"You never struck me as a slavering beast. Something of a wise-ass, maybe."

"Thanks."

A furnace cut in someplace in the long, flat clinic, and the blast of hot air tickled the toes of a skeleton behind Massie's desk and set it dancing in lazy turns. Sam stared at it, trying to pick the right phrases.

"Danny told me he was coming in here before they left on vacation."

Doc Massie said nothing.

"It was none of my business—but we were close and he was shook up. Hell, Doc, the thing was he was going to have a fertility test. He expected to get the results when he came back—only he didn't . . ."

Massie waited and Sam could detect no reaction on his face.

"I know your patient files are privileged information, but the shitty thing is that once you're dead, you lose your rights to privacy. I don't want to force you into anything—"

"What you're asking me is whether Danny could have fathered a child."

"Yeah. Damn it. Yes, that's what I'm asking."

"Sam, you understand that I cannot tell you anything about any *living* patient. That the rules still hold true . . . as far as that goes?"

"I do. I'm not asking anything about anyone else."

Massie whirled in his chair and pulled open a metal file drawer, fished through the tabbed dividers, and drew forth a thick file.

"Danny's been coming in here since he was two years old. My dad took care of him. Small towns, huh?"

"Yeah." Sam waited, although he sensed that Massie had already made up his mind. "Damn few secrets in a small town when it comes down to it."

The doctor read from the last entry in the file. "Daniel Lindstrom, September 2, 1981. Semen specimen presented. Lab report: September 9, 1981. Specimen indicates a disproportionate number of nonmotile spermatozoa. Five million viable sperm per cubic centimeter."

"Five million! Then he was O.K.?"

Massie shook his head. "That means that Danny could not, would not, have been able to father a child. Anything below 20 million—forget it. The chances were that he never would have been able to. I was dreading having to break that news."

"And you never had to."

"No. I never did. No specific reason for it. He was healthy as a horse."

"If it came down to it—and I hope to God it doesn't—we might have to subpoena that file. You understand that?"

Massie stood up and the visit was over. "Have at it. But Sam—"

"Yeah."

"Don't ask me any more questions. Don't even ask me to surmise that something else might be true, because I won't tell you. I won't tell you if what you're thinking is correct, or if it could possibly be correct, or how I think it might have occurred. You know what I'm saying?"

"That's a given."

Massie shook his hand again. "Sam, when your neck is on the chopping block, you do what you have to—and I understand. But if there's another way, a way that will work for you, take it. O.K.?"

"I'm with you Doc. I'm with you all the way on that one."

CHAPTER THIRTY-SEVEN

Joanne's Sunday began before five, long before a flat, dull sun lit the tenebrous sky in the east. She knelt at her window and saw that all the elms and oaks and cottonwoods had gone quite bare of their leaves, that their limbs and twigs seemed charred against the horizon. The crows, sleeping in silhouette, sensed her in the window and woke to mock her.

"Whore! Whore! Whore!"

Even beneath the covers again with her pillow over her head and pressed against her ears, she could hear the black birds' cries. Like all the night sounds that had made her feel protected and cozy when Danny was alive—wind and rain and the whistle of the Union Pacific headed for Spokane—now the crows' cawing only reminded her that there was no hiding place.

She crept back to the window and listened for the river. It was still there, and she could concentrate on its roar and drown out the wicked birds. So close behind the farm property, the river rose high now between the walls of its rock channel after the rain and rain and rain, its current frothing white water over the deep green. She listened to it and smelled its clean, faintly salty smell until she began to shiver in the cold. She pulled on her robe in the dark and walked softly to the kitchen. Her mother appeared almost immediately, pretending she had not been able to sleep either.

"Can I get you something, dear?"

"My pills—I can't find them. I need to sleep."

"Oh . . . Joanne. It's not good for you to take so many pills. I think they just depress you more. Why don't you wait a while?"

"Never mind. It doesn't matter. What time is it?"

"Almost seven. Why don't you go back to bed for a while? Reverend Schuller's coming on at nine—or would you rather watch Oral Roberts?"

"It doesn't matter. Whichever you want."

It didn't matter. She watched her mother move stiffly in the harsh kitchen light and saw that she was old and tired, frail after all the years of being so strong. She should try to be pleasant but the air in the room was heavy and it was so difficult even to talk. The best thing she could do for her mother would be to just go away.

Surely she had been meant to perish on the mountain, and she was suddenly angry that she had not. Each of them—Danny and Duane—had promised her that she was to be with them always. Danny because of love and the other man for a reason she could no longer remember, and each of them had betrayed her. Her life was only left over, a mistake.

"You should get dressed, Joanne, if you can't sleep. Put on something bright and a little lipstick. Someone might come over later."

"Who?"

"Don't jump like that. Only Sonia or one of the girls from the bank, or Mr. Fletcher and, what's her name—the nurse—Mary Jean. They all ask about you."

"I don't want to see anyone but Sonia. Don't let anyone else come. I'm not ready."

Her mother sighed and rose to clear away their coffee cups. "All right, dear. But one of these days—"

"One of these days, I'll be ready to talk to people. I promise you."

I promise you something easier, Mother. And you would thank me one day, if you understood why.

CHAPTER THIRTY-EIGHT

Chelan County's senior deputy prosecutor—Martin Malloy—had watched Nina Armitage in action and under other, more benign, circumstances would have welcomed the chance to confer with her. At present, he was aghast to learn that she—and not Mark Nelson—would be handling Sam Clinton's defense. He had never shared Moutscher's steamroller confidence that they would convict. Moutscher had left too many crevices in the case unchinked; the structure was not as sound as it might be. Even as Malloy stood with wary graciousness and urged Nina to sit down, his hand hovered over the ballistics reports he'd been perusing when her visit was announced. If she didn't have the same reports now, she would demand them soon enough. If he didn't give them to her, she'd scream "Failure to Disclose" and make a jury wonder what he was hiding.

The bullet fragments they'd scooped out of Ling were .38's, jacketed hollow points—police type—but there was no law that stopped civilians from buying them. No lands. No grooves. No firing pin marks. They could have come from either of the .38 pistols recovered, and Armitage would know that and go with it.

He smiled at her and slid the reports into his desk drawer. "Counselor, this is a pleasure."

"My pleasure, Mr. Malloy."

She was relaxed, and that bothered the hell out of him. She seemed already to view him as dead in the water. Why? She was too solicitous, too complimentary about the prestige of his law school, and the unexceptional decor of his county office.

"What can I help you with, Ms. Armitage?"

"I thought we might communicate better if I came in person to tell you I've taken over the case."

"Is that all?"

"I see you have the ballistics report there."

Shit! He slid the ballistics sheets out of his desk and handed them to her, and met her head-on, his voice studiously casual. "Minor consideration, you'll see. A toss-up. Only bullet recovered was in little, tiny pieces."

She read the report without expression, and then smiled at him. "I already have this, but thanks. Ling was *behind* Sam all the time. Sam was firing toward the canyon. Demich had a .22. It looks like the lady may have got a shot off. Amazing, isn't it? She seems such a delicate woman, and from what I've been able to find out, she was terrified of guns. That she could react so quickly, so accurately. What's the pull on a .38? Fourteen pounds, isn't it?"

"That's double-action."

"Of course."

"Single action would be only five to seven."

"You know your stuff, counselor. But you think a mere child could fire a .38 and hit a bull's eye fifty feet away? That puzzles me. It almost seems that someone gave her a crash course, prepared her in case of attack."

"Lindstrom might have. Up there in the woods, he might have shown her how to fire."

"Sam says he tried many times, Mr. Malloy. She wouldn't touch a weapon."

"Clinton is not my most reliable source of information."

"Perhaps not."

She shook a cigarette from her pack, held one out to him and he shook his head. She lit one and inhaled deeply.

"You don't smoke. That's admirable in this business. I suppose you play racquet-ball and lift weights too?"

"Squash." He reddened. The woman was what—ten—fifteen years older than he was, and she made him feel like a gawky student, stuttering before a teacher.

"Have you met Mrs. Lindstrom? Have you talked with her, Mr. Malloy?"

"Rex Moutscher has. My staff members have, and I will. She has been through quite an ordeal, and I . . ."

"What about a polygraph? Voice stress analysis? Did you run her on any of those magic boxes? No? Have you ever considered that it was possible she'd blow ink all over the walls—that she could talk into a PSE and make a lovely line of telling domes? But then, you do have the perfect witness. She's the All-American Beauty, the little heroine, McDonald's, and the Lutheran Church, and . . ."

All her jousting about ballistics had been cat-and-mouse. Malloy saw that she was rolling now, but could not see her direction clearly.

"The tests occurred to us, but it seemed kind of nasty to subject her to all of that when her statement was so straightforward."

"A little like putting the Virgin Mary on the lie-box? It's all right to ask hookers and gypsies if they're telling the truth, but not the kind of girl every man wants to bring hom to Mama?"

"We all make value judgments, Ms. Armitage. Any attorney, any detective, has to depend on his—his instinctive sense. My choices are based upon the physical evidence, on Mrs. Lindstrom's statement, on the medical evidence, and on Moutscher's opinions."

She laughed, almost a happy sound.

"Rex Moutscher can't tell a rat's ass from a primrose. Rex Moutscher let half of the physical evidence slip between his clumsy fingers, and I think, Martin—if I may call you Martin—that his ambition might just possibly exceed yours and mine, and we both admit that we're greedy as hell."

"You coin a poetic phrase, Nina—if I may call you Nina?"

"Of course. I'm only a woman, really, and it's difficult to believe I do what I do, isn't it? A pale flower of a woman cast into the path of ruthless men. Not unlike your little witness."

He leaned back and grinned, but she caught him before his tilted chair hit the substance of the wall.

"Did you know Joanne Lindstrom was pregnant?"

He bounced back with a jolt. Before he could respond, she skewered him.

"Did you know that the late Daniel Lindstrom didn't have enough motile spermatozoa to impregnate a female—not even if they froze thirty ejaculations and stockpiled them? Did you know he was sterile?"

" . . . no. That I did not know." Barracuda. Armitage was a barracuda.

"We have the medical records to prove that. Unless you're anxious to explain to a jury that an immaculate conception took place up there in the greenery, that Joanne is even now carrying the next Messiah, you might be interested in a compromise."

"Fuck!"

"You speak with a certain lyric quality yourself, counselor."

Malloy sighed and she felt a moment of empathy for him, remembering her own losses when victory had seemed so close. Resignation hung heavy over his slumped shoulders. "You're sure about the pregnancy, and the other?"

"Absolutely sure. Funny, isn't it—how many of our efforts come down to the birds and the bees?"

"What do you want? When you speak of a compromise, what would you want from me?"

"Surrender with honor."

"Given the alternative, that seems generous of you. What could you possibly gain from preserving my honor? Your reputation has preceded you, Nina. You've left a lot of opponents twisting in the wind."

"It's not for me. I'm a cut-throat; my client is a man of some compassion. Sam would prefer that the woman not be held up to public ridicule. I don't agree, and I don't really fathom why he isn't itching for revenge. But there you go. For me—for you too—there might be an interesting phenomenon. A defense we could use in the future. I've promised I won't use it this time, but it's happened before and it will happen again. Something weird happened to Joanne Lindstrom and left her brain scrambled; when Moutscher talked to her, she didn't *know* if it was Sam Clinton or Godzilla who shot Demich. I think she may have gotten some of it back by now, and I'm fascinated with the process."

Malloy listlessly arranged paperclips across his desk; he had no enthusiasm for Nina Armitage's psychiatric research, coming as it did on top of the shambles of his best, most glorious, and, yes, most longed-for murder case.

"So then. What do you want?"

"I'm going back to Natchitat. I'd like to take you and Moutscher with me—and we'll arrange a meeting with your witness."

He thought of Moutscher, the outraged disbelief on his face. "Rex is not going to like this at all."

"It might be good for him. Better than a 4.6 deposition from your witness, anyway. From what I've heard, he is a man of little imagination."

"You might say he doesn't know the meaning of the word. He's a cop. What do you expect from cops?"

"I won't tell him you said that. Counselor, we feed off cops. They bring us all their treasures neatly labeled and initialed, and their theories, and their gut reactions, and we make something intelligent out of it. They're our raw materal any way you look at it. From your seat, you need them. From mine—and one day you'll be a defense attorney too because you want the money; you're only here for experience—from *mine,* I get my jollies out of pointing out their overweening stupidity. For now, Moutscher is your cross to bear."

She stood up and smiled again, and he thought he liked her very little. "One thing. Sam Clinton is a cut above them all. If he had had the good fortune to be born meaner, a little quicker on his feet, and a little hungrier, he could have been one of us."

"Is that how he got you for his attorney?"

"That's a long, tired, pathetic story, unfit and uninteresting for your ears." She handed him her card with the Holiday Inn number scribbled on the back. "Can you and Moutscher get down to Natchitat by three or four?"

He reached for his desk phone. "I'll call him now."

"Wait until I leave. I don't want to gloat. We'll look for you by four. And Martin . . . Don't call Joanne first. If she spooks, we'll both be up shit creek."

"You're so damned smug," he said, a bite in his voice that he hadn't meant to betray. "You keep ordering me around and I'll balk. I may just decide to go for a tussle in court. You've got a right to all my paper, but you don't know my battle plan. You could be whistling in the dark, Nina."

"I could be. If today doesn't convince you, then we go ahead into trial. You'll still have your zingers and I'll still have mine. If you do see what I think you will, then we can ask the judge for a 4.9 pretrial conference —clandestinely, as it were, without the press—and we work it out to our mutual satisfaction."

"You've got a deal."

"You don't sound that certain, but I'll shake on it." She held out her hand, and he took it, and found it was only a woman's hand, thin and bony and crushable in his.

"One more thing, counselor—"

"Yes. What else?"

"Do you fool around?"

He laughed and dropped her hand. "With you, my dear, only with the greatest of care."

CHAPTER THIRTY-NINE

Joanne had kissed her mother before Elizabeth left for her day of teaching.

"I love you, Mama."

Her mother could not say it back. "Take care of yourself today. Is Sonia coming over?"

"Maybe. Maybe this afternoon."

"Well, that's good. Try to keep busy."

"I will."

"You're a good daughter."

She heard the car door slam, the whisper of tires moving away over the frosted lane, and then the vast promising silence that meant she was entirely alone.

She was no longer afraid. There was such calmness in her and so much relief that it should be that way. She moved in cool fluidity where nothing or no one could harm. It seemed as if the river already flowed over her, gently forgiving.

She suspected there would be nothing beyond. If there was a God, if the God of her Sunday school days in whom she had believed without questioning still endured, He would not have allowed the red man to have her. It was quite simple. There had been no God to save her, and there was no God waiting now to punish her.

She no longer resented the child. It deserved only the small kindness of dying in her womb before it could be thrust into a world that promised nothing to it.

She had control at last. She had chosen never to be older than thirty-two. She had chosen this day, this last cold Monday for her own, and she had hours of it.

She did her mother's breakfast dishes, wiped the counter clean, and, not satisfied, sprayed kitchen wax and polished the Formica until it glowed. She swept the floor; it was important not to leave a dirty house behind. The effort exhausted her and she slept until two.

When she woke, she took a very long, very hot bath, and felt clean. Really clean, at last.

If she left a note, then Sam would be O.K. They would let him go, and he would forgive her. But she couldn't leave a note. Everyone would know about her. Even when she was dead, she couldn't bear to have them know.

She chose her garments for her own pleasure—if not for pleasure, because pleasure seemed an excessive word, then to her own liking. White. All white. A light cotton skirt that she had not worn for years, and a blouse, long-sleeved and full of lace at the neck. The shoes were her wedding shoes, retrieved from the furthest corner of her closet, and still with a grain of rice clinging to one outdated, pointed toe. A bride rushing to meet no bridegroom.

She wanted something of Danny's, some last garment that had belonged to him, and she found a silk scarf, white too, a gift from her mother that he had worn once to be polite. She twisted it around her and found that it covered the place where she could not fasten the skirt at her waist. She thought she had caught the faintest wafting of Danny's odor when she shook the scarf out.

Joanne had not looked directly at her own face in a mirror since Elizabeth had driven her carefully home from the hospital. She gazed at her image and saw a strange woman with pale lips and lost, faded eyes, such sallow, yellowish skin. She touched her cheek in wonder, and traced the sunken places beneath her eyes.

She brought herself back—the self that she remembered—with an application of liquid foundation, Erace under her eyes, and heavy dusting of Indian Earth blusher. And because it was part of an old ritual, she sprayed her throat and wrists with cologne.

When she was ready, she left the house without looking back. The wind was blowing off the river and she could smell the water the moment she shut the back door behind her.

She looked up at the sound of a heavy footfall and saw them coming toward her. The woman and Sam and Captain Moutscher and the other man that she didn't recognize.

And knew she was trapped. The terror rushed back in as if her body was a shell surrounding a vacuum.

They were staring at her, not surprised, but only curious, perhaps, to find her dressed and coiffed and smelling of roses and on her way to nowhere.

CHAPTER FORTY

"Could we go inside, Mrs. Lindstrom?" Moutscher broke the silence, and Sam saw that Moutscher's hand reaching out to touch Joanne made her shrink back in something very close to panic.

"What?"

"I asked if we could go inside—where we could talk. We're sorry to interrupt you, but something has come up. You look very nice. Were you expecting someone?"

"No . . . no one." She made no move to welcome them in, only stared beyond them toward the river path.

"Then you have a little time for us?"

"My mother isn't home."

Nina's voice cut in, washed of its imperious edge, and Sam breathed more easily. "We know that, Joanne. If you like, you could call your mother and have her come home. We could wait for that—"

"No!" Joanne moved away from the door and held her arm out in an odd wooden motion, seeming to indicate they could enter.

Sam ducked his head at the back door and stepped into the kitchen, and wished instantly that they had chosen some other place for the confrontation that must come. He had been welcome here and was not now. The room was the same still, and he saw ghosts sitting in the empty chairs. He was relieved when Joanne led them into the living room; they had never sat in the "parlor" together. Only at the long kitchen table where Joanne had laughed at them, and with them, and fed them, and rarely spoken beyond her gentle counterpoint to their voices.

She seemed to be aware of his presence in the group, although she had not yet looked directly at him. He could not tell if she was frightened of him or ashamed to face him. She looked like herself now and yet unlike the Joanne he remembered, more uncertain and somehow disjointed. He studied her covertly, this tired, thin girl in white, tried to superimpose the image upon that of the wild brown woman on the mountain and could not.

" . . . coffee?" Joanne's voice was so slight that the ticking clock overrode it. "Would you all like coffee?"

"No thank you," Nina answered. "We've all just had coffee."

And enlightenment and a lot of discussion on how you lied and how they can trap you, Joanne. Joanne looked at Sam, startled, as if she had read his mind. He looked away.

"Does having Mr. Clinton here upset you, Mrs. Lindstrom?" Malloy asked.

Joanne looked at the prosecutor. "I—I didn't want to see him anymore. Excuse me, but I don't know who you are."

"I'm sorry. My name is Martin Malloy. I'm the chief criminal deputy prosecutor from Chelan County. You might say I was your attorney."

"Is this something official?" Joanne started to rise from her chair, as if to take flight, saw that her way was barred, and sat down again. "I need to know if this is official."

"Not really official, Mrs. Lindstrom," Malloy said smoothly. "It's in the nature of a conference—all interested parties meeting by mutual agreement. Is that all right with you?"

"I don't know."

"You would—(Nina caught the word *would* instead of *will* and smiled faintly at Malloy's gaffe)—have to see Mr. Clinton at the trial. A defendant has the right to confront his accuser. That's the law. We all thought it might be easier—talking here in your own home."

"I don't understand." Joanne sat stiffly, her ankles crossed neatly, but her twisting hands in her lap betrayed her. "I thought I would just go to the trial . . . and testify."

"Are you afraid of Sam?" Nina asked bluntly. "Is this room too small? Is he too close to you?"

"No."

"But you were afraid of him before? You were afraid for your life, as I understand your charges?"

Joanne looked toward Sam and made a half-nodding, half-shaking movement with her head.

"Ms. Armitage," Malloy interrupted. "I think—and Captain Moutscher agrees—that we should go at this in some kind of order. I'll speak with Mrs. Lindstrom, go over her statement with her, and then, if you like, you can ask questions. And Mrs. Lindstrom, of course, you may ask questions whenever you like. Would you be comfortable with that procedure?"

Joanne nodded. "Then you're on my side, Mr. Malloy?"

Malloy had the grace to flush as he nodded, "Technically, yes. I represent the state, and you are the state's prime witness."

"And Miss Armitage is on Sam's side?"

"She represents Mr. Clinton, yes." Malloy reached into his sleek attaché case and pulled forth Joanne Lindstrom's statement. "We'll begin at the beginning, as they say, Mrs. Lindstrom."

Don't smile like that, you slippery bastard. Sam looked away from Malloy out over the fields beyond the window, down to the poplars bending in the wind. He did not want to see Joanne's face. He was no innocent sitting in on this massacre; he had agreed to it—to keep himself out of prison. He accepted that, and the guilt that went with it, but he hoped the questioning would not be protracted—that the kill would be quick.

"Mrs. Lindstrom, you stated that you and your husband—Daniel— arrived in Stehekin in September. What date was that?"

"I'm not sure. It was right before Labor Day, 1979."

"You mean 1981, don't you?"

"Yes. 1981."

"Was it on September 4—let's see here, the Friday before Labor Day?"

"Yes."

"And how did you happen to meet Duane Demich?"

"Duane?"

"Yes."

"Duane came into our camp one night. I think the first night—no, it might have been the second night. It was dark, and he sort of loomed up out of the woods and he said a bear had tried to get him, or he'd seen a bear, or something like that. He was a policeman . . ."

"He was *what?*"

"He told Danny he was a policeman in Oregon, and they kind of sat there and talked about people they knew and things like that."

"Why didn't you mention that when Captain Moutscher talked to you before?"

"He didn't ask about that. And Duane wasn't really a policeman. I don't know why he said that. It might have been a joke."

"How did you feel about him? Had you ever seen him before that night?"

Sam listened closely, but kept his head averted.

"Duane? No. I'd never seen him before."

"He was never in Natchitat?"

"Oh no, Mr. Malloy. He hadn't ever been to Natchitat—he told me that."

"How did you feel when he walked into your camp? Were you glad to see him?"

"Danny liked him."

Sam suppressed a groan.

"Danny liked him. How did *you* feel?"

". . . he made me dizzy."

"I don't understand."

"He was a red man."

"A *red* man. I'm sorry. You'll have to explain that to me. Do you mean you thought he was an Indian?"

"He was awfully large. Very, very tall and big, and everything about him seemed to glow or burn or something. It's hard to say—but I was af . . . startled. His hair was red and his skin and eyes were red in the firelight. I guess at first, I thought he wasn't real—or something like that."

"But he *was* real?"

"Yes."

"And he camped with you that night?"

"No. He camped someplace down by the lake, and he was gone in the morning."

"Were you disappointed?"

"What? No. I was glad. I was relieved."

"Why?"

"Because we went up there to be alone, and he was a stranger."

"But he came back again?"

"He came back in the morning. He said there was a grizzly bear on the trail, and that he needed Danny to help him do something—get rid of it, or scare it away, maybe kill it. I don't know."

"You say Duane Demich was a big man. And strong. Were there other trails he could have taken?"

"I don't know. There were trails, I think—but I never knew where I was. He seemed to be very upset."

"Did Mr. Demich have any weapons?"

"He had a rifle, and a pistol, or a revolver, or something like that— something you hold in your hand. And he had a knife in a leather holder."

"But he was afraid of the grizzly bear?"

"He seemed to be."

"What did your husband do?"

Joanne bent her head and stared at her hands.

"Do you want a drink of water?" Nina asked.

"No. I'm all right. I'm trying to remember how it was. I have—kind of cloudy places. It gets black, like black smoke in front of my eyes."

"What did your husband do?" Malloy's voice was a drone, no inflection, no insistence.

"Danny went with him. They pushed me up in a tree. They wouldn't let me go."

"What happened while you were in the tree?"

"The birds came."

"What birds?"

"Little women birds. They waited with me, and it seems as though they talked to me. No. That sounds wrong, doesn't it? I'm sorry—it's not clear. I was very frightened."

"How long were you in the tree?"

"I don't know."

"What happened to your husband and Duane Demich while you were in the tree?"

"I don't know."

"You told Captain Moutscher you saw them fighting with a bear—with a grizzly bear."

"No . . . Did I? I can't remember."

Sam's head came up at that, and Moutscher stood up and strode to the window, turning his back on them. Nina seemed perfectly calm.

"Do you remember anything about the bear?" Malloy probed.

"Duane said it was awful. He said it was the most horrible thing that he had ever seen. He tried to kill it. I think maybe he did kill it. No, something was following us so—so it must have been alive, but there were terrible scratches on his arm when he came back."

"So you remember telling Captain Moutscher about the bear?"

"I must have. I must have forgotten." She bowed her head and stared at her shoes, lined the toes up and waited. The room was too quiet. Her hands flew to her ears. "Ohhh . . . Danny screamed. Somebody screamed."

Nina struck a match and everyone in the room but Joanne looked at her.

Malloy tried another tack. "Why did you tell Captain Moutscher that you saw the bear?"

"I must have. I wouldn't have said that if I hadn't seen it; I just can't remember it now. It's so hard to explain how you can get clouds in your head like this. You try and try to clear them away so you can see, but —"

"O.K. Let's leave that behind for a moment. What happened later? Did someone get you out of the tree? Did someone come back for you?"

"He saved me."

"Who saved you?"

"Duane. Duane came back and saved me." There was something odd in the way she spoke; she lapsed into a kind of sing-song. "I would have died. I would have died if he hadn't saved me."

Moutscher turned around and stared at Joanne, shaking his head faintly.

"How long after you heard the screaming? When did he come back?"

"I don't know. I can see the part where he was in the tree with me.

He held me tight so I couldn't fall. I bit his hand."

"You *what?*"

"I bit his hand. I don't know why, but I left teeth marks in his hand, and it made him sick. But he didn't blame me. He forgave me."

"How did you get out of the tree?"

The clock in the corner chimed four times, and then another in the kitchen answered. When they stopped, the silence in the room seemed heavier.

"Joanne," Malloy tapped her knee lightly to get her attention. "How did you get out of the tree?"

"I don't know. The next thing I can remember is being in a meadow —with a rock. I was holding a rock over my head and—"

"Why? What were you doing?"

"I can't remember."

"A little rock? A big rock?"

"A big rock to smash—"

"What? Were you using it as a weapon—or to cook—or—"

"To smash his eyes."

Nina looked across at Malloy, but he would not meet her eyes. His voice was softer when he spoke to Joanne again.

"Joanne, were you afraid of Duane Demich. Did he attack you?"

"Attack me?"

"Did he—interfere with you sexually?"

"NO!"

"Nothing like that. You're sure?"

"I was married to Danny. I wouldn't let anyone—any man—do that to me."

"Your husband was dead. Didn't he tell you Danny was dead?"

She lifted her head and looked at Malloy. "If he did, I don't remember it. I was all alone. Everyone was gone, and I was lost. He said he would help me—us—get out, and I believed that he would. Don't you see? I—"

"You liked him then. You came to like him?"

She tensed, as if she suspected a trap. "There was nobody else. It wasn't that I liked him or didn't like him. He was all there was. I thought I was going to die. Sometimes it seems as though I wanted to die."

"But he wouldn't let you die?"

"No. He saved me."

Sam heard the same odd cadence in her voice, as if certain phrases she spoke were by rote, like a child mouths poems. It made the hair stand up on his neck. Malloy had become quite gentle with Joanne. Moutscher sat on the window seat and stared at the floor, fidgeting with his socks. Only Nina seemed unmoved and placid.

"Do you know how long you were up there on the mountain?" Malloy asked. "How many days?"

"A month. A couple of months. It's hard to measure time. It was most of the spring."

"Spring? What months? Do you know the months?"

"April. May." She seemed confused. "No, it wasn't spring. There were yellow trees; their leaves were changing, and it snowed some of the time. Didn't it snow?"

"I wasn't there, Joanne."

Joanne looked across the room at Sam and spoke to him for the first time since they'd come into the farmhouse. "Didn't it snow, Sam?"

Malloy shook his head in warning at Sam, but Sam ignored him. "It snowed, Joanne," Sam said softly. "It was autumn."

"Yes. It was autumn. It was October and November."

"What is the date today, Joanne?"

"Could I look at a calendar?"

"Just give us your best guess."

"It's almost Thanksgiving."

"That's right."

"Then it's November."

She was trembling, so faintly that Sam looked again and saw the lacy bow at her neck flutter. It was going on so long. Why didn't Malloy just come out and ask his heavy questions and be done with it? He pulled away from the leather chair and felt his shirt cling to his back, soaked in sweat.

"If it's November now, you must have been home for a long time. What year were you lost?"

"1977."

Moutscher choked and slapped the window seat with his hand.

"After you were in the meadow, what happened?" Malloy plodded on, as if at any moment the pieces of his case would magically come together again. "Was Mr. Demich . . . let me rephrase that: Did Mr. Demich continue to make you feel—'dizzy?' Were you afraid of him?"

"No."

"Did you like him?"

"He was sick. He needed somebody to look after him. Nobody ever had looked after him. He was like a little boy when he was sick, and I think he was frightened."

"So you began to like him?"

"I guess so."

"Did he attempt to rape you, or, let's say did he try to have sex with you?"

"No. I told you he didn't. I don't like that question, Mr. Malloy. His arm was all infected, and it was very hard for us. I thought he was going to die and leave me up there alone."

"But he didn't?"

"No. I had some penicillin which I gave it to him, and he got better for a while. We had to hide."

"Hide from who?"

"People. People following us."

"What people?"

"I don't know."

"Sam Clinton?"

"I don't know."

"You were very frightened?"

"I was always frightened."

"Let's skip ahead. Let's think about when Mr. Clinton found you."

"Do we have to do that?"

"I think so. When did you see Sam Clinton? What was he doing?"

"Could I see my statement?"

"Try to remember, if you can."

"Sam was angry."

"And . . ."

"He was holding a gun."

"Did Duane Demich have a gun?"

"I wasn't looking at him."

"He might have held a gun?"

"He might. He told me that he wouldn't let anything happen to me."

"Did you have a gun?"

"No. I don't think I did."

"Do you know how to fire a gun?"

"Duane showed me how to. In case someone came, someone who was trying to hurt us."

"What happened then?"

"Sam shot Danny." Tears rolled down Joanne's cheeks, although she was seemingly unaware of them. "He shot him and he fell down, and I tried to help him."

"You said Sam shot Danny. Did you mean he shot Duane?"

"Yes. He shot Duane. I meant Duane."

"Do you know why he would do that?"

"No—I guess—no. I guess it was a mistake."

"Did you see another man up there? Did you see Max Ling?"

"I saw him later. After Duane fell over the edge. He was bleeding."

"*Who* was bleeding?"

"Everybody was bleeding. Duane was bleeding, and the little man was bleeding, and Sam was bleeding."

"What was the matter with Sam?"

"His head was hurt in the back. Sombo—something hit him. Mr. Malloy, I would rather not talk about this now."

"We have to go through this before we go into court, Joanne. We could stop for awhile if you think you need to."

"I feel sick."

"Do you want to stop for awhile?"

"No, but that's all there is. There isn't anything else to tell."

Nina had sat so quietly that Sam had almost forgotten she was in the room. She rose and touched Malloy on the shoulder, and he moved over on the couch and Nina took his place. She set her attaché case in front of her and smiled at Joanne.

"Joanne, I have a few questions. Is that all right with you?"

"I guess so."

"Nina," Sam spoke out loud, and they all jerked their heads around to stare at him. "She said she felt sick. Maybe, we should wait, and—"

"No. Sit down, Sam. Let me handle this."

Moutscher was looking at him. Puzzled maybe, not angry, not even annoyed as he would have expected. Sam sat down and looked away from the two women.

"Joanne, let's sum up a little. You've been talking to Mr. Malloy for a long time. O.K.?"

"Yes."

"A very bad thing happened to you, a shocking thing. You lost your husband very suddenly. Very violently."

"Yes."

"And you were all alone with Mr. Demich, and you were terribly frightened?"

"Wouldn't you have been?"

"Of course." But her voice was brusque. "Of course. And you were so confused and things got all mixed up and jumbled around and it's hard to remember."

"I guess so. Yes."

"But you remember when I was here before, when we talked in the kitchen?"

"Yes."

"You asked me how Sam was, didn't you? You asked me to say 'Hi' to him? Why would you care about Sam Clinton—if he did all these things you're accusing him of?"

"He's a person."

"Yes. You care about people, do you?"

"I try to."

"You cared about Duane Demich. You took care of him when he got sick in the mountains."

"I had to. Because—because he was the one who could save me."

"Who told you that?"

"Who?"

"Yes, who told you he would save you?"

"He told me."

"Did he talk to you a lot?"

"Some."

"Didn't he tell you what to think, and what to do, and—" Nina stood up and moved her face close to Joanne's. "*Why were you going to smash his eyes?*"

"BecauseIcouldn'tlookawayfromthem!" Joanne clapped her hand

over her mouth, to stop the words that were out of her control.

Nina moved back, satisfied for the moment, and lowered her voice. "What color were his eyes?"

"Green."

"Always?"

"They were red in the fire."

Malloy's voice cut in, "Ms. Armitage, I don't see how the color of Demich's eyes has anything to do with—"

"My turn, Mr. Malloy." Malloy opened his mouth to protest, thought better of it, and remained silent.

"You called him—what was it?—'the red man.' Why was that?"

"At first he was."

"But later, later he wasn't?"

"No. He saved my life. I would have died if—"

Nina held up one hand wearily. "You've told us that before. Did he tell you to say that?"

". . . no. I don't know . . ."

"Did you love him?"

Joanne was as white as milk, her face so chalky that her white clothes had gone gray in contrast. She swayed visibly, caught in the force of each question. "No. No. That's not true. I was grateful."

"How grateful?"

"I don't know what you mean."

"You do know what I mean. You listened to him, and listened to him, and you began to believe everything he told you. It got very easy, didn't it? It was easier than you thought it would be. It was even easy to have sex with him . . ."

". . . no . . ."

"It was easy to fuck him, wasn't it?"

"Nina!" Sam's voice bounced off the walls and Moutscher jumped. Nina looked at Sam with an angry shake of her head.

Joanne's arms had risen slowly until they crossed over her midsection, covering, hiding. She stared into Nina's eyes, and seemed to have forgotten the men were in the room.

"Please don't say that."

"All right," Nina said. "All right, you don't have to answer that now. Joanne, do you have any children?"

"No."

"How long were you married to Danny?"

"Fourteen years."

"You didn't want children?"

"Oh . . . yes, we always wanted children, right from the start. Always."

"But you never had any children?"

". . . no . . ."

"Did you wonder why?"

"We were trying to find out why . . . when . . ."

"You're pregnant now, aren't you?"

Joanne didn't answer, but her arms drew up tighter around her waist.

"You are pregnant now. I'm a woman. I've been pregnant, and I can see that you are. Why don't you just say it?"

Damn her, damn her, damn me. Sam had asked Nina not to do this. A man could not have done it.

"It seems a bitter thing, doesn't it—to have to go through this pregnancy alone when you both waited so long for it? But then, maybe it's a blessing. Maybe it gives you something to occupy your mind. Did Danny know about the baby?"

Joanne was rigid, a deer caught in the cross hairs, unable to move out of the line of fire. Transfixed.

"Did Danny know you were pregnant?"

"Of course not—no . . ."

"You say 'of course not.' Why?"

"It—it was too soon to tell."

"Oh. Really? How soon was it?"

Malloy and Moutscher looked uncomfortable, more than uncomfortable, aware that they had been led along in something even they had no stomach for. They relaxed slightly when Nina moved physically away from Joanne, striding now in the stance Sam had admired so many years before, moving across the quiet room easily. She seemed to have forgotten that Joanne hadn't answered her question. More likely, she knew she'd made her point. But Sam knew she'd come back to it —bore in until . . .

"Let's go back again to the tree, Joanne. You were high up, holding on for dear life, weren't you?"

"Yes."

"Let's go through it again."

"Please—I'm so tired."

"You can do it. Mr. Malloy, could I borrow your copy of Mrs. Lindstrom's statement? Thank you. 'I looked toward the area where they had gone and saw a very large animal in the brush. I heard a scream. I think it was my husband. Mr. Demich was wrestling with a bear . . .' I wonder how you could have seen that. From that tree, down along the trail, one naturally comes to a wall of rock. You must have amazing vision, Joanne. Can you see around—or through—rock?"

". . . no . . ."

Nina reached into her attaché case and drew forth an eight-by-ten sheet, turned it carefully against her thigh. *"Do* you remember anything, Joanne? What did the red man look like?"

"Oh . . . please. I can't—"

Sam saw what Nina was about to do. It had not occurred to him that she could be so cruel, so willing to destroy. He started to move, but it was too late. Nina turned over the glossy sheet in her hand and thrust the morgue shot of Demich—in full color, eyes open, his long body white against the swollen purple arm—in front of Joanne.

"Is this him? Is this your hero?"

Joanne screamed, a terrible high-pitched monotone sound that had nothing human behind it. The scream went on interminably.

Moutscher jumped between Nina and Joanne, and Malloy grabbed for the photograph and tore it away. And then Joanne slid from her chair as if she had no bones at all and crawled across the carpet, making gibbery noises that struck Sam as far worse than the screaming.

She crawled to Sam, inching along the floor until she could grasp his knees and hide behind them. He lifted her and carried her to the couch. She clung to him, burrowing against him, her face tight against his chest. He looked over her head and saw Nina holding half of a torn picture.

She was still smiling.

"Over there is your rapist and your killer, counselor. You notice that Joanne didn't run to either of you or to me? She went straight to Sam because she's always known he wouldn't hurt her, no matter what she tried to do to him."

"Lady," Malloy said slowly. "You'd eat your own young to win. I'm amazed that you denied yourself the pleasure of doing this in a court-room."

"That wasn't necessary."

"Neither was this. You made your point a long time ago." Malloy looked down at Joanne. "Is she O.K.?"

Sam shook his head. "Call Doc Massie. He's in the book."

The other men welcomed an excuse to leave the room. Nina stood next to Sam as if she expected him to say something to her, but there was nothing to say; all his energy was focused on Joanne. Nina shrugged and left them alone.

Sam held Joanne closely and rocked her. He could hear voices in the kitchen, muffled conversation with no meaning. Nina's mocking laugh rose and stopped half-born when Moutscher and Malloy didn't respond. He wondered for a moment what she could possibly find to laugh about, and then realized that she had won and so had he. That he was now a free man seemed a hollow conquest. The means had soiled the end, and the devastation seemed irreparable.

Joanne clung to him as if he really could save her, and he stroked her hair and whispered, "It's all right now. You're safe. Sam's here. Sam's here. It's all right. It's all over. You're safe. Sam's here." The words he had meant to say on the mountain.

He heard a car door slam and the sound of a car leaving. He was alone with Joanne for a long time, waiting for Doc to come. He heard Elizabeth Crowder's voice, and then Sonia Kluznewski's, but neither of the women ventured beyond the doorway. He kept talking, and Joanne gradually stopped whimpering against his chest. She breathed so shal-lowly that he was alarmed, but her eyes were open and blinking occa-sionally. His bad hip demanded a change of position, but even slight movement set off her trembling, and he stayed still, stroking and hold-ing and whispering with his face against her hair.

When Doc walked in, the two of them together could not unlock Joanne's arms from Sam. He carried her to Doc's car, held her against the night while Doc drove too fast into town, and then carried her into the hospital, and laid her on a bed. She would not let go of his hand.

Doc Massie shut the door against the hovering nurses and filled a syringe.

Sam held his free hand out and stopped Doc's wrist. "What is that?"

"A sedative. She's not going to let loose of you until we sedate her."

"What if she's pregnant? Would that hurt the baby?"

Doc pulled the syringe stopper back and turned away from Sam. "Did I say she was pregnant?"

"No. And I'm not asking you. I said I wouldn't ask you."

Doc turned back and winked, a solemn wink with no humor behind it. "On the off-chance that she's pregnant, that she's carrying Danny's kid, I've got something in there that won't harm it. Nothing I've given her so far would harm it."

"That she's carrying *Danny's* . . ."

"Who else's? And who would know, and who would tell?"

Joanne's features relaxed, her eyes finally closed, and her hand slipped out of Sam's and lay open.

When he was sure that she was really asleep, he walked down the stairway and away from the hospital. The night smelled of chrysanthemums and smoke and apples. His truck was still parked behind the sheriff's office. He drove past the high school and saw the stadium lights were on for night practice.

He drove past the Safeway and went home to feed his cat.

EPILOGUE

NATCHITAT

SPRING, 1982

People forgot. The scandal had burst upon Natchitat already blooming, scarlet flowers budding and fading prematurely; like most gossip, the roots were shallow. It could not survive—at least not with its original glory—the hard winter. Those who knew the truth would not speak of it, and even the most dedicated tale carriers gave up after a while. Without a definite hero (or heroine), or a certain villain, it was too difficult to draw battle lines. In small towns where one can hear each neighbor breathe and laugh and cry, and sometimes in the act of adultery, new transgressions rush in to fill the void. Whatever peculiar secret thing it was that had prevented a trial became part of the folklore of Natchitat, scarcely examined except by old women with nothing better to do, and nobody listened to them anyway.

The winter was bad, full of blizzard and drift, the snows muffling everything and quieting life. The volcano down at St. Helens rumbled and stirred long before spring and threatened to suffocate Natchitat for a second time with eerie and perhaps deadly gray ash. The economy faltered. They closed down the lumber mill and one of the apple packing plants, and people worried far more about running out of unemployment compensation than they did about sin and the possibility of unavenged murder. Jobless, depressed men fought with each other and with their wives in taverns and houses, and when blood is drawn and property threatened, no one looks closely at the deputy who comes to rescue.

Walker Fewell had to take Sam back into his department, a bitter pill to swallow. Under the law and according to civil service guidelines, Sam was without blemish. The rest of the deputies clapped him on the back and made loud, awkward conversation, and then everything was the same as it had been—except that Danny was gone. Sam refused all partners at first, patrolling alone on day watch, but then he accepted the new man, a kid not over twenty-five, who needed a mentor if he was going to make it. And, if the truth were known, Sam was lonely.

Joanne. Joanne went away in a quiet caravan of cars with Doc and her mother and Sonia. They came back without her, leaving her in a gray, quiet, and terribly expensive private sanatorium on the other side of the Cascades. When she came back, she remembered what she had forgotten and understood what she remembered. Except for certain times when the air was a familiar color or when the night was very dark and the wind tore at the moon, she was well. Not wonderfully well, but as well as most.

She came home in January and was welcomed tenderly, all the more tenderly when they saw that she carried her dead husband's child. The women at the church gave her a surprise shower, and she went to natural childbirth classes with Sonia who was pregnant again herself. When Doc Massie saw Joanne for monthly check-ups, he always referred to the unborn child as "Danny's kid," and she gave no sign that she might believe otherwise.

The child within her was active early on, and she stared at her white belly when she bathed and saw its elbows and knees making little bumps there. She was glad that it was healthy.

Sam passed her one day as he patrolled along the Old Orchard Road. She stood at the mailbox and waved him down as he wondered if he should stop. She looked beautiful again, more beautiful, standing there in one of Danny's blue plaid wool shirts, bundled up against the snow. She smiled at him happily and there seemed no reason not to drive her up the lane and sit in the kitchen and drink coffee with her.

It was easy then—more than easy—for him to stop daily. By tacit agreement, they never spoke of the summer or of the trouble in the fall. They were comfortable together. She needed someone to talk to; she was as serene as he had ever known her to be—worried only, she confided, at being alone at night because the snowstorms so often broke the thin black power lines. She would not go to her mother's house in town; she was quite determined about that. He was concerned enough so that he began to sit with her through the long evenings until she was tired enough to sleep. They watched television and talked, and he hugged her when he left, feeling paternal or telling himself that he felt paternal toward her.

It seemed reasonable and mutually beneficial that he accept her offer when Rhodes caught Pistol fouling the laundry room once too often and told Sam to get his trailer out of the park. He moved it to the lower part of the farm property, hooked into the water and electricity lines, and became a sentry at the beginning of the lane. Hidden as the trailer was behind the poplar screen, it was weeks before any passerby noticed it was there. And since he was so close now, it would have been ridiculous for them to cook separately; so he bought the groceries and she cooked for them.

Sam found himself more and more anxious to hurry "home" to Joanne, and she began to listen for the sound of his truck coming up the lane. She had some memory, some old recollection that might not be real, of being safe in his arms.

Three things occurred on the 14th of April, apparently unrelated.

Nina Armitage's bill for "Interest on $5,000.00 loan: $900.00" reached Sam's post office box. He wrote a check immediately, enclosed it in a sweet, flowered thank you card, and mailed it.

The ground in Chelan County thawed, and Duane Demich's body—which had remained unclaimed—was removed from its vault and buried without ceremony in an unmarked grave in a cemetery outside Wenatchee.

And, although the moon was only three quarters full and she had been very careful, Joanne Lindstrom went into hard labor and was delivered of a premature son. Despite his shortened gestation, the baby boy weighed over seven pounds and came into the world with a full head of burnished red hair.

Joanne nursed the infant and rocked it, and carried it close to her wherever she was. He did not have the dull blue eyes common to newborns; his were full of light and intelligence. He clung to her and would have none of Sam at the beginning. But Sam perservered, fascinated by the baby's vulnerability, determined to let this child know that he would not harm it. Gradually it relaxed in his arms as he sat, dwarfing the rocker with his heavy shoulders and sang to it in a gravelly voice that made Joanne laugh.

Joanne named the baby Danny. Hearing her say the name so often first made Sam wince, but he agreed that it was the only choice.

In May, when the apple trees were dotted with pink and white blossoms, they carried Danny outside and laid him on a blanket in the bright green grass so that he could reach out for the blossoms.

"Look at him, Sam. Watch him. He seems so wise the way he stares at us—as if he knows everything and would tell us if he could only talk."

"All babies do that."

"No, he's special. He's really special."

He could not argue with her because she was so happy, and it was good to see her smile again. "Maybe he is. You never can tell."

"I'll love him so much; he'll grow up perfect. You believe that, don't you?"

He looked away from her for a moment, toward the river, and when he turned back her face was suddenly grave.

"You do believe that, don't you?"

He took her hand and lied, "I believe that."

He thought of Nina, who believed in nothing, and he finally let her go. He was not sure what it was that he believed. But the sky was clear above them, and the grass was sweet, and the child too. And there was, after all, only this one place where they were. Only this day.

Also by Cyra McFadden

THE SERIAL

Rain or Shine

Rain or Shine
A FAMILY MEMOIR

Cyra McFadden

Alfred A. Knopf ⬡ New York 1986

THIS IS A BORZOI BOOK
PUBLISHED BY ALFRED A. KNOPF, INC.

Library of Congress Cataloging-in-Publication Data
McFadden, Cyra.
Rain or shine.

1. Taillon, Cy. 2. Rodeo announcers—United States—
Biography. 3. McFadden, Cyra. 4. Journalists—United
States—Biography. I. Title.
GV742.42.T35M34 1986 070.4′ 497918 [B] 85-45597
ISBN 0-394-51937-X

Manufactured in the United States of America
FIRST EDITION

FOR KENT

Acknowledgments

Without the help of my brothers Terry and Tom Taillon, who gave me access to our father's files and scrapbooks, I could not have written this book. They have my gratitude as well as my love.

Rain or Shine

Cy Taillon

INTRODUCTION

When my father died, in April of 1980, newspapers in the West compared him with John Wayne. "Cy Taillon was more than a rodeo announcer," said the writer for the Miles City *Star* in Miles City, Montana, "like John Wayne was more than an actor. Each became an embodiment of an ideal, a spokesman for a quality of life and a way of living it." America was younger when my father left his family's North Dakota farm and Wayne left the football field of the University of Southern California, the writer continued. "It took men of iron will, stout hearts and sensitive manner to tame her. Stubborn men who spoke their minds and minded what they spoke. Times have changed, so has America. And so has rodeo."

He's right about America and rodeo. My father never changed, not in his loyalty to Western values. When his Denver house was burglarized of two hundred dollars' worth of appliances several years ago, he told the Denver *Post*, "I plan to have an armed resident in the house with orders to shoot first and argue later."

Cy was at the top of his profession then. In fact he was the top, with no competition for his title "Dean of Rodeo Announcers," an accolade accorded him by the rest of the rodeo world and almost always attached to his name. Once a rakehell, he'd been respected and respectable for thirty years: well paid, happily married, a family man and a householder. But inside him, beneath his custom-tailored Western jackets, beat the heart of a cowboy. No one stole his toaster while he was out on the road, if he could help it, and walked away intact. A shotgun shell or two should handle the problem nicely.

We were not speaking to each other then. His blue-eyed darling as a child, named after him, dressed like him as a wrong-sex, unusually short cowboy, I'd grown up, moved away from Montana, moved away in heart and mind from my father and shoot first, argue later. I had a couple of degrees, a divorce behind me and a second marriage; a suburban California house; belonged to the ACLU; took part in San Francisco peace marches while my half brother by my father's second marriage was fighting in Vietnam and my father editorializing from the crow's nest, the rodeo announcer's booth, in support of the war.

The last time we'd seen each other, he and I argued about racial intermarriage, hippies, Catholicism as the one true religion and what to have for dinner. We were at an elegant San Francisco Chinese restaurant. My father insisted that we both eat chow mein. I was full of self and my new sophistication and didn't want to sit at the same table with a man who'd order chow mein at Kan's. Especially a man in kangaroo-skin cowboy boots, nipped-in Western suit and diamond pinkie ring.

We were obnoxious in equal proportions, but my father won. He had a voice that could fill a football stadium without amplification, and he was picking up the check.

So he went back to embodying the West while I went back to ACLU meetings. We exchanged letters in which we discussed politics and each other's character defects. Then we exchanged no letters at all, keeping track of each other through relatives, waiting for the other to heal the rift. Cy Taillon's daughter, I am as stubborn as he was. We loved each other, missed each other, and made ourselves miserable, and this went on for years, time for our grievances to harden into granite.

I rankled at a distance about the form my father's letters took, when I was still receiving them. He sent me a carbon of the letters he wrote his entire family. It was a large family. He always sent me the blurry last carbon.

His own grievances predated our quarrel about San Francisco

and whether or not it was part Sodom, part Gomorrah. As a child, I used to meet my father on the rodeo circuit in the summers, in Billings or Miles City or Lewiston, traveling by Greyhound bus, a label pinned to my shirt: "If bus isn't met deliver to Cy Taillon, fairgrounds." On each such occasion, he marched me off instantly to a beauty shop to have a permanent wave, frustrated beyond tolerance that no matter who did what to me, and no matter how much he paid for it, my hair refused to curl. He wanted a daughter who looked like Shirley Temple. Instead, he had a sulky, waiflike child who looked more like Oliver Twist.

The afternoon before we met for dinner at Kan's, he'd made one more attempt. "Go get your hair done," he said, and gave me twenty dollars. At the beauty shop in his San Francisco hotel, a hairdresser tormented me into a lofty bouffant. I felt freakish, and it didn't help our relations that my father was once again disappointed. "I give up," he said when he saw me. I had to put on my dark glasses. Crying, I had been taught long ago, was for sissies.

We were a long time reconciling, and when reconciliation came, it came on my father's terms. He was sick and demoralized after a small stroke. A letter turned up in my mailbox, on his flamboyant stationery, with its cowboy hat, microphone and lariat logo and the legend: "Cy Taillon, Master of Ceremonies and Rodeo Announcer, with records unequaled for consecutive engagements." He wrote that he'd been hoping for a move from me for years, feeling that "any desire to communicate" should originate with me because he was blameless in our estrangement.

I raged at his tone of injured merit; thought about how he always told reporters he had two children, my two half brothers, Terry and Tommy, and not three; remembered every hurt, every slight, and how, when Cy finally left his tempestuous marriage to my mother, he quickly began the process of erasing me from the record of his life along with her.

When we were together, he sometimes slipped and called me "Pat." I was the living reminder that he'd once slept with her, caroused with her, been deeply and destructively in love with her. Respectability had come late and hard to him. I remembered the person he'd been—dazzling, reckless, a drunk.

The day his letter came, I phoned him, and the voice that had made him famous resonated over the line. Majestically, he told me that if I apologized, he was willing to forgive me. He was, he said, incapable of holding a grudge.

We had nine years to make our peace before cancer killed him. I wrote a book during that time, was interviewed by reporters myself and began to tell the ones who asked me where I got my odd name that my father invented it. He was Cy Taillon, Dean of the Rodeo Announcers and living Western legend.

That he was pleased, Terry and Tommy assure me. He also kept articles that I wrote and sent and newspaper pieces in which I mentioned him. What he wrote me was that he was pleased my book was doing well but that the attention paid to it surprised him. He was a writer, too, for Western periodicals, with files full of fan letters. He'd never received as much press as I did, for what was after all a short book. I must have a very good press agent.

In the summer two years after he died, I went back to Montana. This time I went to Great Falls, where my father died and my two brothers live. (I'm dropping "half brother" at this point because we're related not just by blood but by our complicated love for our father.) There I went on a pilgrimage of sorts with Terry, then thirty-seven and a rodeo announcer himself.

Cy was dead. My stepmother, Dorothy, was dead. My mother was failing and close to dying. Even more than Terry did, I felt cut loose from my life as I'd known it until then because my husband of twenty years had died the December before.

In Terry's new Buick Skylark, named "Ol' Sorrel Top," we headed for the Miles City Bucking Horse Sale, the last of Cy's unequaled consecutive engagements. Though Miles City has a celebrated rodeo, our real reason for the trip was to spend time together and to build a bridge between our vastly different lives.

Forty-four-year-old woman, widowed, an urban dweller; kid brother, now grown up and graying, big, barrel-chested, a cowboy. To make the trip and the bridge building go more smoothly, Terry set the car on cruise control and stopped only at crossroads bars.

The road from Great Falls to Miles City heads south across barren, empty country. We peeled away the miles with Jack Daniel's for me and Black Velvet for Terry, while Willie Nelson sang old Hank Williams songs on the tape deck. After spending most of his life on the road, traveling with Cy and then making the circuit himself as a bronc rider, Terry is an expert in dead-animal identification, needing only a blot on the highway, a bit of entrail or a couple of tail feathers, to say authoritatively, "That's your coney" or "That's your magpie."

He said little else as we rolled along, other than "How do you like all this nothing?"

I said it was beautiful nothing. I'd missed it. I also said I wished my husband could have seen it.

"He's seeing it now," Terry said. Full of Jack Daniel's and strong feeling, I had to jam on my dark glasses again.

I did not believe that my dead husband, a man without a religious impulse, was hovering over the road to Miles City and listening, with Terry and me, to Willie Nelson. I also knew that Terry not only believes in heaven, he knows it looks just like Montana.

This book is a memoir of my father's life on the rodeo circuit, his marriage to my mother and my effort to understand the ways in which I am their daughter, who left the West and the world of rodeo behind, full of fear and loathing, to find that Cy Taillon's imprint was indelible. The first writing he ever published was satire; so was mine. We look alike, more so as I get older. Like my father, I love the road show, packing a bag, heading off somewhere or nowhere, traveling light, never looking back over my shoulder. All three of Cy's children, my brothers and I, have the rhythm of the road throbbing in our inner ears, seductive and disorienting if we have to stay in one place for long.

Recently, a friend pointed out to me something obvious I had not realized and found mildly clinical. The daughter of the man with a pipe organ in his throat, a voice that filled me with awe and thrilled audiences, I gravitate toward men with deep, resonant voices. The last time I spoke to him, I knew Cy was dying because his voice on the phone was thin, the cancer having attacked his vocal cords, and the voice was the man. Without it, there would have been no Cy Taillon, no outpouring of tributes when he died, no Dean of Rodeo—a sport that grew more respectable as my father did—championing it articulately, insisting that cowboys were professional athletes instead of hell-raising gypsies.

Our problem with each other was that I loved the hell-raising gypsy who had disappeared, as the years went by, behind reputation and money, the stability of his second marriage and his increasingly John Wayne–like views of how the world should work.

He thought men should be manly, in the traditional Western mold. Women should be their better halves, a role my mother found less than congenial. Male children should call their fathers "sir" and toe the line like West Point cadets. Daughters should defer to them, in matters of politics, religion and what to order from a Chinese menu. Their hair ought to curl.

I became respectable too, though I never deferred to Cy about much of anything, but like him, and like my mother, I prefer the night lights and the bright lights to the daylight, moving restlessly down the road to staying put. It's hereditary, I excuse myself, and fight the pull of the road, the cowboy bars and the signs I pass driving across California, going to visit a friend or carry out a writing assignment: "Oakhurst Rodeo, Saturday and Sunday."

That's going to be a good one, I think. Rowdy and dusty. No sixty-thousand-dollar-a-year All-American saddle-bronc riders. No NBC television cameras. Instead, heat and beer and animal smells, and cowboys from miles around convening in a small town to ride their hearts out and the seats of their pants off. I grip the wheel and keep going only because whoever is announcing, it won't be my father, and unless it's Terry, who says it can't be done, no one will ever preside over the crow's nest with the same style and presence.

Rodeo goes on, better attended and more popular all the time. My brothers' lives go on, and mine does, and through us, our father's name; it's still difficult to pay for a drink, in a Western bar, if your last name is or once was Taillon. But when the Miles City *Star* headlined its editorial: "The Voice of the Bucking Horse Sale is Stilled," it marked not only the end of a man but the end of an era.

Rodeo won't have another senior statesman. Popular mythology aside, there aren't that many gentleman cowboys, perhaps because the gentleman part rubs against the grain, and though some of them are good at what they do, the announcers who now travel my father's old routes aren't in his one-man category. They lack his showmanship and his patrician style.

In Sparks, Nevada, on my way home from Montana, I watched

the movie *The Electric Horseman* on television in my air-conditioned motel room, still suspended between Miles City and San Francisco, my old life and the one I lead now. I'd seen it before, but this time it stirred me, with its elegiac theme of a West once wild and now paved over, once free-spirited and now tame.

Sunny, the broken-down cowboy hero, was reminiscing about his days as a rodeo rider and about Clark Wembley, an announcer with a "voice like runnin' molasses." He made the cowboys, winners and losers, feel special, Sunny says. He encouraged them.

Clark Wembley was Cy Taillon, I knew, and I remembered one of my father's surefire crowd pleasers, a line that rumbled out from the booth over big- and small-town arenas and was followed, after a still moment, by thunderous noise. "Ladies and gentlemen, this cowboy's only pay this afternoon is your applause."

Though the crowd had heard this staple of his repertory a hundred times, and so had I, it always brought us to our feet clapping until our hands ached.

Cy and Pat Taillon in the early years of their marriage

O N E

When they were young, my parents believed they were indestructible, so fast and flashy nothing could touch them. Cy was a lady-killer, a small, natty man whose riverboat-gambler good looks struck women down like lightning bolts. My mother, the former Patricia Montgomery, was a vaudeville dancer, the star of the St. Louis Municipal Opera in the late twenties. When she married Cy, she turned trick rider in the rodeo equivalent of halftime shows. You can take the girl out of show biz, but you cannot take a little girl from Little Rock, or Paragould, which is close enough, and turn her into a house pet.

At least not Pat, with her performer's ego, her longing to shine. Tiny-waisted and white-skinned, her black hair slicked to her cheekbones in sculptured spit curls, she was Cy's equal in recklessness, matching him drink for drink, seduction for seduction, irrational impulse for irrational impulse. Together they shot off sparks and left behind scorched earth, and if they ever thought about how their travels might end, they didn't waste much time on sober reappraisal.

They had more pressing concerns, the main one how to get to the next town with little money, a child and hangovers. My father's schedule took him from Butte, Montana, to Salt Lake City, Utah, from Puyallup, Washington, to Baton Rouge, Louisiana, and sometimes the travel time was a couple of days. We lived in a 1937 blue Packard, spending endless, viciously hot days in it going from Canada to New Mexico and back up to Wyoming, Utah and Idaho— wherever there were rodeos. We slept in that car, ate breakfast, lunch and dinner in it, sang along with the Sons of the Pioneers in it, quarreled in it. My parents must have made love in it, when I was asleep and the Packard parked behind the bleachers in some small-town fairground, waiting for daylight and the rodeo. Between them, there was a strong erotic pull. They walked with their hips touching and had flaming fights over each other's real and imagined flirtations.

Raised on a North Dakota farm, one of nine children of a French Canadian family, Cy had been a law student, a self-taught musician who led dance bands and played in movie-theater pit orchestras, a boxer and a radio personality in Billings and Salt Lake City. In both towns, he was a celebrity, known as "The Singing Announcer" because until a tonsillectomy put an end to this facet of his career, he sang with his bands.

The huge leather scrapbooks he kept all his life document some of these successes; but he claimed triumphs in everything he did, telling a writer for a trade paper called *Hoofs and Horns,* early in his rodeo career, that he'd won a Golden Gloves championship when he was boxing and given a recital at Carnegie Hall as a child prodigy violinist.

How much of that interview is true, I don't know, nor do I think Cy did. For much of his life, he was engaged in the game of inventing himself—adding to what was true what was desirable, stirring counterclockwise and serving up the mix. He must have swallowed much of it himself.

What is fact is that after leaving law school with a theatrical troupe, he ended up, in his early twenties, in Great Falls, where he became a radio announcer and moonlighted as a musician. His hillbilly band, reported the Great Falls *Tribune,* drew 14,600 letters to the local radio station in six and a half weeks. This was roughly half the population of Great Falls at the time. It must have been a letter-writing town.

After two months in St. Paul, Minnesota, as "announcer and entertainer," Cy came back to Great Falls, and in 1929 was leading a trio during the dinner hour at the Hotel Rainbow and picking up other band jobs around town. "The Green Mill gardens, dinner and dancing resort on the paved extension of Second Avenue North, will be formally opened tonight. Eddie Stamy will be director of the orchestra that will play for at least four dances a week. Cy Taillon, Minneapolis, who handles the drums, violin, bells, piano, and most anything else, is charged with providing the sweet numbers."

"Cy Taillon and his orchestra will entertain you again at the Crystal Ballroom . . . Featuring 'The Crystal Ballroom Red Jackets.' "

"Tree Claim Park presents Cy Taillon and his 'Rocky Mountaineers.' Master of Ceremonies, Waddie Ginger, Admission 50 cents."

To the list of instruments he played, another ad for a resort added xylophone, banjo and "relatively smaller string instruments."

The woman who became Cy's second wife got her first glimpse of him during those days. She was a schoolgirl. He was playing one of the twin pianos in the window of a music store. Their eyes met, she told me, and it was Romeo and Juliet, only more intense. If my mother got in their way for twelve years, that was only because Dorothy was fourteen at the time. My father also had his hands full with other women.

A personal archivist, Cy kept copies of every letter he ever wrote, including one to the city attorney of Great Falls in those years. A woman was harassing him, he complained, accusing him of being the third party in a "spiritual triangle" and fathering her three children by remote control. "Further proof she is hopelessly irrational," he wrote, "is her obsession that I have money."

In my teens, I met a woman who knew Cy in Great Falls. "He was the most beautiful man who ever lived," she said. "You don't look very much like him."

She wasn't rude so much as disappointed. I offered to say hello to him for her.

"He wouldn't remember me. There were too many of us. I'll tell you what, though, say hello for the Willis sisters and let him wonder which one."

The student's pilot license Cy took out in 1933 lists his age as

Cy in the mid-1940's, at the time he was doubling for Robert Taylor

twenty-five, weight 139 pounds, height five feet seven and three-quarters inches, hair black and eyes gray-green. It doesn't describe the movie-star handsomeness of his regular features, his olive skin, his wavy black hair and those eyes—as slate green as the ocean, and when he was angry, as cold.

He looked enough like Robert Taylor to double for him, later, in the riding scenes of the movie *Billy the Kid.*

Rodeo stock producer Leo Cremer tapped him for the crow's nest in the early thirties. Cy left radio for what he said was a three months' leave and never went back. Cremer was famous for his Brahma bulls, whose average weight was three-quarters of a ton: Black Devil, Yellow Jacket, Deer Face, Tornado, Joe Louis, Dynamite. He also had good instincts when he signed my father, despite Cy's reputation as a hard drinker and man-about-town.

Because he'd been attracted to it since his childhood, "Roman riding" the horses on the family farm, Cy was a natural for rodeo. He'd mainly swallowed a lot of dust. After he broke a shoulder, he gave up any ambition to be another Casey Tibbs.

He had cards printed, giving his address as the Mint Cafe, Great Falls, and offering "a New Technique in Rodeo Announcing."

A rodeo announcer keeps up a running commentary on the cowboys and the way they fare in the events, calf roping, Brahma-bull riding, bareback and saddle-bronc riding and, more recently, team roping. Cy was the best, a showman who could play a crowd the way he played stringed instruments, by instinct and with perfect pitch. At the piano, he held to the theory that the more keys you used, the better you played. At the mike, he also used the equivalent of all the pedals. "Ladies and gentlemen, this next waddie broke his wrist and three ribs down in Abilene a few weeks ago, and now he's back in competition. That's called courage in my book. Tiny Rios out of Tulsa, Oklahoma, on a mean hunk of horseflesh called Son of Satan. . . . Let's give him a little encouragement."

From his law school days, when he won prizes in debate, he had a sophisticated vocabulary. He used it, never talking down to his audience of cowboys, stock producers and their wives, ranchers and rodeo-loving kids. Nor did he often forget a cowboy's name, or where he came from, or how he fared in previous rodeos, no matter how chronic a loser the cowboy. So they loved him, even when he borrowed their prize money or their wives. He always paid the money back, and the wives straggled home, moony but unrepentant, on their own.

The reviews began to come in early. Cy never got a bad one, any more than he ever took an unflattering photograph, or if there were any, they never wound up in his scrapbooks, a researcher's nightmare because he clipped articles without the name of the newspaper or magazine and frequently without the date. Sometimes he clipped only the paragraphs that mentioned his name, which he underlined. The articles describe him as silver-voiced, golden-voiced, gold-and-silver-voiced, crystal-voiced, honey-voiced. They talk about his clear, bell-like voice. They run out of adjectives and call him the Voice.

In them, he's also spare, handsome and hard as nails; lean, wiry and a natty dresser; suave and dapper; the man who knows rodeo; the possessor of an encyclopedic memory. Said one writer, consigned to anonymity by my father's clipping methods, "Taillon keeps the show going like a golf ball swatted down a concrete highway."

Rodeo was used to announcers who treated the sport as a Wild West show, part vaudeville, part circus. Cy dignified it, with his ten-dollar words, his impeccably tailored, expensive suits and his insistence that the cowboys were professional athletes. When he intoned "Ladies and gentlemen," women became ladies and men became gentlemen; the silver-tongued devil in the announcer's box, as often as not a rickety structure over the chutes and open to the rain, spoke with unmistakable authority. In a world where pretending to be an insider earns the outsider dismissal faintly underlined with menace, he counted as a working cowboy, though he earned his living with his mouth rather than his muscle.

Like the contestants, he lived from rodeo to rodeo, making just enough money to keep us in gas and hamburgers. He worked in all weather: heat, cold, freak rainstorms that turned arenas into mudholes. If he had extra money, everybody drank, and when we rented a room in a motor court, a luxury, cowboys bunked on the floor with their saddles for pillows. Despite his slight frame, he never hesitated about piling in when there was a fight; you had to get through him to get to somebody bigger, and because he was light on his feet and fast with his fists, few made it. Someone wading into my father also had to take on my mother, not one to sit on the sidelines letting out ladylike cries of dismay. A hundred-pound woman can do substantial damage with teeth, fingernails and a high-heeled shoe, and Pat had an advantage going in. No man would hit her back, though she was swearing ripely and trying to maim him, because no self-respecting Western man hits a lady.

The bars were my parents' living rooms. We spent our nights in them, our mornings in the Packard or a motor court—with Cy and Pat sleeping off their headaches and begging me to stop that goddamn humming—and our afternoons at the Black Hills Roundup or the Snake River Stampede, rodeos that blur into one.

A *newspaper photo of the Taillon family "at home" in a Colorado motel, 1937*

Pat sat in the bleachers, if she wasn't trick riding. I sat in the crow's nest with Cy, sometimes announcing the Grand Entry or the national anthem for him or testing the p.a. system. "One two three four, testing testing testing." I wanted to be a movie star. Cy said you had to start somewhere.

The high point of those afternoons, for me, was when Cy played straight man for the rodeo clowns, who sometimes railed at him because he wouldn't allow off-color material, the crude jokes that were a staple. Not present just to entertain, the clowns also divert the bulls or horses when a rider is down. The cowboys and the crowd love and respect them. So did I, and when my father bantered with them from the stand, he took on added luster.

Pinky Gist and his two mules, Mickey and Freckles, George Mills, John Lindsay, the great Emmett Kelly and a dozen others—sad-faced men in baggy pants, absurdly long shoes and long underwear, out in the arena, and my father aiding and abetting them:

"Eddie, there are ladies present here today. Would you mind pulling up your pants?"

"Sure, Cy." Eddie did a flawless double take, pulled his pants up and doffed his porkpie hat to my father. When he lifted the hat, his pants fell down again, revealing long johns with a trapdoor.

"I'm sorry, Cy. I was asleep in the barrel over there and a train hit me. It tore the buttons off my suspenders."

"That wasn't a train, Eddie," Cy said, kingly at the microphone. "That was a two-thousand-pound Brahma bull, and there's another one coming out of the chute right now."

Eddie screamed hoarsely, stumbled across the arena, clutched at his pants and fell over his shoes. "I wondered why I never heard the whistle."

No matter how many times I heard these routines, they never paled for me. Such is the power of early-childhood conditioning that I still love slapstick; mine is the lone voice laughing at a club act in which the comic gets hit with a pie.

I'm less taken with exhibition roping. The great trick-rope artist on the circuit was Monty Montana, a handsome man who could do anything with a rope, including roping Cy Taillon's daughter. On my father's command, I pretended to be a calf; bolted through a string barrier and into the arena; ran like mad until Monty lassoed me, ran down his rope, threw me and tied me. He never hurt me. The crowd loved it. I hated it.

Not to be upstaged, Pat sometimes followed with her breakneck trick riding—headstands at the gallop, vaulting to the ground from a standing position in the saddle. She was so fearless that the cowboys gathered at the fence to watch her, wondering if this would be the night Cy's crazy wife killed herself.

I still have part of her trick-riding costume, a red Spanish bolero with white scrollwork, silver spurs with tooled-leather straps and canted-heel boots. The full-sleeved white satin shirt disappeared, as did the high-waisted red pants that would fit a twelve-year-old boy. Pat's life in those years is recorded in a few bits of her rodeo wardrobe, her own mutilated scrapbook, in which she also obliterated the supporting cast, and not much else.

Constants from those countless rodeos: the smell of sweat and horses that rose out of the open stalls, just below the booth; the fine dust that floated over the arena, powdering evenly cowboys, animals, the crowd, my father's suit and his pointy-toed boots; the haze of cigarette smoke over the stands; the whinnying of horses, the bawling of calves and howling of dogs, left in pickup trucks out in the parking lot.

Always present too were the high voices of women, wives and girlfriends and rodeo groupies, the "buckle bunnies" who were, and are still, the wives' natural enemies. They set the standards of female dress, with their starched curls and their pinkish pancake makeup, ending in a line at the chin. The buckle bunnies wore tight frontier pants and tooled-leather belts, into which they tucked their nailhead-studded shirts. One who was always around, and whom I admired, had a belt with beads spelling out her name, just above her neat rump: "Bonnee."

As for the wives, they were a tight-knit and wary bunch, sitting in the stands afternoon and night, watching their husbands compete and watching the single women through the smoke from their cigarettes. Those that had children left them sleeping in the trailers, and protected their primary interests. Cowboys then, and cowboys now, bear watching.

If the rodeo was in some two-dog town, we might be there for only one daytime and one evening performance, and then it was back on the road again, with a tour of the local bars in between. These had a certain classic similarity—a jukebox playing cowboy songs about lost love and lost illusions, beer signs with neon waterfalls and on the wall the head of a deer with brown glass eyes.

Such bars did not bother to throw kids out, and so we played the pinball machines, or listened to the bragging and the laughter, or put our heads down on the table, among the shot glasses and beer bottles, and slept. Because slot machines were legal in Montana and Nevada, I liked the bars there best; they weren't legal for children, but who was watching? In Helena, Montana, with money I pried loose from my mother by practiced nagging, I won a jackpot. The quarters poured through my hands and onto the floor, a silver river of money.

No one would have thrown me out of the bars whatever I did,

Cyra in cowboy gear at about age two

because I was Cy Taillon's daughter, his namesake, a miniature version of Cy in my own hand-made boots and my Stetson.

Bartenders served my ginger ale with a cherry in it. Cowboys asked me to dance to the jukebox, and asked Pat if she knew my father had himself another little gal. Expansive on bourbon, Cy sat me on the bar and had me sing "Mexicali Rose." I have no voice, and hadn't then, but what I lacked in musicality, I made up for in volume. I could also imitate my father at the mike, booming out: "The only pay this cowboy is going to get tonight . . ." and other crowd pleasers.

Not only did rodeo people live like gypsies, traveling in an in-

formal caravan from town to town; my father and I looked like gypsies, both dark-skinned to start with and tanned by the sun pounding down on us, both with dark hair and high cheekbones. Mine
softened as I grew older. Cy's became more pronounced, until, just
before he died, the flesh receded from the bone. Once, when I was
ten, and he and I were having lunch in the Florence Hotel in Missoula, Montana, a woman asked to take a snapshot of us. She was
from out of town, she said, and we were the first Indians she'd ever
seen. We posed for her in front of the Florence's corny Indian mu-
rals, palms raised in the B movie "how" sign.

All of which I took for granted, when our family lived on the
road, as the way everyone lived, though a social worker might have
taken a dim view of it and I already knew at least one person who
did. It was normal to have a dapper, charming father whose public

An early publicity photo of Pat

self bore little resemblance to the private Cy, the one who drank too much and flared into an alcohol-fueled temper. It was normal to have a trick-riding, ex-chorus-girl mother who still did dancer's limbering-up exercises every morning, sinking into splits and sitting on the floor spraddle-legged, bending her head first to one knee and then to the other. "You better stay in shape when you grow up," she told me as I watched, "because a woman's looks are all she's got."

It was normal to spend days and nights at the rodeo, listening to Cy's molasses voice and the voices of the cowboys, jawing, swearing and bantering with each other, smelling leather, calves in their pens and horse manure; to sit high above the bleachers in the announcer's stand and all but melt with love and pride when, on cold nights, Cy took his jacket off and put it around me.

It wasn't just normal to live in a Packard, it was classy. A Packard was still a classy car when it was ankle deep in hamburger wrappers. Some rodeo people pulled trailers and thus had the equivalent of houses, but most drove pickups or the kind of cars which, if they were horses, would have been taken off and shot.

I also believed then that Pat would stay spirited and taut-bodied forever, like a young racehorse, and that my father, whenever he wanted to, could make himself invisible. He told me that he could, but not when anybody was watching, and in the somewhat deflected way he always told the truth, he was telling it then.

T W O

A few blocks from my San Francisco apartment, a shop sells high-fashion cowboy boots. Custom-ordered from Texas, in lizard, they cost $1,500. The same shop sells stovepipe jeans to tuck into the boots, sterling and turquoise belt buckles and Ralph Lauren's idea of Western wear.

The shop thrives, though there are no cowboys here, and so do similar shops in Beverly Hills, where on quaintly named Rodeo Drive, one sees pencil-hipped, forever blond TV producers in cowboy regalia, coke spoons dangling from the gold chains around their necks.

The West has been reinterpreted by Clint Eastwood, and nothing is more chic on the hills of San Francisco than a pickup truck. But I worry. Does anyone tell the rhinestone cowboys they'll never get the look right until they have broken every major bone in their bodies? That if they wear needle-toed cowboy boots for long, they'll soon have feet as misshapen as a ballerina's, corn-ridden appendages that look like tubers and hurt like hell when the boots come off? That real cowboys don't wear tinted aviator glasses; they either disappear behind ink-black lenses or squint into the sun through eyes red as pickup-truck taillights?

Does anyone warn the owner of a creamy new Stetson that throwing a cowboy hat on the bed is bad luck? The next bronc will

throw you on the same shoulder you broke competing in the bareback event in Cheyenne. Your wife will get tired of watching soap
operas on TV, in the motel, while you're being stuck together with
steel pins again, and leave you, taking the kids, the truck and Bob,
your Aussie dog. Your creditors will close in; many broken-down
bronc riders have few other finely honed skills except spitting for
distance.

Or so it was once. Now some cowboys on the circuit are MIT
graduates or alumni of two years in Nepal with the Peace Corps. A
few are black, finally staking out their claim on what has until recently been an all-white segment of mythic America. San Francisco
has a gay rodeo, though it's not sanctioned by the Professional Rodeo Cowboys Association, and though one brings up the subject in,
say, the Cowboys Bar in Great Falls and then backs slowly, slowly
out the door.

When Cy started out on the circuit, riders were mostly farm boys
like himself, aspiring cowboys who harassed the horses on the family spread until they got their big break at Frontier Days in Fargo,
or Waco, or Mandan. Some of them were fifteen but lied and said
they were eighteen, some were veterans of thirty-five so full of steel
by then you could pick them up with a magnet. Young or old, after
a few lifetimes passed in seconds on the backs of horses named Powder River or Tailspin Terror, they walked like arthritic old men.
Then as now, a few died. "Don't worry about it if the ambulance
pulls out of the fairgrounds and the siren is going," Cy told me. "You
start your worrying when they don't bother with the siren."

Though rodeo claims a good safety record, compared with other
sports and considering the number of participants in it, injuries tend
to be impressive. Horses roll on the riders they've bucked off, crushing ribs. To drive their point home, they trample them. Careering
around the ring, when a rider is down, a bronc kicks with the force
of a heavy-gauge shotgun.

Brahma bulls not only gore their fallen riders but have a knack
for finding the soft flesh of the groin.

You can get hurt before you even get out of the chute, trying to
get a saddle on a bronc that crushes your leg against the chute wall
as easily as bending a straw.

Compared with cowboys, pro football players, in their helmets and padding, are at no more physical risk than chess players. So routine are injuries no one mentions the trivial, the cracked ribs and broken collarbones, and the riders don't cater to them: when my brother Terry was thrown and got his teeth rammed through his lower lip years ago, Tommy mopped up the worst of the blood, packed Terry's lip with ice and pushed his face back into something resembling a human face. Terry got on his next horse and rode.

Children are taught to be stoic before they're taught to feed themselves. Get your finger slammed in a car door at the fairgrounds and an embarrassed parent will swoop down on you. "For heaven's sake, will you stop that bawlin'! You can't get yourself in a lather over every whipstitch."

None of which matters, eternally taped ribs or wives clean out of patience, if you love the road. Cy loved it because he was fiercely independent; he'd sooner starve, he said, than work for somebody else. Pat loved it because it led away from Paragould, Arkansas, and poverty. I loved it because it was the life I knew. By my third birthday, I had logged 150,000 miles, occasion for an AP wirephoto captioned: "She Sees America."

It is inaccurate to say we saw America. What we saw was the western half of the country, the straight highways that shimmer in the heat across Nevada and Utah, the small-town fairgrounds where the rodeo was usually part of a country fair or paired up with a carnival. We saw hundreds of cafes called the Stockman's, the Wagon Wheel or the Gold Nugget, all of them serving mashed potatoes with an ice-cream scoop and offering you your choice of dessert, orange sherbet or orange sherbet. We saw hundreds of bars that still set the standard, for me, of a decent place to buy a bourbon-and-branch (in Montana, called a whiskey ditch).

A bar should be cool and dark, a cave hollowed out of the heat, and it should have a rail, ideally brass, where you can hook your boot heel, the better to settle in and ponder life. The bartender should greet you with "How're you folks today?" and then leave you alone; or if he knows you from other Frontier Days, "Cy, you old son-of-a-gun, how you been keepin'?"

No fake stained glass, no Perrier, and if the bar serves food, no friendly-puppy waiters crying, "Hi! My name is Roger. I'm your serving person tonight."

A decent bar will produce a napkin for a lady, one with cheerfully crass cartoons on it, possibly the only napkin in the place. The cartoons will feature steatopygic women wearing no underpants and surprised by a high wind. Caption: "Just Bummin' Around."

There should be the summer smell of beer sprinkled with salt, the pleasant reek of sour mash bourbon, a rack with Planters peanuts in bags you have to rip open with your teeth, another rack with nail clippers and one with key chains: "Souvenir of Puyallup, Washington." A waitress is optional, but if there is one, her name should be Velma.

Walk out of such a bar on a hot day, into the glare of the street, open the doors of your car, with its melting tires, and you'll get an idea of what it's like to burn in hell.

These are some of the big-time rodeos Cy announced year after year: the Rodeo de Santa Fe, Santa Fe, New Mexico; the Snake River Stampede, Nampa, Idaho; the Pike's Peak or Bust Rodeo, Colorado Springs, Colorado; the Southwestern Exposition and Rodeo, Fort Worth, Texas; the Canadian Western Stock Show and Rodeo, Edmonton, Alberta. The small-time ones all took place, in my memory, in the same smoldering town with a ratty arena and a bar called The Last Roundup.

From the Black Hills Roundup in Belle Fourche, South Dakota, most years, we went to Cavalier, North Dakota, just across the border from Manitoba, and the farm where my father grew up. His father, Eli Taillon, and his mother, the first white child to be born in Pembina County and the former Philomine Dumas, still lived there. Born in 1870, she lived to be eighty-seven and left twenty-one great-grandchildren. Until my generation, it was a good Catholic family.

A tiny woman, Grandma Taillon still made her own lye soap in a boiling kettle in the yard; refused to "hook up to the electricity," so that the farmhouse, at night, swam in the shadows cast by kerosene lamps; killed chickens with fearsome skill. Preparing for Sunday dinner, she grabbed a hen by the neck and swung it in circles until its neck and its will to live gave out. Shrieks and the beating

The "golden-voiced" Cy at the mike

of wings and the figure of my grandmother, upright and still except for her implacably whirring arm. I tried to behave myself at her house.

Of Cy's nine brothers and sisters, all but two had left the farm and its backbreaking days. Uncle Henry worked it, and Aunt Ida, ageless in her great bulk, presided over the kitchen. A sea beast thrown up on land, Ida wore dresses the size of tents, made of printed sacking, and bedroom slippers with the tops of the toes cut out. Though she made shy overtures to me, I thought of her as made of the same dough as the bread she baked every day, soft, white and repulsive, and hurt her feelings by whining for store bread instead. Child of the truck stops, I hated farm food, especially those all too fresh chickens, and longed for french fries cooked in rancid grease.

We never stayed in Cavalier more than a few days. Pat was bored before the car came to a stop in front of the house, feeling correctly that she was out of place there. A woman who never could master the swivel-handled potato peeler, she had nothing to contribute in the way of usefulness, and no one called on her to rattle out a barrage of tap steps or do splits up a wall. Nor did any-one else on the farm own a fitted cosmetics case or wear white loung-ing pajamas. Grandma Taillon and Ida knew nothing about either lip brushes or lounging.

"Go talk to Ida, damn it," Cy said when Pat complained. She and I exchanged horrified looks.

Thirty years later I became curious about Ida, but she was dead and it was too late to ask her why she never left home, never mar-ried, spent her own eighty-seven years at the pump handle and over the wood stove. I am left with her obituary and what it reveals about her lifetime of duty and hard work: charter member of the Tongue River Homemakers Club; 4-H leader; member of the Tongue River Sewing Circle, the American Legion Auxiliary, the Pembina County Pioneer Daughters, St. Bridget's Catholic Church and its Altar Society.

A patchwork quilt she made for us tells the same plain tale. With twenty varieties of fancy stitch, none repeated in the whole, the quilt is the work of a woman who loved her needle. But it's meant for utility, not beauty. The odd-shaped pieces of fabric are homely, cut from the sleeve of a worn cotton work shirt, a pair of whipcord pants or a flannel shirt. How Ida must have longed to cut just one sleeve off one of my mother's silk blouses or one cuff off her bell-bottomed satin pants, to feel the slippery stuff under her needle.

Pat and I were both outsiders on the farm because the language spoken there was mostly Canadian French. Cy spoke it. We neither spoke nor understood it. Much of the time, during those visits, Cy was hidden away, helping my grandmother take care of his father.

Grandfather Taillon was nearly deaf. All communication with him took place by shouting in French, and since he rarely came out of his downstairs room, from which there issued forth bellows and thumps, I thought he was mad. In several visits to Elm Croft, the farm's name, I saw him only a few times, a gaunt old man with Cy's strong cheekbones, yellowed gray hair and hawk's eyes. Though he spoke to me kindly, if unintelligibly, Cy quickly took him back to his room, seeming embarrassed by him and shooing him down the dark hall with what sounded like threats and invective. I think he must have wanted me to think of my grandfather as a gentleman landowner instead of a wild-looking old man, an apparition in long underwear.

Always, Cy's pattern was to treat things as grander than they were, as if the reality would compromise him. When he made me a gift of his ordinary violin many years later—or rather lent it to me, because he soon took it back—he insisted that it was a Stradivarius.

Nonetheless, he loved Elm Croft and the Red River valley in which it was situated, the flat, loamy fields surrounded by woods, the swimming hole with its heart-stopping rope swing and the farm animals, especially the horses.

Mechanization came late to the farm, and its horses were working animals that pulled threshers and bundle wagons for the haying. When Cy was growing up they also pulled the buggy, the light cutter, the sleigh and the Taillon brothers, who skied the frozen ditches in the winter, towed along at bone-rattling speed behind Old Ned, Cy's favorite. Ned, he wrote in an article called "Once a Farm Boy," was a roan weighing 1,250 pounds, "of uncertain lineage, with some Percheron blood."

In the same piece, he writes about the life of the place, the grueling hard work, the rosary his mother recited every night in French, with the family and the neighbors kneeling around her, and the joys of informal evening musicales. The family had its own orchestra of self-taught musicians, with all the children playing instruments— "fiddles, guitars, piano, xylophone, auto-harp, trumpet and drums"—except for Ida. She never learned to play, Cy notes, because she was too burdened with cooking and housekeeping chores.

With the other Taillon boys, he fished in the neighboring streams, hunted in the woods for bush rabbits, partridges and coyotes and ice-skated on the frozen Tongue River in the winters, when the temperatures dropped as low as sixty below zero. He played his fiddle and acted as a caller for square dances in farmhouses "where the musicians would usually stand in a doorway between two rooms filled with sweating and stomping revelers."

Elm Croft couldn't hold him. How can you keep a boy like Cy down on the farm after he's seen Fargo? But it formed him, so that the farm boy remained even when a reporter was describing him as "blasé and full of adjectives as a circus advance man." Resplendent in a satin Western shirt, boots and cowboy hat, on one of those visits he once took me out to the barn, where a colt had just been born. He had me smell its breath. "Sweet as new hay," he said. "Sweet as a baby's."

Yet he seemed happy to have left the place when we were back on the road again, with the world framed by the windshield. Shaking the dust of Cavalier off his feet, Cy merely traded it for different dust, but for him the dust of the rodeo arena was like greasepaint for actors. It had seeped through his skin; he missed it painfully when we were away long. In the winters, when there were no rodeos, he drank with more determination, got into more trouble—the infinite varieties of it having to do with money and women—and was dangerous to be near, volatile and looking for a fight. His restlessness was that of a bucking horse in the chute. My mother's mood wasn't markedly better.

A former chanteuse, as well as the tap-dancing sensation of St. Louis, Pat had a throaty contralto voice. She had no range at all but could have turned "Onward, Christian Soldiers" into a torch song. I remember her singing "Don't Fence Me In" along with the radio. "Let me ride thru the wide-open country that I love . . . Don't fence me in."

It could have been their theme song. I made the back seat of the car into a nest and filled it full of clothes, books, blankets and my collections: matchbooks, bar napkins, rodeo programs and swizzle sticks. They left laundry in towns all over the circuit because they were too impatient to wait for it to be ready; threw the windows and the door open when we slept in motor court cabins, to let in fresh air and cowboys looking for a place to bunk; seemed to think walls and a ceiling would cave in and smother them; rarely made it all the way through a movie. "Come on, now." My mother dragged me up the aisle, still riveted to Yvonne De Carlo, and out of the theater. "I can't stand to stay cooped up in this place."

Somebody usually picked up the laundry anyway, settled our bar bill and paid off the irate owner of the Drop Inn when we left his motor court at dawn, ahead of schedule and the bill. Film crews have retinues who follow them on location, sweeping up rubble and settling damage claims. Cy and Pat attracted a retinue of their own, loners drawn to them as a glamorous couple and admirers who saw themselves reflected in their high shine.

It was a thankless job, in their case. They didn't really care about bills and laundry or about orderly lives. But for the most patient of the loners, it eventually paid off.

Meanwhile we rolled along in the Packard, hell-bent for Dallas, Fort Worth, Baton Rouge and Alabama City. We had our classy car, and gas money. We could sing three-part harmony to "San Antonio Rose." We had the Brahma bull by the tail.

THREE

—————— ᵒᵒᵒᵒᵒᵒᵒᵒ ——————

My mother once told a friend why she left Paragould, Arkansas. "I got tired of grits." Paragould is poultry-raising country. Cold in the winters, it swelters in the summertime. A few years ago, a Deep South heat wave killed off the chickens by the thousands. An Arkansas cousin wrote that they were "keeling right over, already roasted," while in Little Rock, nearby, that same summer, one man shot and killed another over holes made in a plastic wading pool.

At sixteen, Nedra Ann Montgomery fled the climate and the cuisine and departed Arkansas for St. Louis, where she changed her name to Patricia. "Pat Montgomery" would look better on a marquee. Her mother, Minnie Mae, had died of tuberculosis at forty-five, leaving "Baby Sister" in the care of her older sisters, Lucille, Hester, Cleo and Ila Mae. A brother, Rudolph, was in reform school. Their father, Brown Montgomery, was the town drunk and, according to another cousin, Clifton, "mean as a weasel."

Brown was the engineer for the city waterworks. Widowed, he spent his time drinking corn whiskey, tending the boiler at the Paragould power plant and shooting at anything that moved, including Clifton. As a child, Clifton was dispatched to fetch Brown home for Sunday dinner. He remembers with clarity a discussion between them punctuated with blasts from a 12-gauge shotgun.

Because Brown had once been a railroad man, his children could ride the trains on free passes. Nedra Ann got on the train in Paragould, with no one's permission, no profession and no prospects, and got off in St. Louis reborn as Pat Montgomery, dancer and singer; or, as she preferred to call herself, "soubrette."

The next sister up the line, Ila Mae, never forgave her. "Oh no, Baby Sister couldn't settle for honest work as a fry cook."

My mother had always danced, Ila Mae told me in our last conversation before she died. My aunt made it clear she hadn't changed her views on the subject of life upon the stage. "She used to get on an old box, or a tub, or anything she could, and just dance her head off. And she'd say, 'Someday they're going to have to pay to see me.' My brother would laugh, and she'd say, 'Gimme some pennies.' Well, they didn't have one penny between them, you know. But there she was, dancing on some old box out in the backyard like a fool."

Pat got a job modeling for a department store and found work at night as a chorus girl in a less prestigious theater across the street from St. Louis's finest, the Fox. But she had lean times at first, and I suppose she lived then the way poor girls like her have always lived when they came to the city, that she found a man, or men, to serve as her protector while she took her bearings. Souvenirs of her St. Louis days were still among the thin rag endings of her personal possessions thirty years later: a carnelian dinner ring hidden in the back of a drawer, a note reading "After the show, I sure do hate to wait!," a papery pressed gardenia.

Whatever she found in St. Louis, and despite Ila Mae's having followed her there to keep a custodial eye upon her, she didn't go home to Paragould for years, not until she could go back in style. Nor did she attend her father's funeral when he died, widely unmourned. Brown had remarried. His sixteen-year-old second wife had buck teeth. Brown tormented her by telling everyone that Lily could eat an apple through a knothole.

Because Pat was five feet two, she was a "pony," the shortest dancer in a chorus line and the one positioned at the end. She caught the attention of the Fox Theater management anyway and soon moved across the street to its glittering variety show. Vaudeville was flourishing in the mid-twenties. The Fox, Ila Mae recalled, was "really a high-class place, with a big orchestra pit down below, and the orchestra would rise up on a platform. They had all these gorgeous costumes, and beautiful music, and comedy, tap dancing . . ."

Soon the Fox featured Miss Pat Montgomery—"And Can She Sing and Tap!"—as female lead. Cousin Clifton, twelve years old then, rode the magic train to St. Louis, with his mother, to see my mother perform. At the end of her big solo number, the audience pelted her with bouquets. Said Clifton, remembering, "I swear, I thought it was raining roses."

In rapid order, her star on the rise, Pat auditioned as a singer with the Municipal Opera, was hired and became "specialty featured artist." She joined the Missouri Theater's Missouri Rockets— "One of the Finest, Most Versatile Choruses to Ever Set Foot Behind Footlights." She went off to New York with Ernie Young's Revue in the chorus of a production called *Rain or Shine*.

The Revue didn't dazzle New York, but my mother was there long enough to antagonize her four sisters, who thought it was time she settled down, by sending them a postcard: "Have hit the big time." The others were all sensibly married by their late teens, and all were devoted to grits. Only Ila Mae had pursued a career—as a fry cook.

Like Cy, Pat invented herself, with energy and imagination. She rapidly learned to wear stylish clothes, lost her Arkansas accent and became expert at cosmetics. When she finished working with her sable brushes, her pots and jars and hand mirror, her thin upper lip was the top half of a heart, her eyebrows two horizontal commas. Her own eyebrows, she banished, to conform to an ideal of beauty. If thine eyebrow offend thee, pluck it out.

Vain beyond common sense, she thought her size 7 feet were too large and crammed them into size 5½ shoes. I have seen her cry because they hurt so much by the end of an evening, and I have seen Cy pick her up in his arms and carry her to the Packard, wobbling on the high heels of his cowboy boots. It wouldn't have occurred to either of them that Pat could take her shoes off, not when they flattered her ankles and made her look taller, and it wouldn't have occurred to me, either. I shared my parents' highly developed sense of what is important.

Pat was so consistent about this that her scrapbook, like my father's, is a patchy record of her career. She clipped and pasted as selectively as he did and even scratched out other faces in photos. Why should she read about or look at photos of anyone but herself?

What evidence that more or less survived shows that she danced at Billy Rose's Golden Horseshoe, having moved on to conquer Chicago, as well as less glamorous nightclubs. These have names such as the Four Aces (with its Famous Four Ace Band of Rhythm) and the Golden Pumpkin, "The Most Beautiful Chinese Cafe in the World." Signing on with Ernie Young again, she played the Oriental Village at the Chicago World's Fair, where, for reasons that cannot be reconstructed, the group elected to perform something called *Spanish Nights*. The Revue also played the provinces.

A snapshot on which she wrote "My Al, Minot, North Dakota, 1931" preserves the flavor of those tours. A dusty Plymouth sits in

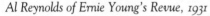

Al Reynolds of Ernie Young's Revue, 1931

Pat on the road in Helena, Montana, 1931

a field, with a line of sagging tents in the background. On the Plym-outh is a placard: "Ernie Young's Productions, Featuring Al Rey-nolds, Chicago's Favorite Son. 50 PEOPLE!" "My Al" leans on the car, looking jaunty in a sport coat, impeccable white shirt and pale striped pants. In front of that tent city in a field, he's dressed for Ascot.

"Always kicking!" reads the caption on another snapshot, this one of my mother braced against a telephone pole in the middle of nowhere, showing off her extension. In still another, she does splits at the top of a flagpole. Caption: "Was it shaky up here? Oh boy and how!" Her good cheer seems unflappable, even when she's waving around in a high wind.

Then she met Cy Taillon, and after a twenty-four-hour court-ship, married him. They must have looked at each other and in-stantly recognized their similarities: two peacocks in a world of mud hens.

Cy was announcing the 1931 Montana State Fair, in Great Falls. Pat was part of the featured entertainment, Ernie Young's road com-pany. The tour was a vacation, she told reporters, before she went off to a starring engagement on Broadway. Enthralled, the Great Falls paper printed her picture, Cy's picture and the headline: "Ra-dio Announcer Weds Revue Girl."

In St. Louis, Ila Mae got a telegram. "She didn't explain any-thing, just said they were married and that was it. My brother Rudy said, 'Oh my God, a radio man. They're as bad as actors. She'll never settle down, she'll dance and dance the rest of her life.' " Ila Mae wired back: "Baby Sister and Cy, Good luck."

They needed it, because as the best man at their wedding later observed, with unconcealed satisfaction, "they didn't have enough sense between them for a good plow horse."

I have said my parents attracted a retinue, people drawn to their specious glamour; they seemed to give off light, noise and gaiety, like a house in which there is a perpetual party going on, and people gravitated to them and stayed. The one who stayed longest was Roy Qualley, my father's friend and self-appointed caretaker.

Eleven years older than Cy, Roy was also from a big family and a farm, this one in Decorah, Iowa. In old photos, the farmhouse springs out of the flat expanse surrounding it like some strange out-cropping. Unsoftened by a single tree, a sprawling carpenter gothic house high off the ground on its foundation, it looks like a model made of cardboard.

Roy's grandparents immigrated from Norway, changing the spelling of their name. Kvale became Qualley. In photos, the family is unsmiling; they all have Roy's stolid, level gaze, parents and children alike looking resigned to hard work, the monotonous midwestern landscape and virtue as its own reward. While they shared little in terms of temperament, Roy and Cy shared a common background and the urge to escape from it.

Roy's nickname was Old Honest Face. It was he who paid the bar bills, extricated my hot-tempered, bantamweight father from fistfights and saw that Cy made it to the radio station most mornings. Square and stocky, already balding by the time he reached his twenties, he had delivered newspapers in Great Falls, sold encyclopedias door to door in Spokane and mined gold in the hills above Helena.

A lifelong self-improver, he clipped from a 1927 Spokane newspaper Mussolini's Efficiency Precepts:

Master your body and mind.
Concentrate on the one thing before you.
Get seven hours' sound sleep.
Never stay in bed after the instant of awakening.
Read the newspapers while dressing.
Shave: I am anti-whiskers.
Drink a glass of milk for breakfast.

The lure of gold brought Roy out West, and once, he struck it. With a partner, he hit what was reported as "an important strike of high-grade gold ore," but something went wrong and the mine and the dream got away. Undaunted, he staked out another claim and clipped another newspaper story that must have held out promise to him: "In His Prison Cell, Convict Turns Sand into Gold — The Secret of the Medieval Alchemists Rediscovered."

Ila Mae thought Cy and Roy met in some Great Falls boardinghouse. Both lived in numbers of them, old houses converted into hotels and catering to single men. She also thought Cy invested in one of Roy's mining ventures, though money, as Roy liked to say, burned a hole in Cy's pocket. He invested it mainly in goodwill. However the connection developed, they were tightly if oddly linked.

Roy worked out on barbells at the YMCA. He took business school correspondence courses and read books on nutrition and hair growth. Cy drank, caroused and still had more hair than he needed.

Roy saved every receipt. Cy was thirty-five before he had a bank account.

Roy said severely that all Cy thought you could buy with money was a good time. Cy said of Roy, "He tried to keep me on the straight and narrow path, and I did his fast living for him. He got to hear about it, and it saved him a lot of money and the wear and tear on his physique."

Theirs was a reciprocal exchange, and when my mother came along, she got Roy as part of the package, inscribing a photo of herself, wearing clinging silk and an ankle bracelet: "To Roy, the Best Pal in the World." Now Roy had not only my father to keep on the straight and narrow but also Pat, who showed a cheerful preference for the wide and convoluted.

He must have liked the amplified job duties. Like Ila Mae, Roy was a born heel snapper, one of the sheep dogs among us who like to nip at other people's ankles and herd them into line. In another throwback to early conditioning, I can recognize a heel snapper on sight, in or out of uniform, with or without brass buttons.

"Somebody has to do it," such people generally defend themselves. In this instance, Roy was right. Put two careless people together, and the damage increases disproportionately—more debts, more broken glass and more threats of lawsuits for alienation of affections. When Leo Cremer, a big, benign man known as a steady hand with horses, contracted with my father to announce rodeos for him, he tried to get my parents to stop doing their imitation of Scott and Zelda. But the life of the circuit, which Pat embraced enthusiastically, didn't help. Unlike their Rodeo Drive imitators, tall

Pat as a young chanteuse

in the saddles of their Mercedes, real rodeo cowboys aren't known for their consumption of white wine and soda.

Rocketing along from rodeo to rodeo, Pat and Cy drove the car they owned before the Packard, a Ford sedan painted yellow. Always, they posed with it in the background of snapshots, the way another couple might have posed on their front porch.

Tireless in her efforts to rehabilitate my mother, Ila Mae had moved from Arkansas to Great Falls to be near them. Now she teamed up with Roy in disapproving mightily of their lives. Perhaps because she was unofficial title holder for world's cleanest woman, she wasn't taken with their style of traveling. "You should have seen that car of theirs. It was *filthy*, and that yellow color showed up every speck of dirt. All those clothes of theirs were stuffed in the back, piled right up to the ceiling. They couldn't be bothered with suitcases, they just threw everything they owned in the back

Ila Mae at about eighteen

seat and went off. Pat drove if Cy was drunk, and she drove like a cowboy, or a maniac." To Ila Mae, the two were one and the same.

She was bitter about life in general. Her husband had run off with another woman, who caught his eye over the grave at a funeral. She'd lost her only child in infancy. There she was, working as a waitress, thirty years old and secondhand goods. Men were lustful beasts, and it didn't improve her state of mind that Baby Sister cottoned to the creatures. "Pat, or whatever you call yourself now," she wrote, in care of Rodeo Headquarters, Deer Lodge, Montana, "always remember our body is a Temple and God means for us to keep it sweet and clean. You showed it off on the stage all those years, *that's enough*."

From her account of my parents, and cousin Clifton's, I see the six years of their marriage before I was born as a frenetic silent movie—the yellow Ford smoking out of some small town, with creditors, love-stricken saddle-bronc riders and faithful Roy Qualley in pursuit; loud quarrels and impassioned reconciliations; a supporting cast of Other Women, Other Men. Pat and Cy competed in sexual conquest as they competed in everything else.

Two small people with enormous egos, they loved each other but needed the reassurance to be found in numbers, the proof that marriage hadn't dimmed their separate luster. When Cy parked Pat on the farm in North Dakota one summer, the better to cut his own wide swath on the circuit, she seduced every able-bodied man for miles. "The only thing you told me not to do," she drawled at Cy when he came back to get her, summoned by his mother, "was smoke in the barn."

Says another cousin, also visiting the farm that summer, "That girl was a living fireball."

Briefly, after this episode, my parents made an attempt at conventional domesticity. They set up a small apartment in Billings, Montana, where Pat kept house and cooked dinners Cy rarely came home at night to eat. He was flying small planes again, too restless to remain earthbound.

Pat teamed up with a male dancer and opened a dance studio. It became a huge success. But it closed a few months after it opened.

"Some jealousy developed between Cy and her business partner,"
Ila Mae said discreetly. "I don't remember just what it was all
about." Pat gave up both the apartment and the studio and joined
Cy on the road.

Ila Mae had married again, to a gentle, round-faced clothing

A newly married Ila Mae with her second husband, Wiley Gosney

salesman named Wiley Gosney, and also moved West. Their own apartment in Great Falls became my parents' mail drop and the place where they bunked when they weren't on the road.

This proved a trial for Ila Mae. She could lecture my mother about cleanliness and its proximity to godliness, and how "undies worn twice aren't very nice." The two couples could share expenses. But Cy tended to disappear for two or three days at a time, coming home when the poker game finally wound down, and docile Wiley, who stayed good-humored even when told to wash his hands ten times a day, was in Ila Mae's view too sorry for Pat and too ready with his ironed, starched handkerchief. Pat became pregnant. Ila Mae had a good reason to ask that they find a place of their own.

Unlikely candidates for parenthood, Cy and Pat made the best of it. They took two rooms in a boardinghouse, with the second for a nursery. I was born, another newsworthy event to the Great Falls *Tribune*. They started a scrapbook for me. Scrapbooks, in my family, are a way of life. You may have nothing else, but you've got your press clippings.

In two weeks, we were on the road again. Where Cy went, Pat was going, with or without a baby. Either she knew better, by now, than to send him off on his own, or he knew enough to insist that she come with him.

Soon I was big enough to be outfitted like a Western Barbie doll and had a role in their long-playing drama. I played what my mother called Little Pat and Cy called Little Cyra and my aunt called "the poor little thing."

And I had a glorious time, as unofficial mascot of the rodeo, from Canada to New Mexico, though my parents sometimes forgot momentarily that I existed. After a long night larking in the bars in Cheyenne, Wyoming, they once left me sleeping in a motor court bed, packed up and headed for the next rodeo. Seventy miles out of town, they had to turn around and go back.

"The poor little thing needs regular hours and good food & training," Ila Mae wrote, in letters that sometimes tracked us down weeks after they were written. Sometimes I stayed with her for a few weeks or a month and got all three of these things, as well as

Cyra at the time she was considered the unofficial mascot of the rodeo circuit

scrubbed inhumanly clean. They held little appeal for me. Mild Wiley watched me chafe under her regime and sometimes intervened. "For Chrissake, let the kid wear her cowboy hat." He only got us both in trouble.

FOUR

"One time I came home, and here was boots and saddles and everything else on the sun porch, and you were in my bed, and Cy and
Pat had took off again." At seventy-five, Ila Mae sounded as irate,
despite the intervening years, as she must have that afternoon in
1940 or so. The problem with Baby Sister, she said, was that she'd
never had proper training herself. "The older girls wouldn't let her
do anything. I did it. I stood on a box and made pies."

When my mother stood on a box, she danced, and I doubt that
her motherless childhood had much to do with it. No one was less
suited to pie baking. On the rare occasions when we had a room
with a kitchenette and Pat cooked, the food was inedible. Food
didn't interest my mother. She'd have preferred to take a pill in
order to stay nourished and not waste time better spent kicking up
her heels.

If she sewed a button on a shirt for Cy, she stuck herself with
the needle and bled on it. She was a copious bleeder.

Refusing to learn the right way to pull a cowboy's boots off for
him, she faced Cy and tugged, instead of standing with her back to
him and straddling his outstretched leg. He swore. Pat rocked his
foot back and forth in her hands and swore back at him. When the
boot came off, she hurtled across the room, caught up in the momentum.

She was a soubrette, not a housewife, and if Cy sometimes forgot it, Pat never did. In our household, what mattered was style, not substance.

They were passionate about clothes, both of them. Pat had a fur coat, made of beaver tails and known as her mink, and dozens of hats that I loved to try on. She claimed that her swirling, bright dresses were made in Paris, France. On the road, in the heat, she wore high-heeled shoes that showed off her legs and wide-legged shorts. In her wardrobe, there were no pastels; she saw life, and herself, in primary colors.

So did Cy, who customarily wore satin and sateen shirts in the colors of parrot feathers, narrow-legged Western pants and the fanciest boots he could find. Straight out of bed in the morning, he pulled them on. He looked peculiar, since he slept in shorts and undershirt, but with his boots on, he was nine feet tall in his own eyes and in mine. It took me twenty years to realize my father was a small man.

Shoes hurt his feet. He owned a pair of black cowboy boots for funerals.

Not left out of all this sartorial splendor, I had my own black felt cowboy hat with white trim and a chin strap, gabardine pants and plaid shirts, neckerchiefs with silver slides and my own tooled boots, the first pair I owned a few inches long. Years later, Cy had these bronzed for me. They came back from the mail-order house that turned them into bookends with a printed card enclosed: "Baby's First Shoes."

How and if these clothes were ever paid for, I don't know. On one desperate occasion, when we needed gas and had no money, we pulled into a one-pump gas station and filled up. Coached by my parents, I used the bathroom, stayed in for a while as a diversionary tactic, then bolted out and jumped on the running board of the already moving Packard. We must not have paid for the gas, because the red-faced attendant ran after us for a short distance, yelling at us.

I suppose my mother's finery was left over from her chorus girl days, a kind of dowry. Cy must have purchased his with charm and credit.

Nor do I know how they paid for all the studio photographs they had taken, recording for posterity the latest additions to our wardrobes. Though Roy said money burned a hole in Cy's pocket, it rarely traveled that far between his hand and the bar. Pat was a two-fisted drinker. Cy was a drunk, charming and good-humored when sober, combative and cold-eyed when full of bourbon.

Their fights began to heat up. Her makeup case on her lap, Pat sat in the passenger seat of the Packard, spitting on a sponge and putting pancake makeup on her black eyes. She'd banged herself up, she told me, bumping into something in the dark.

Those fights were the private side of their lives together. Cy disappeared and reappeared, when we were anywhere as long as a few days, throwing the door of a room open late at night with a bang that woke me and set my heart racing with anticipation. They shouted at each other until Pat hurled herself at Cy like a terrier. They wrestled, lurching back and forth across the room in a parody of the way they danced, bodies locked together. Before I learned not to intervene, I wrapped myself around Cy's pant leg. He reached for his belt buckle.

Belt buckles the size of salad plates are cowboy fetishes. Gold, silver or both, they are awarded as prizes in major rodeos and put up as security for loans. When Cy took off his belt, I knew he was going to use it on my backside, but matters rarely reached that point. All he had to do to reduce me to whimpering panic was reach for the buckle.

When the fight was over and we were all in bed, I heard Cy crying. He was trying to do something, he told my mother, about his "complex."

It wasn't pride alone that kept Pat from cutting and running. She loved Cy with the kind of love that motivates kamikaze pilots. As much as they fought, whittled away at each other's egos and competed for the limelight, they took fierce pride in their respective prizes: the fireball of a woman who stood on the stage in a rainstorm of roses, the darkly handsome man other men liked and other women pursued.

They had a child, for whose affection they also competed. Behind their surface glamour, they were equally insecure. Cy still had to scratch for engagements. Pat had come home from her last tour with a dance company with her tail between her legs. Having ridden the bus nonstop from New York to Great Falls, she ended up on Ila Mae's doorstep. "Half dead, and the dirt beneath her fingernails. I said to her, just wash your hands and go to bed. She must have slept for two, three days."

Between them, they owned a car, not yet paid for, their clothes and a couple of saddles. Together they stood, however shakily, and divided they fell. So they made up their quarrels in bed, and in the morning faced the world again over a table in some coffee shop, joking with the waitress and ordering French toast for me as a signal that the good times were beginning again.

In the car, to get back in my good graces, Cy turned into an affectionate father and a good buddy again, instructing me on the finer points of rodeo: how it was the only authentically American sport. How cowboys had to be tougher than any other athletes. "Put a football player on one of Leo's bucking horses, and there wouldn't be enough left of him to send home to his poor old mother." Why Brahma-bull riders should be small. "They're like jockeys. They've got to be light, because the bigger the man, the slower the reflexes." How misguided it was of outsiders to think the sport was cruel, an attitude that rankled my father all his life.

Bucking horses were born to buck. They liked nothing better than the chance to make some cowboy wish he'd gone into selling insurance. Why weren't the bleeding hearts worried about the riders?

The silver and honey voice spoke only to me, and I forgot the night before and began to think about the next rodeo. If there was a carnival playing the same fairgrounds, Cy would toss me a long strip of free tickets. He had connections. I spent some of the best evenings of my life riding Ferris wheels.

Less happily, we might arrive in town to find "Uncle Roy" Qualley waiting for us. Working a mining claim when he wasn't traveling as a salesman, Roy wasn't in tandem with us as often anymore, but his relationship to our family confused me anyway. I knew Ila Mae was married to Wiley. I still thought of her as married to Roy. It had something to do with their parallel world views.

"Leave the baby with me if you're going to go chasing around the countryside forever," Ila Mae kept urging my parents. Her strong card was my health. I had "spells" of vomiting, was too thin, with sharp knees and sharper collarbones, and couldn't gain weight. I needed liver, spinach and homemade rolls.

Roy was shy with me and issued no edicts about my upbringing, but he doled out dimes and quarters and weeks later expressed dismay that I hadn't saved them. A penny saved was a penny earned. From little acorns mighty oaks grow. He held no brief for investing your capital in slot machines.

Aware that I had to start school soon somewhere, I was afraid Ila Mae would prevail. The last time I'd stayed with her, she'd stripped me naked on the front porch of her apartment building when I came in from the yard, so I wouldn't track dirt into the house. The phrase didn't exist then, but I still consider this child abuse.

That summer started out as another freewheeling season on the circuit. Between rodeos, to keep body and soul together, Cy announced air shows and amateur nights in small-town movie theaters, did some carnival barking—as a personal favor, he explained, to one of the carnies, who was also French Canadian—and took us to Leo Cremer's ranch in Big Timber, Montana, where we rode, fished and played poker. For a few weeks, we lived with a couple named Pearl and Earl in a Billings boardinghouse, which had a resident German shepherd and was generous with the raisins in the tapioca. When we bought a small trailer, no bigger than a pup tent, I knew the purchase meant we were prospering.

Cy told people that he had a "handle on my complex." He wasn't drinking for weeks at a time, intervals when my mother also stopped singing "Stormy Weather" endlessly, her theme song when she had a radio program in St. Louis. They were talking about settling down in Billings for part of the year; I could start school, Cy would work in radio again and Pat would open another Studio of the Dance. Cy said she might be too out of shape. Pat slid into vertical splits up the side of a door frame to prove she wasn't, one of her more startling acrobatic feats.

But she wasn't always kicking that summer, her feistiness intact but her physical vitality dimmed. Afternoons, she lay in bed with a wet washcloth on her forehead, complaining of headaches. Ila Mae rode the bus to Billings and conferred with Cy behind closed doors. The two voices rose and tangled, while I pushed my statues of horses around, in the next room, and tried to eavesdrop.

After one of these conferences, Cy stalked past me, announcing that he was on his way to get drunk. "Poor little thing," Ila Mae said, following on his heels and gathering me into her arms. For something productive to do, she took me off to the bathroom and attacked the skin on my elbows with a pumice stone.

Pat was the beauty of the five Montgomery girls, though studying her photographs, I cannot tell how much of her beauty was nature and how much art. While Ila Mae was also small, dark and vivid, her prettiness was sharp-edged, her animation born of nervous energy. She washed. She sewed, turning out the drab dresses neither my mother nor I ever wore, made of "goods" that would last longer than either of us. She put up jams and jellies, stored winter clothes in mothballs and in the spring, hung them out on clotheslines to air. She sat me down and taught me how to hem tea towels in neat little whipstitches, though I proved to be a bleeder like my mother, and though no matter how neatly I sewed, Ila Mae ripped the hems out and made me do them over again.

Idle hands were the devil's work, she said, and took on the job of my religious education, also neglected. I had to learn to love Jesus, who had died for my sins.

A picture called "The Sacred Heart" hung in Ila Mae's spare bedroom, over the bed I slept in when I visited her—Jesus with reproachful brown eyes, chest open at the sternum, and his exposed heart dripping a single drop of blood. The Sacred Heart gave me nightmares, though it was intended to inspire me to right living and piety, and I threw tantrums over sleeping in the same room with it. "About Cyra's disposition hope it has improved for she has plenty of room," noted one of Ila Mae's letters.

Doctors came to the boardinghouse, carrying black bags, attended Pat, and then drew blood samples from me. She had the headaches. I got stuck with the needles and resented it. The summer that began so promisingly was fading into confusion, tension and the misery of staying in one place for weeks at a time. Ila Mae came and went, telling me to keep my voice down, stay out from underfoot and pray for improvements of my character. God knew everything I did. *Everything.* Not a sparrow falleth, nor a child with a smart mouth on her sass her aunt.

Cy came and went, drunk as often as he was sober. Pat came

and went. Despite orders to stay in bed, she got dressed, put on her makeup, pulled a cloche hat over her spit curls and went dancing with Pinky, a friend from the old days. They were going down to the Club, they said, for a little fun and a Chicken Snack. While Pat dressed, Pinky sat on the bed and sang for me "I Don't Want to Set the World on Fire." Pinky had pink cheeks, pink clothes and pink cotton candy hair. Ila Mae said she wasn't any better than she should be.

Toward the end of the summer, Cy got the first two-day rodeo he'd been hired for all summer, somewhere in eastern Montana. Pat and I went with him. The second night, because I caught "walking pneumonia," we had to go back to Billings. There my parents had their last fight, probably exacerbated by their worries about money.

I watched it from the distance imposed by a high fever, not greatly alarmed. They always fought; they always made up; they were a matched pair, like two pintos with similar markings. The fight took place in the trailer, and I watched with detachment the steps of their familiar, intricate dance.

I fell asleep. In the morning, Cy was gone and my mother was still dressed. She looked at me with the same detachment I had felt the night before and began to rummage in the mess she and Cy had made of the trailer, digging for my jacket. We were going to see Pearl and Earl, she said, so she could use the telephone in the boarding-house.

Privately as well as publicly, Cy's every gesture had flair. Liberating himself from Pat and the wreck of their marriage that night, he unhitched the trailer from the Packard and drove away. He'd "gotten hitched." Now he got unhitched.

Pat made her phone call, and the following day, Roy Qualley came to Billings and performed an act just as tidily symbolic. With the trailer hitch he had brought along, he attached our house on wheels to his own car and hauled us away.

Roy Qualley as a young man in Great Falls, Montana

FIVE

Thus began the next phase of Pat's life, and Cy's, and my introduction to normal living, as opposed to traipsing around on the rodeo circuit. Roy had been in love with my mother for twelve years, he told Ila Mae—biding his time, waiting for the marriage to self-destruct and breathing our exhaust. He'd had time to plan our moral reform.

Pat must have been moved by his patience and his inarticulate longing. She filed for divorce, and within two weeks after Cy signed the papers, married the best man at her first wedding. No more living in a car or in the trailer, which vanished almost as soon as Roy unhitched it. We moved into a small house in Missoula, Montana, where Roy had a job with a wholesale candy and tobacco company and began to learn the ropes of what he called, grimly, "staying put, like sane people."

With his life savings, he took Pat shopping. In Lucy's Furniture Store, in an afternoon, they picked out a living-room suite, consisting of a beige sofa and matching armchair, both high on brass casters, both ponderous and both covered with the same kind of indestructible plush that is used to cover stuffed animals. They bought a Formica dinette set, slippery and cold to the touch, in mouse gray. They chose the china and silver plate that remained unused, thirty-seven years later, when Roy died.

It wasn't genteel to eat off the good china unless entertaining visiting heads of state. We used humbler dishes and graduated, in the fifties, to Melmac. Roy got us a plastic-handled set of knives, forks and spoons with Wrigley's bubble gum premiums.

For my room, they bought a bed, a bureau and a desk, at which I could apply myself to my schoolwork. I had a good mind, Roy told me, but like Cy, I was a grasshopper instead of an ant. With hard work, I could still aspire to ant status.

He put away our childish things, our boots and saddles. We saw no more of Pinky or my mother's other few remaining friends from the old days. We saw as little of Cy as the law allowed. While he was still my biological father, with visiting rights, this was a technicality. A father was the man who brought you up, not the handsome hell-raiser who breezed into town once in a while, on his way somewhere else, and left you "high-strung" for a week. Cy's very existence threatened Roy.

When Pat handed me over to him on the doorstep of the house, with Roy standing silently at her side, the old electricity between them hung in the air, heavy and palpable. They were still in love with each other, their divorce and Pat's second marriage another technicality. I had never heard of sex and I felt the tension between them. Roy felt it, and he had heard of sex.

There must have been hell to pay when the door closed, as there was when my mother got one of Cy's letters addressed to "Dear Cyra Sue and Pat." These, Roy tore open and shook out energetically to show us that no check for child support was enclosed. He also pointed out the obvious, that money doesn't grow on trees.

As a law student in North Dakota, Cy published his first piece of writing, a satire on the Charleston that begins:

> The Charleston is the name of a new form of physical exercise which is practiced on the ballroom floor, in fraternity and sorority houses, or in any place that a mental delinquent happens to become imbued with the desire to execute its intricacies for the amusement of those about him. This violent exercise, which is called a dance, differs from popular previous dance steps in that it requires more dexterity and less intelligence . . .

His prose style hadn't changed much when he began writing to Pat almost daily, ostensibly about my welfare. It was still flamboyant and stylish, full of posturing for her benefit but calculated not to offend Roy, the silent partner in their correspondence, who all but dusted those letters for fingerprints.

He also kept them all. Roy kept everything. Upstairs, in the succession of houses we rented, were the usual domestic trappings. The basements were archaeological sites, embedded with layer upon layer of letters, documents, old candy-order forms; age-whitened Life Savers and fancy boxes of petrified chocolates; every discarded item of clothing any of us ever owned; frayed inner tubes and snow shovels without handles, single surviving gloves of a pair, blankets turned into fine lace by moths. Roy was so compulsive a saver that when Pat threw something away, an old *Reader's Digest* or a soup can full of bacon grease, he went out to the garbage can in the alley, retrieved it and squirreled it away down in the basement.

Bacon grease, he believed, made roses grow to the size of cabbages, knowledge withheld from the general public by the fertilizer companies. We had no rosebushes, but we had our underground bunker full of bacon grease, and mice.

They ate the old chocolate, as well, but they didn't eat Cy's letters, probably because they were difficult to swallow. From Big Timber, where his return address was a friend's car dealership, he sent us a newspaper clipping from a Salt Lake City paper, showing a pretty eighteen-year-old with coyly downcast eyes nibbling on a pencil and contemplating her ballot for an election. "It was rather difficult to talk on the telephone to you the other night, as the young lady pictured on the enclosed was well within hearing distance." Hoping to be hired by one of Salt Lake City's radio stations, he continues, "I occupied myself with assisting at the mortuary." There he worked his magic on the mortuary owner's daughter. "I had informed her that I had no intention of again being married. Under these circumstances, she took enough phenobarbital, morphine and another kind of tablet to kill several persons."

A hardy creature, Miss Winifred L. pulled through, but not without leaving a hysterical suicide note addressed to Cy. "Under these circumstances, I thought it best to leave Salt Lake City."

In another letter, this one from California, he talks about enlisting in the Army so that he can choose his own branch of service instead of being drafted and says that if he's too old for the Aviation Corps, he'll join the Marines. "I would appreciate your reaction as Cyra's mother."

He mentions being delinquent in his child support, which he hopes to pay when he can sell the Packard, "a necessity that breaks my heart." He tells us about radio jobs promised and of rodeos for which he was almost hired before the "machinations" of some other announcer. He signs himself "Yours" and notes in a postscript, "Haven't had even a glass of beer in more than a *month!*"

Brilliantly manipulative, at once genuine and self-serving, these letters must have played chords on my mother's heartstrings. Into them, Cy tucks a picture of a lion cub, for me, and "a brochure with the finest explanation of Christ for a little youngster that I have ever seen. I happened to chance upon it at the mortuary."

Roy notwithstanding, he drops his guard now and then. Pleading to see me before he goes into the service, he tells Pat, "If I should become a casualty, several problems might be solved." I would inherit his service insurance. My mother would be freed of "our situation." All things considered, he might be worth more to both of us dead than alive.

How could Roy have competed with Cy's swagger and dash, or convinced himself that once he married Pat, the two of us would transfer our powerful affections? Though Cy would not agree to adoption, Roy changed my last name to his. He loved me, he told me, as if I were his own flesh and blood. He provided for me, according to his own ideas about what children need to prepare themselves for a world that rewards the deserving and punishes the slothful: brown oxfords instead of cowboy boots, a wholesome diet instead of hamburgers, indoctrination in the theory that whatever the task at hand, you attacked it with disproportionate zeal.

No chore was so routine, so trivial, that you could not compound it, washing the same window and polishing it with a chamois until the glass was so spotless you thought you were buffing thin air. Mowing the lawn in swatches that went up and down, back and forth, and then diagonally, though the grass cried out for mercy and could no longer be seen by the human eye. Sanding and varnishing the wooden panels of the family station wagon until you were hallucinating from inhaling varnish fumes. I still cannot wash a window without seeing Roy's red, sweating face on the other side and his finger tapping on the pane, pointing out an invisible smudge. Work might not give you pleasure but it gave you dignity, which was better than bouquets thrown at your feet. Pat was a lost cause; her idea of hard labor was shaving her legs. My character, or lack of it, was not yet irreversibly determined; I could still be rescued. If only Cy wouldn't keep writing those letters, with plaintive requests that I write back in care of a bar in some cow town, and would stop turning up in Missoula, still nine feet tall to me in his boots and hat, the brim pinched jauntily into a Cheyenne roll. Stubbornly, I preferred boots to oxfords, rodeos to Lutheran vacation Bible camp, neither a camp nor a vacation.

Never one to shirk from duty, Roy found my re-education trying. The fly in the bacon grease was that I had "bad blood," my legacy from Cy.

His marriage to Pat, a consummation devoutly wished, was even more profound a disappointment. Briefly, she convinced herself that security was what she wanted most. She traded passion for it. She relinquished her footloose life, and Cy, for the plain, worshipful suitor who was his antithesis. Almost at once, she changed her mind, writing to Cy and receiving his letters through a post office box after Roy began opening all her mail. When she and I went grocery shopping, she phoned Cy from pay phones. In the back of her closet, she kept a suitcase packed and ready. Before a year was out, she grabbed it, and me, and got on a train. Cy had sent her the money to meet him in Denver, Colorado.

That last act of defiance determined the course of the rest of Pat's life. Whether she acted out of sheer wickedness, as Ila Mae said, or because conformity stifled her, or because of the pull of her feeling for Cy, she paid for it for forty years. The high-spirited colt no one could break, not even Cy, broke herself.

The compost heap that was our basement contained the history of that flight, which I knew little about because in Denver, my parents left me with relatives and took off for those few weeks by themselves. That Roy filed for divorce is on record; the document is intact, pain evident through the legal boilerplate. That Ila Mae got on the bus yet again and came to Missoula to be by Roy's side, I could have guessed. No one loved a melodrama more than she did, nor another piece of evidence that the world reserved suffering for those who least deserve it.

In the best of times, Ila Mae's letters are full of bankruptcies, house fires and illness beyond the reach of modern medicine. "The dr. says he's never seen anything like it, you wouldn't recognize him if you met him on the street, guess it's in God's hands now, he can't weigh more than seventy five pounds." Or: "Poor thing, well guess its for the best. She's out of this vail of tears now."

My aunt saw the world through morose-colored spectacles. If no one she knew was the victim of something sufficiently horrible, she included in her letters clippings from the newspaper: children abandoned by their mother, an old woman robbed on the street, a car wreck in which six people burned to death. Across the front of these enclosures, she scribbles, "Isn't this *terrible?*"

Solidly in Roy's corner, as Baby Sister burned down the barn again, she rose to new heights of outrage, bombarding my mother with two letters daily.

> Dear Pat, just rec your card; Roy called me last nite I was so shocked that it has made me sick.

Ila Mae's health, it was a family conviction, was a fragile thing, her every breath drawn in torment. A lesser woman couldn't have borne it, much less kept on believing in God and putting up her own bread-and-butter pickles.

> I am so disgusted with you to think you & Cy would try & pull something over on Roy . . . I have all ways stood by you when you left Cy for less. But this time I could beat your head off . . . You would have fit if you hadn't got your divorce from Cy so you could marry Roy Then to treat him this way: You aren't a child any more: I think you have back bone of jelly fish.

In the throes of emotion, my aunt always leaves out articles and punctuation.

Pat it isn't funny breaking a person heart and some day you are going to find that out . . . If you go back with Cy I will never visit if you live with him 100 yrs for he doesn't like me & I don't like him if I never see him again will be too soon . . .

Her threat not to visit again might have been a miscalculation, but she wound up with a zinger. "Some day Pat your turn will come to reap what you are sewing." There are a dozen of these letters, all in what Ila Mae would have called the same "vain," as well as more letters from Pat's other sisters, mobilized from campaign headquarters in Great Falls, and a letter from her old friend Pearl in Billings.

This one scolds her at length and then suggests she buy Ila Mae a fur coat: "They're so comfortable for this cold country. It would last for years." Ila Mae, Pearl adds as an afterthought, isn't well, and furthermore, she's a grand sport.

Long-distance phone calls, in those days, were still reserved for major life upheavals, too expensive for casual chat. When she phoned Pearl with the news about Pat, my aunt must have thriftily covered a second subject, the effect of Montana winters on an invalid.

No fur coat materialized as a thank-you for pointing out the path of righteousness. Cy was out of work again, broke again and drinking again. He and my mother must have made love again and fought again, caught up in the patterns of provocation and response that impose themselves upon a long marriage, grooves worn deep because they have been traveled so often.

Pat collected me and came home to Missoula, getting off the train, as she had when she left Arkansas all those years before, transformed. Her illusions were gone, and her fire. A soldier gone AWOL and now back in the trenches, she consigned herself to her second marriage.

Before their meeting in Denver, Cy had been a pariah in our new household. Now he became evil incarnate in boots. I was told not to mention his name.

He had joined the Army, Roy said. With luck, we'd never lay eyes on him again. I absorbed this information and had more spells, severe enough to warrant doctors, more needles and a health regime imposed by Roy.

The main feature was chewing every mouthful of food thirty times to "get the good out of it." Pat was also supposed to chew thirty times, to set a good example. Since we both cheated, Roy sat at the head of the dinette-set table, his eyes worried and watchful, and led us out loud in unison chewing. One, two, three, four . . . fourteen, fifteen, sixteen. The leaves changed color while we sat over a single dinner. Snow covered the ground. Spring came, and summer, followed by fall again. Or so it seemed to me, rhythmically revolving my jaw. Put cottage cheese on fork. Lift fork to mouth. Chew for eternity, while the earth rotates and your lifetime passes.

A health-food fanatic before health food was chic, Roy believed in the digestive tract the way some people believe in the one true path to the Buddha. Whole classes of food, everything I liked, would "repeat on you." French fries coated your stomach with grease, which never "passed"; it just sat there, turning you into a human grease trap. Not only should you eat an apple a day, you should eat the whole thing, core, seeds and stem. Briefly, before it proved unenforceable, Roy insisted that when ingesting oranges and bananas, you should eat the peel.

Harder to endure were his noon-hour tours around the Paxson Grade School playground in the station wagon, making sure I was wearing my snow pants. His method of curing head colds involved "sweating it out of you" with a portable heater and every blanket in the house. He doled out cod-liver oil by the shot glass. He believed in the healthy properties of fresh air.

Winter and summer, we left our bedroom windows open eight inches. At the end of my bed, October through February, would be a drift of new snow.

Worst of all was the mail-order house long underwear he made me wear, a peculiar peach color. Changing into gym bloomers in the school locker room was an exercise in humiliation, one more reason why I was miserable at school.

My speech was then an imitation of Cy's, inflated and full of big words, that made me seem a wizened, pretentious adult, whose only other conversational mode was swearing. Neither vocabulary served me well as an icebreaker with either teachers or kids my own age.

I could already read, also considered eccentric, but read from the last page to the first, the result of long exposure to Burma Shave signs. Thank God no one in Missoula then had heard of dyslexia. Roy would have found a homegrown cure for it.

His anxiety about my health, I know now, originated in something real. If I romanticize Pat and Cy's life together, their great love and greater talent for destructiveness, I can't romanticize the venereal disease my mother contracted before I was born and for which she was being treated that last summer in Billings. It ruined her own health and made the family keep a worried eye on me.

Pat's post office box notwithstanding, Roy early on managed to intercept her letters from Cy. The parts of them he chose to read aloud, he read to her. The paragraphs he chose not to read, he x'd out, with thick, angry black lines. Some of these letters explain Pat's mysterious illness.

"My report came back from the State Board of Health yesterday and supplementing the report of the local pathologist, it was entirely *negative*. Both made Kahn tests in addition to Wassermanns so it would seem quite conclusive that not even the slightest possibility exists that I had ever been exposed." He goes on to beg her for the results of the latest blood tests done on me. Guilt and worry about us both, he says, have given him a great deal of hell.

Venereal disease was considered so shameful then that Roy's and Ila Mae's anxious letters back and forth about Pat's condition used a code word for it: malaria. How her illness must have stigmatized my mother, tying a bell on her as a moral leper. How it must have strengthened Roy's hold over her, the authority of a stern parent over a child.

Only Cy sympathized, and refused to judge her, and Cy could no longer be part of her life. The Denver fling had driven that reality home. It also drove Pat home to Roy, prepared to lie in the bed she had made for herself.

To my Dear Wife Pat.
May all our Days be
as happy as this one Love Ray.
10-19-41

LEE STUDIO
OCONTO, WIS.

S I X

Plain men who marry beautiful women worry. With opportunity ever at hand, will they be betrayed? Jealous of Cy before the Denver episode, Roy had his answer. It filled him not just with anguish but with an increased sense of injured merit. "To my dear wife Pat," he had inscribed the picture of himself he gave my mother on their wedding day. "May all our days be as happy as this one." Now he tore the picture in half, in front of us both so that I would be aware of my mother's perfidy. Later he retrieved it from the garbage and saved it, as he saved his copy of the divorce complaint.

Paragraph II: "That ever since said marriage the plaintiff has been a good and faithful husband and has performed and discharged all of his marital duties and obligations, but that the defendant, totally disregarding the solemnity of her marriage vows, did voluntarily and wilfully commit adultery in that defendant engaged in sexual intercourse with one Cy Taillon."

For years it puzzled me that Roy so carefully preserved evidence of his humiliation. His pack-rat tendencies alone do not explain it. What does is that in the early years of their marriage he saw his claim to Pat, awarded him for years of single-minded devotion, as tenuous. She would leave him, if not with Cy, with some other man, and when she did, Roy would be left with something—pride-saving proof that he was the injured party.

None of us would be allowed to forget this, ever. If insufficiently impressed with my mother's appalling lack of rectitude, I might tap-dance to the same tune.

The torn and patched portrait, the divorce papers and the scolding letters from Ila Mae were also saved for me, hoarded against the day I would renounce Cy. Roy believed he was engaged in a tug-of-war for both Pat's soul and mine. He could not stop tugging long after Cy let go of his end of the rope.

Dear Cy,

I haven't answered your last letter because I've been doing a lot of thinking.

I realize now that you and I could never be together again with any kind of Harmony, too much water has passed under the bridge; but couldn't live with you for almost twelve yrs. without having a lot of memories, and our having Cyra made those memories harder to forget, but I am forgetting them and I know its best for all concerned.

Written in pencil on lined paper, this letter is a rough draft. Though it is signed "Pat," the handwriting is not my mother's but Roy's.

I like my home here with Roy and he has been very good to both Cyra and I and the fact that I am ——— ——— proves that he has my interest and happiness at heart.

My guess is that Roy planned to dictate this letter to Pat, or stand over her while she copied it, when he could think of the right words to fill in the blanks. My mother now conducted all of her affairs, without exception, through her second husband and life manager.

He made her weekly appointment at the beauty parlor, drove her there, waited for her in the car and drove her home. She gave him the grocery list and he did the shopping, abolishing another pretext for her to leave the house and come within dialing distance of a pay phone. When she went bowling Tuesday nights, let out of her cell for an exercise period, Roy and I went along with her. Since

Pat was allowed to bowl only on Ladies' Night, an assignation at the alleys was unlikely. Roy was taking no chances.

He enlisted me in these security precautions, taking me aside and questioning me closely soon after he got home from work. Had Pat talked to any strange men while he was gone? Any man we knew? Any men? If she'd talked to anyone on the telephone, what had she said? He tried for casualness while he conducted these interrogations, but a smiling tormentor is still a tormentor. I remained tight-lipped and wary even when he threw in the promise of an ice-cream cone after dinner.

Half a dozen times a day, he phoned Pat from work, making sure she was still nailed to the floor. My mother took to leaving the bathroom door open while she was on the toilet, offending my sensibilities. I think she did this because it gave her an extra second or two to hitch up her pedal pushers and sprint for the insistently ringing telephone.

Sometimes she and I sat on the front porch on hot afternoons, enjoying a Missoula pastime, watching the lawn sprinklers. Neighboring housewives sat on their front porches too, visiting back and forth and offering my mother the limited social exchange of "Hot enough for ya?" We never had to wait long before the wood-paneled station wagon slowly rounded the corner on patrol. Finding no strange car in the driveway, Roy sometimes rolled down the window, waved and told us he was "just passing by" on his delivery rounds.

Other days, he pulled his hat well down over his eyes, looked neither left nor right and drove on. Now almost totally bald, and self-conscious about it, Roy never went out without a hat. Apparently he thought that if he pushed it down far enough, we couldn't see him.

Evenings we gathered around the radio. Roy lay on the sofa with his arms folded tightly across his chest and his eyes closed. Pat sat in the matching overstuffed chair, chain-smoking Lucky Strikes, and looked at some point in the middle distance. I lay on my stomach on the rug, doing homework.

We looked like a *Saturday Evening Post* cover, the family gathered round the Philco, listening to "The FBI in Peace and War," but this homey tableau was no more realistic than most. We talked not at all. Pat yawned now and then, out of boredom. Roy brooded, or slept, or pretended to sleep while he watched her through almost closed eyes. I tried to look busy over my arithmetic workbook while elaborating on my favorite fantasy: Cy coming to the door, with the Packard waiting at the curb, and taking me back to Billings, or Butte, or anywhere there were rodeos.

He needed me with him, he would explain to my mother and Roy, because he had so much work announcing he couldn't handle it all alone. I was a top hand at the mike and could work the

Pat, Cyra and Roy in Missoula, Montana

crow's nest almost as well as he could, maybe better in a few years when I'd had more experience. So long, and we'd write from the road.

Next reel, me at the microphone, at a night rodeo, high above the arena. I'm spinning out long silk strings of words, like my father. I'm emanating the same star quality. I have new boots, since my old ones don't fit anymore. My hair flows down my back, beneath my white Stetson, and back in its element it is naturally curly. This gives me such a marked resemblance to Margaret O'Brien that everyone who sees me says I'm the spitting image. They're all amazed that they overlooked it before.

Caught up in this scenario, I went off to brush my teeth at eight o'clock dazed as a sleepwalker, and when I was in bed, left the door of my room open so that I could hear the doorbell. It never rang, except at the behest of a Jehovah's Witness or the Fuller Brush man, from whom Pat was afraid to accept the free sample in case Roy thought it evidence of intimacy.

After that first year of their marriage, my mother and Roy went nowhere as a couple and invited no one. A town the size of Missoula has few secrets. Pat's flight with Cy and Roy's cuckoldry had enlivened the party lines over a long, otherwise dull winter. They hadn't been a brilliant success in small-town society even before scandal made matters worse.

Social life in Missoula revolved around card parties, a few couples invited for bridge, highballs and small sandwiches, cut on the bias for elegance and filled with olive-pimento cheese spread. Pat went to these gatherings grudgingly. She hated bridge and played badly. Roy had once enjoyed them, but he did not enjoy being the object of curiosity and pity; and if they'd toughed it out and accepted invitations, they'd have had to reciprocate.

They had played host for their own card party only once. The three of us spent a tense afternoon getting ready. Roy complained about Pat's sloppy housekeeping and her sandwich-cutting technique, pressing the bread down hard with outspread fingers and then sawing between them. The gluey white bread retained the imprint of her fingertips; each sandwich had craterlike squashed places in it.

Pat pursued the logic of the pecking order by yelling at me. In the interest of fairness, I had assigned myself the job of counting all the nuts in the paper nut cups to be sure that each guest got exactly the same number and nobody got more cashews than anyone else. Throughout these preparations, the air vibrated with our respective grievances and hurt feelings.

An hour into the soiree, Pat bungled a bridge hand. Roy addressed the guests on the subject of her shortcomings as card player and housewife, smiling an awful smile that included us all in the joke. My mother took these comments in the spirit in which they were intended, jumped to her feet and upended the card table into his lap.

Nut cups, scorepads, pencils, highballs, sandwiches and bridge mints scattered. So did the guests, thanking Pat and Roy for the lovely evening. The party lines must have hummed nonstop the next day.

Because friends' mothers did not throw tantrums and embarrass people, it hardened my heart against her that mine did. I was judgmental as only children are judgmental. I was desperate to conform to Missoula social norms. I was also too young to know that all parents embarrass all children, if by no overt act, by breathing.

The "good dishes," the green-stemmed wine and water goblets Pat and Roy had picked out together, the silver plate for twelve in its chest—gradually, all were relegated to the backs of the kitchen cupboards, there to gather dust for thirty-five years. The two of them gave no holiday open house with Tom and Jerries served from the cut-glass punch bowl. They invited no friends for supper, so they never needed the mahogany-veneer drop-leaf table in the living room. Roy put an ad in the newspaper and sold these things. Bit by bit, he let go of his own cherished fantasy, the backlit vision of domestic life with Pat he must have clung to throughout all those lonely years in the boardinghouses.

In early snapshots of him is a Roy I never met. He parts his already thinning hair in the middle, slicks it down, smiles dashingly and puts an arm around each of two pretty women in flapper dresses. He poses in the bathtub of a boardinghouse, while one friend scrubs his back with a long-handled brush and another, playing the butler, offers him a bottle of beer on a tray. He visits Yellowstone Park with friends, in an open touring car, strikes pugilistic poses in his boxing clothes and holds up strings of trout he caught. He looks happy.

The yellowing old photos trace his transformation until he became the man my mother met, prematurely middle-aged before he was thirty. He doesn't smile anymore but stares at the camera with a severe, humorless gaze. His body thickens and seems to take on gravity, a body not just heavier but somehow closer to the ground. What the photos don't tell me is what changed him, why he grew old and disappointed while still young.

All the adults I knew—neighbors, teachers, the man behind the grocery store counter—admired Old Honest Face. They told me how hard he worked and how good he had been to my mother and me. I should be grateful to him, they said, for treating me, a child not his own, as if I were his flesh and blood.

I endured these lectures shifting from one foot to the other, felt guilty for not being as grateful as people thought I ought to be and heard a faint undercurrent in all such tributes, the animosity people feel toward goodness that carries with it the whiff of self-congratulation. It won Roy admiration, but it didn't win him affection.

Cy, the reprobate, had hundreds of friends. Roy, virtue personified, had none, with the exception of Ila Mae, a kindred spirit. She visited us so often the intervals between visits seemed shorter than the visits themselves. Arriving on the Greyhound bus, for she and Wiley could not afford a car, she brought preserves, pickles and implacable good intentions.

She took over the kitchen and cooked all our meals, thereby, she suggested to Pat, staving off Roy's and my imminent starvation. She unearthed the chenille bedspreads we never used from the cedar chest, aired them on the clothesline and put them on the beds. "Now isn't that nicer, Patty?" She scrubbed the kitchen walls and woodwork with ammonia and water, bringing on one of her migraine headaches.

"You shouldn't have done it," Roy said. "Not with your health."

"Well, I had to, Roy," Ila Mae said in a small voice, from her bed of pain. She managed to imply that Pat's housekeeping was so bad we were about to be shut down for health code violations.

At dinner, she urged Roy to have third helpings. If there was one thing she loved, she said, it was to see a hungry man eat. Anyone who worked as hard as Roy deserved a good hot supper at the end of the day, and given her many other onerous responsibilities, who knew when she'd be back and he'd get another one?

Roy took her shopping for things she thought our household needed. They came home with a furry cover for the toilet seat, a flowered plastic cover for the toaster and one for the mixer. Ila Mae believed in covering things with other things: beds with bedspreads, chair arms with doilies, my mother with more clothes.

Pat's usual at-home costume was shorts or pedal pushers and a blouse with the bottom rolled up and knotted above her trim bare midriff. Ila Mae bullied her into the housedresses she ran up on her sewing machine, indestructible garments cut like flour sacks. Pat looked self-conscious and uncomfortable, like a dog children have dressed in doll clothes.

The way we were living, my aunt frequently announced, made her just sick. So did an endless list of other things—the inhumanity of man toward man, children who sassed, the absence of a butter knife on a butter plate—but in Pat's lackadaisical housekeeping she saw a chance both to do her Christian duty and to get her own back. No one had ever pelted Ila Mae with roses. It seemed unlikely that anyone ever would. She wasn't the Montgomery sister who'd been the "Toast of St. Louis" and she had few prospects of becoming the "Toast of Great Falls." Even her husband didn't appreciate her.

Gentle Wiley, once the most tractable of men, had learned to resist all attempts to improve his character by practicing passive resistance, paying no more attention to Ila Mae's nagging than to a dog barking somewhere way off in the distance. He spent his time at home barricaded behind his newspaper with a forbidden can of beer within easy reach. He no longer washed his hands on command.

*Ila Mae and Pat on an icy sidewalk during one of Ila
Mae's frequent visits to Missoula*

Only Roy praised Ila Mae, admired her and held her up as an
example to Pat. He fussed over her health. He gorged himself on
her cooking ostentatiously, knife and fork flying to the accompan-
iment of blissful grunts, so that Pat didn't miss the point: Good Man
Eating Good Meal Cooked by Good Woman. At the bus depot,
when Ila Mae headed back to Great Falls, he told her that he
couldn't thank her enough for everything she had done.

Ila Mae always said she only wished that she could have done
more. She began to write to Roy in care of the candy company, private letters that stressed their mutual bond of sympathy. "Please Roy
tear this letter up don't take it home," she begins one such missive,
but she was appealing to the wrong man.

Ila Mae's letters in that period fill a good-sized box that once held overshoes. She wrote once a day and sometimes twice, in her usual breathless style and on any piece of paper that came to hand, including the backs of letters she had received herself. Waste not, want not. For material, she had Pat's infidelity with Cy to chew over, an event that could not be overanalyzed. She had her own frail health and Wiley's illness as well. In his mid-thirties, he'd had a stroke and was at death's door, she narrates, though his condition seems to exasperate more than worry her. She had her own romance with Roy's brother Vin.

Consummated or unconsummated, the product of her imagination or a real love affair—the details are missing, in the interest of discretion or because there weren't any—this passion flowered from one of her visits to us when Vin was visiting too.

Vin was a bachelor. Though he came to Montana looking for work, he spent his month or so with us lying on the sofa, drinking beer and snapping dish towels at Pat's rump, an entertainment that infuriated her but sent both Vin and Roy into fits of high-pitched whinnying. He was no charmer, in my opinion, since he had little use for children other than as beer bringers, but Ila Mae found him more attractive than I did.

It would seem hypocritical of her to chastise Pat for a love affair and then indulge in one herself. But my aunt's extramarital adventure, her letters make clear, bears no resemblance to Pat's whatsoever, since Ila Mae's was divinely ordained. "Some how I have a Feeling that God intended for Vin & I to meet for God knows we couldn't help it."

Though written English fought her all the way, she gave Cy stiff competition as a masterful manipulator. Writing to Roy, tirelessly stirring up domestic unrest, she sought not just to conquer but to divide.

Monday morning

Dear Roy:

Well how are things going better I hope. Roy, Pat hurt my feelings when I got ready to leave she never even as much said thanks all she said was, she was glad that I came over, ask Vin for he was there. But I know how you felt about it: for as I told you that I will all ways help you In any way That I can. any time. You just let me know.

    I know she was glad when I left.

    The dinner at the restaurant was very nice & She was nice as she could be . . .

"As nice as she could be" is a conventional phrase. Ila Mae somehow gives it the subtext "which we both know isn't very nice at all."

Wiley is in such condition I called the Dr. have appoint-ment for 8 this evening he is going to have ex ray somehow I know that we will have to give up the House before Long & I just can't go back to his mother's to live. I will let you know how things turn out.

Finally comes the main business at hand:

. . . Pat has written to Hope about Cy calling all the time & Hope is such cat that she has spread it all over town. I told Pat long ago that you can't trust her. Please Roy don't tell her any thing I tell you because I know you are right & will all ways do the right thing.

"Cy calling all the time . . ." The words must have detonated within Roy like a bomb. He could intercept letters and destroy them. Must he also have the phone ripped out? Surround our bungalow with a moat? Hire a team of sharpshooters trained to fire at anybody wearing a cowboy hat? Leaving him reeling in the shock waves, Ila Mae winds up briskly.

. . . Will let you know how Wiley comes out he looks half dead.

Busy though she was fanning all those flames, Ila Mae did not neglect my mother's moral guidance or mine. To Pat, she wrote:

"Pat dear you have such lovely home & the grandest husband I pray to God to help you & keep you good sweet & loyal all ways." And to me: "Hello Susie have you been good little girl. Remember when you are naughty that God puts a mark on the Board."

She closes with the promise that she is going to send me "nice Bible book." I doubt that I so much as looked at the pictures. To my well-intentioned aunt, I owe my continuing resistance to all forms of religious belief. Though her own faith was genuine, and though she believed that godliness was next to cleanliness, she instilled in me the conviction that God, like Ila Mae and Roy, was a keeper of old scores, the type cowboys would say had Himself a burr under His saddle.

S E V E N

Wiley recovered and went back to selling men's clothing at Strain Bros. department store, where he got a little respect as "our Mr. Gosney." Vin went back to Wisconsin, without Ila Mae. She wrote Roy that she would not have gone with him even if he'd asked. My mother and stepfather went on with the accommodation that would become a long marriage. Inscrutable, I once considered it, but I am now older and I do not think of marriages as scrutable.

Theirs made as much sense as any. Pat was childish herself, incompetent at the practical business of living and saddled with a young child. She needed refuge and may have thought of it as temporary, from one day to the next, until the days added up to years and she no longer thought of it at all. Roy was used to disappointment: the gold strike, when he was a miner, that somehow made someone else rich, the innocent schemes for self-improvement he pursued—business school correspondence courses, health food and miracle vitamins, potions and unguents for growing hair—that led nowhere and left him unchanged. His marriage to my mother was just one more.

Roy never gave up trying to reverse his baldness. It pains me still that I once humiliated him by giving him a pair of military brushes for Christmas. He opened the package, then left the room, choking out that I'd done it now and this time I was going to catch it. Pat laughed helplessly. I wondered what I had done and why he did not like my gift. It wouldn't help matters now if I could explain to Roy that I didn't see him as bald because I didn't see him at all.

While I had not seen Cy for months either, he still held me in the same thralldom and his distant star eclipsed Roy. The parent on the scene making the rules cannot compete for glamour with the one who is not there, and when the rules include chewing each mouthful of food thirty times, there is no contest.

Nor could Roy compete with Cy in knowing how to charm me, though he longed for my affection and tried hard to win it. He gave me a watch for my birthday, a gift he could ill afford. Cy sent a telegram, delivered to our front door by messenger, and dazzled me; I knew of no other child who had ever received a telegram. "Isn't that just *typical*," said Ila Mae, who was there. "Scaring us all like that. I thought sure it was from Wiley, and his mother had passed away."

For Christmas, Roy gave me the bicycle I'd longed for, second-hand but lovingly repainted, and had to watch while I exclaimed over it briefly, set it aside and went back to pawing over Cy's gift, a package full of smaller packages. Individually wrapped, these contained every food I loved and was no longer allowed to eat: a tall jar of stuffed green olives, the kind I used to fish out of my parents' martinis; animal crackers; Kraft's caramels; marshmallows; Tootsie Rolls; a dozen Hershey bars. Roy's face told me that before I had taken a bite out of these, he could hear my teeth starting to rot.

Cy's letters came, addressed to me. A man was entitled to write to his daughter, if not to his ex-wife, so Roy reluctantly let the mail go through. Though I could read them perfectly well myself, Pat helpfully volunteered to read these letters to me and was less puzzled than I was, I'm sure, by such information as: "In the event you are interested, I haven't had a date in the last two and a half months. I tried keeping company with a girl in Salt Lake City but despite the fact that I am continually lonesome as Hell for someone . . . I haven't been able to make a go of it and despite myself have been drawn into a shell from which it is difficult to emerge."

He was bouncing around the country again, finding little work and hard up. From Tucson, and Phoenix, and a dozen other western

towns, he wrote letters, ostensibly to me, about prospects and re-
versals. "Next week, M-G-M begins the filming of *Apache Trails*
here and I hope to obtain work on that until my shows get under
way." "I was offered a show at St. Louis for March 25–April 1st
but I guess my price was too high as I have not heard from them."
"It will be necessary for me to dispose of the car in some manner
which I hope to determine within the next few days. There remains
a balance of $272.20 and I do dislike to lose an investment of
$1300.00 because of that amount. Yet . . . I have to have some cash
to go on until February unless something breaks in the meantime."

He didn't get the job as a movie extra. He didn't get the radio
announcing job he wanted at a small station in Harrisonburg, Vir-
ginia. He left a job as a ranch hand because "the situation there
became practically unbearable" and holed up on another ranch
owned by a friend, to "get out the scores of letters incident to lining
up my itinerary for this, my final year in this game."

Desperate, he finally sold the Packard, in Salt Lake City, for a
few hundred dollars. It broke his heart, he wrote, and it also broke
Pat's. Reading this news to me, she cried.

The midnight-blue Packard had been our announcement to the
world, and ourselves, that we Taillons were winners. It had style,
that ephemeral thing Pat and Cy valued above all else. It repre-
sented the old, footloose high-roller days, and no sensible Plymouth
station wagon, its fenders and hood a muddy maroon, could inspire
the same pride of ownership. That Cy would part with it was un-
thinkable.

Roy, Pat and I all knew that Cy could not have brought himself
to sell the car unless he was flat broke. Only Roy found that knowledge heartening. Though Cy enclosed a crisp fifty-dollar bill, in par-
tial payment of overdue child support, the money was not as
welcome as the news that "the Big Shot," as Roy called Cy, was in
a tailspin and rapidly losing altitude.

My parents' divorce agreement, unusual at the time, provided
that each had custody of me for six months of the year. Pat was to
take me for the school year, Cy for the summers and school vacations.

My spending school vacations with him was impractical, since

he was usually thousands of miles away. Summers were also out of
the question. He was working rodeos then, and in Roy's and Ila
Mae's views, couldn't take care of me properly. Still spindly and
neurasthenic, I could not survive three months of hard travel, hamburgers and Hershey bars. So I saw Cy only when he came through
Missoula. Because these visits were infrequent, and because Cy
staged each like a Broadway play, they became big events not just
for me but for Missoula, anticipated with as much interest as the
opening day of deer-hunting season.

Missoula is a pretty town with numerous virtues. Spectacle and
diversion are not among them, unless one counts watching car
crashes at an intersection called "Suicide Junction." Cy's appear-
ances were at least as exciting, and nobody died.

Forbidden by Roy to come to our house anymore, he picked me
up at Paxson Grade School. I knew he was in the building before I
actually saw him because he stopped in at the principal's office to
find out which classroom I was in. Through the office secretary, or
a miscreant kid putting in detention time, word leaked out the door
that some cowboy movie star was in our midst.

Next came the sound of Cy's boot heels down the hall, accompanied by pairs of other feet. In the course of his progress from the
first floor to the second, he'd picked up a retinue. Trotting behind
him were the principal, female teachers and kids who were supposed
to be somewhere else. All that was missing was a marching band
playing "I Love a Parade."

I'd hear his unmistakable baritone, pitched for the bleachers,
telling how he'd always wanted to teach school himself, because
there was no job like it. Oh, not for the material rewards, maybe,
but for the satisfaction.

Finally he stood in my classroom door, handsome as Gary
Cooper, in his whitest hat and nattiest Western shirt and narrow-
legged pants, with his beautifully manicured hands resting on an
enormous silver and gold belt buckle. "Cy Taillon," he introduced
himself, lifting his hat to my teacher, who looked breathless. On
one of these occasions, he got a spontaneous round of applause from
the third grade.

Manic with joy at seeing him again, I was anxious to leave school

Cyra (first row, second from left) in her skinned-back-pigtails stage

and have him to myself, but not Cy, surrounded with admirers. He let himself be persuaded to give an informal talk about rodeo, the only all-American sport, while the principal beamed and took a seat and thought this was his own idea. "I guess you've heard about enough," Cy said, at intervals. "No, no," screamed his rapt audience.

He'd seen what looked like a fine instrument through the open door of the music room, Cy mentioned. He played a little piano himself. Soon he was installed on the bench putting the old upright through his rendition of "Springtime in the Rockies," heavy on trills suggesting birdsong. He captured everyone within range of his voice, roughly the southwest quadrant of Missoula, with stories of his travels across America, the grandest country in the world. He had us all, kids and adults, jumping through hoops.

Cy was not being paid for this performance, but things were slow on the circuit and an audience was an audience. He would have gladly done two shows, called a square dance and then pitched War Bonds in front of the PTA. Appreciation was the little bottle labeled "Drink Me" whose elixir made him tall, taller, taller still.

By the time I finally got him out of there, by threatening to have hysterics, he had a date with the red-haired music teacher to discuss my buried talent for music (still buried so deep it has never surfaced); an ink stain on his middle finger from signing autographs with a school pen; a satisfied flush under his suntan. The music teacher believed Cy had always wanted to be a concert pianist—if only he could have had lessons, instead of being entirely self-taught. The principal knew Cy thought being principal of Paxson Grade School the noblest of callings. The girls in the class all wanted to grow up to be Miss Rodeo America and the boys champion bronc riders.

Was everybody happy? Everybody except my father, who deflated visibly when we were by ourselves and the performance was over. Demonstrating that he was not bound by Roy's relayed injunctions, he took me out for greasy food. He told me how much he'd missed me and read the report cards I'd saved up for him. But he was restless, gazing out the car windows as we sat in the drive-in parking lot, not even bothering to flirt with the car hop.

He asked me about my mother. How was her health? Did she have headaches anymore? How was she wearing her hair now? Did she still sing that damned song all the time around the house? He meant "Stormy Weather," Pat's staple along with "Rain or Shine." She was fond of songs about love under assorted climatic conditions.

Before he dropped me the block from home Roy permitted, Cy gave me a letter for her, with instructions to deliver it when Roy was not around. It was nothing to do with Roy, he said, just news about old friends.

I gave him the letter Pat had tucked into my lunchbox, uneasy because I was sure that Roy would not approve and that he would find out. He missed nothing, my stepfather, no invisible speck on a freshly washed window, no blade of grass left standing on a lawn mowed so closely it looked as if it had been cropped by sheep, no subversive act of Pat's or mine, real or suspected.

Sometimes I stared at him absentmindedly. "I know what you're thinking," Roy was inclined to announce on such occasions. Whatever it was, he didn't like it and repaid my stare with odd forms of reprisal. Most unbearable was no reading other than school books, enforced by night raids to make sure I wasn't reading by flashlight under the covers. Second most unbearable was helping clean out the garage, a useless undertaking consisting of shifting piles of things, the overflow from the basement, from one damp, spider-infested corner to the other. As a middle-aged adult, I have yet to live in a house with either a garage or a basement.

What form Pat's punishments took, I don't know, since house arrest does not permit many embellishments. Whatever the risk, she continued to stay in touch with Cy by whatever means she could contrive.

In 1942, a few months before he enlisted in the Army Air Corps, Cy wrote Pat a three-page typewritten letter advising her to have an abortion. Her own letter to him, appealing to him for advice, had followed him around for weeks, from temporary address to temporary address. It filled him with confusion, coming "as a considerable additional shock to those of the past few years." He had no right to enter into any decision she might make, he wrote, but he was full of concern for her state of mind—"It is the grossest kind of an injustice to bring an unwanted child into the world"—and her health. "You are still taking treatments and if you intensify these again as you did before, there is a great possibility that your health will be impaired to a great extent. Moreover, in consideration of the fact that this condition of yours continues to persist, you will be taking a tremendous chance for the baby. Do you think it would be fair to subject an unborn one to the chance?"

They were lucky with me, he says, in that my periodic tests do not indicate any disease. Pat cannot count on being as lucky a second time.

His usual eloquence trails off into near-incoherence: "Regardless of what our actual feelings toward each other may be—or, regardless of what may develop in the future—if you do feel as you have indicated, and, in consideration of all that you are going through now . . ."

Beginning "Dearest Pat" and ending "All my love," this is my father's valedictory letter to my mother. It hints at their continuing longing for one another while acknowledging that he has no further claim on her. "In the light of your quickly chosen circumstances, I really have no right to make any further suggestions regarding you or your relationship to me." It tells her that "the thoughts that your letter aroused in my mind are far too involved to write." Write him as soon as possible with regard to her decision, Cy pleads; he will always be of any help he can be to her. But he was letting go of her at last. Whether she had the baby or not, Pat was pregnant by Roy. There could be no more tangible proof that she was his wife now.

No baby was born. My mother's medical condition may have made it possible for her to have a legal abortion, or she may have made the private arrangements women then and now contrive to make if they are desperate enough. I don't know, either, whether she ever received Cy's letter or whether Roy intercepted and with-held it. All I do know about her pregnancy is that Ila Mae was never consulted. Had she been, another boot-box would have bulged with her counsel on the subject, along with privileged information on what God thought about it.

Later that year, Pat had a nervous breakdown. I was told she was visiting Ila Mae. She was actually in a sanitarium called Warm Springs. A ceaseless flow of letters from Ila Mae harangued Roy about feeding me properly and seeing that I went to Sunday school, discussed Pat's "malaria" as the cause of her emotional problems and blamed Cy for her physical and moral deterioration. "Before she met him she was sweetest thing ever lived." Ila Mae hadn't thought so at the time but she wasn't a slave to foolish consistency.

Roy should "keep chin up," she told him, and enclosed a note for Pat telling her to think of Roy and do everything the doctors ordered, "for they know what's best for you."

My mother's sister Lucille also wrote to her, from the Wisconsin dairy farm where she lived with her second husband. Her first had been a Filipino railroad engineer named Pedro Magatutu, a union that must have raised eyebrows back home in Paragould. Pedro was seduced by the music of the rails, and vanished. Lucille settled down with Henry and the dairy herd. "You make Roy happy and *forget* the past,"she wrote Pat. "I know about the haphazard life you've led, & dear was it worth it? I'm lots older than you and I want you to be happy with Roy as I am with Pa. It takes a man with a little more age & yes common sense to make a woman appreciate her good fortune."

Did Pat hear, in her sisters' words of comfort, their mutual belief that she was being punished for her sins? Her therapy involved drugs, spinal taps and something called "brain waves"; she must have been ready to believe it.

Once in the two months she was gone, she phoned, reassuring me that she was all right, only having such a swell time with Ila Mae that she was staying longer. She also told me to be good, one of those parental injunctions she rarely uttered. She'd been on the receiving end of it too often.

No uncritical expression of love and sympathy came from Cy this time, for no one told him about Pat's breakdown, though Lucille's letter mentions that she and Pa have heard from him. "Cy writes us he may join the Army, just where he belongs." The family's consensus was that he was in no way involved, other than as a guilty bystander.

While my mother was gone, Roy and I made a qualified peace with each other. He lectured and scolded me less. I tried harder to please him, aware that something I did not understand was causing him pain and worry. In return for my grudging efforts at housekeeping, he granted me an allowance for the first time, a quarter a week. All his life, Roy carried a change purse, an old-fashioned black leather pouch with a clasp that opened with a snap. Doling out my allowance, he opened it slowly and deliberately, shook it to inspect its contents and then handed over the two dimes and a nickel with care, as if the coins were breakable.

What money Roy earned, he earned for six-day weeks of hard work, and though he managed to put a little aside, he never had more than he needed. The trouble he had parting with it was commensurate with the trouble he had getting hold of it in the first place.

It puzzled me, his insistence that even a penny was precious, worth stooping to pick up from the sidewalk. It angered Roy that he could not get it through my head that money was not manufactured inside slot machines and that before it ended up carelessly scattered up and down a bar, the shiny silver dollars and the crumpled bills, someone had to earn it. I thought money fell out of the sky, he said, like Cy, and would end up the same way, broke and a bum, unless my quarters went into the bank he gave me and stayed there.

They went in, but they came out as fast. I had learned to work the coins out through the slot on top, armed with determination and a table knife I kept hidden underneath my mattress. An adult lifetime later, I still feel guilty when I spend money and guilty when I save it, caught between two powerful object lessons.

What money buys, Roy taught me, is security. What it ought to buy, Cy taught me by example, is self-respect, that fragile intricate form of it that people understand only when they have no security whatsoever. The ethic of the rodeo circuit was that if you won prize money for an event, you paid some less fortunate cowboy's entry fees in the next event. You also saw to it that he could hold his head up in the bar after the rodeo, which meant not buying a drink but buying a round and leaving the bartender the change. The money was a loan, but a loan that would never be called in.

The ethic around our household in Missoula was that self-respect came only at the price of honest labor. A handout, however well meant, degraded the receiver. In those post-Depression years of the early forties, tramps appeared at our screen door sometimes, asking to cut firewood, or mow the lawn, in exchange for a meal or a dollar. They terrified Pat, but Roy had forbidden her to turn them away, no matter how shabby they were.

Tell them to come back in the evening, he made her promise. If they did, he found some job for them and showed them where we kept our tools in the garage. He never stood over their shoulders while they did some task that did not really need doing, or conducted an inventory of the tools before they left. When the man came to the back door again, Roy met him with change purse in hand. "Here's your wages," he said gravely, and shook hands.

My father and my stepfather both understood dignity. They only understood it differently, a matter of temperament. Both were midwestern farm boys who left home and came out West, where there was room for ambition. Both fell in love with Pat, whose attraction for them must have been that she embodied no trace of girl-next-door, unless you happened to live next door to a burlesque house. They were more alike than they knew, and had my mother not come along, they might have remained friends until they were old men, Roy riding the tail of the comet, Cy grateful for the ballast.

EIGHT

As good as his word, Cy enlisted in the Army Air Corps. Friends had urged him to somehow remarry my mother in order to avoid the draft, he wrote to me, but he was outraged "at the apparent fact that someone would think that I would use the subterfuge of hiding behind the skirts of any woman to escape an obvious duty." "Subterfuge" sent me to the dictionary at school, to look up the word. Cy's letters frequently sent me burrowing through the dictionary, educational fallout from his letter-writing style.

He was ready to dispute with anyone "that I should fall into the category of being a coward," a thought that would have occurred to no one, not even Roy, who'd ever seen my bantamweight father pile into a fight. I was proud of him and terrified. From the way Roy and Ila Mae talked about Cy's joining the Army, I had the strong impression that he'd get killed, at least if he had enough decency left in him to do the right thing for once.

The months before he was assigned to duty were the worst months of his professional life thus far. Rodeo job after rodeo job fell through because of cancellations. The country had other things on its mind, and without the Packard, Cy had to travel between the few announcing jobs he scraped up on crowded wartime trains. While this was expensive, he wrote, it was still cheaper than trying to run a car in the face of gas and rubber shortages.

To keep body and soul alive, he went back to Salt Lake City in the hope of getting a job at the Remington plant there, but he could not hold out for the two or three weeks it took to get hired and so signed on as a track laborer at an ordnance plant, for sixty-five cents an hour. He said the job saved him money on manicures.

What money he did not need to live on, and he was living cheaply, he'd send on to Pat to buy school clothes for me. Though Roy kept pointing out that Cy was a deadbeat, who owed him hundreds of dollars in child support, he took his obligation seriously at that point, and when he could not send cash—always the crisp new bills he liked to carry instead of worn ones—he at least worried about it. Again he mentioned the $10,000 in service life insurance he was assigning to me. He too seemed to think it likely I would collect. The drifty, demoralized summer behind him had left him pessimistic about his prospects in general.

An old shoulder injury, the result of his last attempt at bronc riding, kept Cy out of combat. As he'd feared, he was too old to be a pilot, a major disappointment. For all his posing and posturing, his idea of serving his country involved more than the public relations slot he soon found himself in. He sent clippings of himself, dapper in uniform, leading dance bands and acting as m.c. for bond drive evenings and air shows. As usual, he underlined his name, frequently misspelled, in case I managed to miss it while reading the photo captions. Letter after letter, he fumed about being on the sidelines of the war and vowed not to give up on being assigned to combat duty. Having failed other tests of manhood, in others' eyes and his own, he longed for another, one he knew he would pass.

Then his letters stopped coming, an unprecedented and alarming lapse. Though my own letters were less frequent than Cy's, though I saw him briefly and seldom and though I was settling into my new life with my mother and Roy, I basked in the certainty of my father's love. He sent me birthday telegrams and Christmas boxes full of things that were associated, in my mind, with the old days. He still addressed me as Taillon instead of Qualley, though Pat instructed me to write him that she could call me anything she wanted. He wrote me every two weeks, even when I didn't write back or wrote the letters children write when they are rebelling against an emotional claim: Dear Dad, How are you? I am fine. I got a B in spelling. P.S. My mother says to tell you she needs the money and send it.

Never had he stopped writing, no matter where he was or what was happening to him. As the months went by, I began to believe that he had been killed.

Even in peaceful Missoula, reminders that there was a war on were constant. At school, we took up collections to buy War Bonds. At home, Roy started a Victory garden, digging up our backyard and planting carrots, potatoes and onions, "good keepers" in case our food supply was cut off. A skillful farmer, he grew so many vegetables that we could supply our neighbors and still have enough to stockpile in a dank corner of the basement, smelling of earth and filling me with horror. I saw a lifetime ahead of eating cooked carrots.

Like everyone else, we saved flattened tin cans, cooking fat and string. When kids asked why the soldiers needed cooking fat and string to fight the Germans, no convincing answers were forthcoming. Adults didn't seem to know either. It was all part of "the war effort." We got the impression that they considered the question smart-alecky if not treasonous.

Ours not to question why. Ours to compete over who could make the biggest string ball and thank our lucky stars we weren't the children of Europe, who were being bombed and starving. When the March of Time newsreel at the Wilma Theater showed air raids, the cylindrical bombs dropping from the bellies of the planes, a girl I knew, at the movies with her parents, screamed that we were all going to be killed, a possibility that visited itself upon me as her parents led her, sobbing, up the aisle.

I caught her fear. The sight of a plane in the clear skies over Missoula turned me weak-kneed and made me lose bladder control. In bed, I heard the snarling engines in the newsreels again and waited for the explosion that would blow us all to smithereens.

Don't be ridiculous, Pat and Roy said, standing in the doorway of my room when nightmares made me cry out. Nobody was going to bomb South Central Avenue. The war was a long way away. We were winning it.

Kids who'd lost their older brothers came to school silent and swollen-eyed and suffered the awkward, unctuous sympathy of the rest of us. The newspaper announced additions to the list of "Gold Star Mothers." Evenings, the kids on my block were shooed out into our front yards while our parents listened to the news on the radio. When we were called in again, to sit down to supper, they were in no mood to tolerate complaints about the ration-coupon fare.

The adults knew more than they were telling us, it was clear, and maybe what they knew was that we weren't winning at all. We were losing. Still no letters from Cy; I knew he'd been sent into active combat, as he longed to be, someplace where the bombs were falling.

"You do what your father tells you," Pat said to me over the dinner table one night, backing Roy up on some point of contention between us, such as the palatability of turnips. "My father's dead," I said, and burst into noisy sobs that were both self-dramatizing and born of real fear. Only the vehemence with which Pat denied it convinced me otherwise. My outburst caused the blood to drain out of her face and make her hands shake, so that she couldn't steady the match to light her cigarette.

Roy pushed back his chair and left the kitchen table. I bolted from it too, and in my room went back to work rolling string, superior heavy cord that Roy brought home for me from the candy company. It came on packing crates, he said, and if I kept up the good work, rolling it nice and tight like that, I might get a prize from the War Department.

I had the awards ceremony planned out in my mind, complete with a band and a famous general presenting me with the plaque. It pleased me to think how the people who found me an oddity, too fond by half of ten-dollar words, would have to revise their opinions and apologize or not get a seat in the auditorium.

When I'd last heard from my father, he'd been stationed in New Jersey. I wrote him a long, patriotic letter that would reach him somehow, I thought, if he were on some secret mission but still alive. I wrote him again, and again, and when I could find nothing to write, sent him newspaper clippings, content irrelevant; the point was an excuse to ask Pat for a stamp. I changed my tune and wrote dramatic letters berating him for not writing to me anymore, his very own daughter, the best string saver in Missoula. No answer over the weeks. I wrote him that I had a fatal disease and was dying. Weak as I was, and despite how hard it was to hold a pencil, I wanted to say goodbye.

Though Cy knew this was hokum, concern about my health must have been at the back of his mind constantly. He called Pat, late at night after I was in bed. She told him I was just fine, and what was it to him? He told her that he was getting married again. He must have stopped writing because he was afraid to break this news, not to me, but to her.

Pat's replay of this conversation to me was flat and don't-give-a-damn. She couldn't remember the woman's name, she said, and offered no information except that she was twenty-eight. An old maid.

My reaction was outrage that Cy hadn't consulted me. I made up a form to send him regarding my future stepmother: name, date of birth, height, weight, hair color, color of eyes, hobbies, favorite movie star, health (good? average? excellent?) but I lost my nerve before I mailed it.

They were already married by the time I met Dorothy, the girl who had seen Cy playing one of the twin pianos in the window of a Great Falls music store, when she was fourteen, and told a girl-friend, "Someday I'm going to marry him." The story was one newspapers loved and reprinted for thirty years.

An Army nurse, Dorothy had masses of auburn hair, a volup-tuous body supported on short, thick legs, and enormous green eyes, extraordinary eyes that seemed to fill up her entire face. They glis-tened as if with tears all the time and gave her a wistful expression even when she smiled. She emphasized them with emerald-green eye shadow and a heavy black line on each upper lid.

Her hair was shoulder-length and artfully curled. She wore styl-ish, fitted gabardine suits, never slacks, and high-heeled backless pumps, called "Spring-o-lators," always color-matched to the rest of her clothes, heavy pancake makeup and jewel-toned pillbox hats. Her earrings matched everything else, her perfume preceded her into a room, and young as she was, she had adopted a notion of el-egant style, furred, hatted and gloved, suited to a much older

Dorothy Cosgriff in her high school years

woman. One thing you could say for her, she said of herself, was that she knew how to dress.

I'd never seen anyone as glamorous as Dorothy and was stunned. She must have been taken aback by Cy's rail-thin, somber daughter, dark-skinned, pigtails pulled so tight they made my own eyes look slanted. Having prepared for our meeting by reading etiquette books in the Missoula library, I greeted her with "It's a pleasure to make your acquaintance."

This did not get our relationship off to the smooth start I had intended, but nothing I could have said or done would have improved matters much. For Dorothy, I was evidence that my mother existed; that she had been Cy's wife for twelve years; that while Cy could sever every other tie, he had a child by a former show girl whose own beauty and style had made her a celebrity in Dorothy's hometown. I was the hard fact that interfered with the mythmaking of perfect love, burning uninterrupted with a true flame since the piano player and the schoolgirl locked eyes through the music store window.

The two of them were staying at Dorothy's parents' house in Great Falls, home on leave, when I went to visit, riding the bus as I'd always ridden the bus to catch up with Cy somewhere or other. The Cosgriff family, Dorothy's parents and a sister living at home, took me in warmly. They were a close, devoutly Catholic bunch, one with whom Cy must have felt at home, and they seemed to have enough of everything to go around and extend to me, rooms, beds, delicious food and tolerant good humor. If they also found me exotic, a gnome inclined to oratorical flourishes, they were kind about it. They were getting used to Cy's oratorical flourishes and willing to get used to mine.

Dorothy took my hair out of the pigtails and rolled it up on metal curlers. Like all previous efforts to curl my hair, hers failed. The reason, she told Cy and the rest of the family, was that I had impossible hair, as straight and fine as a cat's. She let me rummage around in her jewelry box and gave me a pair of earrings she no longer wore because they matched a dress she no longer had. I had no use for earrings but knew she meant the present as a goodwill gesture and was so effusive in my thanks I must have unnerved her again. Letting me try on one of her uniforms, she pointed out that her own waist was so small it almost fit. My mother had a really tiny waist too, I said, and got a look from Cy that created a wind-chill factor in the warm room. When he and I sat side by side on the sofa later that same night, Dorothy came into the room, ignored a pair of empty armchairs and wedged herself between us.

"Dorothy, for god's sake," Cy said, at once amused and irritated. I moved over so that the three of us were not squeezed together but felt like an inadvertent troublemaker again.

I went back home to Missoula a day later, and with some childish impulse to wound, regaled Pat with praise of Dorothy, her auburn hair, her green eye shadow, her diamond engagement and wedding rings and her Spring-o-lators. I told her about the photo I'd seen of her in her nurse's uniform, carrying the American flag at the head of a parade. To my disappointment, Pat asked no questions at all, nor showed any interest in this monologue. Only when I produced the plastic button earrings Dorothy gave me did she betray curiosity. She took the earrings over to the kitchen window and turned them over in her hands, examining them as if they were jigsaw pieces.

Whether by remarrying, or drying out, or both, Cy had redeemed himself in Ila Mae's eyes. She had seen him and Dorothy when they were in Great Falls, my aunt wrote to my mother, and "Pat you wouldn't recognize him he different man, handsome as dog." The drying out was Dorothy's doing. "He hasn't had single drink for mos. She said it was either the bottle or her take his choice. They don't any of them touch a drop, any of her people." This was a miracle and proof of God's grace, as Ila Mae had told Cy to his face. As for Dorothy, she had to give her credit. Before she came along, he was headed "straight for gutter."

I was sixteen or so when Dorothy gave me her own account of Cy's reform. She had not only made him swear that he would never take another drink, but on their wedding night had insisted that he get down on his knees and pray to God, for help in keeping his word, before he climbed into bed. She and I were in a motel room in Puyallup, Washington, waiting for Cy to come back after announcing a night rodeo. When he appeared, I could not look him in the eye and snapped on the television set.

The scene stays in my mind still, hilarious and disturbing as a Thurber cartoon. In it, Cy kneels beside the bridal bed in his boxer shorts and his cowboy boots.

Some women believe that the right woman, loving and resolute enough, can dry out a drunk and turn a lady-killer into a happily monogamous husband. In my view, this is like believing you can win at three-card monte. Yet with Cy and Dorothy, I saw it happen. My father became a man I barely knew, a new Cy impeccable in his starched uniform, clear-eyed and confident, within months after their marriage.

He walked differently. His old swagger had given way to a brisk, military step compromised somewhat by his bowed legs but impressive anyway. His manners with Dorothy were courtly; he opened car doors for her and held her coat, each of these acts ceremonious. To me, he observed that ladies did not sit with one ankle perched on the other knee and that there were also places well-brought-up little girls did not scratch. When I swore in his presence, he threatened to wash my mouth out with soap. Shades of Roy and Ila Mae. I was amazed.

Through laser looks and a stiffening of his body, as he sat behind the wheel of a car or on the sofa in Dorothy's parents' living room, he let me know that our old lives were now off-limits in conversation. "Remember . . ." I would begin, or "We used to . . ." and there would emanate from Cy what felt like a blast of cold air, freezing out both reminiscence and me.

The same cold draft chilled us all when Cy addressed me as "Pat," a mistake he corrected in the same breath but that left him flustered and Dorothy annoyed each time it happened. How much or how little Dorothy knew about Cy's first marriage, the powerful attachment, the destructive behavior and the refusal to acknowledge that it was over, she knew enough to feel threatened. If mentioning Pat was unavoidable, my mother was "Her." "You'd better call Missoula and let her know when Cyra's coming home." The pronoun came out of my stepmother's mouth with backspin on it. Without having it spelled out for me, on my short and infrequent visits, I knew that Dorothy felt the sooner I was back on the bus, the better.

Soon after the marriage she resigned her commission, while Cy, unwilling to be outranked by his wife, went into Officer Candidate School. Dorothy became pregnant. My brother Terry was born, the event marked by a printed announcement headed "Taillon Stampede" and listing the doctor in attendance as the Arena Judge and the nurses as Pickup Riders. Along with everyone else on their mailing list, I got this announcement and glued it into my scrapbook, beside clippings about my mother's bowling league. It was the first piece of mail from Cy for nearly a year.

Ila Mae wrote, full of goodwill toward the reconstituted Taillons and breathless about the baby. Cy was sorry now that he had named me after him, she said. Otherwise Terry could have been Cy

Jr. Always practical, she suggested that since "Cyra funny name anyway as I have all ways said," the problem could be solved if Roy and
Pat changed my name. Her suggestion was Minnie Mae, after my
maternal grandmother, who was "living saint until God took her
to be angel."

Longing to see the new baby, I got my chance at last. Cy was
stationed in Oakland, California, and was coming home, briefly, to
get Dorothy and Terry. He'd found an apartment, no easy task in
wartime. Before they left, he called and arranged for me to visit the
family in Great Falls. I went, and through no fault of mine or anyone else's, became a burden on Cy and Dorothy's marriage that both
of them deeply resented. During that week, Pat had her second
nervous breakdown. This one was so severe she was sent back to the
hospital at Warm Springs immediately.

Behind the closed doors I had learned to associate with trouble,
Cy talked to Roy on the telephone. Afterward, in the upstairs bedroom of the Cosgriffs' house, he and Dorothy shut themselves away
for hours, conferring over the crisis. The room was thick with smoke
from Cy's cigarettes, his remaining vice, when he emerged to tell
me that I was coming along with him, Dorothy and Terry to Oakland. He had the grace to tell me what was going on this time,
though I dimly understood "nervous breakdown." Roy was too upset himself to take care of me, he said. He also agreed with Cy that
the cause of Pat's illness was overwork. "She had to go and start
another damned dance studio."

Several months before, Pat had launched "Patricia's School of
the Dance" on the ground floor of a moving and storage company
in Missoula. It offered tap, ballet and exercise classes for what ads
forthrightly called "fatties" and was an instant success.

The money must have come from Roy, not a large investment
in that it involved only rent and equipping the place with mirrors,
ballet barres and exercise mats. It must have been large to him, and
how my mother talked him into freeing her from her captivity, as
well as backing her financially, I can't imagine.

That Cy was remarried may have had something to do with it,
in that he no longer posed so grave a threat. It may have occurred
to Roy that having married his dream woman, the glamorous show

girl, he had turned her into a household drab. Hidden under a
bushel, or one of Ila Mae's housedresses, Pat's light cast no luster
on him. Whatever negotiations took place behind the scenes, Patricia's School of the Dance opened with fanfare.

The Daily Missoulian ran my mother's press release, the same one
she'd used when she opened her Billings studio years before. It out-
lined her theatrical career, with flourishes, and included a high-
minded statement about Dance and the Whole Child. We held an
open house for prospective customers, with iced tea and bakery
cookies. Old publicity pictures of Pat filled the big window facing
the street: Pat in a feathered headdress doing the splits, Pat waving
from the door of an airplane, "en route to further studies in Paris."
Had she really been to Paris? I asked her, dying to hear all about it.
That's what it said, didn't it? she snapped.

By the end of her first month, she had so many students, kids
taking tap after school and their mothers sweating through acrobatic routines mornings and evenings, she had to hire an assistant
instructor, a high school girl who had mastered the time step and
could lead Beginning Tap, over and over, through "East Side, West
Side."

Roy kept the books at the studio and spent all his evenings there.
I reported to the place after school and ran errands, among them
checking out library books on ballet for Pat. She knew virtually
nothing about it but was teaching it anyway. Her students mainly
learned to stand on one leg and point their toes.

I loved the school. One large bright room with a hardwood floor,
it smelled of sweaty rubber mats and floor polish, the ammonia with
which Roy and I cleaned the mirrors, and take-out food. With no
time to go home for dinner, the three of us ate in the partitioned-
off office at the front, on Roy's secondhand wooden desk. Though
Roy claimed he went out for hamburgers and milk shakes only because no drive-ins offered take-out spinach, he loved the greasy food
he preached was poisonous and fell on it with as much appetite as
my mother and I did. Scratch a food faddist and you'll find a man
whose erotic fantasies center on french fries.

Still slim and supple, no longer isolated from the world outside
our bungalow, Pat turned into a beauty again. My mother was one
of those women who can dazzle one day and the next look plain,

gray-faced and lifeless. In retrospect, I can reconstruct the periods before her breakdowns by remembering how she looked. Light went out of her face a little at a time, as if behind her eyes she were pulling down a shade. As a child, I hadn't learned to read the signs and had no clue. So when her second bout of mental illness shattered her, life upended itself without warning. With my father and his new family, I left Great Falls in a few days, on a train packed tight with servicemen and headed for California.

The four of us had two seats. Dorothy sat in one holding Terry, whose restless crying rose up with the crying of other babies. I sat in the other, watching the landscape go by until the overhead lights dimmed and it was black outside. Cy stood for the whole trip in the crowded aisle, holding on to the overhead baggage rack and refusing to trade places with either Dorothy or me. His notion of chivalry dictated that he stand for eighteen hours or so while his wife and children sat.

My parents' shared-custody agreement, a cousin told me later, had resolved a deadlock. Neither parent wanted full-time responsibility for me. In fact, neither wanted custody. Cy wanted to pursue his rodeo career. Pat wanted to pursue the fantasy that she was still a show girl despite her marriage to Roy. They weren't enlightened but self-centered.

Wasn't that a fine kettle of beans? the cousin asked. Didn't it just make me want to shake the two of them until their teeth rattled?

Of course it did, but memory is selective. One couldn't live with it if it weren't. I prefer to remember my mother all dazzle and snap, leading her dancing classes at the studio while I gloried in gilt by association. I prefer to remember Cy swaying in the aisle on that trip to Oakland, gallant and asleep on his feet.

N I N E

The apartment in Oakland, dark and smelling of mildew, was in the basement of a stucco house on a hill. The rent for it was extortionate, Cy complained, wartime profiteering on the part of our landlady, who lived upstairs, scolded every time we turned on our radio and threatened to evict us when I picked plums from the tree in the backyard. She didn't mind if they rotted unpicked, or if birds ate them, only if tenants' children did.

Without my being there, Cy, Dorothy and Terry would have been cramped in their three rooms. Cy's soldier's pay had to stretch farther than my father and his new wife anticipated. They had no privacy and countless practical problems, from putting me in school somewhere to getting along without a car, never easy in California. Because our hill was so steep, Dorothy could push Terry's buggy down it to shop, but not up again. She had to wait on the corner for Cy to come home on the streetcar, in the evenings, with her buggyload of baby, laundry and groceries.

Far harder on her, the apartment teemed with mice. Dorothy was in terror of them. I wasn't, and when she and I were at war with one another, I could always pretend that I had seen a mouse. It gave me a satisfying sense of power to see her standing on a kitchen chair, white-faced and helpless—my powerful stepmother reduced to powerlessness. She and I had quickly arrived at the relationship we never substantially altered. With equal vehemence, we detested each other.

So jealous of Cy she resented even the fraction of his affections I claimed, Dorothy was a setter of snares. In her version of our skirmishes, she made heroic efforts to please her stepdaughter. I failed to appreciate these efforts, or appreciate them enough, or appreciate them in the proper way, impossible because there was no proper way. "I'm not angry, I'm only hurt," was her litany.

"I'm not hurt, I'm only angry," I screamed back at her, and caught hell from my father for "sassing back." Like most men, Cy hated what he called "a cat fight," friction between women. His un-Solomon-like solution was to join in the shouting himself, until the landlady wielded her gavel, a broom handle, and brought us all to order by pounding on her kitchen floor, our kitchen ceiling.

Dorothy escalated our hostilities every chance she got. I became ever more resentful and cagier, as good at provoking her as she was at provoking me. She spent a lot of time on that kitchen chair, cowering from imaginary mice, and was subjected to worse forms of terrorism. Carrying the baby across the room, I got good at faking a stumble and making it look as if I were about to drop him on his head.

This hateful behavior I look back on without guilt because I was up against an equally unprincipled opponent. What affection I can find in my middle-aged self for Dorothy is based on what a worthy enemy she was, how determined and how inventive. I got up the Irish in her, she said, but what I really brought to flower in her was tactical genius. One has to respect the domestic Desert Fox who never deploys the same weapons in the same place or repeats the same maneuver.

I had few clothes with me in Oakland, only those I would have needed for a few days of visiting in Great Falls. Ila Mae's handiwork, these clothes were dowdy even at Our Lady of Lourdes, the Catholic school at the foot of the hill where Cy enrolled me. Other girls my age wore skirts and sweaters, he noticed, when he escorted me there on his way to the Army base in the mornings. I alternated among three skimpier versions of the housedresses Ila Mae made for Pat, cotton print sacks cut like those worn by early female missionaries.

As tight as money was in the household, my fashion-conscious father insisted Dorothy buy me a pleated plaid skirt and matching sweater.

Dorothy set out on this mission alone. With unerring instinct, she picked out an outfit that made me look even more sallow and wizened than I already looked, the skirt two sizes too large and so long it came to the top of my socks, the sweater a yellow-green never seen in nature, seldom in art. My skin took a greenish sheen from it even under the low-wattage light bulbs our landlady made us use.

Cy looked at me and registered the same despair he had felt when he paid ten dollars for a permanent wave and my hair didn't bend. His expression told me he had a hopeless case for a daughter: deck her out in a brand-new green sweater, and the whole kid turned green.

Dorothy told me how much these clothes had cost and the trial-by-streetcar she had gone through to buy them. All that money, and all that work, and one could tell from my sour look that I didn't like them. It just went to show that as far as I was concerned, she could do nothing right.

As soon as I put on that sweater and skirt, I knew they made me look like an organ grinder's monkey. I also knew it was politic to make a show of appreciation and launched into one fit for a cast of thousands. I jumped up and down, squealed, hugged Dorothy, hugged Cy, hugged Dorothy again. I said the skirt was the most beautiful skirt in the world and the sweater was even prettier. I claimed to want to sleep in these clothes, so that we would never be parted. Oh thank you thank you thank you thank you. I concluded with a clog dance meant to convey wild excitement.

My stepmother watched. Her shoulders sagged and a pair of perfect tears spilled from her luminous green eyes. "You know," she said, "even if you don't like a present somebody gives you, you could pretend to be grateful."

That I remember this incident, so far in the past, is a sign of arrested development. I do remember it, and after thirty-five years, compulsively thank telephone solicitors for calling.

Our time in Oakland must have passed slowly for Cy and Dorothy as it did for me. Cy was just one more lieutenant, and the man hated being one more anything. Dorothy, a gregarious young woman, was far from her friends and family, trapped in a basement with a new baby, a loathsome stepdaughter and mice. Only Terry, blond, sunny-tempered and sturdy, thrived. The world's prize baby, in Cy's view, Dorothy's and mine, he made us into a family of sorts, in spite of ourselves, because we all thought of him as under our care and joint proprietorship. At Our Lady of Lourdes, I got into a fist-fight with a girl who claimed her baby brother was walking before he was.

There, too, I was baptized as a Catholic at my own insistence. Frantic to conform, as usual, I had undergone a conversion of epic proportions, complete with religious visions lifted from *The Song of Bernadette* and an inner voice announcing I was destined to be a saint. When I wrote home about it, the baptism caused proportionate religious hysteria on my Aunt Ila Mae's part, and prompted one of the few letters Roy ever wrote me.

In his surprisingly elegant hand, he informed me that no matter how much holy water the priests and nuns had made me drink, I was a Lutheran. While he had no religious faith of his own, Roy knew all about "mackerel snappers" just as he knew all about house cats. Cats jumped on your chest and sucked out your breath while you were asleep. Catholics sucked out your soul, sold it on the soul market and turned the proceeds over to the Pope.

Ila Mae changed church affiliations frequently because she and the minister differed on some fine point of theology. Her restless quest stopped short of Catholicism, however, and she also wrote furious letters to Cy and Dorothy, more letters to me. In mine, she pointed out that Catholicism was for foreigners and I had been born right here in the U.S. of A.

I must have known that the Catholic Church and I were just one of those things, and that when I went back to Missoula, it would be all over between us. Certainly I threw myself into my new faith the way one hurtles into doomed love affairs, with such excessiveness the nuns at school were alarmed rather than pleased. I prayed for hours at a time, in front of the statues in the chapel; genuflected deeply upon entering and leaving the pews, as if taking a curtain call; told my rosary beads at recess and lunchtime, while everybody else ate. I had a brown-bag lunch but was fasting. No opportunity for a pietism got by me. I was ready with "Bless you" before anyone within miles thought of sneezing.

Though Cy looked at his prospective saint askance too, he arranged for my baptism, and never one to miss an opportunity, asked his CO from the base to be my godfather. I do not remember that imposing gentleman's name because I never saw or heard from him again.

Because of my prayers, I felt sure at the time, the war finally ended. Cy took me to downtown Oakland, the streetcar we rode inching through the crowds in the street, to see the victory celebration. Confetti poured down on us from the tall buildings. Car horns blared. Men pounded my father on the back, because he was in uniform, and weeping women kissed him. Caught up in all that emotion, I had a satisfying cry too. Somewhere in the back of my mind was a release from the fear I had felt back in Missoula—that Cy would die in the war, that bombs would fall on the peaceful town, that there was no such thing as safety anymore, or sameness.

I was right about the "sameness" part. In a few weeks, I was back in Missoula again, my temporary family and I having made another long train ride home. And while Missoula was intact, not bombed into oblivion, my mother wasn't.

Though she'd been withdrawn sometimes before, I'd never seen her so old-looking and dispirited. She padded around the house in bedroom slippers, incurious about the time I had been away. Patricia's School of the Dance was empty, I could see through the dusty windows, except for the ballet barres that still lined the walls. No sign out front, no mirrors, no rubber exercise mats on the floors. Roy must have sold the fittings secondhand and closed the place while she was in the hospital at Warm Springs.

At first I wondered if Pat missed the school, then if she remembered that there had been one. She moved around now in a fog of her own making, smiling when she sensed that a response of some description was called for, picking up small objects—ashtrays, copies of the *Reader's Digest*, pots and pans—and then putting them back where she got them. She seemed to be keeping herself busy, but the busy work accomplished nothing and her monotonous slow pacing led nowhere. Roy told me to be nice to her and made an exhausted effort to be nicer to her himself.

Why it takes so many years to forgive one's parents their failings and sympathize with their disappointments, I cannot explain. Nor do I know why that sympathy comes so much harder than the tolerance one summons easily for friends, or strangers. All of Roy's long life, I thought of him as a tyrant, my mother his helpless victim. Now I know he was a victim of their marriage as much as she was, a man who didn't miss the brass ring but had the misfortune of catching it.

My stepfather must have lain awake nights, during those years, comparing the fantasy of Pat to the damaged woman sleeping in the other room. He must have felt he had two children, my mother and me, neither one loving him and neither really his. He was subject to night terrors, bad dreams that made him cry out so loudly, I would get out of bed and wake him up.

To stall off the moment when I would leave him alone again, Roy told me about these nightmares in detail. Large animals sprang onto his back and dug their claws into him; no matter how he struggled, he could not shake them off. Gaping pits opened in front of the station wagon while he drove around Missoula replenishing vending machines. Someone close to him died, in dream after dream. Roy stood at the graveside, grieving deeply, but did not know who lay in the coffin.

From Wisconsin came word that his brother Vin actually had died, of bronchial flu. A sister wrote a long letter describing his last hours in the hospital and the funeral arrangements. "The casket was a very lovely one. The pillow was a sort of ashes of roses color and a third of the cover was too and a little in the scarf over the casket. You see he was so dark & thin we didn't want him to lay on white or cream."

Roy sat up all night, for a week, reading this letter over and over again. In the mornings, I'd find him in the same chair in the living room, the lights all on and cigarette smoke dense in the air. So superstitious he'd make a U-turn and drive around the block rather than let a black cat cross his path, my stepfather must have blamed himself for Vin's death, believed that his nightmares had been prophetic. If he fell asleep and dreamed the same dream again, someone else might die, one of the few other human beings to whom he felt connected.

What little he revealed of himself served only to make him more opaque. We lived, when I was ten years old, in a house that had two bedrooms facing the street, North Avenue East. In mine one winter evening, I sat on my bed reading, in my Montgomery Ward catalogue mail-order underwear. Roy drove past, coming home from work, hurtled into the house and my room and stood there, still with his hat on, red-faced and wild-eyed. On his forehead, a vein pulsed.

He snatched up a blanket and threw it over my spindly form. "My God, woman," he shouted. *"Are you mad?"*

What quirk of his sexual nature led him to see a forty-pound child, in peach-colored cotton vest and knickers, as Susanna tempting the elders? What other quirk caused him to express his outrage in language that might have come from Edgar Allan Poe? My stepfather remains as much a mystery to me now as he was then, a man whose mind resembled the curious hodgepodge he had created in our basement.

I have a copy of a book he sold door to door in 1921, *The Standard Dictionary of Facts*. He must have studied it extensively himself and had chosen to underline "100 A.D., The Huns Migrate Westward" and "1834, Robert Peel, Premier, Difficulties in Canada."

I have representative volumes from his library on baldness remedies, cancer cures and the diagnostic talents of the lower bowel. Also heavily underlined is a book entitled *Making Yourself Taller*.

Though I have moved numbers of times myself, I have carted along Roy's canvas boxing shoes, in case I ever need them; a leather miner's apron and a Life Saver display rack from the candy company—useless artifacts, all of them, and impossible to discard. I keep expecting them to unravel for me that dour, inscrutable man who wanted to be taller, and hairier, and no doubt happier.

I leave him behind, for the moment, with his impracticable dreams and his night terrors, in order to catch up with Cy; but my stepfather will be back. Roy Qualley was tacked as closely to Cy Taillon's heels as his shadow.

TEN

In 1945, after his discharge from the Army, Cy set out on the rodeo circuit again. He had promised Dorothy that when the war was over he would get a steady job, the kind that came with a regular paycheck, and that the family would settle down somewhere. No more gypsying; she had his word on it. In its place, security and a life that made sense.

He could no more have kept this promise than squeezed his feet into shoes without complaining that they pinched intolerably. My father was destined to announce rodeos the way other people are born cellists or water diviners. Keeping regular hours and leading a normal life, he would have vaporized, like the wicked witch in *The Wizard of Oz*, leaving nothing behind but gray ash and a pair of cowboy boots.

Whatever her preference in the matter, Dorothy went along with his change of heart, becoming an expert packer of suitcases, spending her evenings in motel rooms, with the baby, while Cy was at the fairgrounds orchestrating the roar of the crowd. Blessed with more sense than Pat had, she imposed the condition that Cy come straight home after the rodeo.

My newly respectable father did. For the first time in his life, he welcomed domesticity instead of finding ways to avoid it. He opened the first bank account he ever had and stayed out of the bars, which meant he had money to deposit in it.

That first year on the circuit after the war was as lean as the prewar years. Cy's itinerary for 1945 shows few bookings and entire weeks followed by the notation "To be announced at a later date."

He was on his way to a successful career notwithstanding. After 1946, and the Great Falls air show disaster, these itineraries run to three double-spaced pages, the rodeos so close together he had to fly, rather than drive, between some of them.

You can still hear firsthand accounts of this event over a whiskey ditch at the Cowboys Bar, across from the fairgrounds where it took place, and if you linger there long, you will. Calling itself a bar and museum, the Cowboys is lined with rodeo photos and populated with the former riders in them. These men, soft-bellied but with handshakes you can feel in your shoulder blades, reminisce about favorite Brahmas as if they were much-loved household pets. They also reminisce about what proved to be the turning point in my father's life on the circuit.

Pete Logan, another announcer, described it in a tribute he wrote, for *World of Rodeo and Western Heritage*, when Cy retired. Noting that his longtime colleague "left indelible footprints along the long and lonely rodeo road," Logan tells what happened that afternoon in a style that suggests he would have also made a first-rate documentary filmmaker:

August, 1946. Great Falls, Mt. A hot August afternoon. Within seconds it got much hotter.

For some reason known only to God, the Air Force decided to fly three fully fueled airplanes past a grandstand that was occupied with no less than ten thousand people. An Air Force person was to comment on this as the rodeo waited. Without warning the planes collided. Bits and pieces of metal started falling. One plane ploughed into a race barn not three hundred yards from the grandstand and exploded, killing horses and people. A second one crashed into a hillside less than a quarter mile away and exploded. The third was able to stay airborne and stagger back to the Air Force base.

The Air Force person froze, unable to say a word. Cy immediately took over and calmly explained that there was no danger now. And as the heat from the burning plane, the awful smell of death permeated the atmosphere, the people remained pretty much as they were, transfixed at the horror of what they had seen. The slightest suggestion of uncertainty or panic would have resulted in the death of scores of humanity. A then 17-year-old girl remembers bits of metal falling by her, with tiny sparks falling in her hair, the heat from the burning gasoline, and thru it all, hearing Cy talking to them.

Perhaps it was the same woman who told me her own version of this tale, a few summers ago, and in the course of it issued the definitive statement on Cy's voice. "I don't know what God looks like," she said, "but I know what He sounds like."

His presence of mind brought my father a citation from the Air Force and masses of publicity. Newspapers all over the country ran the story and his picture; intrigued with the strikingly handsome man with the profession no one outside the West had ever heard of, they also ran sidebars discovering rodeo. Bookings began to pour in, not just for rodeos but for public events of all kinds. After all the lean years of eating more dust than steak dinners, Cy was established.

At least he was established in most people's eyes. After the Great Falls air show disaster, he sent me a clipping. The story notes breathlessly: "In addition to his announcing experience he has been a theatrical producer, vaudeville performer, songwriter, dance musician, amateur boxer, airplane pilot and radio producer." Written beside this list is an addition only Roy Qualley could have made—"& Bum," it reads.

Westerners love a hero, and when the hero is one of their own, a cowboy, their pride does not diminish in a small matter of four decades. On trips back to Great Falls now, I size up the fairgrounds and wonder how such a small place could have held ten thousand people. I listen to eyewitness accounts of that afternoon and ponder their discrepancies. As the bourbon flows, the number of people killed increases, the explosion virtually wipes out Great Falls and

my father remains at the mike while flames lick at the wooden announcer's stand.

I swallow my skepticism, along with the drink I am never allowed to pay for. As my father's daughter, I should know that mythmaking has its own logic.

I also know less about Cy, at that point in his life, than do the
tale tellers, for just when he stepped to center stage, I drifted off into
the wings and our long estrangement began. While I still joined Cy,
Dorothy and Terry on the circuit from time to time, or spent a school
holiday with them in Great Falls, I was never part of my father's
household again after Oakland. As was inevitable, after his remar-

Cy, Tommy, Dorothy and Terry on the road between rodeos

riage the father and the child of his first marriage began to grow apart.

Cy had two sons now, two future cowboys. My brother Tommy's birth in 1947 occasioned another announcement in the form of a mock rodeo program, reproducing the logo from Cy's letterhead. The Second Performance of the Taillon Stampede noted that Tommy Louis was the brother of the previous world champion baby boy, Terry James. Along with the Arena Director, the Pickup Riders and the Judges (Cy's mother and father), this edition lists Mr. and Mrs. Cy Taillon as Producers and Cy Taillon as Announcer. Cy thus managed to get his own name in print twice.

He had his pretty second wife, who had transformed his life and made him infinitely happier. So domestic she made up motel beds in the mornings, with neat hospital corners, Dorothy was the wife my mother had refused to be, the woman behind the man instead of the one constantly stepping in front of him.

He had both the freedom of the road and a place to call home, the Cosgriff house in Great Falls. The family made its base there during the thirty days a year or so they weren't traveling.

Cy's voice boomed through that house and his proprietary presence filled it. His previous addresses had been boardinghouses, motels and favorite saloons. In Dorothy's mother's house, he enjoyed comforts ordinary to other people, extraordinary to Cy, such as beds without lumps in them, home cooking and full-sized bars of soap in the bathroom. His mail was waiting for him there, instead of bouncing from General Delivery in one town to General Delivery in the next.

Best of all, none of these things threatened to curb his independence because the house was not Cy's own. He could come and go, unencumbered by anything but his luggage. No one expected him to run errands or take down the storm windows; his arrival was an event, another personal appearance. My father never walked into a room, anywhere, without expecting faces to turn toward him and at least a silent round of applause. If one read a magazine when he was present, or listened to *Amos 'n' Andy* rather than to Cy, he sulked.

He knew no more drunken nights and unspeakable mornings.

Nor did he start the day rummaging for enough change to put a few gallons of gas in the car. With his career thriving, Cy had become an astute businessman, acting as his own agent, commanding high fees. The first year he needed a tax accountant, he passed the news on to me, and thus to Pat and Roy, in Missoula. He was so busy now, he wrote, he could not keep track of his complicated financial situation.

Roy took the opportunity to deliver an address on the subject of Cy's unpaid child support. He never tried to collect this money, because he found it more satisfying that Cy owed it, but when Cy sent me a crisp new twenty-dollar bill for Christmas, Roy placed a personal lien on it. He opened a passbook savings account for me, at the First National Bank in Missoula, and soon had cause for more anger and indignation. No banking laws prevent minors from drawing their money out of savings accounts and investing it in Fred Astaire movies.

I would have preferred one of Cy's old Christmas boxes, full of stuffed olives and animal crackers. Cy didn't know about this because we knew less and less about each other. When I came to visit him, infrequently, we were taken aback by how the other had changed and how the familiar had become strange.

As I grew, I stayed thin and became gawkier, the kind of pre-adolescent poltergeist who can't move about without tripping over her own feet. From across a room, I could cause Dorothy's Hummel figurines to fall off their shelves. My hands were too big for the rest of me and hung at the ends of my wrists like a pair of empty gardening gloves. They were shaped like Cy's meticulously manicured hands, but his were deft, while what I did with mine, mainly, was drop things.

Immune to the sulfurous-smelling anti-acne cream Dorothy bought me, I broke out in blotches; was a demonstration model of nervous tics and twitches; still cried when spoken to sharply. In Cy's view, accurate in this case, I was also freakishly bookish. Normal twelve-year-old girls, by way of making conversation, did not recite "Hiawatha." After I confessed to Terry, who blew the whistle on me out of astonishment, that I had always been afraid of horses, my father knew no blood ties existed between us. My strongest memory

Cyra in Missoula at about age twelve

of him then is Cy staring at me, with his heavy black eyebrows raised. He must have been trying to figure out who I was.

He seemed as alien to me. For years, Cy shared with champion bronc rider Casey Tibbs the title "World's Best-Dressed Cowboy." This accolade, awarded him by the Western Clothiers Association, my father earned with his wardrobe of dozens upon dozens of cowboy hats: soft grays and beiges, black, white and mossy green. Twenty color-coordinated outfits accompanied him on the road, Western suits made for him by a tailor in Denver out of fine, lightweight gabardine. Dorothy packed them all in layers and layers of tissue paper, so they emerged from suitcases without a wrinkle. His cowboy boots were also custom-made, of kangaroo skin. Cy had found that kangaroo skin was the softest of leathers, he told reporters. Now he could wear nothing else.

His shirts crackled with starch when they emerged from their own tissue-paper clouds. He held his tie in place with a diamond horseshoe stickpin fashioned from his mother's wedding ring. His best kangaroo-skin boots had gold- and silver-inlaid heels, and a leather hanging bag made for him by a fan had his profile at the mike tooled into it and the legend "Cy Taillon, World's Greatest Rodeo Announcer." Even his tuxedos, he told the Denver *Post*, were custom-tailored and Western-cut. The former peacock in the bright satin shirts had adopted his own version of quiet good taste.

At the curb in front of the Cosgriff house was the latest of his Buick Roadmasters. By 1959, Cy was driving 65,000 to 80,000 miles a year. By 1971, he had worn out nine of these cars as well as ten Cadillacs. Before he announced his last rodeo, he had put another half dozen cars out to pasture—in Western parlance, tuckered out.

One of these Roadmasters was salmon pink and silver, with my father's initials on silver plaques on the doors. At thirteen, I took

A teenaged Cyra leaning against the Buick Roadmaster in front of the Cosgriff family home, 1954

Cy Taillon, "World's Greatest Rodeo Announcer"

it for a spin around the block, at his insistence, and almost put us both through the windshield when I stepped on the power brakes. Cy said I drove like my mother and asked if she had put me up to killing him.

He was a fixture, by then, at all the big rodeos with the romantic names, the Snake River Stampede, the Pike's Peak or Bust Rodeo, the American Royal Horse Show and the Calgary Stampede, as well as thirty smaller ones a year. By the late fifties, he estimated that 87,000 people had heard him announce. When he began presiding over rodeos on national television, the number shot up, and he received requests for signed photos, as if he were a movie star.

Announcing in Madison Square Garden, he even impressed an eastern sportswriter and got a good if condescending review, one that suggested he was not as provincial as New Yorkers might expect: "His diction is excellent and he speaks gentlemanly English with a faint touch of Westernism."

We went nowhere, when I traveled with the family, where my father was not lionized and where people did not crowd around him, dogging his gold and silver heels and hanging on his every word. To these people's amazement, he remembered all their names from one year to the next, cowboys, local rodeo officials, fans and without exception, reporters. No wonder it irritated Cy that I would not wear cowboy boots anymore; that I'd as soon watch television in the motel as sit through every performance he gave; that when I did go, while he enthralled the rest of the rodeo crowd, I sat in the grandstands and read.

Out of necessity, I had ceased to be a satellite spinning in his orbit. So there he was, with his rodeo-loving sons, his tireless press agent of a wife and a daughter who looked like him, was named after him and had decided "seen one rodeo, you've seen them all."

Public speakers always find themselves preoccupied with the face in a crowd stretched into a yawn. Mine must have been that bored face Cy picked out, blandly disengaged except when a calf got its neck broken in the calf-roping event.

On these occasions, infrequent though they were, I registered moral outrage. Rodeo was cruel, I said. This attitude my father could not tolerate, not from me, not from journalists and, most of all, not the self-righteous, lily-livered SPCA.

Cy no longer "cussed." He made an exception for misguided critics of the sport that was his life as well as his livelihood. In a piece he wrote for *Western Horseman*, he tells of trying to convert some SPCA officials, at a rodeo in Chicago, "to my honest belief that any cruelty in the game applies more to the contestants than to the stock." Bucking horses did not work over five minutes a year and "enjoyed the greatest freedom of any animal." Thousands of calves and steers "were slaughtered every day, without a sporting chance, in order to provide meat for our tables. . . ." As for injuries, "a ratio of about ten contestants were injured for any animal hurt in any way."

Soon after the Chicago rodeo began, a quarter horse burst out of the chute without a buck-jump. "Attaining great speed, it veered sharply to the left and exploded into the concrete wall from which it rebounded with an obviously broken neck: With tongue lolling grotesquely, the animal gave a few convulsive jerks and was dead."

From the crow's nest, the Voice of the West announced that this animal was merely stunned. "I also expressed the hope that it would soon recover."

The audience, including the SPCA inspectors, was not convinced. It booed and hissed. Cy ducked behind the chutes for a desperate consultation with the stock producers.

The dead horse had been dragged out of the arena, in full view of the hostile crowd. Later in the rodeo, notwithstanding, my father announced that it had been "frightened or confused by the lights" and was once again in perfect health. Into the arena charged a similar horse, flummoxing the Chicagoans, who couldn't tell one horse from another. "We went on to complete one of the most enthusiastically received performances of the entire engagement."

My rodeo heritage aside, my heart still goes out to the steer when the rope snaps taut around its neck. I wince when the rider jumps from his horse, runs down the rope and twists its neck in a hammerlock. But I have come to accept the sport on its own terms and keep my remaining objections to myself. Call this craven if you will. Then ponder what might have happened to a daughter of Manolete, at the bullring in Madrid, who was moved to wail, "Oh, the poor bull."

ELEVEN

In an old "Red Ryder" cartoon panel, the strip's creator, Fred Har-
mon, has Red say to Cy Taillon, "It wouldn't be a show
without your silver-tongued palaver." I'm sure my father liked the
exposure and that he took exception to the word "show." A major
concern of his, as he refined and developed his style at the mike,
was that rodeo develop a more dignified image as well. It was a sport,
not a carnival act, and it behooved everyone who had anything to
do with it—sportswriters, fans and contestants alike—to remember
that.

Bronc riders and record-time ropers, a modest lot, rarely wave
their hats at the crowd or give each other "high fives" at the end
of a ride. Any who did would have felt the cutting edge of Cy's silver
tongue.

The reporter who wrote about colorful buckaroos putting on a
daredevil Wild West show soon had a wrathful Cy on the other side
of his desk, his expensive boots parked on it and his voice making
the paper clips rattle. Rodeo belonged on the sports page, not in the
entertainment section, and the correct term was "rodeo athletes,"
not "cowpokes."

The fan who caught up with him to tell him he and the wife
thought those hands sure could ride was set straight. Rodeo contestants were not ranch hands but professional riders and ropers.

"They have developed such skill with rampaging livestock," Cy thundered at a writer for a Fort Worth newspaper, "that the average ranch hand would be licked hands down in competition with them." Putting an ordinary ranch hand in the rodeo arena, in fact, would be like "letting a sandlot baseball player in the World Series."

The writer had said in print that cowboys were cowboys, not athletes. When my father got through with him, he published a follow-up column deciding that he "just possibly was wrong."

Cy wore the Western equivalent of Savile Row tailoring because he wanted to look like a man presiding over a major sports competition rather than like a barker for Annie Oakley or Wild Bill Hickok. He pioneered the "straight man" style of announcing, even when the cowboys themselves told him he sounded like a storefront lawyer, because he thought the old style of cornball comedy from the crow's nest was an affront to both competitors and audience. Says Pete Logan, who began announcing rodeos the year after Cy did, "At times he was stubborn, uncompromising and difficult, but always a dedicated professional. He was acutely aware that his conduct and appearance reflected on our profession." Thus he set standards that those who followed him had to have "if they ever expected to get out of the bushes."

Much of the impetus for these reforms, I am certain, came from Dorothy, who turned Cy into a gentleman by being a lady, unmistakable as anything but one, in a world that divided women into two categories. One was what my brother Terry calls "twinks, scuzzbutts and squirrels," rodeo groupies. The other was good ol' gals, female counterparts of their Western men.

Good ol' gals wore jeans and boots. They hauled horse trailers as handily as they hauled their husbands from a bar, or someone else's bed, and had what Dorothy called "mouths on them." They could tell dirty stories, drink men twice their body weight under the table or ride a breakneck barrel race.

Dorothy stuck to dresses and high-heeled shoes, though there are no heels high enough to traverse a rodeo grounds and end up smelling like a rose. She never laughed at a dirty joke, much less told one, and had a way of causing the joke teller to wither and mutter, "No offense intended." In her mink-stoled and perfumed wake, gentility followed, trotting to keep up.

So did the old-fashioned gallantry cowboys accord "ladies" and grudging deference from members of her own sex. Somehow my stepmother spent her long married life on the circuit without its rough-and-tumble rubbing off on her. Instead, she rubbed the rough-and-tumble off the circuit, and Cy. It was a point of pride with her that the house the family eventually bought in Denver showed "no trace of any Western influence." Neither did Dorothy, she emphasized to an interviewer in Sydney, Australia, where Cy announced the riding events at the Royal Easter Show. While she professed to love rodeo, she disliked Western dress, would never wear it and made only one concession to it. This was to wear clothes made in the same fabric as her husband's suits. "The dress I wear merely complements his outfit."

No cowboys bunked on the wall-to-wall carpet in that house in the suburbs of Denver. My father's collection of Western bronzes was consigned to the den. It could have been the house of a branch bank manager or a dentist.

The sport was changing along with Cy, rubbing off its rough edges. Back in 1945, a group of rodeo contestants had founded the Cowboys Turtle Association, so named because they had been so slow in seeing the need for it and getting it started. The organization was a union of sorts, its intention to cut riders and ropers in on a fair share of the profits.

Before the Turtles, promoters could stage rodeos and skip out with the gate. Contestants' entry fees were not added to the prize money for an event; the cowboy paid for the privilege of risking life and limb, while the promoters scooped in both his entry fees and the money fans paid to pass through the turnstiles.

The organization became the Rodeo Cowboys Association and eventually the Professional Rodeo Cowboys Association, which now regulates all phases of the rodeo profession. One of its rules is that entry fees must be added to the prize money. Though he may have to enter ninety or a hundred rodeos a year, sometimes competing in two on the same day, a top cowboy can keep himself in Holiday Inns, Levi's and orthopedic surgeons. If he's a champion, and his kids don't insist on enrolling in rodeo school in Henryetta, Oklahoma, or Clovis, California, an all-American bronc rider can put them through Yale.

These gains came hard, over the objections of the producers. The producers hired Cy and issued his contracts—more often than not, in the form of a handshake—and signed his paychecks. Because his sympathies were with the cowboys, he joined the RCA anyway and promoted it from the beginning. One cowboy who approved wrote the following poetic tribute: "Cy Taillon tossed his Stetson aside / And kissed the girls goodbye. / This is one big show he can't announce, / But he's workin' it high."

Numbers of more formal testimonials followed. Over Cy's desk, in later years, was a display of awards, including one from International Rodeo Management naming him the 1966 "Rodeo Man of the Year." My father rode tall in the saddle in the eyes of money men and cowboys alike.

How could we find common ground anymore, when he became such an estimable personage, his daughter and the Voice of Rodeo? Never a shy wood violet, Cy now took himself seriously indeed. He became an avatar of traditional American values and a pre–Ronald Reagan symbol of political conservatism. He grew cocksure of his judgment even when it made little or no sense, as when, though a Republican, he voted for John F. Kennedy "to show that Catholics aren't prejudiced."

He claimed intimacy with the rich and powerful, beginning sentences with "When I went fishing with Ike Eisenhower last summer . . ." or "I've been in touch with Lyndon about that, and he told me confidentially . . ." His name-dropping made me writhe. So did Dorothy's claim, in the press, that my father's most notable characteristic was his modesty.

In Denver, he ran a Captain Queeg–like tight ship. All hands on deck for an early breakfast, permission to go ashore viewed with suspicion, liberties canceled for infractions. As what I still think was a mildly rebellious adolescent, I managed to break every rule in his book when I was around and inspire the issuing of new ones. Cy once woke me out of a sound sleep to point out my lack of consideration for others, in the form of a single hair in the sink.

No one is purer in thought, word and deed than a reformed rake-hell. No one is as insufferable. Cy now expected hero worship, but he was not going to get it from me, and what he got instead were reminders that I had known him for a long time and did not look upon him as a candidate for Mount Rushmore.

Nor had time altered my relationship to my old antagonist, Dorothy. No longer the insecure young woman I thought of as my wicked stepmother, she was still doing a convincing imitation. She had gained weight, had a matronly quality now and dyed her hair its former auburn. What had not changed was that she still resented my existence, as evidence of my mother's existence. In actuality, she explained to me once, I didn't exist.

She reasoned as follows. Cy was Catholic. My mother wasn't. If Cy had married outside the Church, he hadn't really married. If there was no first marriage, there could be no child born of it.

With the test of this syllogism standing there, living, breathing and marveling, some accommodation had to be made. It stopped short of the reality principle. I think my stepmother convinced herself that my attachment to the Taillons was the result of a mix-up in the record-keeping procedures of Deaconess Hospital.

With Terry and Tommy, I was on more tolerant ground. They thought me prissy. I considered them a pair of roughnecks. We formed close ties despite all this, probably because they too were riddled with faults, and heard about them. Scatter them thousands of miles apart, and the children of the same family remain an affinity group. Growing up, always, is a matter of "us against them," and in relation to Dorothy and Cy, my brothers and I were the "us."

All three of us were proud of our father and longed for his good opinion. All of us fell short of his standards and ignited his short fuse. I fought him with words, the torrents I could produce as part of his genetic legacy to me. As a teenager, Terry once fought him physically.

Coming in late one night, he found his small, stainless-steel father waiting for him in the kitchen. The two enacted the universal father/son scene: Where have you been? You've got your mother worried half to death.

Strapping teenage son: She can go to hell . . .

Cy escorted Terry out to the backyard to discuss their differences. He had not lost his skills as a Golden Gloves boxer. Says Terry, "The next thing I knew, I was on my back, looking at the stars. He really Powder Rivered me."

According to the code of the West, one does not disparage motherhood, or its embodiment, Mother. Whatever the law in the rest of the land, we lived under that code, with Cy keeping a boot on the back of the neck of the lawless element. He revised the code as he went along but never its underlying tenet: thou shalt honor thy father the rodeo announcer, or encounter his ire, backed up, if necessary, by one hell of a punch.

He was impossible, I thought then, a tyrant. I still think so but give him credit for consistency.

My mother had done battle with Cy toe to toe, as incendiary-tempered as he was and as fond of a good brawl. Far more intelligent than Pat was, Dorothy employed guerrilla tactics, tears and wounded feelings. These always won the day because Western men hold the unexamined belief that they "can't stand to see a woman cry."

They believe this about themselves because they learned it from their mothers. For the same reason, they believe that women are the weaker sex, that men are their strong protectors and that a man's house or mobile home is his castle. These inculcated attitudes leave Western women a lot of room to wield the power behind the saddle, without appearing to come anywhere near it. My stepmother knew this intuitively, and in her traditional femininity, her furs, bangles and beads, must have been more terrible to Cy than an army with banners. You can't challenge a lady to come out and fight like a man.

I fought with my father because I wasn't a lady, I was a teenager and thus a rolling gland. I fought with him because while I did not miss Cy the reckless drunk, I missed the Cy who had been fallible. I fought with him because he was bigoted against Jews, blacks, Easterners, intellectuals, hippies, draft resisters, Democrats, city dwellers and sopranos.

I liked to listen to opera on the radio. Cy called it "caterwauling" and imitated the female singers in falsetto.

The more he believed his own press, and saw himself as exem-

plar of the best of America, the more he railed against what he saw
as the worst, anything that did not fall within the narrow confines
of his values. What was most maddening was that he thought of
himself as the model of tolerance, some of whose best friends were
hippie Jewish sopranos. Arguing with him was tilting at a wind-
mill of rectitude, and one always ended up unhorsed. Over the
telephone, my father once drove me into an incoherent, stuttering
rage. He waited it out and asked me if there were psychiatrists in
Missoula.

Cy's politics and his all-round conservatism were not unusual
in his part of the world and still aren't. In a coffee shop in Montana
just a few years ago, I heard one man in cowboy boots tell another
that England ought to "stop pussyfooting around and bomb the living shit out of the Falklands."

I leaned over the leatherette booth between us and asked why.
He told me that you had to stop the Commies somewhere, little lady,
and apologized for having said "shit."

I knew I was home, and felt the same mixture of helpless affection and anger I often felt toward Cy. Most people live with vacil-
lation and doubt. Men like my father have no doubts and never
vacillate: the natural order of things is as clear to them as their favorite trout streams, or the Rocky Mountain air, and on the cloud-
iest day, they can still see forever.

What Cy saw was a landscape of immutable certainties, one I
have sometimes longed to rest my eyes upon as he did. Always seeing
himself as acted upon, rather than acting, he was a stranger to the
paralyzing emotion I know best, vague, all-purpose guilt. I drag
quantities of it around, like a suitcase full of bricks. My father once
spelled out his version of self-blame in a letter to me.

He was not only at odds with me just then but disappointed in
my brothers. "I am probably unfortunate," he wrote, "in being a
most sensitive person and having an all encompassing love for those
I had a part in creating."

I stopped visiting Cy. He stopped visiting and calling me. He
collected more accolades, and made more money, and became still
better known. I went about my own life, reading about him more
often than I saw him. For source material I had the private museum

for which my stepfather Roy served as curator, the mentions of Cy that came over the teletype machines at *The Daily Missoulian*, where I was known as a copyboy, and the clippings Ila Mae sent.

In our Missoula house was a large wooden desk where no one ever wrote a check or affixed a stamp to a letter; its function was to serve as one more hollow log where Roy could stuff things. In its drawers, along with thousands of pipe cleaners, a massive collection of No. 2 pencils and, eventually, thirty-seven years' accumulation of unopened junk mail, Cy's onetime best pal stuffed articles torn out of magazines and every scrap of print about Cy he could get his hands on.

He pushed these into the backs of the drawers, burying them under the pipe cleaners. I rummaged for and found them. Such was the strength of Roy's mysterious obsession that he kept tracking Cy long after I left home, tearing the one-line listing out of *TV Guide* when Cy announced rodeos on national television, unconsciously imitating Cy by underlining my father's name.

The great river of letters Ila Mae wrote, going for the record in Sheer Volume of Personal Correspondence, had Cy as their major subject—every sighting in Great Falls, every bit of malicious gossip she could glean from unnamed sources. "Heard something wrong with Cy, he losing His Voice. Their trying to keep it hush but he in trouble now. The paper said he was taking vacation, he really have operation at the Mayo Clinic."

My mother seemed to have forgotten Cy at last, as she had forgotten so much else, but as his status as living Western legend grew, no one else who'd ever met him seemed immune to my father's fascination. Even my high school teacher collected clippings for me, asked to be introduced to him someday and told me how they'd heard him, sometime, somewhere, and never forgotten his mighty Wurlitzer voice.

My sense of his powerfulness increased, and my determination not to become fixed on him, ever again, as the pole star. Not only had that misconception caused me pain in the past, I could see its effects on my mother.

The large Taillon family boasts a great many cousins, one of whom has her own theory about why my father and I quarreled so long and bitterly and why, after I was fifteen or so, I had to take his all-encompassing love for his children on faith. Her reason is less cerebral than mine are.

"Don't you know what you did to cross Cy?" my cousin Sis asked me. "All of a sudden, you shot up and got taller than he was."

T W E L V E

It took him twenty years, but my father finally managed to arrange an annulment of his marriage to my mother, thereby ratifying his long, stable marriage to Dorothy. Pat had been a youthful mistake. Dorothy was the helpmeet and full-time companion for whom Cy always came first, and my father adored her.

She traveled the circuit with him, though it meant leaving Terry and Tommy, whom she also loved with fierce possessiveness, in charge of housekeepers much of the year. She selected his clothes, color-coordinating them as relentlessly as she did her own. Without complaint, she lived out of suitcases and motel rooms, spent the rest of her time in automobiles, traveling the same roads year after year, and became as skilled a promoter of Cy's business interests as he was.

Typical of their marriage was that my stepmother never learned to drive. She merely came along in the passenger seat while Cy steered their joint course. Even Ila Mae approved of her vocation as the woman behind the man and expanded on it in one of her treatises on marriage. "I always say it important for man to be king, thats the way it has always been with Wiley and Me, for God created he woman out of mans rib. The man came first Remember That Pat."

Her attitude would have come as news to Wiley, but he wrote no letters and issued no rebuttals. Instead, he spent his days trying to become invisible, keeping his nose in the sports pages, his feet off the ottoman and his head off the crocheted doily over the back of the chair. If he left shoe-polish smudges on the upholstery and hair-oil stains on the doilies, it wasn't for lack of trying to pass through his own household without a trace.

My uncle sought not earthly rewards, nor pie in the sky when he died, but domestic tranquillity. He might as well have aimed at being the first men's clothing salesman on the moon. His hundred-pound spouse had the stamina of a jockey, the eye-hand coordination to snatch a speck of dust out of the air before it settled on one of her end tables and an insatiable appetite for reform. In this, the world stubbornly continued to defy her, going its own untidy way. Crime raged in the streets. Promiscuity grew rampant. Drugs ravaged America's youth. Wiley shed cigarette ash on the carpet.

Ila Mae wrote on, her pen the weapon she wielded against chaos. Her stream-of-consciousness prose reveals her vision of the interconnectedness of all things, sometimes with alarming clarity. "Two young girls were robbed & stabbed here that worked at the taco treat, they caught the men. One blessing they didn't rape them. Know what I would do if I got my Hands on them, Wiley have cold he leave filthy Kleenex all over the Place."

All the years he had been married to my mother, Ila Mae thought of Cy as the Prince of Darkness. Now that he was successful, and happily remarried, and no longer a drunk, his former sister-in-law reinstated him back into the human race, and ever magnanimous, appointed herself his best friend and spiritual adviser.

My father rarely called her and never went to see her. She interpreted his neglect as proof of their indissoluble bond, intimacy so profound it threatened Dorothy. "Cy was here and he didn't come to see me, guess Dorothy wouldn't let him. Her sister say he always asks about me. For he know I always have good cup of coffee for him if he need somebody to talk to." She had advice ready to serve up with the cream and sugar. Dorothy should stop dying her hair, Cy was ruining his feet in those cowboy boots and my brothers were going to end up in jail if he did not stay home with them more often. Teenage hoodlums were the product of "broken homes."

Cy never came around to profit from this wisdom. It accumulated, doing no one any good, until Ila Mae bundled it off to us in Missoula. She must have known her constant reminders of Cy caused unrest in our household but attributed to herself only the purest of motives. "Know Susie would want to know about Cys throat, she could send him a get well card & maybe a letter."

I'm sure my mother did not want to be reminded of Cy at all, or to hear about Dorothy, the paragon. Roy could have taken no pleasure from Ila Mae's description of Cy's house in Denver, which she had never seen but described as rivaling the Taj Mahal. Her misinformed medical bulletins upset me and got Roy's hopes up until Cy turned up on television again, the voice as sonorous as ever, the man as dapper and handsome. When it came to malicious mischief, my law-and-order aunt was a repeat offender.

Cy and I lived at such physical and emotional distance from one another by then that I knew almost as little about him as Ila Mae did. My visits were occasions for friction, my view of my father the blinkered view of an adolescent in revolt against a parent who overwhelmed me. Terry and Tommy knew another Cy entirely, and loved him so much less critically, their adult lives are memorials to him.

I found him heavy-handed on the reins, and bucked, and reared, and finally bolted out of his reach. My brothers found in him the model of a Western man, with the perfect mix of toughness and tenderness, and as soon as they were old enough, took to the circuit as rodeo cowboys. They knew his hard anger too, but looked upon it as strength; could have chosen lives outside the rodeo but never considered it; believe that while none of us can ever measure up to our father's stature, we were privileged to see the mark made on the wall.

The father Terry and Tommy grew up with instructed them in the deft and serene art of fly fishing. He taught them to put out a line as lightly as a sigh and to smell a trout swimming in some dark eddy, smugly assuming it is going to die of old age. He spent their thousands of hours on the road together teaching them about wildlife. Both my brothers can spot a mountain goat on a mountain-goat-colored rocky promontory or an eagle so high overhead it looks like a wren. Accurate within a few hours, they can predict the first snowflake of winter from the quality of a chill in the air.

Terry, Cy and Tommy

Both are dead shots. Though Cy's passion was fishing, he saw to it they learned to hunt, because in Montana hunting is not only a rite of manhood but a means of filling the larder. At a cousin's house in Billings a few years ago, the dinner entrée was antelope tacos. Terry had shot the antelope, and split an elk with a hunting buddy the past winter, and took great glee in telling me what I was eating. He was reminding the sister from San Francisco who she really was and where she really came from. The antelope tacos were good but greasy. We washed them down with quarts of orange soda pop.

Tommy stores Cy's files, his scrapbooks and copies of the articles he wrote for Western publications. In them our father reminisced about favorite horses, adventures on the rodeo circuit and his love for wild birds. Sentimental articles, written in Cy's literate, ornate style, they brought him more recognition and more fan letters. My brothers tell me that the wild birds he wrote about ate out of Cy's hand.

We are children of the same man, the three of us, but of different memories, and when we're together now, we spend much of our time trying to make those memories mesh, living testimony to the staying power of his presence. The public Cy looms as large, still written about frequently years after his death.

That Cy, the rodeo announcer, never missed an engagement. In health or shaking in his boots with a fever, he turned up at the microphone and routinely gave a performance that earned a standing ovation. As an especially lyrical reporter put it, "He can fairly make you hear the cling-clang of spurs, the snap of leather, the furious snorting of the bronc demons as they come kicking, leaping, swirling out of the chutes defying any man to stay aboard."

The remarkable part of this description is that Cy made the reporter hear all these things in a newspaper office, a week in advance of the show.

Long after he became successful, he would drive all night to appear at a small-time rodeo because his being there guaranteed a crowd. Cy said he chose his profession because he wanted to be his own boss. In reality, he worked for the sport he loved, so slavishly that he rarely took time off.

He caught colds working in downpours in roofless announcer's booths, sweated in heat waves without loosening his tie or taking off his jacket and went out to the fairgrounds two hours before a performance to study his program notes, intent on coordinating the flow of events seamlessly. There he also made rounds, shaking hands with veteran cowboys, meeting the green kids riding in their first rodeos and wishing them luck. His compendious memory tucked away their names and histories. The green cowboy plummeted out of the chute on a bronc demon to the sound of Cy's voice, introducing him as glowingly as if he were a champion.

His closest rival for the rodeos that meant big money and prestige was Pete Logan, whom Cy respected as another dignified professional. Cy never tried to move into Logan's territory, Logan wrote, though "he has had several chances at me I am sure." Not only would doing so have been unethical, but "Cy [never] tried to replace anybody that was doing his job."

The onetime rounder had become principled, hardworking and reliable, a man whose handshake was as good as his signature on a contract. If he seemed pompous to me, swollen beyond recognition with pride, he would have argued he had earned that pride. The early years of Cy's life were a trajectory toward crash and burn, alcoholic drifting and a marriage that threatened to destroy him with its violent emotional extremes. He climbed out of the rubble determined never to look back.

From my vantage point as part of my father's past, I resented the extent of that resoluteness. I might have been more sympathetic to it had I been able to look upon my mother's course as its alternative. Though she functioned more or less normally for periods of weeks or months, by the time I was in high school the fogs closed in again without warning. Pat wandered off into them, in the clutch of private misery that put her out of Roy's reach and mine. During one of these withdrawals, she dug her old, cracked Samsonite suitcase out of the basement, packed it with odds and ends of her clothing and sat in a chair, waiting, as if the Missoula house were the Milwaukee Railroad depot downtown, near her former School of the Dance, and she were ready to go wherever the next train would take her. She came out of her lassitude to struggle with Roy when he took the suitcase away from her, more roughly than was necessary.

From Great Falls, Ila Mae assumed responsibility for her medical care, genuinely concerned about Baby Sister, taking her usual pleasure in a crisis. She pelted us with the names of doctors and clinics, legal expertise—"There would be no public hearing no one would have to know about it, just be signed by a Judge"—and pep talks urging Pat to cooperate in her own healing. "The treatment have to be given in closed ward hospital where they have special trained nurses for it . . . so Pat don't you think if you could be cured six weeks would be worth it . . . Some times we have to do things we don't want to."

Roy, Ila Mae and Wiley

My mother's breakdowns embarrassed Roy, as did all information about the family that became known outside it, lumped together as "washing your dirty laundry in public." He waited the latest illness out, forbidding me to talk about it, raging and weeping if it went on long. I marched back and forth to school and to my job at *The Daily Missoulian*, removing myself from a situation I felt powerless to change, protected by my own isolating fog. Ila Mae scolded. And scolded.

"Dr. Layne is a very brilliant man & he has gone out of his way to be helpful in this case. Roy, bring her, I would take her my self, I could do all the talking for her."

I don't think Roy ignored my aunt so much as he no longer heard her. Too many letters, over too many years, fell through the mail slot in our front door twice a day, filled every crevice in the house and exceeded his capacity to absorb them. Roy was like a soldier in combat who had learned to sleep through machine-gun fire.

Trivial or consequential, Ila Mae's letters are one long letter, really, no installment ever complete. She folded up her sheaf of blue-lined sheets, put all those words in an envelope and sealed it. Irresistible impulse seized her, and on the outside of it, she scribbled a recipe: "One can potato soup condensed, 1 can milk, handfull of cheese cheddar, mix well, shredded wheat, bake. I serve with jello mold fruit cocktail in it."

We heard about every head cold, every dish Ila Mae washed and every insight that came to her as she struggled to make sense of human existence: "I always say God have a plan," she wrote when she had some painful dental work done. "My gumbs hurt so bad today tho don't ask me what it is."

We knew about every change in the weather in Great Falls, Montana, over forty years. Ila Mae took blizzards as personally as she took holdups at the Taco Treat, as visitations upon her by a malevolent universe.

When the spring thaws came, she raised her voice in seasonal rhapsodies. The crocuses pushed through the ground, the birds sang and her arthritis no longer troubled her. "This winter so long I thought God trying to kill me."

Her never-ending letter testifies to the need to chronicle one's life, lest its events have no significance beyond oneself, and the trouble with them is that in our household they turned into cries of "Wolf!" so familiar they lost the power to mobilize the villagers.

Ila Mae's health preoccupied her, the migraine headaches that run in the family, arthritis and a painful chronic ailment described only as "My Colon." As frequently as she switched from one church to another, she went from doctor to doctor. Her search wasn't for one who could cure her as much as it was for the one doctor who would understand how much she suffered, who would set aside whole afternoons for her visits and pick up his telephone each and every time she called.

"I in Hell and He out playing golf," she wrote when one doctor defected from his full-time responsibility. She intended to sue him, because, for once, she wasn't going to take it lying down.

The woman downstairs would testify in court that she'd seen Ila Mae that day looking half dead. Ila Mae had demanded her medical records, which would have kept the few copying machines in Great Falls busy until both plaintiff and defendant had died of old age. A new doctor took the place of the target of her wrath and created a diversion. He performed surgery on My Colon, apologizing on behalf of the entire medical profession that it hadn't been performed long ago. My aunt wrote that "they took out practically the whole Thing." The fragment remaining still hurt, though not as much as that source of indescribable torture, her bridgework.

Roy telephoned Wiley, while Ila Mae was in the hospital, and sent flowers that "set him back" ten dollars. My mother listened to the detailed bulletin he relayed to us with one of her almost invisible eyebrows raised. Pat had stopped wearing makeup and now had a face that was a clean slate, whatever went on behind it unwritten for anybody else to read. Her raised brow bone was as eloquent as if she'd stuck her tongue out and told us what she thought of her sister's latest brush with the Grim Reaper.

I assumed that nothing much went on in my mother's mind and that she had somehow unplugged it, so that the clatter of life going on around her was barely perceived background noise, elevator music. I thought the woman I remembered had burned herself out and had no joy left in her, and no memories, and certainly no traces of Miss Patricia Montgomery, St. Louis's bright star of the stage.

Pat outraged me, when I was a junior in high school, by proving

Cyra's high school graduation photo, Class of '55

just how wrong I was. A date picked me up to take me to a movie. He arrived half an hour early, and from my bedroom, as I hurtled into my clothes, I heard my mother's low voice, talking about how hot it was for April and what a suntan she was getting, just sitting out in our backyard.

She sounded social and relaxed. The boy guffawed at something she said. I snagged a stocking, tried to put my neck through the arm-hole of my dress and jerked the curlers out of my bangs. Frantic with anxiety, I made my entrance. My mother had pulled up her blouse and was showing my date her smooth brown back, with the white band of her bra bisecting it, while he looked on grinning foolishly.

I dragged him out of the house and jumped into his car before he could open the door. "Your mother's really something," he said when he came around to his side.

"You shut up," I said.

Though both would have been as shocked as I was, and would have let my mother the exhibitionist hear about it, I never told Roy or Ila Mae about this incident. I didn't warn them that the show girl was still in there, and that she still had a high kick left in her. I kept my own counsel, not because I was kind, but because I was thrown so badly off balance.

I had burst out, "Mother!" Pat looked at me with amusement and no apology at all. Lazily, she tucked her blouse in, said she hoped we had a nice time and trotted out her honeyed southern drawl to tell my escort, "Nice meeting y'all."

What made me want to kill her on that occasion, I know now, was that she had a powerful sexual edge on me. An aged crone in her forties, my mother could call up her former seductive self effortlessly, a genie out of the bottle, and make her nubile daughter vanish from sight, print summer dress, Cuban-heeled shoes, Fire and Ice lipstick and all. Worse, she thought this was funny.

Now that I am her age then, I remember this scene with pride in Pat, and a whiff of middle-aged envy. Her second marriage turned the living fireball into a cowed creature who no longer knocked over bridge tables when belittled beyond tolerance, and whose dancer's body had lost its taut-muscled definition. Obeying the rhythm of her illness, she checked in and out of Roy's life and mine like a weary salesman checking into another cheap hotel, indifferent to the decor and the company in the dining room.

She could still transfix that teenaged boy with the baring of her suntanned back and her husky drawl, the low murmur that turned talk about the weather into an intimate treatise on the pleasure principle. As that unworthy audience for her female magic observed, when Pat chose to be she was still really something.

THIRTEEN

At eighteen, shortly after my freshman year in college, I got married. My mother and Roy gave me a steam iron. Ila Mae gave me two sets of sheets and pillowcases she had trimmed with embroidered borders, a lecture on sex along the lines of "we all have to do things we don't want to do sometimes" and two dozen blank thankyou note cards. Cy walked down the aisle as stiffly as if he were nailed to a board, after a sharp exchange between us in the anteroom of the Lutheran church in Missoula. I was wearing a white knit dress, a white satin pillbox hat and white satin pumps with three-inch heels. I loomed above Cy, who told me that I wobbled when I walked in those things and seemed to want me to take them off and make my journey to the altar stocking-footed. He must have thought I should make some concession since he couldn't wear his cowboy hat.

Roy boycotted the wedding. I had asked my father to give me away instead of asking him. He wouldn't come at all, he said, because I had shamed him so cruelly by this act of repudiation he couldn't face people. Nor would he ever set foot again on the same ground, hallowed or otherwise, with Cy.

Ila Mae and Wiley brought Pat, who took one of her rare stands against Roy's authority by telling him she would attend whether he came with her or not. For the occasion, she resurrected a rose silk dress that must have been twenty years old but still had flair, even though it was tight for her and had the only shoulder pads left in Montana. A neighbor gave her a home perm that turned her hair, mostly gray by now, into tight corkscrews. She made up her face and crammed her feet into ancient alligator pumps with open toes.

She looked very pretty, I told her as I pinned on her gardenia corsage. My mother smiled with great sweetness and apologized for her hands, holding them out for me to inspect. Her fingernails were clipped short, and as they had been for many years, were without nail polish. She said she had wanted to "do" them but had no manicure tools anymore. Did I know what had happened to the set Cy gave her, in the red leather case?

I said it didn't matter and wondered when she had last seen that manicure set. I also knew what had happened to it. Anything Roy knew that Cy had given either of us disappeared, sooner or later. We had both learned early on not to ask what had become of "junk" like missing manicure sets or plastic statuettes of horses.

Pat and Dorothy met for the first time at that wedding. They introduced themselves to one another politely enough but could not conceal their mutual curiosity. Dorothy stared at my mother's thirties dress, the two round spots of rouge on her cheeks and her Little Orphan Annie permanent wave. My mother turned her good child's open gaze on Dorothy, in her mink stole and kelly green everything else.

Neither matched the other's image of her old rival for my father's love, a contest that never really existed other than in my stepmother's mind. Pat expected the auburn-haired nurse I had described so effusively as a child. Dorothy expected the face that had launched a thousand bronc riders. They looked at each other as if neither could believe her own eyes, two women thickening into middle age who had in common only that they had married the same man. When they weren't staring at each other, they stared at Cy, who was frozen with discomfort, as if searching for some clue to his inexplicable tastes.

Of the dearly beloved gathered together, only Ila Mae enjoyed that somewhat forlorn wedding, my leap into the idea of normalcy that prevailed at the time. Many of my high school friends were already married. Some of them had babies. Instead of pursuing acting careers, they were settling for what was possible, and greeted with warm approval in Missoula, and seemed smugly happy in their roles as young housewives. At her request, I had given one of them a rolling pin as a shower present; she wanted a new kind that one filled with ice water because it made flakier piecrust.

In the back of my mind, I knew mine was a mismatch, and walked through the ceremony, head held high, as if I were auditioning for a role I knew I would not get. My father and my bridegroom, my college drama professor, looked down upon each other, neither of them impressed by the other's credentials, and Cy played father of the bride with bristling irritation. For Dorothy and Pat, the other woman was the Ancient Mariner, though disappointingly devoid of glittering eye. Instead, my mother looked mildly out from beneath her horizontal-comma eyebrows, drawn on with the old painstaking care, and as it usually did, Dorothy's mascara ran.

That left Ila Mae to rejoice in the ceremony, which vindicated her formative role in my upbringing. I was being sensible, for once, instead of following Pat into the world of greasepaint and loose morals. I wouldn't be exposed to the rodeo circuit anymore and so wouldn't relapse into swearing when I wasn't showing off my vocabulary, like Cy. Though he had earned back Ila Mae's good opinion by becoming respectable, she still thought plain speech was good enough for the Bible and ought to be good enough for him.

Before my new husband and I drove away in a shower of rice, my aunt passed on to me her accumulated domestic wisdom, standing on her toes so that she could look me in the face or at least in the chin. I was to remember who was the boss, never send shirts to the laundry, save the ends of bars of soap and press them together to make new bars, and when I no longer needed the diapers, hem them and use them for dish towels. I was not pregnant. Ila Mae was looking ahead.

My husband learned in her parting address to him that I was clean about my person, made my own clothes on my Singer sewing machine and could learn to cook if I put my mind to it. I had eaten good food at her table all those years, and so knew what it was. If my household management was so inept at first that he needed expert help, she was just a phone call away and would be there before he could say "too much starch in the collars." Into his jacket pocket, because I was carrying a nosegay rather than a purse, she tucked her recipe for icebox rolls.

Though it did not last long and caused as much pain as most failed marriages, mine freed me, finally, from my family. It removed me physically from my mother, whom I loved but whose custodianship Roy expected me to share, all the while pretending that Pat wasn't ill and needed no custodianship. By staying home from my wedding, and staging a noisy weeping scene behind his closed bedroom door while I was in my own room getting dressed in something old, something new and something borrowed (my bridegroom would slide on the blue garter, for the flash camera of the photographer), Roy hardened me against further emotional appeals he might make. He had a legitimate claim on me. It wasn't the claim he was making, one that precluded all other loyalties and that I had been resisting with more assertiveness as I got older.

He had raised me as Qualley. On my eighteenth birthday, I took back my legal name, Taillon.

As for Cy, my marriage elevated me, in my view, to parity with him. It proclaimed that I was an adult, who could do what I liked without his consent, and for whom another man was more important than he was. For the satisfaction I took in shooing my father off to the wings, for once, instead of being ushered into them myself, I was willing to master my aunt's icebox rolls and give up my career as the next Helen Hayes.

My husband and I moved to Oregon. Though none of us was in a league with Ila Mae, my mother, Cy and I kept in touch through letters. I rambled on cheerfully about married life, which wasn't cheerful in the least. My mother wrote about large events in her life, such as a new refrigerator. The refrigerator was the first major household purchase she and Roy had made since they'd set up housekeeping, in one afternoon, at Mr. Lucy's furniture store fifteen years earlier. Ila Mae's comment on this acquisition, when Pat wrote her about it too, was "too bad it had to be a Kelvinator."

Cy sent me twenty-five-dollar checks on birthdays and on the birth of my first child, and the unreadable last carbons of his sched-

Cyra

ules and his letters to the whole family. I had not seen him for two years when I made a last visit to him and Dorothy in Denver. Now that I regarded my father as an equal, I regarded Dorothy as an equal too and met her hostility head-on. Under the guise of girl talk, we sat in her spotless kitchen, over coffee, and skewered each other like chickens for the barbecue.

Dorothy told me how pretty I'd be if I ever learned to dress and if my skin ever cleared up. I told my overweight stepmother about the terrible metabolic curse I was under, how I stayed thin no matter how much I ate. I sighed and added that I guessed I was just like my father.

While we never tired of this sniping, and both perversely enjoyed it, Cy did, in a hurry. He turned his coldest green look upon me, one that could have frozen Lake Michigan in July, and got the same cold look back. It told him that his anger no longer turned me into a whimpering heap. Having no way of knowing that a nervous tic pulsed in my eyelid, he tried impressing his daughter into the deference due him.

At dinner one night, when there were guests present, he brought a bottle of Chianti to the table with a white napkin draped over his arm, ceremoniously pulled the cork and announced that he would pour it after it had time to breathe. I suggested maybe he should keep an oxygen tank around, in case the wine didn't start breathing on its own.

He itemized how much everything in the house had cost and showed me Dorothy's Grand Baroque sterling silver, "the most expensive pattern made." I thanked him warmly once again for his most recent twenty-five-dollar birthday check.

He told me he now drove Cadillacs, rather than Buicks, because he had "a certain image to maintain." I told him I thought Cadillacs were ostentatious and for a split second thought my father was going to swing on me.

Similarly, Dorothy gained no admiration from me through her own steady stream of self-praise, a conversational style she may have picked up from long intimacy with Cy. For modesty's sake, these compliments were always attributed to others. The man who laid the wall-to-wall carpet had urged Dorothy to become a professional decorator; he had never met anyone with her color sense. Someone had stopped her on the street in San Francisco to tell her how nice it was to see an elegantly turned-out woman for a change.

Years later, also in San Francisco, my stepmother startled me and a nearby table of diners with the most singular of these spontaneous tributes. Her gynecologist, she announced loudly, had said to her, "Mrs. Taillon, you have the uterus of a young girl."

My father and Dorothy were equally unimpressed with me, a young woman with intellectual pretensions and a pugnacious set to the jaw. It never occurred to Cy that I had his temperament, as well as his bone structure. He and Pat had taught me never to run or even walk away from a fight, a rule of life still dear to writers of Western songs, and neither had thought to mention that I need not go out looking for one.

What angered Cy most in me was what he knew was also true of himself: that he was stubborn, demanded unqualified love from others and found it hard to forget, impossible to forgive. What angered me most about Cy was his rigidity, his total lack of warmth. Put my arms around him, and I was hugging a telephone pole. We kept our distance after that visit because father and daughter knew we had the same inflated pride, as well as the same cheekbones, and what we saw when we looked at each other made us both flinch.

I had to ask Cy for two hundred dollars when I fled my bad marriage. This wasn't the hardest part of extricating myself from it, but it was far from the easiest. He sent the money promptly, suggested that I live with a cousin in San Francisco while I was getting on my feet financially and emotionally, and filled two single-spaced pages with "if you had listened to your older and wiser father in the first place . . ." That he was right this time made his pointing out the obvious almost unbearable.

Cy announced the Grand National Western Livestock Exposition, in the San Francisco Cow Palace, for thirty-one consecutive years. The Cow Palace is a cavernous building shaped like a giant Quonset hut on the southern margins of the city, the rodeo a prosperous one whose main sponsor, for years, has been Winston cigarettes. A jumping-horse competition gives the proceedings an overlay of proper English classiness. Banners and flags fill the huge hall, floats are lowered from the ceiling and at the Grand Opening ceremonies rodeo dignitaries come out at the full gallop on horses doubly weighted with the silver on their saddles, bridles and stirrups. The cowboys who walk or limp away from the various events as PRCA champions have won as much as eighty thousand dollars for the year, as well as glory.

The riders and ropers at the Cow Palace are the best. The buckle bunnies are the prettiest, in their pearly cowboy hats and sprayed-on Western shirts and pants. Their boots are meant for dancing the two-step, after the rodeo, rather than riding. Their pink mouths open to let out piercing shrieks of "Ride 'em, cowboy! Hang in there, baby!"

Behind the arena and the chute area, where the vendors sell beer and hot dogs, the livestock exhibitors scrub bulls the size of small buildings with brushes and soapy water, rub them down as carefully as if they were fragile Chippendale chairs and await the judges with the clipboards, who'll get down on their hands and knees and inspect their entries from every angle. They're looking for perfect conformation, and Prime-grade flesh on the heavy bones, but it's a fair guess that when one is inspecting the undercarriage of such an animal, it gets a few points for having a friendly attitude.

The massive Winston scoreboard prints out times and scores electronically. When the honor guard rides out with the flags of the United States and California, their black horses have sparkle dust on their rumps, and the audience that applauds is saluting superb horseflesh along with all else for which America stands. Hats over their hearts, the crowd stands erect and still for the playing of "The Star-Spangled Banner," watching a faceted, reflecting ball revolving in the ceiling. It's the same lighting effect, but not the same crowd, one would find in a disco.

My father loved the Cow Palace rodeo, commanding the lavish spectacle and filling the enormous space with his voice from an announcer's stand almost lost in the vastness.

He liked descending on the big city in his latest Cadillac and taking up residence in his hotel just off Union Square. If people on the street did a double take at the sight of the small man in the Western suit, high-heeled boots, big hat and diamond horseshoe stickpin, they were simply struck by his fine clothes and good looks. He paraded fur-stoled and hatted Dorothy on his arm, fragrant in a cloud of perfume, as if the two of them owned the San Francisco sidewalks and no doubt wondered why I hung behind, studying department store windows.

The Cow Palace board of directors included some of the city's prominent citizens, fine men Cy was proud to call his friends. The proprietors of his favorite restaurants recognized him from year to year, as they could hardly have failed to do, and Cy gave them both his patronage and tickets to the rodeo, expensive box seats he produced with a flourish. I also got free tickets, and one year shared a box with two Chinese cooks from Johnny Kan's and an Italian waiter from Fior D'Italia.

That was the year Cy deposited me in a downtown beauty salon to have my hair done before I appeared out at the Cow Palace. As I shook hands with the members of the board of directors, big, hearty men, I was miserable with self-consciousness under my bouffant, which looked as if it should have swallows nesting in it.

San Francisco was the high point of the circuit for Dorothy too. It was sophisticated, and unlike Chicago or Dallas, did not reek of the stockyards. Most of all, she liked the sidewalk flower stands, where my father bought violets for her furs. The city to which I had moved nonetheless alarmed them. Even before the hippies came along in their madras bedspreads of many colors, it had a reputation for both hedonism and excessive liberalism. It was full of interracial couples and homosexuals. I was involved with a man who was thirty-two years old and had never been married.

The dress code Dorothy remembered fondly, from years ago, no longer existed. Hatted and befurred women were the exception, not the rule, and Dorothy sighed for San Francisco's lost elegance.

The shape of my life further alarmed them. I picked them up one night in my male friend's old Volkswagen, veteran of so many spray-paint jobs, ranging from beige to army green, it was now mottled like army camouflage. I lived in a neighborhood not in the guidebooks, in an apartment above a grocery store reached by three flights of odorous stairs. I had joined a "Communist front organization," the ACLU. Cy was deeply relieved when he determined that I still used my married name.

I was too busy supporting myself and a child to be looking for fights anymore, especially not with my father. We fought constantly anyway, over whether the city I had embraced was or was not a cesspool. We fought over the man I would later marry, who never bought clothes and always needed a haircut.

"Your father's a short man," he said to me as we drove home from the rodeo one night. "You always talk about him as if he were a six-footer."

"Not short, *medium* height," I said. I thought I was abnormally tall, a giantess, and that this explained why I could look down on the top of Cy's hat.

I separated the man and the Western myth long enough to quarrel with Cy definitively, with such lingering wounds we did not see each other, and wrote no letters, for nearly eight years. In the early sixties, he and Dorothy came to San Francisco for the Cow Palace engagement as usual. They called me a day before they were about to leave. I rushed from the office where I worked to pay the short court visit that was all time allowed.

In the course of it, Dorothy suggested that I should put my young child up for adoption—I'd have a better chance of making an advantageous marriage. Considering the way I lived, in what amounted to a tenement, it was the kindest sacrifice a mother could make.

Did he agree with this advice? I asked Cy, who was roaming the room, gathering up notes and getting ready for the evening performance. We locked eyes for a long time. Of course he did, Cy said finally.

I walked out of his hotel room, determined never to see him again. And for years, when the rodeo was in town, I told my second husband that I was going to a movie and drove out to listen to my father's baritone voice rolling out in the darkness of the Cow Palace, setting off seismographs.

What a cornball the man is, I thought, what an insufferable strutting rooster, what a showboat. Then I'd think, you've got to hand it to him, though, he can sure as hell work a crowd.

FOURTEEN

Until Cy's offer to let me apologize arrived, after all those years of silence on both sides, my only contact with the immediate family was with Dorothy. Shortly after I marched out of that San Francisco hotel room, she wrote me a letter she must have been composing as long as we had known each other. Its expressed intention was to make a better woman of me.

Again, she charged me with being an unfit mother, one who lived in an unfit apartment. She complained about the large sums of money Cy had given me, pointing out that when I lived with them in Oakland, she "went without to see you had decent clothes to go to school." The neon-green sweater and plaid skirt haunted her as much as they haunted me.

Most recently, they had invited me to Denver, where my time "was spent mostly in the company of that professor from Boulder. Who had quite a reputation as we bothered to find out."

Cy made no child support payments after the first years of his legal obligation, and few of them then. The professor was a seventy-year-old expert on George Bernard Shaw, with whom I'd had dinner once during my stay. If he had vices other than compulsive reading—bizarre sexual practices or heroin, say—he chose not to share them with me.

Dorothy's indictment ran on for two pages, unanswerable because her anger was irrational and bottomless. My former husband had not beaten me, she wrote. I must have divorced him because he did not make enough money "to give you the life you wanted." I had left my marriage because I was miserable in it, the reason most people leave marriages. My Catholic stepmother seemed to think the only grounds for divorce were compound fractures.

I knew Cy had read this outburst because Dorothy made no move without consulting him, not even planning the dinner menu. He added no postscript reading: "Disregard the foregoing." From that point on, Dorothy's resentment sat in the road leading to reconciliation between us like a heavily armored tank. I think we had equal respect for its fighting capabilities.

For Cy, Terry and Tommy, my stepmother's love was inexhaustible as the life force. By serving as my father's handmaiden, as well as his wife, she made Cy possible; her faith in him and her devotion to his career allowed him to become the man he became.

For her sons, she would have swum oceans or got between them and a hand grenade. Their joys were Dorothy's joys, their setbacks her heavy blows, felt more profoundly than her children felt them.

But I was another woman's child, Cy's role in my existence irrelevant. He had "his own children" to consider, Dorothy told me once, when I asked him for a loan. It was a small loan. I needed it badly. Instead I got a forthright spelling-out that there was no room in my stepmother for what was not hers. Any defection from this view of things, on my father's part, would be seen as betrayal, parceling out his affections rather than delivering them whole.

What prompted Cy to write to me anyway, after nearly a decade, was learning that he had cancer. "This CA thing," as he called it, frightened my father and set him conducting a retrospective on his life, including the part of it he had banished from his résumé. From me, as well as from my brothers and Dorothy, he needed comfort, and moral support, and affirmation of his worth. The worst of his medical problems had been occasional laryngitis. Now he had cancer of the prostate; was ordered to quit smoking after forty years; had to endure treatments that he found painful and humiliating.

Other signs of physical failure assailed him, the loss of sight in his right eye for a few days and what sounds, in his highly circumspect description of it, like a stroke. He rolled a sheet of his letter-head into his portable typewriter and sent me a stiff-necked but un-mistakable appeal for help, in toughing out the rest of his life and in mending his broken fences.

I wanted them mended as much as he did, though there was one section I was unwilling to prop up. "Life is too short to go on nursing old grievances," my father wrote me, meaning my grievances against Dorothy. "My own version of 'life is too short,' " I wrote back, "is that it's too short to keep beating one's head against the same stone wall." I could not forgive my stepmother her mean-spiritedness any more than Cy could forgive me for what he perceived as not loving him enough.

To his wife and sons, and to his fans, he had no flaws. To me, he had the usual number. Shaken by his illness, my father began to entertain the notion that while this was extremely unlikely, it was possible.

For the first time since I was a child, he wrote me personal let-ters instead of sending me carbons, telling me about money worries and disappointments. A rodeo he'd worked for thirty years had not renewed his contract for the following season. "Some of the younger announcers have greatly exaggerated my condition, and taken ad-vantage of it."

Terry was wounded in Vietnam. Tommy was badly hurt in a bull-riding accident. My brothers made impulsive young marriages, as I had, and both were divorced. Cy told me how much anguish these events caused him, both on paper and on the phone, his voice querulous with complaint. "Cyra, old age is hell," he blurted in one conversation. My father was then in his early sixties.

Equally startling to me, because it was uncharacteristic, was his speculation in a letter that "perhaps I am now being punished for things I have done in the past." I replied that cancer was as arbitrary as a roll of the dice and that if there was a God, he hired no goons and kneecapped no one for being fallible. "Your ability to write is certainly reflected in your last long letter of November 2nd," Cy told me, moved by my mixed metaphors. I could recall no previous compliment from him, ever, and joked to my husband about hiring a stone carver.

A somber Cy in his early sixties

Slowly, my father and I undertook the task of getting to know each other again, the most important in a long history of such efforts. Because I had not been around to see the process under way, I found it hard to grasp that Cy was as old as he was. My image of him was frozen in his early fifties, when I had last seen him, and even then I had not seen him realistically. Superimposed, always, on Cy in the flesh was the image of himself he'd invented and lived, the dashing cowboy celebrity. I had not seen him on the screen, doubling for Robert Taylor. One more ticket buyer, I had sat in the uppermost reaches of the Cow Palace, watching and listening to Cy a quarter mile away in the announcer's booth. On such occasions, the man for whom I was named was as unreal as an actor in a Western movie, and as inaccessible.

Nor had he any sense of me, living in the suburbs, remarried for ten years, going to school as a "re-entry woman." He did not know if there were "any little McFaddens," misspelled my daughter's name and could not remember how old she was, and politely asked after friends I had not seen since I was seventeen years old. Did I still keep up with my music? he inquired. I had no music to keep up with, as Cy damned well knew; listening to me attempt the national anthem with the rest of the crowd at rodeo openings, he'd shaken his head often enough and told anyone around it was a shame I was tone deaf.

I worked as a secretary for the San Francisco Opera for a few years, and must have told him about it. My job description underwent a transformation when he got hold of it and came back to me later, from someone he knew, as "I hear you sing with the opera company out there in San Francisco." "No," I said, and then, furious with Cy, added, "that was my mother."

It would have bewildered my father, with his P. T. Barnum approach to press agentry, that I did not appreciate his promotional efforts on my behalf. In wanting him to recognize that mine was a reasonable sort of life as it actually was, I was expecting a sculptor to put down his chisel and leave a block of marble intact. For Cy, the showman, one started with fact and took it from there, as far as invention would go.

A crowd at a rodeo was never a few hundred shivering souls, it was a thousand people cheering their lungs out. The hotel and dance-hall bands he had led, in his pre-rodeo days, became the Benny Goodman band and Cy the xylophone soloist. The radio program that featured my mother, in St. Louis, was the most popular program in the country and Pat competition for Sophie Tucker.

I was used to this facet of my father's character, and amused by it, but when it extended to me, I felt compromised. I was in my thirties, with children of my own, and Cy still hadn't acknowledged that he was stuck with the person I was, who would go to my grave with the same straight hair, would never be named Miss Rodeo America and was unlikely to shrink much.

Our letters were affectionate, when they began to travel back and forth every month or so. Cy congratulated me when I got my bachelor's degree. I congratulated him when he got favorable medical reports. Neither of us suggested meeting. We knew that we had best conduct our new accord at a distance, one at which we could sustain it. Had we risked getting together, other than on paper, we would have debated the shape of the conference table, my stepmother's motives and which station to listen to on the car radio.

Parents generally try to dominate their children. Children struggle to break free of them. My father's and my variation on this theme was that neither of us would yield a millimeter of ground, ever. Civilized in our relations with other people, we squared off at each other like a pair of pit bulls.

After twenty-five years of avoiding the mention of her name, Cy asked about Pat. He wanted to know about the state of her health, and whether she was any happier these days, and confessed to an uneasy conscience about her. "In retrospect, I cannot help but believe that much of the difficulty between your mother and me was my own fault—much of it resulting from my immoderate drinking." As if this admission were disloyal, he followed with a paragraph about what good care Dorothy took of the house and of him, despite "a problem involving the nerve endings." Either he was being circumspect again or the problem had not yet been named to them. My father's much-loved wife and my old nemesis was in the early stages of Lou Gehrig's disease.

Pat and Roy in their late years

Pat and Ila Mae in Lincoln, Montana, in the early 1970's

At a twelve-hundred-mile remove from them all, I began to realize, through their letters and calls, that my parents' lives, my step-
parents' lives, Aunt Ila Mae's and Wiley's were winding down,
trailing off into an accumulation of illnesses and disappointments.
Like Cy, all seemed to feel obscurely betrayed, only Pat incapable
of surprise.

She wrote of breaking her leg in a sand trap while playing golf.
Roy had taught her the game, the one form of recreation they
shared. Fearful of telling him that she had been so clumsy, after she
fell she played on until the leg was swollen and painful.

Pat's account of this accident is almost jaunty; it restored a little
drama to her life. "I have to wear a cast!" she says, sounding pleased,
and then pulls herself up short and adds a rote, Ila Mae–like pietism: "However, with God's help I will golf again."

From Roy, not long afterward, I heard of a more serious event
in her life, a radical mastectomy. I'd fly home, I told him. Roy was
mysterious about the reasons, on his end of the phone, but made it
plain that he did not want me there. The house was too small. The
trip would be a waste of good money. In the summer, he said, he'd
bring my mother to California to visit my family instead.

Although I could have pointed out that I'd been home many
times before, and the house had held us all then, I didn't argue. For
years Pat had not been more than a few miles from the block on
which they lived. Such a journey, for her, would be on a scale with
Lindbergh's in "The Spirit of St. Louis." My less altruistic motive
was that I hated the Missoula bungalow, with its storm windows in
place the year round, so that the air inside was stale and oppressive,
and its peculiar smell of vitamin capsules and the sprouted wheat
Roy grew in the bathtub.

His health-food preoccupation had become a passion. We
started the mornings there with the viscous brew he whipped up for
breakfast in his indispensable blender, blackstrap molasses and
twenty-one other ingredients outside any normal definition of food.
By now, my stepfather's theory was that if it tasted good, it was trying
to kill you. Behind his back, Pat and I made terrible faces over our
khaki-colored health shakes. Roy left for the candy company. We
poured them down the toilet in the bathroom, making our way
around the amber waves of grain.

The Ila Mae Chronicles escalated my mother's loss of a breast to both breasts and stated darkly that her doctors weren't telling her the whole truth. "Once It get started it go right thru you, they can cut It out but It pop out somewhere else, Susie her Days Are Numbered. I can't do anything for her only Pray, that I do for the whole world."

She moved on to world affairs:

> Our town is full of Rape stabbings and dope. Last night 12 year old girl was stabbed six times in her home. He tried to Rape her. Didn't make it, he was just out of prison. Few weeks ago 9 year old girl was Raped all most died they haven't caught the man yet. The police said no woman should be out after dark.
>
> So have good day for I love you all.

The blow dealt Wiley worried me more than the latest crime wave in Great Falls. For thirty years, he worked for the same downtown department store, selling suits, ties and what he considered the height of elegance for men, white-on-white shirts. The store was a genteel anachronism, with a cafeteria in the basement that offered weary shoppers chicken salad and angel food cake, and a staff of Wiley-like employees, old family retainers who'd spent their adult lives behind its counters writing up sales of Ladies Necessaries and Better Chocolates.

In the seventies, the store was sold to a large chain. The chain fired Wiley a few weeks before he would have been entitled to retirement benefits. He got a job at J. C. Penney's after a few anxious months, but at Penney's he was no longer "our Mr. Gosney." Ila Mae wrote that he had developed a bleeding ulcer and that the piped-in music in the menswear department made his ears ring.

My mother and father had been adventurers, performers who wrote their own scripts, starring themselves, and expected even the people they loved best to function as the supporting cast. Dorothy played her own fulfilling role as wife of the great man. Wiley plodded along, not thinking very deeply about where a day led. Ila Mae saw the world through her kitchen window but took her limited raw material and wrote it large, interpreting life for the rest of us in its rich, rape-and-murder-ridden variety. Roy made a vocation of injured merit. Now, with the exception of Pat, who accepted broken legs, mastectomies and wheat in the bathtub with the same passivity, they all seemed to feel they were the victims of injustice, in the form of mortality.

At Christmas, Roy sent me a gift subscription to *Prevention*, a magazine that reflected his views about diet and health maintenance. "Your health is all you have got," his card read. Pat's motto had been "Your looks are all you've got." Ila Mae lived for Judgment Day, when God would reward the good and punish the sinners. My father wanted above all to be Somebody. With the end of his rodeo days in sight, he felt the way he must have felt without his cowboy boots on, insubstantial and reduced to ordinariness.

Through their letters ran a strain of melancholy: where had their lives gone? Even Ila Mae, awaiting vindication beyond earthly glory, had doubts about her belief system. God would pin a good conduct medal on her for the suffering she'd endured, she knew, but he was unaccountably taking His own sweet time about it.

FIFTEEN

Wiley was the first to die. He left the world without a fuss after an illness of a week, a workhorse dropping in his traces. My aunt mourned him so deeply we all worried about her. Their marriage, to outsiders, resembled a Punch-and-Judy show. Mysteriously, it was a close marriage all the same, Ila Mae's nagging and Wiley's automatic "Aaa, shut up" their own form of intimate communication.

Cy was on the road when Wiley was buried, but he called on Ila Mae when he was back in Great Falls, the first visit he had paid in years. Time was tearing down barriers between my father and the people he cared about when he was young, or who cared about him; he was seeing his life whole now, rather than in installments. Coming full cycle, he and Dorothy had sold the Denver house and moved back to Great Falls, a few blocks from the house in which Dorothy grew up.

Roy was next. The oldest, he was also the sturdiest, because of his health regimes or in spite of them, and at seventy-eight was still working part-time at the candy company. No longer on the payroll, he helped out at inventory time, in the warehouse, and spent the day he died shifting packing cases. Neighbors called me late the following night to tell me about his death. My mother, they said, had just remembered she had a daughter in California.

At the airport in Missoula, where they drove her out to meet my plane, Pat waited behind the barrier, wearing a cheap platinum-blond wig, slightly askew, and her sweet, vague smile. "Why, hello, dear," she said, surprised. If she knew why I was there, the information was tucked somewhere back in the reaches of her mind. Behind her, the husband of the neighbor couple tapped the side of his head significantly and rolled his eyes

My stepfather died of a sudden heart attack. Pat called 911, rehearsed by him in how to pick up the receiver and dial the three numbers, but he was dead when the ambulance arrived a few moments later. She told the story while I helped her get ready for bed, anxious about getting the details right but dry-eyed. Roy seemed to be vanishing from her memory as quickly and painlessly as he had died in his easy chair, still wearing his hat and overcoat. In his musty room, with its lonely double bed, I lay awake chain-smoking and thought how quickly the house would burn if I were careless. The rugs were thick with dust, the windows hermetically sealed and hung with moldering curtains, the room strung with a maze of frayed electrical cords. Health-food books, piled up on the bureau, on Pat's long-unused vanity table and along the walls, made the passage to the bed a narrow tunnel. I knew why Roy had fended off visitors.

The man who'd had the terrible nightmares in that room lay in a local funeral home, which had left several urgent telephone messages. The gist of these was that the deceased aren't good keepers. I knew Roy wanted his body flown home to Wisconsin, because Pat had come out of her stupor long enough to tell me so, and I got out of bed to look for his address book. For most of the night I went through drawers stuffed full of paper, finding only old order pads, yellowing junk mail and on a closet shelf a paper bag criss-crossed with Scotch tape. On it, Roy had written: "LAETRILE. *Illegal.* Pat, do not tell anyone, in the event of my death, destroy." The contents looked like fine brown dust.

My stepfather and mother, Ila Mae and Wiley had come to see me and my family two summers ago, as Roy had promised. They made a slow trip in the Dodge Dart Roy bought when the station wagon began to send up clouds of smoke, stuck close to my suburban house for a week and then set off for home and safe haven again. I made them promise not to continue a practice that terrified me when I rode with them on their lone excursion into San Francisco, stopping in the middle of the freeway to look around. Cars skidded and blared around them. Roy studied the map unhurriedly and honked back at them.

The Dart had less than a thousand miles on it. Like Roy's bed-room, it smelled musty, and it started hard because it was driven so little. Stalling at every intersection, it made my mother and me late for Roy's funeral two days after I arrived.

In the interest of saving money, I had picked out the cheapest coffin in the funeral home. I regretted it when I saw my stepfather laid out in what looked like a Styrofoam picnic chest. The under-taker had rouged Roy's cheeks and made his mouth rosy with lip-stick. I felt an acute pang of sympathy for him, looking androgynous, and mortified about it, beneath his layer of makeup.

Another pang seized me when the few mourners arrived, mem-bers of Roy's Masonic lodge alerted by the notice in the newspaper. The lodge brothers did not know him. The older he grew, the more reclusive Roy became, imprisoning himself and Pat in the airless house, venturing out to buy more lecithin capsules and the sacks of worm-infested grains that filled the kitchen cupboards. Equipped with his blender and a few pots and pans, he had taken over the cooking. At the all-you-can-eat smorgasbord where I took Pat for our meals, I watched her pile her tray with plates of cream pie.

Although she cried at the funeral, her tears were perfunctory, as if she sensed that tears were expected of her. She and I were to fly Roy's casket home, to be buried in the family plot, the following day. That night I began clearing out the refrigerator, empty except for the ranks of brown bottles full of vitamin capsules. Pat was asleep. I worked quietly so that she would not see me performing this task and be upset by it.

My mother appeared in the kitchen doorway, in her nightgown. She saw the trash bag at my feet and reached into the open refrig-erator, picked up a bottle and slammed it into the bag, with the speed and coordination of a major-league pitcher. Before she went back to bed, she joined me in a beer and a cigarette. I spent a ma-cabre morning filling out shipping orders for Roy's remains, referred to by the airline personnel as Mr. Qualley and "it." Pat sat in the waiting room, her suitcase at her feet, restless with anticipation. On the plane, she sat pressed to the window, looking out into the cloud banks, until the stewardess brought lunch. "This is on me," she told me graciously. "I insist." In Roy's sister's house in Oconto, over and over, she told the assembled family about the manner of Roy's death.

"He said to me, 'Dear, I'm tired. I think I just want to sit here and rest.' Then he said, 'Sweetheart, I've got a bad pain in my chest, call the ambulance.'" Each time Pat told the story, enjoying being the focus of attention, she incorporated more endearments into it, loving pet names Roy had never spoken. She was describing their marriage, for posterity, not as it was but as she wanted it to be. In the coquettish blond wig, from which she refused to be parted, she put on a last performance, transforming life into art.

The Wisconsin relatives, kind people who liked "Patty," listened and nodded and wept with her. I went into my Aunt Babe's kitchen and drank with Uncle Norman, Roy's oldest brother.

Norman preferred bourbon to the hot dishes and sheet cakes neighbors brought to the front door all that week. In the pocket of his plaid wool jacket, food-stained and tobacco-smelling, he had a pint flask, from which he poured an inch into a cheese glass for me. In silent complicity, we bolted the bourbon down, then stood leaning against the counter. "Poor old son of a bitch," Norman said gravely. He had pronounced his brother's most eloquent eulogy.

A young Lutheran minister delivered the more formal eulogy at the graveyard, where I was shamed again by my taste in coffins. In late October, in Wisconsin, snow lay on the ground. A gray sky sent down a drizzle, and Aunt Babe passed around umbrellas to the dozen of us present. Pat cried once more, tears that stopped almost as soon as they started, but seemed more bewildered than grieving. Among her clothes, I'd had trouble finding a dark dress that fit her and a warm coat. The garments I had finally packed were so old they gave her that look, again, of a woman in a period movie.

Now that the week of sorting out Roy's affairs was behind me, it struck me with full force that my mother was helpless, a woman who had not driven a car for twenty years, could not write a check and responded to my "It's Cyra, Mother" on the phone with a thoughtful pause followed by "Who?" Back in Missoula, I began the paperwork for putting her house on the market and found a convalescent home for her.

The day I took her there, my stomach churned with guilt. I was the parent now, and she was the child, and I was abandoning her.

Pat bounced on her bed, testing the mattress, put her clothes in the bureau and the closet and in a cracked mirror applied lipstick to her mouth with her little finger, peering closely at her reflection. She was in some small town in the Midwest, forty years ago, getting ready to play the provinces.

After the long, stifling captivity of her marriage, my mother found the convalescent home stimulating and wrote me cheerful letters about small events in her day. To make the letter writing easier, I sent her stamped envelopes with printed return-address stickers on them. She crossed out "Mrs. Roy Qualley" above her address and painstakingly lettered in "Patricia."

Cy asked me to convey his sympathy, when I told him about her new circumstances, and wrote that he would contact her "at the first opportunity." That he never did had nothing to do with insincerity but with his wariness of the past, and the pain that confronting it held for him. Everyone who knew the ruinous rakehell in the old photographs had forgiven him except for Cy himself.

"Don't come to see him Susie," Ila Mae wrote. "You wouldn't recognize him & he wouldn't want you to see him This way." Cy was a walking skeleton. Dorothy wasn't much better. "She have some terrible disease, some famous baseball player got it. It incurable." Terrible diseases being no excuse for letting oneself go, she noted that Dorothy had gained more weight. "Also, she *huge*."

My aunt sounded the death knell for Cy prematurely. Though he pared down his schedule to a dozen rodeos a year, he kept on working, telling people that he was retiring and would spend his time writing and trout fishing. In 1977, taking note that he was not appearing at the Cow Palace as usual, a writer for the San Francisco *Examiner* referred to him as "slick Cy Taillon . . . a legend who looked like Spade Cooley and sounded like the Reverend Billy Graham."

In Lewiston, Idaho, a reporter wrote of "a voice that rose and fell with each passing crisis on the arena floor below, investing even the prosaic with an element of excitement." By then Cy had announced the Lewiston Roundup for twenty-nine years.

Thirty-one years at the National Western in Denver. Thirty-eight at the Western Washington State Fair, where, for a decade, photographed as a six-year-old in cowgirl regalia, I had been a poster girl. These rodeos were constants in my father's life, and he kept presiding over them despite depression, trouble breathing and "the increasing pain and distress . . . of this cancer thing." Part of the Western ethic was that cowboys die with their boots on. Reading me the latest tribute over the phone, marking his farewell appearance one place or another, he told me irritably, "They're lining up behind the bone wagon, and I'm not even dead yet."

In 1979, a package arrived from him. He was going through memorabilia and thought I might like to have my baby pictures.

I knew that if I didn't see my father soon, I wouldn't see him alive again. I stayed home in California. By the time Cy was hospitalized for what was to be the last time, in 1980, my husband had borne out my theory of the randomness of the lightning bolt. He also had terminal cancer.

Don't come, Terry said on the phone when I made a halfhearted offer. Remember him the way he was. My brothers and I had not seen each other for ten years either, but out of empathy for me, as we watched the people we loved best dying, Terry let me off one more emotional hook. So did Cy. "It wouldn't do me any good," he said the last time we talked on the phone, and seeing him could only cause me pain. At least, he assumed it would cause me pain.

"You know it would," I snapped.

"Well, I certainly hope so," my father snapped back. For us, this exchange was an unprecedented admission of love.

My brother Terry has a growly, good-old-boy Western voice. "We lost him," it told me when he called in mid-April of 1980. Agonizing as it was to see him go, he went on, it was a mercy. Cy had been in terrible pain for days, and so heavily drugged he wasn't anyone we both knew. "Cyra," Terry said through tears, "he was as spaced out as a soup sandwich."

I said I'd lost Cy a long time ago. My brother took exception. "He always loved you."

I wanted to believe this. I also wanted the impossible: to live my life over again, with Cy remaining present in it, not as the parent I could not please but as the father I remembered from my childhood, dangerous but dashing, who'd taught me the words to "San Antonio Rose." Into my scrapbook, Cy Taillon's daughter in spite of him and myself, I pasted the newspaper editorials that people I barely knew sent me from all over the West.

Dorothy followed Cy a few months later, and in some unfathomable scheme of things, it was her deathbed that found me in attendance. Pat had suffered a series of strokes. I went to Missoula to move her into a nursing home. Before I turned around and went back to California, I drove to Great Falls to see my brothers, as adults. With my family "passing away," in the gentle euphemism, one after another, I felt the need to hang on to the relatives I had left.

I stayed at the Cosgriff house with Dorothy's sisters, in the bedroom I used to stay in all those lifetimes ago. We went out to dinner at the same steak house across the Misssouri River where we all used to go when Cy was in town, and where he'd once exasperated me by sending a bottle of wine back. He claimed it was "off."

As is usually the case in Montana, the wine was chilled just short of being frozen solid. Alexis Lichine couldn't have pronounced on its merits or said, for sure, whether it was red or white. Cy still got a stricken apology from the waiter, who brought him another bottle, or possibly the same one, bowing from the waist.

"Much better," my father said regally, without tasting it.

Dorothy was in a nursing home too. She had asked urgently that I come to see her, her sisters said. I went, reluctant but deeply curious; what did she want from me, near the end of her life, and what could we find to say to each other? The nursing home turned out to be the hospital in which I was born, fallen on hard times. My stepmother had done her nurse's training there, under the watchful eye of the nuns. It was hard to imagine the young, auburn-haired Dorothy, in her starched white cap, as the same woman who lay in bed, almost immobilized, no longer my antagonist or anyone's.

Her eyes were as extraordinary as I remembered, large and brilliant, with the familiar wistful expression. They locked on me as I stood beside her and listened to her tell me about her marriage to my father, "the greatest love story ever told." Their ashes would be mingled, she said, so that the two of them would be together in death as they were in life.

While she spoke, I looked at the picture of Cy on the wall of her room, an enormous blowup of a black-and-white photo. In it, he accepted one more award, a plaque or a silver and gold belt buckle, a compellingly handsome man in a Western suit and cowboy hat photographed from somewhere down around his knees, so that he looked tall as a tree.

He not only loomed above me, he loomed above Dorothy. Of all the people who had loved him and lived in the shadow he cast, I thought, only my stepmother had never felt diminished or chilled by it. With an exhausting effort of will, she was serving the legend still, testifying to her part in it to me, the only unexplained interruption of the tale of the schoolgirl and the piano player. I needn't have worried about what to say. I had been summoned there to listen.

S I X T E E N

Cy said that Bennett Cerf urged him to write his autobiography; his was a singularly colorful American life. I began my version the year before he died, intending it to be a journalistic account of his career. The book refused to remain the one I set out to write, the one Cy himself might have written. It wasn't Cy Taillon the celebrity that I needed to make sense of but my onetime polestar, and Roy's obsession, and the hell-for-leather cowboy my mother had sung about loving come rain or shine.

Two years after our father's death, I asked Terry to take me to Miles City, where he had announced his last rodeo. Cy's ghost would be there. I thought it would be pleased to know his adult children, strangers for so long, had reclaimed each other as family, and that I was in the process of reclaiming him.

My brother and I traveled the same route that Cy took out of Great Falls, across eastern Montana and vast expanses of sagebrush, sand cliffs and emptiness. The landscape is dun-colored except for white spots on the horizon, the tails of grazing antelope. Alongside streams, cabins with no roofs stand abandoned, swallows their tenants. The cold winters, or the loneliness, proved too much for the homesteaders who built them. Said Terry, pointing to one of them, "Somebody's dream . . ."

With years as a bronc rider and a rodeo judge behind him, Terry had begun announcing. He was not appearing at Miles City. Though he is following in Cy's bootsteps, he is reluctant to step in them. "Those boots left holes too big for me to put my feet in."

The Western songs he played on his tape deck were the old songs. The bars we stopped at were the same bars, timeless, preserved in their amber light. When we pulled into Miles City on Friday night, the town was unchanged to my eyes although I had not been there for twenty-five years. The false-front one-story buildings on Main Street still looked like the set for a Western movie. Had I leaned against one of them, I would have expected to plunge through a plywood façade. The sale started on Saturday, but Miles City was already full of horse trailers and pickup trucks, the Olive Hotel bar full of stock contractors.

Solidly muscled men, nicknamed Red and Scrapiron, the contractors "signify" because they have earned respect on the backs of broncs or in brawls, the kind Miles City talks about the way veterans talk about the Normandy landing. Shoulder to shoulder in the bar, with its low-lying pall of cigarette smoke, they traded jokes and set up drinks for each other and for us.

Though the Bucking Horse Sale is a relatively small rodeo, it is famous in the West because producers come there to bid on the horses that may make them rich. Cy announced it one last time, on a rainy weekend, when he was easily exhausted and in pain. If it's not hot in Miles City in May, it's so cold that after a few hours at the fairgrounds on the outskirts of town, slogging through icy mud, you keep looking down, making sure your feet have not been amputated. The cold must have penetrated Cy's bones.

The traditional Friday-night itinerary is to go from one of the bars that line Main Street to the next. The Bucking Horse Sale is a notoriously rowdy event that turns Miles City inside out once a year, to the collective civic pride of the place, and alcohol fuels the good fellowship and the fights. Until recently, the city aided and abetted the drinking by closing off several blocks to truck and car traffic, so that celebrants could go from one bar to the other with drinks in hand. The sale was a drunken orgy, local clergy and an out-of-state newspaper complained, telling Miles City what it already knew, and finally, the city sighed and passed an open-container law. Now the contractors, the cowboys and the crowd that comes simply to whoop and holler have to stand packed together inside the bars and relay drinks over each other's heads.

At the Bison, where Terry and I dug in for the evening, the passing of drinks resulted in frequent deluges down the backs of our necks. Conversation blurred into an amorphous roar. Somewhere in the back, a Western trio played to nobody in particular, the lot of musicians in bars the world over. Brusque and efficient, the bartenders wore Gay Nineties dress. They darted back and forth like water bugs while I knocked back whiskey ditches with Terry, calculating his body weight as opposed to mine and wondering if we'd eaten dinner that night. Approximately 960,000 people live in Montana. Most of them seemed to be in the Bison, pleased to see Terry and deaf to my pleas of "Oh no, thanks a lot, but really, I've had enough." His eyes hidden behind black sunglasses, Terry grinned down at me. One of my brother's favorite sayings is: "If you can't run with the dogs, don't piss with the puppies."

So I drank with him, and the rest of the crowd, and tried to catch the punch lines of the stories that all begin, a popular joke has it, "This ain't no bullshit . . ." The press of other bodies, and pride, kept me upright. Around midnight, beside me in the crush, a young cowboy tapped me on the shoulder. "I must be taken into consideration," he said.

Echoes of Willy Loman and "attention must be paid." "How come?" I asked.

"Because I lost my hat. Somebody done took it."

"You can get another one."

"I can't, neither. That was the Beethoven's Ninth of hats."

This exchange seemed hallucinatory, but so did being back in my father's world. I had walked away from it. There it was, tapping me on the shoulder and insisting on being taken into consideration. I knew that to Terry, and to the genial crowd at this bar, Cy had epitomized the last line of defense in a country gone to the dogs, the liberals and Gloria Steinem.

The Western wives I remembered were present too, handsome women who sat a barstool as stylishly as they sat a horse and who told the same breathtakingly sexist and racist jokes their husbands told. "This is a good one, honey," they said, launching into them, friendly and welcoming. They reminded me that the West is still a male world, one in which women are admired for how well they imitate men. On the ranches, these women did the same hard work, taking the pickup out in blizzards to hay the horses; shearing the sheep on sheep ranches and putting up with the smell that permeates clothing with a foul lanolin reek; sharing the driving on the rodeo circuit, with the kids, the blue heeler dog and a horse trailer in tow. I decided not to lobby for the ERA that night.

These women enjoy the lives they have chosen, thank you, and if I saw them as patronized, they didn't. Nor did they mind the affectionate references to "the ball and chain here," perhaps because they knew that if they got fed up with his chippying around, they could bring their man back into the corral like any experienced pickup rider. Lecturing a Montana ranch wife about women's lot at the hands of the male oppressor is asking to get your face rearranged.

The Bison closed at three in the morning. Terry and I were propelled out into the street by a flying wedge of merrymakers behind us. We stood swaying on the sidewalk, confronted with a line of helmeted policemen fingering riot clubs.

Miles City brings in police from Billings to maintain order for the Bucking Horse Sale, a hopeless undertaking. In the afternoon, they had patrolled in pairs, checking out the bars and making themselves visible. By seven o'clock, they traveled in fours. At bar-closing time, they were deployed eight strong, figuring that their small margin of strength lay in numbers. The Billings police are deeply resented, by the rodeo crowd, as foreign mercenaries. For some atavistic reason they were resented that night by me. "I hate those old boys," my brother said. His arm, draped over my shoulder, felt weighty as a redwood log. The two of us fixed the police between us and Terry's car in a hostile gaze.

"Hell," I heard myself saying. "They're not so big, let's take 'em." I had picked out my four, and Terry's, and this idea seemed entirely reasonable.

My brother wrestled me to the car and drove back to my motel. Before he said good night, he told me I was showing signs of turning into trouble.

Saturday morning, badly hung over, we drank Bloody Marys and pushed around eggs in the motel coffee shop, where the breakfast special was twelve-ounce buffalo steaks. More friends of Terry's, and Cy's, stopped by our table to say hello. "Cy's daughter," they said to me. "Well, I'll be damned, where you been?" They were open, and sociable, and I still found them unnerving, these men whose gaze was skilled at appraising horseflesh.

By the time we got out to the fairgrounds, Miles City was running true to form for the Bucking Horse Sale weekend. The rain fell steadily, wetter than other rain, and in the arena, gumbo mud turned the rider who got bucked off his horse into a human Fudgsicle. Gumbo is slick and black, with enough suction to swallow a three-year-old child. You can't walk in it without using both hands to pull one foot clear, and then the other, and if you drive through it, it becomes part of your car. In a reaction to the rhinestone cowboy syndrome that brings out the Taillon in me, I had worn shoes to Miles City instead of boots. I own cowboy boots, but so do computer programmers, hairdressers, rock stars and buyers for Macy's. They belong on cowboys.

The result of this principled choice was that I sank into the freezing gumbo up to my ankles. It climbed my pants legs and oozed over my shoe tops. Said Terry, looking at my feet with compassion and scorn, "You forgot. Never go to a rodeo unless you don't care what you step in."

The only events at the rodeo were bareback and saddle-bronc riding, intended to show off the horses rather than the riders, some of whom were weekend cowboys and young kids from the surrounding ranches. Since 1951, the contractors who supply rodeo stock have come to the Miles City sale to buy bucking horses at auction. Immediately after each ride, the auctioneer starts the bidding. While sellers bring in horses from all over the West, many are local. A rancher finds he has a horse that bucks, a trait that cannot be bred into an animal and makes him useless as a working ranch horse. He brings him to Miles City and hopes he'll show what he's made of, thereby entering the ranks of the elite in the rodeo world. Highly prized, bucking horses have careers that outlast those of the cowboys who ride them and who get to know every horse on the circuit—their cranky personalities, their bone-shattering moves. As catered to as coloraturas, these horses become legends in their own right.

The sale published a Collector's Edition program that year, one with a moving tribute to Cy in it. It contained a lengthier tribute to a horse named Skyrocket. "There were many other great horses, like Limber Jim, Bovee Grey, Flying Devil and the Spinner, but Skyrocket captured the heart of Montana." Six men managed to ride him before he died, after twenty years of putting cowboys in full-body casts.

Terry explained the scoring to me as the first rider shot out of the chute, to be bucked off, hard, when the horse nearly lost its footing. Both rider and horse are judged; the scoring is 1–25 for the rider, 1–25 for the horse. There are two judges, for a total of 100 possible points.

The horses are judged on how high they buck and how powerfully. "Look for the extension of the back legs in the kick, and at the withers. That's where the power is in a bucking horse."

Riders are judged on how securely they sit, on how far forward they keep their feet and on their spur stroke. The rider should spur the horse from shoulder to rump with smooth strokes of blunted spurs, which agitate but don't hurt the horse. Though the spurs will sometimes draw blood on a thin-skinned thoroughbred, bucking-horse stock is too highly valued to be abused. Over the afternoon, at the end of the auctioneer's glossolalia, sales prices ranged from one hundred thirty to twelve hundred dollars, for a black horse that tried to dismantle the bleachers and the cowboy on his back. In previous years, horses have sold for as much as the compact cars most cowboys still wouldn't be caught dead in.

The metal grandstands were open to the weather. I had not brought enough warm clothes with me to Miles City, and the rain drilled through my city slicker. My head throbbed from the bourbon I had drunk the night before. My throat closed on the hot dogs I tried to put down it, the only fare at the concession stand besides beer. Amazed at how much, I missed Cy's voice over the p.a. system; the pilgrimage I had insisted upon struck me as a mistake, a trip back to a world in which I did not belong, and hadn't for most of a lifetime.

Beside me sat the brother I scarcely knew, his cowboy hat soaked through despite its plastic cover, immune to the cold. Terry worked the chutes when he wasn't dutifully keeping me company. He wished he were riding again, he told me, and I wanted to shake him; hadn't he broken enough bones yet? What he replied paraphrases loosely as "A man's gotta do what a man's gotta do."

Tommy, too, was waiting to turn forty so he could ride Brahma bulls in "old-timers" rodeo, held together though he was with steel pins and Superglue. Tending bar in Colorado once, my younger brother had been shot in a fight he was trying to break up. In Great Falls, before Terry and I left, I asked him for particulars. Tom said it was no big deal, the gunshot missed all of his vital organs and the helicopter that evacuated him to the nearest hospital got there right away.

Our father had spent his life promoting this chest-beating ethic. I realized that I'd found it more comprehensible as a child than I now found it as an adult, and as the rodeo and the rain continued, worked myself into a fouler and fouler mood.

Terry, Cyra and Tommy together in 1982

Interspersed with the bareback and saddle-bronc riding at the Bucking Horse Sale are quarter-horse races. It was already dark, at midday, when the track announcer took over for the rodeo announcer, who, at the beginning of the day, had called for a moment of silence in memory of Cy Taillon.

The track announcer asked us to put money in a hat over at the beer stand, a collection for "a cowboy who planned to be here today but didn't make it. He was in a car crash, and had an ear tore off and other minor injuries." This appeal sank in slowly. When it did, the crowd burst into mighty guffaws.

"What do you suppose a major injury is?" my brother asked, laughing so hard himself that his eyes were watering. I didn't know, and couldn't have answered through my own laughter, but I didn't care: that only-at-a-rodeo announcement had replaced my feeling of strangeness with familiar affection, for Miles City, for the sport my father loved, and for Cy.

Even when he was close to dying, he would have been in his element here. He would have made us forget the cold, by stamping our feet and cheering the riders on; pulled out the organ stops until the hat at the beer stand overflowed with money; forgotten his own discomfort, and all else, as long as he had a microphone in his hand.

I thought, with no irony at all, that it wasn't cancer that had killed my father, it was being unplugged.

C O D A

Here are some excerpts from the yellowing pages I carry around from one side of the country to the other, in old hatboxes that once belonged to Roy.

Ila Mae to Pat, sometime in the spring of 1982:

Dear Pat, It has been such long time since I have had any news from you you are all ways on my mind cause I love you . . . Please dear let me hear from you. Some one will read this for you Some one will write note for you. I worry about you . . .

Roy to me, undated:

I know you have to consume spirits at all the partys you attend and possibly more than is good for you. If such is the case, you should eat a lot of asparagus, that cleans out all the ammonia in your system. The least harmful of all liquors is vodka made from potatoes; and be sure you get a lot of B-vitamins in your diet. I hope you have a nice exmas and take care of your health. As ever.

Cy to me, 1975:

I must tell you how proud I am of you in your pursuit of an
education and in the reaping of the fruits of your efforts now.
The important thing now is for you to realize happiness in
the short life span allotted to all of us . . .

Ila Mae to me, undated:

Well Dear Keep up the good work just remember that John
comes First. This clipping was in our paper the Great Falls
Tribune, isn't this terrible? . . .

Each time I move, I ask myself why I keep this accumulation of
letters. The writers are all dead; throwing away their correspondence could offend none of their sensibilities. Yet I preserve all
these thousands of words, Roy-like, as if they were encoded and someday I will crack the cipher, understand the nature of my family's
affections and jealousies. I will learn to see them all through their
own eyes, instead of imperfectly through mine.

Ila Mae tyrannized Baby Sister from their days in Paragould,
chastising her for everything from marrying Cy, to leaving Roy, to
crooked seams up the backs of her stockings. In the months before
she died, she wrote Pat almost daily, telling her how much she loved
her, and instead of newspaper photos of child polio victims, enclosed dime-store valentines. Their mottoes read: "You're sweet as
honey" and "You're very special, be mine," and they are meant for
small children.

Roy named me his heir, after my mother. The language of his
will says he does so "because I look upon her as my own flesh and
blood."

When we drew close again, at our cautious remove, Cy wrote
often about how proud he was of me for getting a book published.
All the praise he had withheld for a lifetime, he heaped on me
then, sending me interviews in which he mentioned me as "the
other writer in the Taillon family." A sentence in his will ex-
cluded me. I wanted nothing from him, and expected nothing,
but found it painful to be struck once again from the rolls of his

children. He had acknowledged my existence intermittently. It made me smile a peculiar smile that my copy of the will, mailed to me by a North Dakota law office, arrived with fourteen cents postage due.

My mother, the one who had the greatest capacity to surprise, gave me the most unassimilable proof that I had not really known her. Soon after my husband died, I drove to Montana again to visit her. We sat on the porch of the nursing home, in a thin winter sun, and I told Pat that Ila Mae had died a few months earlier, news I had withheld because I wanted to tell it to her in person. She received it calmly, the way she had accepted Roy's death and my phone call telling her that we were both widows now.

Her most recent stroke had taken away her ability to speak clearly. She communicated with smiles, or arranged her face in a frown, but neither smiles nor frowns had much to do with what anyone said to her.

The nursing home staff was fond of her because Pat was the only patient who never complained.

She seemed pleased to see me, if not entirely sure who I was. A radio played somewhere inside, and she hummed tunelessly along with the music and moved her swollen, slippered feet, a seventy-two-year-old former dancer, who in some core of herself was still a dancer. "I guess I ought to tell you that Cy died too," I said. I thought Pat was entitled to know, and that this knowledge could not touch her because nothing could. As we sat together, her glance had flicked off me and the cars in the parking lot with equal disinterest.

She turned and stared at me, through glasses smeary with thumbprints, and made a sound I interpreted as "What?" "He died, Mother," I said again. "He'd been sick for a long time. It's sad, isn't it? I'm sorry too."

The noise that ripped out of her throat froze me. "No!" My mother's hands jerked up from the arms of her chair and struck at me, catching a finger in one of my hoop earrings, and the keening sound poured out of her as I took the earring off and reached over to comfort her. Her face contorted, she batted my hands away.

"What *on earth* did you say to her?" asked the nurse who came running out to us, alarmed. I let her lead Pat inside and went and sat in my car, too shaken to start it and drive away.

I thought I had guessed correctly at what Pat had forgotten. I'd been massively wrong about what she remembered.

"She couldn't adjust to that life back on the road, with you," Ila Mae had told me, talking about her sister's early life. "Maybe Cy wouldn't come home all night, and that left her in some little room alone with you. She called me and said 'I don't know where Cy is and I haven't known for two days. Can you come over?' I came and got you, and we didn't see anything of him for two or three days. He'd been gambling in a crap game."

The Cy my mother mourned was not the man who parked her in motel rooms and disappeared, not the man who had blackened her eyes more than once, nor the man Cy became, the senior statesman of rodeo. Like me, she mourned another Cy entirely, the husband who had picked her up and carried her, when they danced the night away, because out of vanity she insisted on wearing shoes a size and a half too small. Nothing—not time, not Roy, not other losses—had erased that memory for her, any more than time had erased it for me.

I put this book aside finally, wondering if anyone ever makes sense of fathers, or families, and whether their daughters perceive all fathers as part men, part myth. Whoever the man with the golden voice was when he took his high-heeled boots off, and his tall hat, and the diamond horseshoe stickpin, and the pearl buttons marching up to his elbows, I missed him when he unhitched our trailer in Billings decades ago. I missed him as a child and as an adult, every time I saw him and then didn't see him. And I go right on missing him, even as he eludes me again.

I tell myself that I would be less Cy-like if I had the chance to grow up all over again, less stubborn and more forgiving; that I'd judge Roy and Dorothy less harshly; that I'd understand my mother fully and tend the spark that remained in her, underneath the ashes. I'd do a better job of loving this time, and so would they, and we'd be that domestic group in the *Saturday Evening Post* covers, strangers to both reality and regret.

Then I realize there are no rodeo announcers in those illustrations, no soubrettes, no auburn-haired nurses and no earnest Old Honest Faces—also no daughters with the temperament of bulldogs. I accept the lot of us, at last, as who and what we were: just one more group of people joined together as that mysterious and complicated thing, a family.

A NOTE ON THE TYPE

The text of this book has been set in Goudy Old Style, one of the more than a hundred type faces designed by Frederic William Goudy (1865–1947). Although Goudy began his career as a bookkeeper, he was so inspired by the appearance of several newly published books from the Kelmscott Press that he devoted the remainder of his life to typography in an attempt to bring a better understanding of the movement led by William Morris to printers in the United States.

Produced in 1914, Goudy Old Style reflects the absorption of a generation of designers with things "ancient." Its smooth, even color, combined with its generous curves and ample cut, marks it as one of Goudy's finest achievements.

Composed by Creative Graphics, Inc.,
Allentown, Pennsylvania

Printed and bound by Halliday Lithographers,
Hanover, Massachusetts

Typography and binding design by
TASHA HALL